A TALE OF SOMETHING BORROWED

D. S. McCOLGAN

BOOK 3

A Tale of Ltd

Published by
A Tale Of Ltd
Unit 133388, PO Box 7169
Poole, BH15 9EL
UK

www.ataleofbooks.com

Cover design by Lukas Lauener, instagram@lks_dsn
Map Art by KJ Reading, instagram@kjr.art
Edited by Leona Skene, www.intuitiveediting.co.uk
Proofread by Phillipa Haskins

ISBN 978-1-7385050-9-8

This book is dedicated to my little family, my husband and my daughter, who had to live with a hermit crab because I had decided I could write a whole new perspective in less than three months.

Dear Victoria
thank you for joining
El on his quest to
get his Liliana back
and also find his
inner balance!

xx
Damaris

The Moorlands
Crimson Plains
Rabenmoor
Alfort
The Lowlands
The Harshlands
Jasnok
The Highlands
Evernight Valley
Hohburg
The Silver Coast
Finsterwald
The Lakelands
Dimas
Mirror Lake
Seefurt
Aradad
Trinago
Silver Coast

To be alive means to change.

Chapter One

Eldric roared at the top of his lungs. The demonic sound was repelled by the rocks and thrown back as if by a gigantic shield. The rest of the surroundings lay still. Everything with a pulse had long disappeared.

Kill. Them. All. He would return and tear down that hallowed castle. He would rip it all apart, shred it into small pieces, scatter the organs of the inhabitants across the walls. He would make them bleed, scream, beg …

Enough. With a forceful jerk, Eldric withdrew his powers. They writhed and hissed hatefully but obeyed. The cutting cold in his veins melted away. It was no use. He had to walk through the fury until he reached the other end, and he had a pretty good idea of what awaited him there.

The water splashed on his bare shoulders. He concentrated on his breathing. The familiar feeling of drowning rose inside him, up to his chest, into his throat. He gasped as the horror of those moments caught up with him. His limbs trembled and cramped, suddenly seized with panic.

Eldric continued to hold back his powers, not allowing them to obscure what was stuck in the back of his consciousness like shards of glass. This time he had to feel it with all his body and soul – or it would begin to fester inside him. Annie's whimpering and the fear in Liliana's eyes, Morton's laughter ... The helplessness swallowed him.

Desperately, he struggled for air. Everything was fighting back, resisting the reality he was experiencing. He gasped and gasped and couldn't stop.

He had known it. He had known it would end like this, and he had given in anyway. Her softness, her warmth had tempted him to become soft, too. And now exactly what he had feared most had happened.

Eldric wanted to scream these terrible feelings out of his lungs once more, but instead, he threatened to suffocate for good. His own shocked panting took over his senses until he could no longer perceive anything but the dreadful pressure on his chest. This pain … no air …

I should never have allowed this to happen. I should never have brought her here and lost my heart so completely to her.

He should not have let the entanglements and the danger, that were meant for him, spread to her. He should have locked her away forever in that sacred tower, where nothing and no one could get to her. And he should have kept what he felt for her locked up, too.

The sound of the water around him mingled with the rushing in his ears. He had failed on every level. A multitude of unfortunate decisions, a mixture of overconfidence, wilful optimism and deluded infatuation had brought him to this point.

Eldric continued to gasp for air, panting and wheezing. Only when he thought he might lose consciousness did he allow his powers to kick in and drive away this horrific episode.

Simultaneously, he broke through the surface, and the lake that represented his emotional world froze over. His feet found a foothold on the ice, which spread out and separated him from the treacherous depths. He traced the anger, untangled the chaos, until he found the line that led to cool resolve.

His breathing slowly found a regular rhythm, his lungs relaxed … He had managed to mediate between the demon and his human side. At last, he felt like himself again.

A different pain replaced what he had felt before, and he almost welcomed the angry stinging and burning on his back. This, he could deal with more easily; his powers would heal all physical wounds sooner or later.

He stood here, under the waterfall, his legs planted firmly on the stones in the pool. It was over. He was free and in possession of his usual powers. Morton was dead. Annie slept safe and sound in his room.

Eldric shook his head and limbs, savouring the power the Curse sent through his veins. It had taken him an almost infinite amount of willpower to subdue his demonic powers, trapped in the Light chains while Morton had shown him what he was truly capable of; how far he was willing to go just to torment and humiliate Eldric. But he had relied on his wits, on the only chance he had left, which was to save his strength for as long as possible.

In his urgent fear for Annie, he had flown straight into a trap. Without Liliana and Albert's rescue operation, Morton would have tortured and killed both Annie and him.

Eldric stepped out from under the waterfall and brushed a hand over the waist-high water. He should have stepped into the pool with Liliana back when she'd invited him to. The cold had been an excuse. After all, he was willingly putting up with it now that the weather had turned springlike again despite the onset of summer.

Who would have thought that Albert and Liliana, of all people, would follow him to the Crimson Plains? Yes, Liliana could be incredibly persuasive when she wanted to be. And daring, too! Following him into the jaws of the enemy with a hodgepodge of ancient Light weapons ... He snorted, half amused, half indignant, and brushed the damp hair from his forehead.

This crazy human woman had saved his life twice already. During the short time she had spent in the castle, she had become his safe haven. In her arms, he had felt a strange peace alongside overwhelming desire. There was something terribly confidence-inspiring about Liliana. She tried to convince him of her world views, but she did so openly. She didn't manipulate, she didn't deceive, she didn't take advantage.

Her presence had been so captivating that he had been able to forget the rest of the world. When he closed his eyes, he could still taste her, smell her skin, feel her body against his.

Eldric sighed and waded out of the water. He felt lost in the emptiness she had left behind ... sore outwardly and inwardly. Where was the old Eldric, who witnessed a violent slaughter and then buried himself comfortably in a novel?

Well, this time it had been *very* personal. He hadn't fully realised, or perhaps hadn't wanted to realise, how far he and Morton had grown in opposite directions. And the danger hadn't been to just anyone, but to Annie and Liliana. Of course, by removing Morton from power, he had prevented him from ruling their lands in open oppression. But what good was it for him to be Lord of Finsterwald if he couldn't protect those closest to him? His earlier disinterest in political intrigue had taken its revenge. He had not been aware enough of the inter-family feuds to correctly assess the extent of the additional danger his connection to Liliana would bring her.

He had always wondered whether he had it in him to defeat his brother in a duel to the death. At least that one question had been answered. Fate had entertained with another irony, namely that his greatest weakness, his fear for Liliana and Annie, had enabled Eldric to achieve this victory in his desperation.

Do you know what that means, Morton? Two to zero. I escaped death twice, while you met your end at the very first real opportunity. You lost. How do you like that?

Eldric growled and grimaced. Determined, he reached for the towel he had laid out and rubbed himself vigorously. His back burned.

If Morton was watching from the other side, he was in for a terrible ride. *He* could no longer win; his actions had caused his time to run out prematurely. Eldric, on the other hand, was alive. And as long as he was alive, he could fight for what was important and precious to him; he could exert his influence and direct events. He would overturn everything Morton had wanted to achieve.

Since Sartiria had extracted her powers and thus her soul from her former body, it should be possible to repeat the process. He would hold on to this and pore over the books with Albert until he found a solution. He couldn't give up on Liliana.

Was that ...? The smell of a vampiress made him look up. How long had she been standing there among the trees? His thoughts and the sound of the waterfall in the background had made him largely oblivious to his surroundings. Hopefully she hadn't been watching his pathetic panting. He dressed quickly.

'You could have made yourself known.'

Rosalia put one ankle boot in front of the other and crossed the narrow embankment to him light-footedly. 'I take it my curfew has been lifted, under the circumstances?'

He could hardly remember the punishment he had imposed on her, it seemed so long ago. 'That is negotiable.'

'How so?'

His cousin knew how to dress to flatter her curves. She smiled and brushed her hair back to reveal the nape of her neck. Eldric only marginally took notice, crushing the first signs of demonic lust before they could properly crystallise.

'What kind of negotiation do you have in mind?' she asked.

'A binding one.'

Rosalia scrutinised him insistently. The teasing expression around her eyes disappeared. She lifted a hand and touched his cheek.

'It was Morton, wasn't it? The one who did this to you. You killed him for it. That serves him right.'

Eldric sighed. News definitely had wings among the vampires in the castle, if even those under room arrest learned what he hadn't told anyone. Kathleen was apparently back and had coaxed the rough happenings out of Albert.

'Did you follow me? I came here because I wanted to be alone.'

'You're not the only one who likes this waterfall.' Her fingertips stroked his almost healed lower lip. He involuntarily shivered under the touch. 'I'm glad you're still alive.'

Her heart began to beat faster, and his followed suit. She leaned forward and kissed him. His powers swelled and swirled around her with interest. Her lips felt soft; soft and pleasant. She smelled—

No. He hastily stepped back. Liliana had been right. He shouldn't have drunk Rosalia's blood. He had sent the wrong message. Giving in to one kind of temptation only created more temptations.

Couldn't they leave things as they had been? Although his aloof manner generally kept people at bay, he had occasionally had to fend off the advances of other nobles or overzealous maids. But this was different. Rosalia was both friend and family. They had known each other since childhood. How he wished he could have avoided this conversation!

He cleared his throat. 'You will hardly need to hear it affirmed from me. You are as desirable as ever. But I am afraid I have a matter to settle in this regard. Liliana is—'

'I know what you're going to say. I'm not stupid, El.' Rosalia stared at him with her cat-like eyes. Her voice quivered. 'So, she's not dead, then.'

'No.' He wanted – he *had to* believe that Sartiria had lied and Liliana was still there.

'But where is she? Why did you leave her behind if she means so much to you?'

'Because she ... has turned into someone else.'

'What do you mean?'

'The powers and thus the soul of an ancient vampiress have taken possession of her.'

'I can't say that bothers me all that much.'

Eldric smiled painedly. 'You must understand that I will do everything in my power to win her back.'

'Wonderful. You want her, even when she's possessed.' Rosalia pushed her lower lip forward. She seemed more fragile than he was used to. 'What I don't understand is why we can't both have you. I can come to terms with having to share you.'

Eldric faltered. He bent down for his coat to gather his thoughts. Rosalia's affection did not leave him cold, and the offer took him by surprise. She would stoop to sharing him with a human? He hadn't expected such strong feelings. Her engaging, flirtatious ways simply seemed to be part of her nature. How was he supposed to know that they took on a special meaning when directed at him?

Admittedly, he had been vaguely aware in the moment that drinking Rosalia's blood wasn't exactly a smart thing to do. But he had let the demon's hunger get the better of him. Compared to the devastating consequences of biting Liliana, this was the lesser of two evils by far. Still, he had neither anticipated how strongly she would react upon finding out, nor how much Rosalia would interpret from his lapse.

They hadn't taken the oath, but Liliana had made it clear that she expected exclusivity – which was a very welcome development. He meant what he had told her in the library about that one special book he never intended to let go of again. He, too, didn't like the idea of having to see her in someone else's arms.

Eldric had never bothered to gather friends around his person to be popular, and he didn't see the point in showing off with romantic conquests like some vampires did. How meaningful could relationships be if they were so easily interchangeable? Maybe he was, deep down, a hopeless romantic, or maybe he found it scary enough to open up to just one person. And Rosalia – as attractive as she might appear – had never really embodied what he was looking for.

He took a deep breath and straightened up. 'I couldn't. That simply wouldn't be me. I don't want to string you along. I value you, and I don't want to put our friendship at risk.'

Her eyes glistened like the surface of the pool. 'You already have!'

He swallowed and returned her gaze. 'I am sorry. I acted foolishly. But it will be better if we—'

'Why does it always have to be all or nothing with you?' She wiped her eyes with the back of her hand and glared at him.

He suppressed the urge to take her in his arms. 'Not least for your sake. You deserve more than I can give you.'

'What do you hope to gain from this human female?' She suddenly leaned towards him, as she had done when she'd kissed him, but this time, she hissed through her teeth. 'Or is it just that? Is it because she's human? Does the latent danger of your absurd union appeal to you?'

'What? No!' Eldric moved his upper body back a little. 'Only because I went a little too far in that one moment, and—'

'Or is it because you want to play the hero? Because the poor, defenceless thing needs you?'

'No, it's she who—'

'Or is it a new manifestation of your urge to be different? You always have to stand out, don't you? One might think you've grown tired of being one of us!'

Eldric growled, shook out his coat and slipped into the first sleeve. 'That is not true! I'm proud to be part of the family.'

'You think you're something special, just like Morton! The demonic powers have gone to both your heads. An ordinary love affair wouldn't be good enough for you!'

He remained silent and slipped into the second sleeve. Rosalia knew him well. Her words chafed at his already battered self-image. He obviously placed more value on her opinion than he had previously thought. Perhaps it was because she noticed things about him that others in his close circle of friends did not. Was her criticism based on honest deductions, or was she trying to offend him because she felt rejected?

'I didn't choose a human on purpose. I'm no masochist. Do you think I would have wished for all these difficulties? But it is no use trying to deny the truth. I have realised what those feelings mean, and I will act accordingly.'

'Blessed be your stubbornness!'

Rosalia turned her back to him on the spot and transformed. Then she took off in such an indignant flurry that her wings would have swept Eldric off his feet had he not dodged. With a deep sigh, he sat down on one of the stones and put on his shoes. That was exactly why he avoided such confrontations when he could. Should he have gone about it more gently? The result would have been the same. Regardless of the approach, it would have remained a painful experience – for both sides.

He stood up and looked out over the rushing, swirling water with his hands buried in his coat pockets. The memory of Liliana swimming in it played itself out without him consciously summoning it. He missed her refreshingly uncomplicated nature, her scent, her soothing touch. What he would give for one night, just one more night ...

He extended his wings with the same abruptness as Rosalia before him and launched himself into the air. If there was a way to bring Liliana back, he would find it.

Chapter Two

When he arrived in his study with Annie, a tangle of odours swirled around. Eldric was glad he had waited until things calmed down a little before having this discussion.

Lola and Kathleen were arguing on the sofa while the twins whispered in the background. Tripp leaned against the desk, scraping dried blood from under his nails with Eldric's letter opener, his elbow coming precariously close to the flame of the candle behind him. The moonlight through the stained-glass window bathed his fair hair in red and green. Beside him, Albert scanned the titles of the documents on the shelves, obviously unsure why he had to be here at all.

Kathleen raised her head and gave Eldric a venomous look as soon as he entered. 'What took you so long?' she hissed.

He ignored her and turned to Tripp instead.

'Let me guess. There was no attack on Rabenmoor. Or the attack was in fact directed against you.'

'First guess, I'm afraid,' Tripp grumbled. 'You had all the fun while we flew to Rabenmoor so Tara could claim she didn't write the letter.'

'Do you believe that?'

Eldric put Annie down next to Lola on the sofa and looked over at his sister. The little girl continued to cling to him, however. With a heavy heart he sat down and held her on his lap. Ever since they had returned from the Crimson Plains, incessant fear had clung to her. The others must have noticed it, too, because no one complained about her presence.

'Tara suspected one of her cousins forged the letter. He had challenged her to a friendly duel, wrung her blood from his clothes and used it for the signature. Hina executed him.' Kathleen had her arms crossed and was drumming the fingers of her right hand on her upper arm. Her face was a neutral mask, but her powers wafted around the room unbound.

Hina ... That was a name he hadn't spoken in ages. His heart skipped a beat but quickly calmed down again.

'Is that possible?' Kathleen continued, 'Yes, it is ...'

'But?' Eldric asked.

'But it's just as possible that Tara betrayed us. That bitch!'

'I don't esteem Tara as the kind of Lord who doesn't keep her word,' Eldric said. 'Breaking a treaty signed in blood calls for blood. It would be tantamount to an openly declared feud between our families. I can't imagine why Tara would want that.'

'She will have organised it so that she is not directly to blame,' Lola said.

'Could she have been blackmailed?' Zac suggested, eager to contribute.

His brother was staring holes in the air next to him. Normally, his nephews would not be present at such a meeting, but since they had answered Tara's call for help with the others and flown back without having achieved anything, no one had sent them away.

Kathleen pursed her lips and remained silent. She took any affront to Finsterwald as a personal insult. Perhaps the fact that she had been the one to insist on a defensive pact with another family made her even angrier.

'Tara would rather throw herself into a hopeless fight than be blackmailed by anyone.' In the affairs of nobility, however, things were rarely black or white. 'If she didn't write the letter herself and just happened to make sure a small amount of her blood found its way to someone who had fallen out of favour anyway ...'

'And this someone either wanted to prove himself to Tara or was trying to undermine her ...' Lola continued.

'... then she could keep her hands clean and only refer the right person to our enemies.' Kathleen snorted and shook her waves of hair. 'If she thinks she's leading us around by the nose, she's got another thing coming.'

'What do we do?' Zac asked.

Eldric sighed. 'Not much for now.' Or rather, nothing they wouldn't have done anyway. 'As for Sartiria ...'

'Oh, yes!' Albert raised his head over by the shelves. 'We should invite her to Finsterwald Castle as soon as possible so we can learn more about the Four Hundred Years' War. We will never find a more direct source than her.'

'I don't think she will let herself be *invited*,' Eldric replied, stretching. His hand twitched towards his coat pocket, where he kept the empty glass beads of the necklace.

Everything in him had pleaded to return that first night and force Sartiria to give up the body she had stolen. But the shock and the emotional overstimulation had thrown the inner balance between demonic madness and his human mind dangerously out of kilter, so he had done what he always did when he felt overwhelmed: he had withdrawn.

Sartiria possessed an alarming amount of power. In his drained state, she could easily have killed him. Even in top form, it would take an elaborate ruse for him to take her somewhere against her will and hold her long enough to ... Well, he didn't even know if and how her soul could be forced back into the necklace.

'Eldric?' Kathleen looked at him sharply.

He cleared his throat. 'Yes?'

'I said that if this wartime vampiress joins forces with the Crimson Plains, it could become a problem for us. Morton and Farkas were plotting to pit the noble families against each other and establish themselves as rulers of the Continent. At least that's what Albert told us?'

'Unfortunately, Morton did not have the generosity to inform me of their plans,' Eldric replied. 'I can't say for certain whether they will be pursued further. Besides, we don't know Sartiria's motives.'

'Yes.' Kathleen's powers had settled down. She smiled in much the same way she had before the duel with Harlan. 'The Crimson Plains have pulled a joker card.'

'The loss in numbers should temporarily curb their plans,' Lola remarked and continued directed at Eldric, 'Judging by what Albert told us, it will take them a while to recover from your presence there.'

'You mean, from their own stupidity in setting a trap for El?' Tripp examined his nails with a scrutinising glance and placed Eldric's letter opener on the desk behind him. Then he grinned broadly. 'I always knew you were stronger than Morton.'

'Just about,' Eldric said quietly, yet he felt a similar grin creep onto his lips.

Morton was dead. They were finally rid of him without Eldric having to break his principles. In the moment, he had been too focused on what was happening, on the fight and on his fear for Liliana and Annie, to feel anything like satisfaction. Tripp's obvious gloating, however, fuelled this emotion in him.

'I only regret not being there.' Tripp put on an effusive expression. 'You let Albert and your human lover help you out, of all people?'

Eldric nodded while Albert rubbed his numb hand and grumbled into his dishevelled beard, 'How am I supposed to take that?'

'No offence, but I didn't think you'd have the guts or the necessary, ahem, punch.' Tripp took three quick steps around the desk and patted Albert so generously on the shoulder that he almost buckled. 'Good work! All those stars and glass spheres have proven to be useful after all.'

Albert looked a little taken aback but not necessarily unhappy about Tripp's gesture. 'They were originally intended as weapons, you know.'

'Have you got any more?'

'Sadly, there are only a few specimens left. Which does not mean that further excavations couldn't yield results.'

'Maybe I can help you with that sometime.'

An amused spark lit up in Albert's eyes. 'I didn't think you'd have the necessary, ahem, patience for it.'

'So, Berlinda was the traitor,' Lola mused. 'Who would have thought?'

'None of us for sure, or else it wouldn't have come to all this.' Kathleen continued to smile grimly to herself. Eldric thought he knew what the recent incidents meant for her. On the one hand, like everyone in the room, she was glad to be rid of Morton. On the other hand, she had lost a trump card that she could have played against him by indicating she might switch sides if he kept ignoring her demands. 'If the other families find out about this ...'

'But why did Berlinda side with Morton?' Albert followed the conversation with mild interest. 'Wasn't she happy with the tasks entrusted to her?'

'Can you repeat what she said to Liliana?' Lola asked.

The mention of her name drove an iron claw between Eldric's ribs. His grip on Annie tightened.

'She said that Farkas would swear to her after he took the Continent.'

'Oh, of course.' Kathleen's expression turned disparaging. 'Hence it was a fanatical crush that led her to betray her own family.'

Zac shrugged his shoulders. 'Theoretically, Morton was also in the—'

Kathleen silenced her son with a curt, indignant flick of the wrist. 'Shh ... Anyone who harms the family should be excluded, not supported. Morton knew no moderation. He would have brought us into disrepute with the other noble families in no time at all.'

'Berlinda must have thrown your bust into the fire herself!' Tripp slapped his flat hand against the side of Eldric's shelves, making them shake. 'She left the key to the library in the lock on purpose.'

Had she also persuaded Rosalia to ignore her room arrest in order to create a distraction? Eldric wouldn't have predicted that she could be so cunning.

She also murdered Martha. The loss still smouldered inside him. He wished he could have cut the traitor's throat himself.

'She deserved to die, if only for killing Martha,' Lola said sternly. Perhaps she had sensed the brief uprising of his powers and guessed what he was thinking. Anger made it harder to keep them in check. At least Annie didn't seem to be intimidated by them any more.

Tripp scratched his head. 'Do you think Berlinda also arranged for the Crimson Plains to invade our territory, to intercept Liliana when she tried to escape from the tower?'

'Well, she might have found out indirectly through Tiomon – may his soul hunt in peace.' Eldric glanced over at the twins, who were each studying a different wall of the room. 'Please tell me she didn't instigate you copying the key to help Liliana escape in the first place.'

'She did *not*,' Zic claimed stiffly, and Zac shook his head wildly.

'Be that as it may, we clearly underestimated her,' Lola said.

'What a waste of a skilful manipulator.' From Kathleen's lips it sounded more like a compliment.

'To get back to Sartiria.' Albert looked directly at Eldric and plucked at his tangled, grey-spotted beard. 'I think we should try to find out more about her. She's mentioned by name in the diaries. What a treasure trove of knowledge she must harbour about the old nights and the Light magic ...'

'I agree with that suggestion.' They would be able to investigate the circumstances under which she had transferred her soul, and that was the first step towards getting Liliana back. 'I will prioritise it over all other tasks. Maybe we can uncover more about her motives.'

Eldric stood up with Annie in his arms. He endeavoured to restrain his heartbeat and the urgent impatience inside him. Nevertheless, Kathleen measured him with a disapproving look. Was he becoming increasingly easy to read, or had his sister always been so frighteningly good at guessing what was driving him?

Luckily, she contented herself with a pointed smile. 'Do what you can't help doing. In the meantime, I will take care of the real issues and find out who knew how much about Morton's plans.'

Chapter Three

'Nothing,' Zic said tonelessly, and dropped the book on the floor next to him. He sat cross-legged on the soft, red carpet of the library, in the centre of a structure that resembled a messy incantation circle of printed matter.

His brother hung over a chair behind him and groaned demonstratively. He turned his book this way and that, as if he hoped the secrets inside would simply tumble out at some point. 'What does that even mean? *Bimetallic corrosion* ... And what does it have to do with old frippery? If anyone here is corroding, it's me.'

The twins had joined Eldric and Albert, and even Tripp had volunteered to help them, while Lola checked the border posts and Kathleen wrote sharp-tongued letters and engaged their aunts in chit-chat. His blond friend had long been bobbing his feet, constantly shifting from one sitting position to another on the windowsill and staring at the pages in front of him as if they had murdered someone. Eldric suspected that the only reason Tripp hadn't given up yet was because he wanted to prove something to Albert.

He let his gaze wander over the rows of high, neat shelves. Since the fire, there was still a hint of smoke in the cracks of the walls and what was left of the carpet. Although he had already replaced the furniture and many of the books, entire subject matters were missing and needed restocking. For the sake of tradition and aesthetics, he would eventually also replace the two missing busts.

Annie nibbled on a biscuit and, for the first time since her return, seemed a little less anxious as she studied books with colourful pictures. Perhaps he shouldn't have been surprised, especially as her parents both had a penchant for reading and Liliana had often brought her here. Liliana ... *If only I knew whether she is still here ... whether she is suffering or whether she is all right ...*

Eldric closed the opus in front of him and pushed it away, against the pile on the table. So much knowledge, so much recorded research and experience, and yet they had been poring over it all for hours without having discovered anything useful. Yes, Sartiria's peculiar experiments with captured Lightsmiths were mentioned in the diaries, but that was all. The literature dealing with the Curse had nothing to offer as to how she had managed to remove her soul from her body and store it in that blasted necklace. His leather-bound friends had let him down.

Someone had to fly to the Crimson Plains to find out what Sartiria was planning in Liliana's body. The idea of facing her tugged at him in two opposite directions. He missed her closeness. The need to speak to her, to inhale her scent, to touch her, was overwhelming. At the same time, he was put off by the power she had radiated ... the presence of the Curse that she had always rejected ... the strange hardness in the now-shimmering green eyes ... the thought that she no longer reciprocated his feelings ... It made him want to tear out his hair.

Instead, he leaned back in his chair and began to laugh. Apart from Albert, the others in the room seemed to take this outburst as an opportunity to interrupt their search as well.

Annie detached herself from her pictures, plodded closer in confusion and hugged his right leg. 'Daddy, why you are laughing?'

Tripp jumped to his feet and held out his book to him. 'Can we swap?'

Slowly, Eldric shook his head, and his laughter died away as abruptly as it had come. 'It's just ... we have made no progress at all, and the sun is about to rise.'

Tripp frowned in disappointment and lowered the outstretched book. In the meantime, Zac began to poke his brother with a single claw and giggled when he snatched at him and missed.

Eldric pushed his feelings aside and cleared his thoughts. He needed someone who could suppress his powers to enter the Crimson Plains undetected and look around, by day if necessary. On the surface, he was the best choice. However, he could hardly bring Annie with him, and worried about how she would react to being separated so soon. Besides, he would be instantly recognisable if he was forced to show himself. Lola and Tripp would face the same problem and would have to starve themselves a little in advance. He looked thoughtfully at his nephews, who were trying to tickle each other.

Was it a wise idea to send the twins off on a potentially dangerous mission? Kathleen never did anything without an ulterior motive, and taking her sons to Rabenmoor seemed to be a hint. She wanted Zac and Zic to be more involved in what was happening. Meaning, she thought they were ready to take on more responsibility.

Annie continued to clutch Eldric's leg, and he stroked her head until she decided to return to her biscuit and pictures.

'Has anyone ever pointed out to you that you tend to laugh in inappropriate situations?' Albert asked, without looking up from the diary in front of him.

'What inspired this conclusion?' Eldric asked, unsure whether he really wanted to hear the answer.

His healthy hand in a glove, Albert carefully turned a page. 'My own observations. Most vampires laugh when something gives them pleasure. Zac and Zic laugh when they hatch something or when they are involved in some kind of game.'

The twins paused in their bickering and listened as their names were mentioned.

'Tripp laughs when he does something daring and uses his powers. Or when someone has a mishap.'

In the background, the aforementioned pushed his lower lip forward, thought for a moment, and then nodded approvingly.

'Kathleen's laughter is very social. She laughs when she wants to encourage someone or to communicate her approval or disapproval, for example when someone breaks an unwritten rule of conduct. Many vampires also laugh when something surprises them.'

Albert frowned and turned another page. 'Morton used to laugh whenever he won. When he could prove once again that he was better or stronger, preferably by inflicting pain or humiliation on someone else. But you ...' He hesitated and then raised his eyes to scrutinise Eldric. 'You laugh when you should be in poor spirits.'

'Not only then,' Eldric emphasised. 'I, too, laugh when I feel joy, like when I'm flying or ...' His thoughts wandered back to Liliana, and he cleared his throat. 'I guess I laugh when I am relieved or in need of relief.'

'I see,' Albert replied thoughtfully. 'Your laughter is a relaxation mechanism.'

His brother had a habit of analysing the behaviours of others, just as he noted compounds of chemical substances or pieced together a mental image of a historical place from fragments of old writings. He was rarely wrong, but his statements sometimes came across as strange. Although everyone was constantly observing others and drawing conclusions from what they revealed about themselves, it wasn't exactly pleasant when pointed out so bluntly.

'Yes, probably,' Eldric admitted. 'However, I doubt that I am the only one. I listen to jokes all the time from certain persons who feel the need to lighten the mood.'

Tripp only grunted in response to this last remark. Zic rolled his eyes, and Zac sulked. 'Make up your own jokes if you don't like ours,' the latter grumbled.

'I didn't say that.' Eldric reached for the next book, but apart from Albert, nobody seemed to have the motivation to continue with their investigation.

Tripp even stretched out on the windowsill and placed the open book over his face.

Zic yawned and rested his head on his wall made of books, while Zac went back to his chair and plopped down on it. In his eyes lay one of those appraising looks Eldric knew from Kathleen.

'Uncle El, why do you love books so much?'

He had expected a different ending to the sentence, one in which *her* name fell again, and had already steeled himself inwardly for the appropriate response. Now, he paused for a moment. 'Because they never complain.'

'No, seriously. My mum says you used to be more interested in letters than other vampires.'

Eldric sighed. That was a short explanation, but it was nevertheless a serious one. One could pick up a book on a whim or put it back on the shelf and leave it there for years; it never grew resentful because it wasn't paid enough attention. At most, it became a little dusty. Books had no expectations. They only wished to communicate their message and left it up to the reader what to do with said information. If Albert hadn't been engrossed in his reading again, he would certainly have agreed with this notion.

'There is something about the written word that fascinates me,' Eldric said. 'It's nothing but ink on paper, and yet that ink brings whole worlds to life in our minds; stories, ideas, connections ... It's like an immersive kind of listening, where we can make up our own minds and repeat a particular passage as many times as we like until we truly understand it. If we read a book from the past, we receive messages from the dead.'

Zac grinned at this last remark, showing his dimples, so El continued. 'Admittedly, at the moment it feels like we are groping our way through impenetrable darkness. But this library alone contains more knowledge than we could ever acquire in an entire lifetime.' He leaned forward towards Zac and lowered his voice conspiratorially. 'And knowledge is a form of power. I think your mother understands that. She simply deals with other offshoots of knowledge.'

This aroused Zic's interest. He blinked and raised his head.

Eldric remembered well what it had been like to be passed over as a child and then – when it turned out that he was in no way inferior to Morton in terms of demonic powers – to be confronted with extremely high expectations. He didn't want to overburden his nephews, but he also knew how much they craved an opportunity to prove themselves. Furthermore, the likelihood of them being easily identified if the Crimson Plains vampires caught sight of them was minimal. He had not yet sought Kathleen's opinion on the matter, but time was of the essence, and he suspected that he would be better off informing her only after they had left.

'Speaking of *knowledge*,' he began, 'what are your thoughts on undertaking a delicate investigation for me?'

Zac's eyes immediately lit up. 'What kind of investigation?'

'We need to find out what Sartiria is currently up to in the Crimson Plains, and unfortunately, no books can tell us that. Would you dare to go?'

'Yes! Yes, absolutely.' Zac grabbed his brother's arm, and Zic nodded eagerly.

'Look around without being noticed. I need to know if Sartiria is still there, how extensive her control over Liliana's body is, and if she has allied herself with the family of the Crimson Plains. Bonus points if you can catch anything about the Light chains we left behind ... the chains Morton was trapped in. They must have been buried when the dungeon collapsed.'

He gave them a stern look. 'That shall be all there is to it. Do not take any unnecessary risks. I'd rather you return unharmed and without any useful information than be captured and force us to launch another rescue operation.'

'Understood!' The youngsters stood at attention as if he had shouted orders at them.

'Good, I'll expect you back in three nights.' Eldric hesitated, but he suspected this would only increase their enthusiasm for the task, so he added, 'Go as soon as you can get ready, and make sure your mother doesn't notice.'

'Don't worry.' Zac winked. 'We are masters at secretly disappearing.'

While his nephews scurried out of the library, Eldric sorted out the books so that they could be returned to their assigned places. He turned around when he heard someone approaching.

'I see you are hard at work here.' Smiling and with a slinky walk, Rosalia entered the library. 'I am currently underemployed, if you could use another pair of eyes. What are you looking for?'

Eldric hesitated and went back to his chair, where he stopped with one hand on the backrest. The question was, what was *she* looking for? Did she merely long for company, or had she come here in the hope of finding him alone?

'Since when have you been interested in scientific research?' Tripp lifted one half of the book from his face and squinted out from under it.

'And you?' Rosalia replied tersely. 'What do you have to contribute, apart from silly remarks? You don't even know which way to hold a book.'

Ever since Eldric had found out about her attempts to murder Liliana through Tripp, Rosalia had not been on particularly good terms with the latter.

'At least I was asked to be here,' Tripp replied.

Rosalia glared irritably at him before regaining her good humour and turning to Eldric. 'How can I help?'

'We are looking for information on the storage and transfer of demonic powers.' Engrossed in his reading, Albert hadn't noticed his brother's indecision, and pointed to the half-dismantled circle of books that Zic had left behind. 'That is our pre-selection. You may help yourself to it.'

'Actually, we were about to call it a night,' Eldric said. But Rosalia bent over, picked up one of the books Albert had mentioned and sat down at the table.

Only after she had skimmed through the table of contents did she raise her eyes. 'You said you valued our friendship, El, and so do I. We can remain friends, can't we?'

Eldric didn't know the answer to this question, although he would have liked to agree with her. 'I suppose that depends on whether you can see me and treat me the same way you would, for example, Tripp.'

'Impossible,' Rosalia claimed mockingly, tossing back her hair. 'You are our honourable Lord, and Tripp is an impulsive fool.'

'I'm right here,' Tripp grumbled from the windowsill. 'I can hear you.'

'All the better.' Rosalia smirked and turned her attention back to the book in front of her.

Eldric finally sat down. He didn't want to discuss this further in front of Albert and Tripp, and he couldn't see any obvious signs that she was plotting something. Still ... Could she put her feelings aside so quickly? If she hadn't yet realised the connection between their research and Liliana, she soon would.

Chapter Four

According to Ernestine of Finsterwald, author of *Hunters of the Night*, there were three categories: blatant hunters, stealth hunters and seductive hunters. These categories certainly had their justification. Yet, Eldric had observed vampires whose hunting style could not be conclusively categorised. Lola was one such case, as she showed no particular preference and was skilled at all three styles. Olin jumped from one thing to the next when hunting, as he did in everything else, and Albert's demonic powers were so tame that he scarcely hunted. Even if he supposedly flew out for that very purpose, no one would have been surprised if he were conducting some kind of natural science or historic research instead.

Although Eldric was never obvious about it, Rosalia had an uncanny sense for when his blood levels were getting low. Today, she had intercepted him in the courtyard and tried to persuade him to go hunting with her. But he wouldn't make such a similar mistake a second time. Rosalia hunted by seduction, and he would make sure to stay away from her whenever one of them was hungry.

Their hunting styles didn't match anyway, because Eldric himself was a stealth hunter. He liked his prey happy, free, unsuspecting and uninfluenced until the last moment. These humans laid down their lives to preserve his, and he thanked them by not frightening them unnecessarily. His victims died within a single heartbeat. Of course, Liliana had this idea that vampires shouldn't kill humans, but that was just the way things were. Foxes hunted rabbits, wolves hunted deer, and vampires hunted humans. Wolves would also eat a human if they were hungry and got hold of one. Even a simple house cat, given the circumstances, would probably eat a human. Nobody despised them for it.

In his thoughts, he could hear Liliana's rebuking voice and see her glaring at him for calling her prey. It wasn't nice, but that was rarely reality.

You have more intelligence than an animal, she would say. *You vampires lie to us and manipulate us.*

Yes, they did. Every species drew on the abilities it had at its disposal. Animals outwitted other animals, too. They hid, lay in wait, tried to lure others into traps. Packs of wolves coordinated their hunt, enclosing their prey wherever possible. Vampires also manipulated, lied to and killed each other. In this respect, they treated humans no differently from their kind.

But you are more than just clever. You philosophise, you make moral decisions, you create art. You are capable of empathy. You *are capable of empathy, El.*

Yes, he was. And that was why he submitted himself to these strict rules, even though he didn't really have to. That was why he never took more than he needed. But he did need human blood.

Eldric flew a daring arc around a rock formation and turned south. He had never understood Liliana's initial fear of heights. The ability to fly was the best of all the privileges the Curse granted them. Eldric loved the feeling of being carried on the wind by his wings. Especially in the mountains around Finsterwald Castle, where there were many places one could only reach by flying. One also acquired a much better understanding of the geography of an area from the air. Everything suddenly looked neat and picturesque.

To improve his vision, he loosened the grip on his powers. The hunger grew immediately, clawing at his consciousness. There was still nothing moving beneath him to attract the attention of his hunting instinct.

Humans, too, could starve, but nothing matched the greed the Curse instilled in him. It was insatiable and unbending. Well, he was able to bend it a little here and there. However, if he neglected the demon's needs for too long, it always took its toll at a particularly inconvenient moment.

Many of the authors in this field compared the desire for blood and hunting with sexual appetite, which was certainly true to some extent. It was a kind of desire that took possession of his body as well as his mind. Both were by nature deeply rooted instincts.

In addition, both of these urges helped to spread the Curse. Producing many vampire children also increased the demon's influence on the world, just not as effectively. Albeit in Eldric's case, this relationship was reversed. In him, the Curse failed to fulfil its purpose in the sense that none of the humans he bit could live with it. Perhaps he really was something of a monster, an anomaly. Then again, the Curse would dilute as it was passed on. As long as those bitten by him lasted long enough to bite someone in turn, it was possible for the bitten of the bitten of the bitten to survive.

Most vampires didn't worry too much about it, but Eldric had always endeavoured to keep his human and demonic sides separate, or at least to pay attention to where he was on that spectrum so that he didn't slip too far to the side where madness crept up on him. Tracing these intertwined needs and untangling them with precision was what helped him stay sane and grounded. He had become accustomed to careful self-examination. The better he was able to assess his own reactions, thoughts and feelings, the better he was able to deal with them properly. No other living vampire on this continent knew how to decipher and control their powers and urges as precisely as he did.

He had acquired this ability with iron discipline, because the sheer extent of his powers forced him to do so. And since Liliana, this discipline had become twice as important. With her, Eldric had sensed how the needs of his demonic and human parts suddenly overlapped in a strange way, which had confused and unsettled him at first. By now, he had learned that the crucial difference was the heart. The demon was incapable of love. This feeling came solely from his human side. Therefore, in Liliana's presence, he only indulged in those parts of his lust that included his heart.

Eldric startled and realised that he was already hovering over the villages just before Seefurt. A night-time stagecoach sped along the road below. As the sky was overcast, the darkness would help him stay undiscovered by weak human eyes. So he lowered his flight path and ventured closer to the coach, but not so close that the horses would notice him and start to baulk. He allowed his powers to expand. His senses were completely focused on the possible prey inside, the trail of scents that the vehicle was dragging behind it. His powers urged him to strike immediately, but instead, Eldric dropped back and spiralled upwards again.

Unfortunately, there was no one with a promising smell in this carriage. Since he only allowed himself to hunt as often as was truly necessary, he was not satisfied with just any prey. Especially in summer, he stalked various potential victims and spent two or three nights or even longer looking for the best blood. In contrast to other predators, who had to contend with sparser hunting opportunities in winter, the short summer nights made it more difficult for vampires to find prey. By the time the sun had finally set, the vast majority of humans no longer had any honest work to do outside, and the vampires had to concentrate more on the towns, on pub-goers, travellers and those who met in secret because they were not engaged in honest work.

Attractiveness was a strange thing. A person with particularly flavoursome blood running through their veins did not necessarily have to be attractive on the outside. Eldric's last prey had been an older, sinewy craftsman. However, if he felt a certain physical attraction to a human, he could predict with confidence that the demon inside him would also find their blood particularly enjoyable. For this reason, he didn't even want to know what Liliana's blood tasted like. He had been presented with the opportunity to try it many times – too many times, really. And each time he'd had to make a conscious and valiant decision against it.

If he were to bite Liliana out of sheer carelessness or a lack of self-control and thus hand her over to the demon's madness and certain death, he would never be able to forgive himself ...

What if she was already too exposed to the madness, with Sartiria inside her? The idea that the powers of a vampiress from the time of the war could be whittling away at her mind, her soul, with every passing minute, tugged at his nerves. Seeing her as she was now, with that strange, hard look in her eyes and the overflowing powers, was unsettling. At the same time, he longed for her. *He*, Eldric, longed for her as much as the demon longed for human blood. Except that in addition to his body and mind, his heart was affected, too.

Kathleen had accused him of having turned into a drooling fool. As if she wouldn't moan if her devoted Richard suddenly left her. The abrupt break, the change from spending every spare moment with Liliana to complete abstinence from her presence, was understandably a shock to his system. He hadn't ever been able to confide in anyone as unconditionally as he had in her. Therefore, his feelings did make sense, didn't they? He could list at least a dozen poets who had written lovesick poems or entire ballads. Waldemar's 'The Sweetness of a Wild Rose' and 'Moonlit Crests of Hills' had clearly been addressed to a woman, or possibly several women.

As a youth, he had dabbled in poetry himself, but had quickly given up after Morton had recited his most unsuccessful lines in the courtyard for everyone's amusement. That had been one of the episodes during which his father had sat on him for three hours, pinning him to the ground so that his sons wouldn't slit each other's throats.

As a result, Eldric had limited himself to factual essays and eventually stopped writing down his thoughts altogether. Because everything that was written down could be used against him. If, despite seemingly everyone trying to kill him, he was to ever reach an old age, he could still write a book to pass on his wealth of experience in dealing with demonic powers to future generations. Until then, however, he would keep everything to himself that gave him an edge over potential opponents ... with the exception of the lessons he taught his nephews and individual confidants.

Like all the cities in his territory, Seefurt had long outgrown its original fortifications. Regular holes and indentations, as well as inaccessible sections without stairs, still bore witness to the wooden fixtures that had once completed the wall. As the common folk had lived in peace for centuries under his family's rule, they had made generous use of the freely available material.

Eldric approached from the lake side. Here, sections of the wall were still standing because the residents had built right into it to gain access to the water or to enjoy the views over the lake from their homes.

He retracted his wings at just the right moment, landed, and nimbly took off onto the first roof. From the ground, a human would only be able to recognise the dark outline of a person that disappeared after a single blink.

The old town was a winding labyrinth of narrow alleyways, but from up here, he could read it like a map. For the purpose of hunting, the many hiding spots were extremely helpful in a place where there were potential eyewitnesses. Because cities never really slept.

He spotted a staggering pub-goer on his way home and jumped onward. His great-grandfather, Rodon of Finsterwald, had introduced a rule that buildings in a city could not use flammable materials to build roofs. While Hohburg exclusively used slate in order to preserve the uniform, natural appearance of the cityscape, the majority of roofs in Seefurt were made of reddish clay tiles.

In bad weather, and especially if the tiles were covered in moss or algae, it was easy to slip on a roof. But tonight it was dry, and he was wearing his good boots. Besides, he had always caught himself so far, and even a fall from this height would only do lasting damage to his pride.

If he concentrated hard enough, he could feel the heartbeats of the peacefully sleeping inhabitants below his feet. As the influence of the nobility was greater in the cities, there were hardly any offshoots of the religion of Light here and therefore no blessed dwellings. Nevertheless, as Lord, Eldric did not allow intrusion into homes.

The wind direction changed, and a sudden surge of his powers told him that particularly delicious blood was within reach. He turned south-west, trying to pick out the scent from the general mix of heated stone, wood, smoke and animal and human evaporations. He didn't possess Boras' nose, but once he had picked up a promising scent, he never failed to track down the corresponding prey.

He dashed across the rooftops and caught up. The Curse gave him strength and suppleness, filling him with cold determination and confidence. *This prey is mine.*

A woman, perhaps twenty years old, discreetly perfumed and a little anxious, but above all joyfully excited ... and *close.*

Delicious. Hungry. Crouching down, he leaned over the gutter and scanned the alley below him. There she was!

Despite the mildness of the night, the human woman wore a scarf. She kept looking around as she walked, as if afraid of being discovered. Judging by her scent, she was on her way to a meeting with friends or, more likely, a secret lover.

He waited until she had turned the next corner, clung to the edge of the roof and listened briefly for footsteps before dropping to the floor. As soon as his feet hit the cobblestones, he pressed himself against the wall of the building he had just been dangling from. No startled heartbeats, no noises or panicked odours nearby? Good.

As he stalked along the alley, blending with the shadows, he used only as much of his powers as necessary to keep the human from sensing his approach. He might not be able to glide silently like an owl, but on the ground, he was just as silent and just as deadly.

He drew even closer. Her breathing, the soft scraping of her footsteps ... everything reached him demonically amplified and crystal clear, especially her smell and the tantalising pulsating of her heart. His senses latched onto it, and the other impressions – rubbish in the gutter, beer and the muffled noise from an inn – faded. Her anticipation mingled with his own, and his powers now threw themselves with all their might against the cage of his imposed restraint.

Hunger. Blood. Drink. Now!

His mouth immediately began to water. His jaw muscles tightened almost painfully. His fingers trembled and twitched with a thirst for action. The demon wanted to spread his curse. His powers needed this blood; *he* needed this blood.

His prey stopped, placed her fingertips on the wall of a closed grocer's shop and peered out onto a wider street in front of her. He couldn't wait any longer.

Eldric let his demon take over. A heartbeat later, he was at her side, wrapping one arm around her from behind and pressing the other over her mouth. His teeth sank into her skin before she realised what was happening, and the clawed hand that had gripped her ran across her throat at the same moment as the Curse ate into her mind. There was no scream of agony; she merely gurgled and went limp.

Good. While he did enjoy the power it lent him, he didn't wish his curse on an unprepared mind. His demon feasted on the fresh, warm blood. The need to suck as much life out of her as possible began to fill his entire field of perception.

He drank hastily, filled with that greed bordering on desperation that felt so familiar and a little frightening at the same time. His powers flooded his body and mind with deep satisfaction and renewed vigour. It felt so right. So exhilarating ...

But as soon as the woman lay in his arms drained of blood and he took a deep breath, he heard her voice. *Then at least I know where I stand. How you see me.* Liliana's face appeared again, her eyes glittering with rage after he had pointed out that she was still potential prey.

What had that blue-eyed human done to him?

Chapter Five

Eldric looked at his sleeping daughter and played with the glass beads of Sartiria's necklace. At last, her heart was beating regularly and her breaths came calmly. It amazed him every time he held her that he should somehow have been involved in bringing this innocent new life into the world. How was that possible? His role in it had been precariously small. But without him, she would not exist. A part of him had reproduced in her; his powers flowed through her veins.

Unfortunately, they had not yet made themselves known. All children showed only small amounts of power before they reached adolescence. But at least a hint of Darkness, a demonic tickle, should be noticeable. Well, Annie was a special case, and apart from waiting, there was nothing he could do; at least nothing he could do without incurring Liliana's wrath ... once she returned.

There was an oppressive emptiness in Liliana's room. Lying between the sheets, which still smelled of her, would only have made his longing worse. So he had simply moved Annie's bed into his bedroom. It was a little cramped between his bed, the bookshelves and the narrow desk, but that was the preferable inconvenience.

Originally, he had hoped that nature endowed fathers with an innate knowledge of how to care for their offspring. Either that wasn't the case, or nature had skipped him in this respect. He may have flown around the mountains and played with her, but being there for her all the time was something else entirely. The library had a few books on raising children;

however, he didn't find any of them particularly helpful, as none of the authors had found it necessary to write about human children.

After the first few nights – and days – without Liliana, he had to admit to himself that he had grossly underestimated how exhausting it was to look after a small child. To constantly provide food and drink for her and put her on the toilet was one thing. But Annie didn't want to be separated from him for a single moment, which on one hand was endearing and understandable after everything she had experienced. On the other hand, though, it was a hindrance to everything else he should have been doing. She distracted him in the midst of private conversations, and when he tried to correspond in writing, she insisted on writing, too, scribbling on his documents and dripping ink on his trouser leg.

Only when he was searching the books did she content herself for a while with reading individual letters or looking at pictures. Still, now that the twins were no longer there to play with her, she was often bored. And boredom, apart from hunger, was obviously the worst thing that could happen to a child.

Then there was the problem of sleep. After Victor's betrayal, he could not bring himself to leave her to the servants. Vampire mothers had it much easier, because vampires, whether big or small, slumbered from sunrise to sunset. Humans, on the other hand, especially young humans, seemed to have a habit of lying in bed for a long time without falling asleep, and even once they did sleep, they often awoke again. He, on the other hand, did not wake up once he had fallen into his vampire sleep. Annie could cry her eyes out, scream for help and shake him desperately; he wouldn't notice. That meant he had to stay awake all day to be there for her. He took turns with Sebastian, but the lack of sleep already showed in his increased irritability.

'Daddy, I'm scared,' was Annie's most common reason for staying awake. 'There is an evil monster.'

'I'm the most dangerous monster here,' he assured her each time. 'All the other monsters are afraid of me.'

'No, Daddy, there is a monster behind curtain.'

'There is nothing there, Annie. I could smell it if someone were hiding here. Lie down so you can go back to sleep.'

'You have to look, Daddy.'

'I promise you, there is nothing there.'

'I'm thirsty.'

'I have already brought you a cup, twice.'

'I have to go wee-wee. I don't want sleep. I want to play. Where is Lisi? Where is Mummy?'

This last question bothered him the most. How did one explain to a little girl that while her mother was still there, she was no longer her mother?

As much as he wished things had turned out differently, he wouldn't have done anything different in Liliana's place. Was it his fault that it had come to this? Morton had been right. If Eldric had killed him during his captivity, he could have prevented all of this. But what good would that have done him? Without his self-imposed rules and convictions, the ice he walked on quickly became very thin. No, if Morton had done nothing, Farkas would have tried on his own, or Indira or someone else.

Not all his memories of Morton were bad. In the beginning, Eldric had always measured himself against his brother and downright idolised him. Morton had loved having a younger version of himself following him around and mimicking everything he did. He had taught Eldric many of the skills that vampires needed, and flashes of that time still accompanied him today. How he dealt and caught his first punches ... How Morton scolded him for stepping on a branch and startling the deer they were trying to catch ... How he jumped off a cliff to Morton's cheering shouts, tumbled through the air and collided with a tree trunk as he attempted a swift turn ...

But when Eldric experienced his first surge of powers shortly after his thirteenth birthday, everything had changed. Lord Thormund, his previously oh-so-busy father, suddenly began to take an interest in his third son. In

Morton's eyes, this meant he had risen from entertaining toy to rival. From then on, every game, every outing together became a competition, and Morton realised that his appendage was quite capable of forming his own opinion. This opinion differed more and more from his. While Morton enjoyed frightening his victims, Eldric specialised in stealth hunting. Morton increasingly spent his time in wine sprees, dice and card games and ordering the servants around, while Eldric immersed himself in the world of books. Morton gathered his admirers around him – Edward, Axton and, at the time, Tripp and Boras. Eldric, on the other hand, began to make friends with Albert, Lola and Rosalia.

The further the brothers grew apart in their personal development, the bloodier the competitions between them became. Fortunately, Eldric was a quick learner. His powers continued to grow, and his skill increased, especially once their father was training him also. Thus, Morton looked for other ways to demonstrate his superiority. Eldric had of course noticed his teasing and spiteful behaviours towards those of the castle's inhabitants whom he disliked. Then he found out what it really meant to be at the receiving end of those vulgarities.

Another crossroad in their relationship was the night Morton persuaded him to visit the grotto at Mirror Lake. There, at the tender age of twenty – inexperienced and barely older than the twins were now – he had discovered a side of himself that he deeply rejected.

The Mirror Lake had heated underground pools built on the island, and several times a year, orgies were held there for special guests. Surrounded by fragrant rose petals, touched by naked, faceless bodies and drenched in copious amounts of blood and wine, he fell into a trance-like state. Morton called it a celebration of their true nature. For Eldric, it was an incontinent and pernicious unleashing of the demon. He hated the feeling of losing control over his powers and had not known that it could be deliberately induced. Unlike bloodrage, this loss of control did not stem from unquenched thirst and the need to survive but from excess, from an obscene over-satisfaction of demonic urges.

It was rare for a vampire to actually go into bloodfrenzy during such an orgy and for the demon inside to take over completely. But when it happened, the vampire in question was doomed. That night, Eldric had willingly allowed himself to be led straight to the abyss. Morton had no doubt enjoyed seeing him like this, knowing that a little push from his side would be enough to rid himself of his brother for good. He would have never returned from the chaotic, destructive and lustful madness of his demon. His own powers would have consumed him, body and soul.

It was then that Eldric had realised how profoundly different he and Morton were. And he had decided to only ever take what he truly needed. Everything else was a waste of life – his and that of the humans who died for their blood – and dangerous to boot. He wanted to remain master of his senses, his mind and his actions. For he was more than his demon, just as he was more than the human body in which he dwelled.

This experience motivated him to find out as much as he could about the Curse. He devoured everything books had to offer and practised tirelessly – holding on, letting go, holding on, letting go just a little, holding on once more ... The instinctive use of his powers had become conscious, meticulous control, repeated until it became intuitive again, like the muscles that moved his legs to walk.

A knock snapped him out of his thoughts. Hastily, he stowed the empty necklace in his desk drawer before he went to the door, slipped through the open crack and closed it behind him. Olin stood in the corridor in his demon form and thrust his protruding chin even further forward. Eldric sighed inwardly. He knew what that meant.

'Annie has just fallen asleep,' he said quietly.

'You promised me a duel,' Tripp's father rumbled.

'When the appropriate opportunity arises.'

'And when is that? Last time you—'

'Last time I was on my way to pursue Morton because he had kidnapped my daughter. Before that, my library had gone up in flames.'

As a Lord, he couldn't afford to turn down a duel, and he hadn't wanted to immediately crush Olin's eagerness to avenge the death of his vowed partner. On the other hand, he couldn't be responsible for the demise of both of Tripp's parents.

'Can't your revenge wait until there is a bit of peace around here?' Which would probably never happen. And that suited him just fine in this case.

Olin crossed his muscular arms. 'I know what game you're playing, Eldric. You're hoping I will forget my challenge. But I won't.'

In fact, that would have been the easiest solution. 'Olin ... Do you seriously think you can win a duel to the death against me?'

The man he spoke to shrugged his shoulders. 'We will see about that.'

Eldric suppressed the impulse to grab him by the collar and shook his head. 'Don't you recognise my intention? I am giving you the chance to get on with your life and save face. You've issued your challenge. I have accepted it. As long as I stall you, no one has to die.'

'But that is not what our honourable traditions dictate.'

That didn't mean they had to be enforced at all costs, bless it! Arguing with Olin could be frustrating. Did he *want to* die? Did he miss Luella that much? As Eldric pondered this possibility, footsteps approached from the stairs, swift but unhurried. Sebastian.

The valet stopped when he found his Lord at the door with the transformed Olin. As he bowed, his long ponytail slipped over his shoulder. 'Please excuse me, Lord Eldric, Sir Olin. Am I interrupting? Is your daughter asleep, Mylord? Shall I relieve you?'

Before Eldric had time to reply, he heard more steps approaching.

'Where are my sons?' Kathleen's voice echoed through the corridor as she hurried past the lancet windows, her skirts billowing. Richard and Ava trotted after her. 'For two nights, *two nights*, I haven't heard a peep from them. No one claims to have seen or smelled them, and they were last in your care in the library.'

He raised his brows. 'And, therefore, I am supposed to know where they are hiding out?'

'*Eldric!*' Her clove perfume masked other body odours, but her heart was beating unusually hard and her flushed cheeks owed nothing to rouge. 'Two of our horses have also disappeared. You sent them over the border, didn't you?'

Sebastian's ears twitched; Olin fanned his wings softly.

Eldric had intended to keep their mission quiet for as long as possible, but his guilty conscience started to rear its head. Kathleen had to be rather upset to reveal so many pieces of the puzzle in front of everyone present.

'Nothing bad will happen,' Richard said. He and Kathleen's maid had caught up with his vowed one, and he put a hand on her arm to reassure her. His reddish beard was perfectly trimmed, as always. 'Eldric knows what he's doing.'

'Oh, does he?' Kathleen's accusing forefinger pointed at his chest.

'Perhaps we don't want to discuss this matter here and now,' Eldric suggested. 'How about you come to my study later? Then we can—'

'We don't know what this Sartiria wants, what she is capable of!'

'That is exactly why someone has to check on site.'

'The youngest members of the family, of all people? My sons and Medina?'

Eldric creased his forehead. 'Medina? I didn't send Medina anywhere.' When was the last time he had even seen her? The night Berlinda had freed Morton and kidnapped Annie with Victor's help? His mind had been too preoccupied by that incident to remember the silent shadow of his cousin – who was also his niece – in the background.

'But you sent Zac and Zic,' Kathleen hissed.

'No one in the Crimson Plains will recognise them. Besides, I was under the impression that you wanted a more active role for them.'

Kathleen snorted. 'Of course I do. But not without being consulted first. This is dangerous!'

'Not if they don't do anything stupid.'

She stared at him wordlessly, and Eldric sucked his cheeks in between his teeth to suppress a grin. He had worded his answer that way on purpose, and Kathleen rewarded him with an angry frown. By the Primordial Demon, Albert was right. He found inappropriate things funny.

'It is a simple observational task. They were told to look around, nothing more. I forbade them to reveal themselves or interfere in anything. At worst, they will be captured. Then the Crimson Plains will inform us and demand some kind of compensation.'

'You must have a little faith in them.' Richard patted Kathleen's arm, her index finger still hovering in the air in front of Eldric.

'After all, you took them to Rabenmoor yourself so that they could gain experience,' Eldric added. 'A battle was to be expected. I only tasked them with an investigation.'

'Yes, but they were with me, and now they are *alone*.'

'They have each other. And isn't that the next natural step?'

'What if they try to force information out of them?' Kathleen hissed, and Richard's eyes widened beside her. Apparently the idea hadn't occurred to him yet. 'What if they take revenge on them for the pile of corpses you left behind? What if their spurts aren't over yet?'

'I consider all of that to be highly unlikely,' Eldric replied calmly, 'otherwise I wouldn't have taken the risk. I have to employ the vampires under my authority according to their abilities. Zac and Zic have learned a few skills thanks to my guidance. They are up to the task. However ...'

He let his powers flare up and took on a threatening tone. 'You have my word. If they are not back by the appointed time, I will deal with this personally. And that is certainly not what the Crimson Plains wish.'

Although Kathleen's eyes continued to spark, her hand finally dropped.

A whimper from his room made Eldric flinch. 'Wonderful. Now she's awake again. Sebastian, come with me. The rest of you ...' He glanced at Olin, Kathleen and Richard. '... can lodge a written complaint if you don't like my approach.'

He swivelled around and pushed the door open. Back to another seemingly never-ending struggle.

Chapter Six

Eldric tied Shadowprancer to the trunk of a birch tree. The rope wasn't really an obstacle and would not stop the stallion if he wanted to run away. It served more as a reminder for him to stay close by.

'If you wait here for me, I'll bring you a rabbit,' he promised and rubbed the horse's flank.

Shadowprancer only snorted in reply. It was a hot night, and Eldric was grateful for the wind that rustled softly through the leaves of the oaks, beeches and chestnuts above them. He soaked up the smell of the dry forest floor.

'And what am I supposed to do?' Tripp asked, swinging off his mount. 'Catch rabbits, too?'

'You can do whatever you want, as long as you are prepared to follow me into the enemy castle, should I not be back by midnight.' In case a trap awaited him, he had arranged for a rearguard this time.

'It's long past midnight. Do you want me to sleep out here with the horses?' Tripp searched the ground until his gaze travelled upwards and caught on a fork in a tree branch.

'Or you can practise staying awake. I'm leaving the decision to you.'

Zac and Zic hadn't returned after three nights as agreed, and that was, admittedly, worrying. He hadn't waited for Kathleen to storm into his bedroom and remind him of everything that could have gone wrong but had left immediately. Medina hadn't turned up yet either, despite repeated searches, and the suspicion that she might have joined Zac and Zic hadn't been born out of thin air. After all, she often clung to the only other family members her age. Conversely, it would be a gross miscalculation on the twins' part to involve her in a secret investigation.

Should Medina also be sneaking around the Crimson Plains castle, he would have to drag three adolescents home by their ears ... or free them from the jaws of the enemy.

He didn't like leaving Annie behind. But what else could he have done? Stealing away had seemed wrong to him, so there had been a tearful farewell. Lola had returned from the border posts and would look after Annie with Sebastian. The two of them had gone to great lengths to distract the girl with her new doll. But this doll wasn't Lisi, and Mummy was gone, and Martha, too, and Daddy didn't want to take her on his trip.

He had promised Kathleen that he would personally take care of the matter. And ... although he was somewhat dreading meeting the possessed Liliana, he could not deny that the longing to see her face, to hear her real voice, also spurred him on. If he could speak to her, if he could somehow get through to her ...

Eldric gave himself a jolt and straightened up. 'By the way, your father has reminded me once again that I owe him a duel to the death.'

Tripp clicked his tongue and whirled round to face him. 'That blessed dimwit.'

'To be honest, I didn't expect him to show so much resolve. But I take it you understand that as a Lord, I can't simply turn down such a challenge.'

Tripp's left foot scuffed the ground while his fingers played with the bridle. 'You know, I don't miss Luella. She wasn't much of a mother and never looked after us. The old wet nurse Camilla brought me and Axton up. But Olin is ... he's become ...'

'He has become even more unpredictable?' Eldric finished the sentence.

Tripp nodded without returning his gaze. Instead, he wove the leather strip between his fingers. 'I think he misses her. And he may be crazy, but he has his version of pride.'

'It looks like it.'

For a nobleman, Tripp wasn't particularly good at hiding his feelings. He said what he thought and showed what he felt. And at the moment, that was an extremely uncharacteristic concern.

Although he acted loutishly, Tripp respected authority. He was one of the vampires who had internalised the law of the strongest and abided by it even when it didn't work in his favour. Even more than the fact that Morton had played him badly on several occasions, his decision to join Eldric was due to the conviction that he was the stronger of the brothers – or at least possessed a combination of strength and intellect that made him the better Lord. Their friendship had developed later, owing to the joint hunting of strays, training border guards, flying races, playing card games and the discovery that they could rely on one another.

'Tripp,' Eldric said earnestly, 'I'm not going to kill him. I will find a way to keep stalling.'

'I know, I know.' Tripp let go of the reins and made a dismissive gesture with his hand, while stretching his spine in relief. 'I'll see you soon.' His toothy grin flashed. 'Are you sure you don't want me to come along and let a few heads roll? As advance payment for whatever atrocities they come up with next.'

Eldric shook his head and released his powers without letting his wings sprout. Then he took off running, dashing between the trees, ducking and leaping at high speed. The demonic powers accelerated his heartbeat, strengthened his muscles, increased the capacity of his lungs, sharpened his hearing and dilated his pupils. The air rushing past him cooled the sweat on his skin.

In no time at all, he left the forest behind, crossed several meadows and fields and hid behind a hay shed to catch his breath and listen into the night. The flat landscape meant that the Crimson Plains castle was visible from afar, but potential intruders were also easily spotted. An approach from the air was therefore out of the question if he did not want to attract attention.

Sartiria was a general from the war; at least they knew that much. And someone like that would thoroughly secure the castle after his last visit.

As a stealth hunter, Eldric had the advantage in that approaching unnoticed came naturally to him. He knew without thinking where to merge with the shadows, how to move silently, when to advance and when to stay still. He had memorised the aerial view on his last visit and studied it beforehand in his mind's eye. The south side seemed best suited for crossing the inner castle wall, as it bordered an orange grove. The outer castle wall was too narrow for a guard's walkway and therefore unmanned. Presumably, the area between served as a buffer zone.

When nothing moved, he sprinted on, straight out into an open wheat field. In doing so, he risked being seen by people, so he ducked down at regular intervals and kept still. Possible witnesses would hopefully think him a delusion. However, it was more important not to be spotted by the guards. If rumours of unnatural passing shadows spread around the area, that wasn't his problem. But if he had to fight his way through the guards, it would give his presence away. So he made sure that the last building before the outer castle wall was always between him and that wall.

When he reached the building – a simple, white-plastered house with a stable – he pressed himself against the wall on the side facing away from the moon and dropped into a crouch. The last section before the wall consisted of a dry field from which a few sad poppies sprouted, and he wanted his crossing timed just right.

Patience was another virtue of a stealth hunter, and his was being tested as the first reddish tinge appeared on the horizon and the occupants of the house began to stir inside. He ignored the demon's craving for the blood that coursed through their veins and waited for the first signs of fatigue. It always began with a gentle pressure that increased in severity until he either had to lock his powers away completely or lie down and sink into unconsciousness.

Now.

His feet raced across the floor; dusty earth swirled up beneath them. He pushed off, pulled himself up, and paused for a moment in crouching balance on top of the outer wall, his senses heightened to the point of overstimulation. Mice, nightjars, a fox – nothing bigger.

A narrow path led right through the thicket that grew between the outer and the inner wall. The Crimson Plains had hired human guards for this ring. The quicker he disappeared again, the less likely he was to be discovered.

The inner wall rose up an estimated thirty feet. He looked for movement or human outlines, spotted no one, and jumped. As he landed on the path, branches whipped his arms and thorns tugged at his clothing. Eldric ignored them, smoothly transitioning into another pike jump over the remaining bushes, rolling off and stopping his momentum by hitting his forearm against the outside of the inner wall.

Were those voices? Two humans – they were approaching from the west, two hundred feet away, still concealed for the moment by the curvature of the wall. Well, he hardly had any time left, anyway. The heaviness of the rising sun was already tugging at him.

He jumped, found grip with his fingertips in the furrows between the stones, channelled his powers there, extended his claws and pulled himself up. Five seconds later, and he was over the battlements, falling downwards on the other side of the wall walk.

This landing was rough, but the pain in his left knee disappeared almost immediately. He threw himself completely to the ground, remained there and sent out his senses – smells, sounds, heartbeats. Then he jerkily withdrew them before his consciousness began to fade. As always, his demonic powers resisted being suppressed, but years of practice made the process much easier. His self-regulation blocked the inflow of power like the gate of a sluice.

He grinned. Time was up. The day had arrived. And no one had discovered him because the humans were too slow in the undergrowth of the buffer ring and the vampires had fallen asleep behind closed doors.

Out of sheer caution, he waited a while after the human guards on the other side of the inner wall were out of earshot. Then he got to his feet, patted off his clothes and looked around.

The oranges around him smelled delightful, even to his limited human nose. Behind them were more fruit trees, the green of a well-tended hedge showing through their branches. He looked up at the wall walk. In his human form, that was a height from which he would probably have broken his legs. Fortunately, he hadn't waited a moment too long to get over it.

The vampire families had built their castles in such a way that they were difficult for humans to storm. Finsterwald Castle and the castle of Evernight Valley could only be properly entered from the air. This one in the Crimson Plains was the most exposed, and he couldn't imagine the nobility entrusting themselves entirely to human guards. It was therefore reasonable to assume that there were also vampire guards patrolling in daylight, even if they had to go hungry to do so.

He crept through the castle grounds towards the main building – if it could be called creeping, in this form. Liliana would certainly have liked the gardens. That was one of the disadvantages of a castle on a steep cliff: there wasn't enough space for groves and flowerbeds. However, it offered her a marvellous view of the mountains, and that was magical, too, wasn't it?

Where could she be now? Was she sleeping, locked in one of the rooms like the other vampires? He shook his head. One thing at a time. First, he had to find his nephews. If Zac and Zic had indeed been captured, he knew where the dungeon was. But since it had collapsed, they might be locked up somewhere else. Unfortunately, without his powers, he couldn't break down any doors. Assuming they hadn't been caught and had been delayed by some other incident, where would they be hiding?

Eldric recalled the aerial view. Greenhouses, a labyrinth, rose gardens, ponds, stables, the servants' quarters ... Finding someone when you were without demonic powers was drudgery. With any luck, they weren't inside one of the buildings. He himself would have hidden outside, in a place where, firstly, he couldn't be locked in, secondly, no one passed by often, and thirdly, he would be sheltered.

He found the labyrinth deserted, as well as the pavilions covered in jasmine. Eldric strode through the ornamental shrubs and approached the main building via detours. While Finsterwald Castle had grown organically upwards and sideways from the original core, the builders of Crimson Plains Castle had planned and laid everything out meticulously. Only the observatory – which he had heard was Aleksander's pastime – and the pillars on the roof terrace appeared to have been grafted on. Everything else was subject to a deliberate aesthetic, yet Eldric liked the wild playfulness of his home better.

The sun continued to climb towards its zenith. He took off his coat, put it over his arm, undid the top buttons on his shirt and rolled up his sleeves. How could humans work in this stifling heat?

All entrances and windows had to be locked; anything else would be reckless. If he found a suitable stone or shovel, he could try to break a window to get inside. But he would certainly attract attention, and if he did that, he might as well wait until evening and use his powers to break an entry.

Out of the corner of his eye, he noticed a movement and ducked behind a bush that was trimmed to a spiral. Guards? He peered out from behind the dense growth. A figure flitted from bush to bush on the other side of the gravel path. Out of habit, Eldric sniffed, but noticed nothing but grass, flowers and dust.

He hid behind his bushy spiral and waited until the person had reached the same height on the other side of the path. Then, grinning, he stuck his head out from behind the foliage and raised his hand in greeting.

The figure flinched and widened its bronze-coloured eyes. 'Uncle El!'

Chapter Seven

He took a quick look at the wall, which from here was still as high as his outstretched hand. When he didn't spot anyone, he beckoned Zic over to him. The young vampire dashed over. He looked a little meek, as if he wasn't sure whether he should be happy or prepared for a scolding.

Eldric tried not to let his relief show and instead put on a stern face. 'How is it that I had to come and look for you here rather than listening to your report at my desk? Your mother is worried.'

'We, uhm ... The family swarmed out and we followed them. They are gathering people and bringing them here to be bitten.'

'They are recruiting vampires ...' That was a bad sign. 'Do you know what for?'

'Not exactly. But I think they want to recoup their losses?'

'Why haven't you returned with this information? Where is your brother? Is Medina with you?'

Zic's eyes briefly jumped to the main part of the castle in front of them.

'Have they gotten themselves caught?'

'What? No. I mean yes, but on purpose. And only Zac. He let himself be recruited.'

Eldric raised his brows. 'He did what?'

'You taught us how to suppress our powers almost completely in order to appear human.'

'Human blood tastes different.'

'That's what I said, too. So we came up with the idea that he would let one of the people who had already been turned bite him before it was his turn.'

Eldric nodded curtly. 'That could work.'

'It did work,' Zic replied with a hint of defiance in his voice, brushing a dark curl from his forehead. 'Only now he's sitting in the storage cellar with the actual bitten recruits.'

Being locked in a room with the newly cursed while they were still wrestling with demonic madness wasn't a pleasant thought. But it didn't pose too much of a threat to a vampire perfectly capable of defending himself.

'And Medina?'

'What about her? I haven't seen her in forever.'

That was exactly the problem. 'Could she have followed you here?'

'No. Why would she do that? No one saw us sneak away from Finsterwald. I swear.'

Well then, Medina's disappearance had to be related to something else. If she had defected to the Crimson Plains because she blamed her own family for Berlinda's death, Zac and Zic would have noticed. Or she could have overheard about Boras being her biological father and flown away from home out of protest.

'And what are the next steps in your plan?'

Zic showed his dimples. 'We found your Light chains.'

'You have?' Eldric remarked appreciatively.

'We broke down the door and released the prisoners. Amidst the confusion, we searched the collapsed dungeon. Zac took the chains and hid them in a chest of drawers that was standing around. In the banqueting hall.'

'Do you mean the ballroom?'

'Yes, that's where they took all the furniture and valuables from the storage cellar because the dungeon was destroyed.'

'I see.' Eldric switched from a lowered voice to a whisper. Someone had appeared on the wall, and he pulled his nephew closer to him behind the bush. 'Then we'll get Zac and the chains out after nightfall and leave.'

'No. We can take care of Liliana if we stay here. Uhm, Sartiria ...' A sudden redness climbed up Zic's neck.

His secret crush on Liliana had not escaped Eldric's notice. But it was just that, a youthful crush, and since Liliana had no idea, and Zic would hardly confess it to her any time soon, he saw no reason to comment on it.

He smiled. 'I thank you for your thoughtfulness, but I wouldn't want to—'

'We can find out a lot more if we mingle with them. What exactly this Sartiria is up to in Liliana's body, whether they are preparing to fight us, or ...' Zic fumbled for words and waved his right arm, which Eldric quickly grabbed and pushed back to his side, out of sight of the wall.

His suggestion was by no means bad: no, it was in fact very tempting. Having loyal informers was invaluable. And if someone could stay here and stand by Liliana in an emergency ...

'We take turns with the role of the recruited vampire, so we don't tire ourselves out too much,' Zic added eagerly.

'And how do you plan on communicating with us?' Eldric asked.

Zic bit his lower lip. They hadn't thought about that yet. 'With a written message?'

'Who will transport the message to Finsterwald?'

'My father does his bat breeding ...'

'The Curse makes the animals more persistent, but they are still a long way from being able to deliver messages.'

'Or whichever of us isn't playing the recruit can fly to the border and deliver the message there.'

'Hm.' That would leave one of them alone for a whole night. 'In an emergency, yes. If time is not of the essence, you could send a letter to our official letterbox. By post.'

'By ... post?' Zic repeated incredulously.

'Since you are here on your first unofficial assignment from the Lord of Finsterwald, I think it may be time I told you about the letterboxes. When an informant sends us a message that cannot be delivered in person, he sends it to a so-called letterbox, a contact who forwards the message to one of the border towers. Such a message must, of course, be encrypted. It reaches the mailbox in the normal way via human postal service.'

'Wouldn't carrier pigeons be much faster and safer?'

'A little faster, yes. Safer? No. A carrier pigeon can be intercepted. So can a stagecoach, I suppose, but the nobility is not interested in the personal affairs of the common folk. Yet every territory has a relatively efficient postal system.'

'Er, should I just walk into a post office?'

'Yes. Ask for it in the next town.'

Zic blinked as if he needed a moment to digest this news.

Kathleen would not be pleased with his decision. But Eldric was impressed by the cunning and swift determination with which the twins had manoeuvred themselves into a favourable position.

A rustling in the bushes further back made him perk up. But only two sparrows hopped onto the gravel path.

'What do you do if you get caught?'

'Flee.' Zic grinned sheepishly. 'Or assure them that our kind uncle will pay a large ransom for us.'

'Well ... I'll leave it up to you. If you prefer, I will break Zac out of the cellar at sunset and consider your job done. If, however, you want to stay here as informants, I won't force you to return to Finsterwald with me.'

'We're staying,' Zic replied, puffing out his chest and crossing his arms.

'I hope you understand the risks. I can't imagine you getting killed if you were captured. You are too valuable for that. But you could be held hostage.'

'We're staying,' Zic repeated resolutely.

When Eldric awoke, he was enclosed by unpleasant stuffiness. The odours of earth, wood, dried plants, metal and heated stone were pervasive. His hair and clothes stuck to his skin. Zic had led him to the greenhouses, at the back of which was a shed where the gardeners stored their tools. They slept there, uncomfortably cramped between pots and spades, until the sun went down.

He stretched, loosening his stiff limbs and allowing his powers to dispel the fatigue. Then he took the coat that had been rolled up as a pillow and massaged the back of his neck while he slipped Zic a gold standard to exchange to local currency. Before he said goodbye, Eldric made him repeat the postal address of the letterbox several times.

Outside, fresher air greeted him, though this inadequate freshness could not compete with the mountain breeze in Finsterwald. As soon as he had checked that no one was around, he set off. Lest his powers betray his presence, he reserved them to the minimum he needed to keep his senses heightened. It was still early enough for him not to encounter anyone. But the castle was coming to life, and he felt the otherworldly vibrations, the collection of individual offshoots of demonic power, like echoes of the same chaotic presence that inhabited his inner workings.

He stuck to the ornamental bushes again and stalked back to the main building, to one of the patio doors. There, he placed one flat hand right next to the door handle, the second hand over it, and pushed with a concentrated burst of demonic force. The wings of the door swung open with an indignant crack.

Eldric hurried inside and looked around for the chest of drawers that Zic had described to him. Wisely, he or Zac had wrapped the Light chains in a piece of clothing to keep them from glowing suspiciously. Besides, no cursed person could touch them with bare skin. He tied the chains around his waist with two torn curtain cords and buttoned the cloak back up. If it came to a fight, this wouldn't last long, but it was enough to smuggle them out of the castle unseen.

Footsteps and muffled voices could now be heard in the neighbouring entrance hall and on the floor above. It was time to retreat. Even if no one had heard the doors bursting open or noticed the sudden surge of power, there was a good chance that traces of his smell would linger in the poorly ventilated hall and be detected.

He stepped back to the broken patio door, listened and peered out before sneaking from the building. He paused briefly behind the ornamental bushes next to the path and then left in the direction of the orange grove. As there were no shouts from the wall, he assumed that the guards had not noticed him. If he disappeared without being tracked down, the broken door would cause a stir and the Crimson Plains vampires might come looking for intruders, which would be bad for Zac and Zic. Although, on the other hand, if he was discovered, the break-in would be blamed on him ... and sooner or later he would find himself face to face with Sartiria.

Something inside him tightened, and he took a deep breath. But the decision had already been made. He couldn't leave without seeing her. He had to try to get through to her somehow.

Eldric hid behind a small wall to let a group in white uniforms pass him by. When he reached the orange trees, he sat down under one of them and waited. Here he was already close to the inner castle wall, in the place closest to the grove where Tripp was waiting for him.

Gloomy clouds gathered in the sky from the west. He bent one leg and rested his head against the tree trunk. Five nights had passed since Sartiria had taken possession of Liliana, of her body and her spirit. At first, he had still harboured a desperate, tiny spark of hope that she would stabilise and return to him of her own accord ... out of her love for him, out of her love for Annie. If he was honest with himself, that spark of hope was still glinting.

The takeover is complete. Liliana's cold voice repeated in his memory.

Even if ... her soul couldn't just disappear. She had absorbed Sartiria and her demonic powers, but nothing had been taken from her. So she must still be there, huddled in a corner of her consciousness.

Grass rustled diagonally behind him. Someone was creeping up on him. The guards would have raised the alarm if they suspected an intruder, so this person had not yet recognised him. It was probably ... His heart skipped a beat.

Whether it was her scent, her powers, or something else that gave her away – Eldric sensed it was her. The prospect of seeing Liliana but speaking to Sartiria made his nerves flutter. As she stalked closer, he slowly, very slowly, filled his lungs with air, held his breath for ten heartbeats, and exhaled just as slowly. He tuned into the bumpy rhythm pounding in his chest, bringing it back to its usual regularity bit by bit.

However, this exercise cost him the few moments she needed to approach him. When he opened his eyes, she stood between the bushy branches a few steps away.

She was wearing a hunting outfit consisting of trousers and a simple shirt-blouse. Her hair ... the flowing golden brown that Liliana had been so proud of had been trimmed to just below her ears. Distrust shone from her large, shimmering green eyes. The demonic powers flowed from her centre with a steady hunger. But she still looked painfully beautiful. The sight choked his throat.

'What are you doing here?' she hissed.

She didn't want to kill him, otherwise she would have struck immediately. She made more of a lurking, waiting impression.

He kept some of his attention focused on his own bodily functions – breathing, heartbeat, muscle tension – and continued to force himself to calm down. Slowly, he got to his feet.

'So, you've discovered me,' he said with all the composure he could muster.

She smelled so confusingly strange and familiar at the same time. Unlike most ladies of the noble class, Liliana had never perfumed herself, apart from rose oil in her bath or rosemary in her hair, which was a blessing for his nose and soul. After all, anyone who didn't cover themselves up with distracting odours had nothing to hide. This circumstance, coupled with her beating heart, enabled him to read her feelings as if from a book ... his favourite book, the only perfect book that he now had to discover in the hands of someone else. This someone tore out pages at will, scribbled inappropriate comments in the margins and dripped blood wine on the cover.

'How did you get into my castle?' she asked with a grim look on her face.

'*Your* castle?' he replied, raising his eyebrows. 'What I've heard is true, then. The Crimson Plains have a new Lord.'

Of course, he had heard nothing of the sort. But someone had to replace Farkas, and as a wartime general, Sartiria was used to taking command. She possessed a level of power and a lifetime of combat experience that made her a suitable and dangerous candidate. The fact that she did not contradict him confirmed his suspicions: either she had already been given the title, or, at least, she intended to take it.

'I will ask again. What are you doing here?'

'I had a little errand to take care of. Now that we have bumped into each other, I would like to take the opportunity to deliver a message.'

Despite the anger he felt, the desire to take her in his arms, to touch her and feel her close to him, grew with every moment he spent in her presence. This confusing contradiction grated on his controlled poise. Barely moving of his own accord, he approached her, his gaze fixed on her face, on her eyes, and stretched out a hand towards her.

What could he say to reach her? Could she even hear him, or was she asleep in there somewhere? Had the two souls mingled? If so, he would have expected more signs of the transitional process, such as confusion, pain, delusion or other fluctuations.

Before his fingers touched her shoulder, she knocked his hand away. Her powers seemed to want to keep him at a distance as well. 'Don't touch me! If you think I am going to put up with that ...'

His hand sank down. He stared at her. *She is still there. She* must *still be there.*

'I know she is still somewhere inside you,' he murmured. 'Liliana, if you can hear me ...'

He hesitated, waited, hoped in vain for a sign, a smile, a twitch or a blink, some indication that the woman he missed so painfully was standing in front of him. Nothing. There was so much he wanted to say to her; so much he should have said to her when he'd had the chance.

All he could utter was a promise. 'I'm not giving up on you.'

'What are you doing?' She lifted her chin as if trying to look down on him despite the difference in height. Her contemptuous snort hit him like a fist to the stomach. His powers reacted as if she had actually hit him. *Take revenge. Bite back.*

'That useless human female is gone for good and will never reappear.'

His claws shot forward. The ache and anger that suddenly flared up inside him had tempted him to give in to the impulse of his powers. As expected, she dodged skilfully, and he pulled his arm back. Her reflexes were excellent. Unfortunately, the Light chains around his centre slipped a little as he moved.

His heart was pounding now. He held back, growling, prepared for a possible counterattack from her side. Instead, Sartiria stood rooted to the spot. A light gust swirled the odours of earth, oranges and leaves around them.

Drink. Drink her.

The Curse in him sensed the human soul in her. He almost laughed.

Then her smell changed, became more attractive, more enticing. He wanted to pull her towards him, press his lips to hers. She gasped, and her eyes widened.

Eldric understood instinctively. Although Sartiria had no deliberate access to Liliana's memories, her subconscious and her body were still reacting to him as before. And because of this reaction, she had just realised the nature of their relationship.

But he fared no better. As easy as it was in most circumstances for him to keep the Curse's greed in check, it was just as easy for Liliana – or what was left of her – to trigger more of it. He didn't want to expose too much of himself to Sartiria, who had apparently sided with the Crimson Plains. Moreover, the Light chains he had tied around himself were slipping lower and lower.

He took a hasty step backwards before wrapping an arm around his middle, summoning his wings and taking off. He ignored the shouts of the guards that followed him as he flew over the inner castle wall. Sartiria was the only one who could have stopped him, but she didn't.

Chapter Eight

Eldric drew in his wings and knocked on the balcony door. He heard a soft tap, felt the heartbeats behind the drawn curtains. When no one opened, he hit his knuckles harder against the reinforced glass.

'Kathleen?'

The double layers of mulberry-coloured fabric were pulled aside, and the maid, Ava, unlocked the door from the inside. She curtseyed politely to him. 'Lord Eldric.'

'Ava.' He forced a smile and nodded at her.

'Thank you, dear,' Kathleen said, rising from her dressing table. 'You may go now.'

The maid said goodbye and slipped out into the corridor.

'What do you want so late?' Kathleen's hand stroked the wooden edge of the table in front of which she had paused. 'Is this about my sons?'

Eldric hesitated at the threshold. There was something unusually intimate about the scene of the couple getting ready for sleep.

He hadn't entered Kathleen's bedroom since he was thirteen, and the décor didn't match his memory. She knew how to furnish opulently without cluttering a room. The same fabric that covered the windows hung draped over a floating ring and the four gold-trimmed posts around the bed. Under it sat Richard, the summer blanket pulled up to his waist, bent over an open book on his lap. It was probably a study on bats or horse breeding. He looked up briefly, greeted his brother-in-law and pretended to continue concentrating on his reading.

On a small table between two armchairs stood a decanter and two glasses, from which he smelled the remnants of blood wine. The door to the dressing room was half open, and behind it, the bright colours of skirts, shirts, jackets, hats, lace-ups and stockings shone out between their black counterparts. The portable statue of a naked Ragna lolled on a chest of drawers next to a fragrant bunch of sweet peas. Above it, his parents, Amalia and Thormund of Finsterwald, beamed down at the viewer from a portrait.

'Are you waiting for a prompt?' Kathleen waved him in impatiently. 'The sun will be up soon, so you can hurry up a little with that urgent message you're obviously holding on the tip of your tongue.'

'Of course.' How easily she could mix rebuke and invitation. He stepped inside, closed the balcony door behind him and drew the curtains before walking towards his sister.

In her slate grey nightgown, she made a peculiar impression on Eldric. He hadn't realised how deliberately she used her appearance as a tool. Without the usual make-up and her elaborate wardrobe, Kathleen appeared less imposing, older and younger at the same time; older because small blemishes, such as wrinkles or irregularities of her skin, were not concealed, and younger because the absence of splendour and colour made her appear less authoritative. Even the usual cloud of cloves that surrounded her had dissipated by the end of the night.

'The good news is that Zac and Zic are fine.'

'And the bad?' she asked immediately.

Despite the cool sharpness in her voice, Eldric noticed the tucked corners of her mouth and the quickening pulse. And for the first time in a long while, he saw in her neither the thread-puller who crouched like a powerful spider at the centre of her web of intrigues, nor the big sister with whose favour his title stood or fell. Right now, she was just an anxious mother.

So, he refrained from stalling her any longer than necessary, even though the thought appealed to him. 'The bad news is that, as you can see, they stayed there.'

'Why?' Richard wanted to know from the bed.

'Because they managed to worm their way into the ranks of new recruits.' Richard was not usually privy to delicate details, but there was no doubt that his sister trusted her sworn partner completely.

'You call that an observation assignment?' Kathleen flared her nostrils. 'And Medina? Wasn't she with them?'

'No. There was no sign of her for miles around. There must be another reason for her disappearance.'

'So ...'

'I want to emphasise that the twins' ruse directly contradicted the instructions I gave them. But ...' He grinned. What she needed to hear from him was confidence and appreciation. 'They have made themselves indispensable.'

'In-dispensable.' Kathleen repeated the word as if savouring the sweetness and bitterness in it one after the other. The conflict in her chest between pride and concern was palpable.

'We don't have any reliable informants in the Crimson Plains. The twins realised that this was just the right opportunity to infiltrate them. They also managed to recover the Light chains for me.'

Kathleen's fingernails tapped the tabletop she had been stroking earlier. Her gaze was directed into space. 'So the family is still pursuing Morton's plans?'

'I can't say that for sure. What I can confirm, however, is that Sartiria is already their new Lord ... or will be shortly.'

'We should pay them an official visit.'

'I agree. And preferably before they have had a chance to properly prepare for said visit.'

'Then we'll dispense with an announcement.' Kathleen's smile returned in cunning anticipation.

'Yes, but ... I don't want you there.'

'Excuse me?' she hissed.

'I understand that you want to see Zac and Zic, but I'm afraid your smell, or even just the outward resemblance, might give them away.' Or any sign of affection ... a secret smile, a heartbeat when their paths crossed. 'And we should carefully spread the information about a new Lord in the Crimson Plains to keep them on their toes ... in case the other families haven't heard yet.'

'Do you doubt my restraint?' She glared at him, which created a less dramatic effect without the coal-black lines around her eyes. 'I am not going to throw myself at them. And I don't see why newly bitten recruits should be present on an official visit.'

'To stand guard, for example.' He was not only concerned about the mother and her possible reaction but also about the sons. 'That's not the point, though. We want to avoid any additional risk, don't we?'

'Yes, of course,' Richard intervened from his bed. The book lay now closed on his bedside table.

'I will, of course, listen to your advice on exactly how to proceed,' Eldric assured Kathleen.

She snorted and glanced at the thick curtains. Morning was approaching; they could all feel it.

The idea that he might still be standing in the middle of their bedroom while Kathleen and Richard sank into a deep sleep had to be uncomfortable for them. It wasn't appropriate to watch someone fall asleep with whom you weren't prepared to share a bed. And you only ever shared a bed with babies or a vowed partner you trusted with your life.

He did not need to let his sister in on the fact that he hadn't been too strict with this unwritten rule since his time with the humans. It was probably an open secret among the servants and had therefore already made the rounds as a rumour. If he was lucky, he would eventually be labelled a crazy oddball like

Albert or Olin. If he was unlucky ... well, then this would just become another minor issue to use against him.

'I will make sure the information about Sartiria becoming the new Lord spreads,' Kathleen said. 'The other families will have at least heard of an incident in the Crimson Plains, due to my previous explorations and their own informers. Therefore, all ears will be open to snippets about this.'

'Excellent. I thank you in advance.'

'It shall be my pleasure.' His sister twisted her lips into a grimace that couldn't really be called a smile. 'And now please remove yourself from our private chambers, Lord Eldric.'

He couldn't help but raise a mocking brow. 'As you wish, dearest sister.'

Turning to leave, his gaze once again lingered on the portrait of their parents. His father showed his teeth in a broad grin and had his arm around his mother's waist. She must have been a little younger than Kathleen when the painting was commissioned. Chocolate brown hair flowed in thick waves around her shoulders and there was a playful look in her eyes. The couple looked as if they could conquer the world together.

Eldric paused. This image ... if only this image could replace those that were forever etched in his memory. His father, gurgling and crawling across the floor with the last of his strength, his face contorted with pain and rage ... and his mother's empty eyes as she slipped from Morton's arms with her throat slit.

Chapter Nine

Eldric had been sitting on the roof of the west wing, reading *Ten Groundbreaking Inventions of the Century*, when he felt an explosion of demonic power. The roar that immediately followed shook the walls of the castle.

It was a mild autumn night, and Eldric had enjoyed the peace and quiet to himself. He tucked his book under his arm, ran up, crossed the roof ridge and crouched down by the eaves. Excited voices floated up to him. The whole family seemed to have gathered along the arbours and at the front end of the courtyard. He perceived the assembled heartbeats as a faint, mingled thump.

His father was fighting a duel down there. Tradition determined that any member of the family could challenge their Lord to a duel to test his claim to the title. Although in theory, a Lord was free to refuse the challenge, he lost credibility and respect in the eyes of the others, which was why this never happened in practice. If someone defeated the current Lord, he did not automatically have to give up his privileges. But it weakened his position, reminded everyone of his fallibility and that it might be time to replace him with someone better suited for this honour.

Thormund had never lost an official duel before. But this was no ordinary fight. Eldric had recognised his opponent's power signature from its incredible scale alone: Morton had challenged his father himself. No wonder this duel had lured everyone out of their rooms. There hadn't been a direct confrontation between Lord Thormund and the son who had already seen himself as his rightful successor for a decade.

Eldric watched as they struck at each other, trying to predict their next moves a split second before they were made. It gave him a certain satisfaction to guess whether his father would strike from this side or that, and how Morton would block or dodge the blow.

His own powers tried to escape from the cage inside him, crawling over his skin, watching, too, hoping for an opportunity to interfere. He may have refused his father's ambitions for some time now, but whenever he asked him to a practice fight, Eldric would agree. Apart from his father and Morton, whom he was increasingly avoiding, no one had managed to overpower him one-on-one for a long time. The difference between him and Morton was that he did not trumpet this fact to every corner of the Continent.

Blood spurted ... an alarming amount of blood ... The vampires down in the courtyard gasped in chorus. His father roared angrily, and the mood changed. Eldric narrowed his eyes and gripped his book tighter. Even from up here, he could see the gaping wound from which his father was bleeding across his chest and stomach.

An eerie coldness gripped him. Morton meant business. This was not a mere challenge to see who was stronger. He was going to kill the Lord of Finsterwald! And he had surprised him with his covert killing intent.

The fight turned from a boastful display to dogged brutality. Before Eldric knew it – before anyone knew it – his father was writhing on the ground. He gurgled, heaved himself up and slipped in the scarlet pool beneath him, swallowing and spitting out his own blood. While his demonic powers still clung to life, attempting to heal the damage to his lungs and other organs, Morton kicked his throat with all his might. The strange wet bursting sound pierced marrow and bone.

Without using his wings, Eldric jumped onto one and then the other canopy and landed on the cobblestones. By the time he slid into line beside Lola, his father's heart had already stopped beating. It was shocking, and yet part of him wasn't as surprised as he should have been ...

Morton was firmly convinced that he was entitled to this position anyway. After all, their father had corroborated exactly that all these years. Now he had become tired of waiting and had simply claimed it ahead of time.

Eldric tried in vain to swallow the bitter taste on his tongue. *If you hadn't treated him so blatantly as your favourite, perhaps Morton wouldn't have behaved so high-handedly. Then perhaps you wouldn't have died prematurely at the hands of your own blessed son.*

Covered in blood and grinning like a pig, Morton threw his head back and laughed. The movement of his wings spread red speckles across the ground. Edward howled triumphantly, and some of the onlookers applauded hesitantly. The courtyard was drenched in the all-pervading smell of vampiric blood, tinged with the vapours of excitement and confusion. Eldric pulled up his upper lip contemptuously but said nothing. Then he caught sight of his mother, and his heart tightened.

With tear-filled eyes, Amalia rushed forward towards the place where her husband's body lay. Her silken, pine-green skirt fluttered behind her. But Morton blocked her path. His voice boomed over her, directed at everyone.

'I understand you, *Mother*. You loved him more than even *your children*. You want *revenge* for the heart I stopped.'

She transformed into her demon form and hissed, sobbing. 'Why? Why did you do that?'

'Because *I am the stronger one* now. That's the way of things. The *new generation* is replacing the old.' Morton spread his arms. 'Come, avenge your loved one's death, *as you swore to do!*'

Amalia stood in front of him, her chest rising and falling convulsively. She cried out desperately, and her claws did race towards Morton's face. But it wasn't a successful attack. Morton blocked her arm, pulling her towards him by the shoulder into a violent embrace from behind. The movement with which he ripped open her carotid artery was so fast that Eldric would hardly have noticed had it not been accompanied by gushes of blood.

He stood there and watched his mother go limp while a larger and larger area of her dress turned dark in colour. Her eyes, which had a second ago glinted with life, went out. In the horrified silence, his ears heard the soft rustle of fabric and the dull thud as her body slid from Morton's arms to the floor.

My mother ... It was as though the earth was giving way beneath him. The world had shifted – in a way that could never be reversed. The feeling of suffocation enveloped his chest.

No one, not even Morton himself, said a word. Eldric had believed his brother incapable of empathy because his emotional world was so shallow. But he realised with nauseating certainty that he'd been wrong. Morton understood exactly what was going on in his mother's heart. He understood her, and he had exploited that understanding shamelessly.

In a fair fight, his mother would have presented him with a real challenge, especially after Morton himself had received a few cuts and bruises from the duel with his father. Had he waited too long, some of the bystanders might have intervened. So he had goaded her, had played on her vow and the upholding of honour that came with it, had used her shock and her grief against her because he had known full well that his mother could never bring herself to kill her own child, despite everything he had become. In doing so, he had prevented his mother from voicing her concerns and possibly swaying the family's support for him to become Lord.

Eldric raised his eyes and noticed that those present, the family, the servants and even the guards at the top of the entrance gate, started turning in his direction one by one. As if they were expecting something from him ...

He swallowed. The silence weighed infinitely heavily on his shoulders. What did they want from him? Did they think he could raise the dead? This was not his battle. He had long withdrawn from the unnerving contests with Morton.

Kathleen's features had turned into a mask of neutrality. The clenched fists at her side trembled. A worried Richard held her by the arm. Beside her, Tristan's eyes had widened in disbelieving shock.

Even Morton turned towards him, growling. 'What?' he snarled, as if Eldric had hurled a reproach at him.

Eldric did not answer. He gritted his teeth. His surroundings blurred. His mother's motionless face at Morton's feet seemed to accuse him. *Why didn't you do something?* He hadn't intervened, hadn't prevented her death. And now ...

Cold burned through his veins like stinging crystal shards. His demonic powers raged and shrieked inside him. He staggered, searching for a foothold, a supporting arm to hold on to. No ... He had to stay in control.

He remained frozen in the midst of this storm, naked and lonely, exposed to the lust for revenge and the biting fury of the demonic powers that were tugging at him from all directions. Horrified, he detached himself, took a step back and looked at himself as if from the outside. No ... He could not afford to lose to the rising madness. He could not afford to feel these all-consuming emotions.

And so, he left that version of himself behind. He walked away from that lone figure, the helpless Eldric in the storm, and went to a place of calm and control.

He looked into Morton's triumphant face and felt ... nothing.

This was the crowning glory of half a lifetime of taunts and provocations. Morton had unintentionally prepared him for this. Eldric hadn't cared when he'd convinced the servants and all of his friends to pretend he didn't exist for a whole year; he hadn't cared when he'd torn up his favourite books or spread rumours about his genitals being missing; he hadn't cared when he'd blamed Eldric for his theft of two hundred gold standards from Finsterwald's treasury. And he wasn't going to start caring now. It was all the same to him. He had never asked for his overwhelming powers. He had never wanted to become Lord of Finsterwald.

He raised his eyebrows and asked in a bored tone, 'Are you finished here?'

Morton's jaw dropped open. His powers flickered for a moment. No doubt he felt for a wild drumming in his brother's chest and instead found only the beat of cold-hearted indifference.

The corners of Eldric's mouth twitched. Morton might have won everything his filthy heart desired tonight: the fight with his father, the title, power over his own mother. But he had not granted him this last victory. He was denied the satisfaction of tasting Eldric's pain.

Without waiting for an answer, he turned away and strolled down the steps into the castle, leaving Morton and the stunned gathering behind him. He left them just as uninvolved as he had left himself in the storm.

Two nights later, Morton commanded the vampires of Finsterwald to kneel before him and swear allegiance. It was a meaningless ritual that he had invented to showcase his authority. Eldric endured it with the same disinterest with which he tied his shoelaces or flicked a fly from a plate.

No, he didn't care. All this theatre, the posturing for power and position, the fears and expectations ... His parents were dead, Morton was the new Lord, and he didn't care.

A week later, Tristan disappeared without a trace. Eldric secretly took part in the search, but the family soon concluded that his death must have been directly or indirectly related to Morton's takeover.

Two weeks later, Lord Adorjan of the Crimson Plains appeared with his escort to welcome the new Lord of the Finsterwald to the circle of the Vampire Council. Eldric flew around the mountain peaks, discovered an eyrie and two new caves and read all eight volumes of the *Adventures of Wild Werner* to a young silver fir.

Five weeks later, the other Lords had also made their visits. Kathleen gave them a proper reception, as she had done countless times under Amalia's guidance.

Six weeks later, Morton had appointed new justices of the peace in all the cities of Finsterwald and declared it no longer necessary for vampires to hide from the humans under his rule. In the same breath, he complained about the other Lords of the continent interfering in the affairs of his territory.

Ten weeks later, as Eldric sat on the windowsill, soaking up the familiar smell of paper, leather and dust and staring out of the window lost in thought, Morton entered the library. Eldric ignored him, not even bothering to pick up his forgotten book and pretend to read.

Morton stopped intrusively close before him and nudged him on the thigh with the tip of his boot. His voice sounded like greased gears. 'I *knew* I'd *find you* here sooner or later.'

Eldric twisted his head and returned his brother's gaze in silence. As always when Morton was nearby, he was ready to unleash his powers if necessary. A little surprised, he noticed Rosalia next to him. He hadn't recognised her by her scent because she had sprayed herself with some heavy, flowery perfume. Her eyes looked even more feline, her lips an even deeper shade of red than usual.

With a loose arm around her, Morton waited for a reaction from his side, which never came. If Rosalia liked her place at the side of the Lord of Finsterwald, that was her business. Although judging by her heartbeat and shallow breathing, she didn't necessarily feel comfortable. However, lacing that was too tight could cause similar symptoms, and her dress was obviously *tight*. She avoided Eldric's questioning glance.

'I have a *suggestion* to make,' Morton finally said.

Eldric was tempted to simply turn away again. He had to clear his throat before he managed to speak. Perhaps Morton had ordered the whole castle not to talk to him, or perhaps everyone simply hated him after he had put up no resistance to Morton's takeover. In any case, no one had spoken to him since then, not even Lola or Albert. He couldn't remember seeing his eldest brother among the crowd that had witnessed their parents' death that night. But he must have been there somewhere, like everyone else.

'What do you want?'

'You'll *like* my suggestion, stupid,' Morton claimed. 'Come *along!*'

What was that? Was he trying to pretend they still had something to say to each other? 'Thank you very much, I can do without your suggestions.'

'*Eldric*, you're behaving like a *child*,' Morton snarled.

He had no leverage over Eldric, and that made him livid. He couldn't beat him into submission using physical force because he was just as dangerous in a straight-up fight. Eldric had practised his cool equanimity long enough. There was nothing Morton could use to seduce, bribe or threaten him. Therefore, even though Morton was Lord of Finsterwald, in his perception, he had no real power over him.

'I have a *request* for you, an important task,' he began again. 'You also belong to this *new generation*. Wouldn't you like to be part of the *progressive government* that I intend to implement?'

He grinned chummily and pinched Rosalia's buttocks.

'It's nothing dangerous,' she hastened to say, but continued to avoid looking Eldric in the eye. 'And it won't take long, either.'

Just because something wasn't dangerous didn't mean it was pleasant. Unfortunately, Morton didn't let go once he had gotten his teeth into something.

Eldric rolled his eyes. 'Just tell me.'

'Enough of this,' Morton growled. 'Come on now!'

He walked away, dragging Rosalia with him. Suddenly, to Eldric, she seemed more like a hostage than a lover. Morton stopped at the entrance and waited for him to catch up with them.

Sighing, Eldric stood up and put the book, which he had only read halfway through, back on the shelf before following Morton and Rosalia through the corridor. They had already stopped at the first door, and Morton pushed it open with attitude. Behind it was Thormund's old study.

Eldric entered and immediately stopped. Morton had barely made changes, but what he had changed was grotesque. In place of the comfortable arrangement of chairs and armchairs, a seat made of pure gold sat against the opposite wall, between the tiled stove and the oak desk.

He laughed loudly. 'You had a throne built for yourself? Did you want to show me how you can ruin classic aesthetics with misplaced splendour? This room is far too small to do justice to your level of self-importance.'

The two vampires, who had been waiting in the room as if they'd been ordered and not collected, gave him long looks. Tripp was fiddling with his cufflinks, while Lola had her arms crossed and her lips pressed together to a single, thin line. Why were those two here? They smelled of tension and discontent. Where were Edward, Axton and their silent follower, Boras?

Morton grinned, but Eldric could sense the smouldering anger behind it. 'What do *you* know about aesthetics? That's *not why* I let you come here. This is why!'

He pointed to the desk, where letters, reports, accounts and other documents accumulated in a messy heap. 'You like papers, and I need a scribbler to deal with this stuff.'

Brows raised reproachfully, Eldric approached the desk, fished one of the letters out of the pile and skimmed it quickly. 'This appears to be an overview of the yield, expenditure and income of one of our mines in the Thomlin region.' He lowered the loose sheet and looked at the mess again. 'You really do need help.'

'Yes, yes.' Morton made a patronising hand gesture. 'That's what I said.'

'What do you spend your nights doing? Did you think the administration would take care of itself?'

Morton glared at him as if he had insulted him in the worst possible way. Then his face smoothed, and he gave Eldric a frighteningly charming smile. 'You withdraw too much. It will do you good to have a purpose, to enrich your life with something *meaningful*. I don't shy away from public appearances or making important decisions. But this—' He nodded towards his desk. 'This is giving me a headache. I need someone *like you*, Eldric. Someone who can handle the boring stuff and make sure our territory *thrives*.'

He was not wrong. Eldric was indeed interested in how the various ventures, resource extraction licences and negotiations with the cities worked.

'Well,' he replied, half reluctantly, half curiously. 'I can at least have a look at it.'

'I *knew* I could count on you! You can start at any time, of course.' Eagerness lit up in Morton. 'But you know what we should do first? Go hunting *together*! Like the *good old nights*.'

Eldric realised how he involuntarily returned his smile. He had been avoiding Morton for so long that he had forgotten how infectious his enthusiasm for a cause could be. Did he think all was forgiven and forgotten just because Eldric had temporarily agreed to his request?

'I prefer to hunt alone.'

Morton winked as if they were once again the inseparable brothers from Eldric's childhood. 'We can make a bet out of it. If I *track down* my victim *faster* than you, you'll accompany me on my next official visit to Dimas. If you win ... well, you can *choose* your *prize*. What do you say?'

'I'll get in on the bet,' Tripp remarked, eyes shining dark and feverish. He looked as if he were about to jump out of his skin with tingling impatience. How long had Morton kept him and Lola waiting here?

Morton wrinkled his nose. 'The bet only applies to those of us who have *actual brains* in our skulls.'

Tripp growled but didn't argue. How did Morton have him in his pocket? Or did Tripp feel he had to follow him solely because of the title and the vocal support his mother Luella had given Morton?

Meanwhile, his hand stroked Rosalia's side, from her breasts to her waist to her hips. She smiled and snuggled up to him, but there was something wrong with the picture they presented.

In the background, Lola leaned against the wall and averted her eyes. Eldric finally realised why she was here. Morton pursued a specific purpose with everything he did. Most of the time, that purpose was to ensure his dominance and, if possible, amuse himself in the process. Lola had to have feelings for Rosalia, and Morton tormented her with having to see her with him. He tormented Tripp by letting him be both part and not part of his close group of friends. But Rosalia ... what was he using to torture her?

'Fine,' Eldric said. 'If I win, you and Rosalia will split up.'

At last, she looked up. Her heart was pounding faster, whether in anger that he had made her the object of a bet or out of interest in a little thrill, he couldn't tell.

Morton bared his teeth. 'It's *a deal*. We'll start at one of the north-west border towers near Roinnenstadt. And to ensure there is *no cheating*, we will ask the honourable Lord Adorjan to be our *impartial witness*.'

Chapter Ten

Eldric stepped out of the carriage and turned his head to either side until his neck cracked. No one came to receive them and tend to the horses. Old Herder put the whip over his knees and looked around.

'Where did they all go?' Tripp asked after jumping out of the vehicle behind Eldric. He busily rolled up the sleeves of his shirt.

'I'm sure we'll run into someone sooner or later if we just march into the castle.' Lola stepped up beside them and the three of them made their way to the main building.

Since no one opened the door for them, Lola pulled open one side of the gate for her Lord. As it turned out, the clan of the Crimson Plains had gathered in the entrance hall. The guards must have announced their arrival because servants scurried into neighbouring rooms with flower arrangements and crystal glasses. However, most of them stood rooted to the spot as soon as they beheld the uninvited guests.

Eldric grinned. They had succeeded in their surprise by crossing the territorial border unnoticed during the day. Issuing himself the permission to do so hadn't been particularly difficult, and thanks to that little trick, the Crimson Plains hadn't expected them to show up until the guards on the castle's inner curtain wall had spotted them. Of course, this could be seen as an unauthorised intrusion but seeing as they were officially waiting on the new Lord at the same time, this interpretation was easy to challenge.

Amidst the tense silence, they walked across the marble floor that shone in the light of the restored chandelier.

'Does it always stink of fear here, or is this a special welcome for us?' Tripp whispered out of the corner of his mouth. He had found a splinter of wood somewhere and was picking his teeth with it in front of everyone.

At the top of the balcony, to which curved stairs led up on both sides, stood Sartiria, scowling down at them. *She's still there, inside her. She is fine.* Eldric breathed in and out deeply. In fact, even the thick clouds of perfume could not hide the traces of general uncertainty and excitement.

'What is he doing here?' Lola hissed to his left.

Only then did Eldric's gaze fall on the young man with the protruding, rust-coloured eyes, who was whispering something to Sartiria. *Victor.*

He felt his powers stirring and slammed the door to his consciousness in their face. By the Primordial Demon! She had taken Victor into her service. What did this faithless vampire know about him and Finsterwald as a whole that he could pass on to her? Besides, Victor would easily recognise the twins. Or had he already recognised them, and they were now in custody? That would be a very bad starting point for negotiations.

He should have killed him. He should have wrung his sacred neck, so they wouldn't have had this problem in the first place. But ... No ... *Killing an attacker is defence,* he reminded himself. *Killing someone who once harmed me is revenge. Killing someone who could harm me is cowardice.* Only the last two points applied to Victor.

Nevertheless, Eldric growled softly. 'Traitor.'

As if he had heard him despite his lowered voice, Victor cowered behind his new Lord. Eldric didn't need to feel his heartbeat, seeing as he was sweating with fear.

He believed his assurances that Berlinda had persuaded him to commit his misdeed under threat. Consequently, he was susceptible to such threats. If they marked their presence in the Crimson Plains from the start, they might be able to keep him quiet if he had not yet blown the twins' cover. The only question was for how long ...

Aleksander broke away from the other family members and bowed. Eldric remembered seeing Farkas' younger brother briefly at the last Vampire Council. He was only just forty years old and his long, dark hair fell silkily over his cobalt blue tailcoat, which he had combined with sand-coloured trousers and an orange waistcoat. Compared to his late brother – Kathleen had described their relationship as strained and tense – he was less broadly built, but his features showed the same classically handsome symmetry.

Before Aleksander could address him, Sartiria's powers surged. 'I didn't expect to see you again so soon, *Eldric*,' she called imperiously from the balcony.

He bowed his head. 'Custom calls for such a visit.'

Sartiria came down the stairs at a moderate pace. 'The other Lords announced their arrival in advance.'

'We were in a hurry,' Tripp remarked, not taking his eyes off Victor, who crept down the steps behind his Lord and then squeezed himself into a corner as if imitating a mural.

'Due to the lack of advance notice, we were unfortunately unable to arrange a proper meal or other amenities.' Aleksander made a reproachfully apologetic gesture and pointed to one of the doors at the side. 'After the meeting, however, our servants should have prepared some refreshments.'

Without another word, Sartiria strutted past them. She barely gave the servants the opportunity to open the room before her, which was intended for such official meetings. There she took a seat on an armchair made of ornately carved cherry wood. Opposite it stood less extravagant chairs in a semicircle. Porcelain vases with bouquets of dwarf sunflowers, spherical glass lamps and gilded statuettes of birds such as peacocks, pheasants, swallows and ravens were displayed on waist-high pedestals along the walls.

Apart from Aleksander, Sartiria must have chosen Nusa as her close confidante, for she settled down next to Sartiria's throne chair after him. The smell of the slumbering infant in her arms triggered a feeling in Eldric that he had otherwise only known from his time with Annie. He gave the sleeping child and its mother a brief smile. Nusa had tied her blonde tresses loosely together with a hair clip. The upper part of her dress consisted of two overlapping panels of fabric; presumably to facilitate access to her breasts when she wanted to feed the baby. Perhaps it was also intended to provide a little distraction. Both Tripp and Lola showed a discreet interest in her generous cleavage, and Eldric's thoughts were caught up in the question of whether he might have missed something because he had never seen Liliana as a nursing mother.

Nusa was the vampiress they had pledged support to with the intention of destabilising the balance of power in the Crimson Plains a little. Unfortunately, she had broken off contact after Annie's abduction. He hadn't been able to find out why, although his guess was that her brother Ned dying alongside Farkas had something to do with it.

'Who would have thought that we'd be sitting opposite *you* like this...' Tripp leaned back with his legs crossed as soon as he had plopped down on a chair, and his grin travelled from Nusa to Sartiria.

Aleksander tilted forward indignantly. 'I must apparently remind you that this tone is not fit for addressing a Lord.'

Eldric also gave him a warning look, and Tripp sighed. 'Apologies, *Lord Sartiria*. I can't quite get your old persona out of my head.'

Sartiria smiled casually, and Eldric involuntarily dug his nails into the arms of his chair. It was the same smile Liliana wore on those lips when she mused to herself while brushing her hair or sewing up a hole in Annie's stockings. Only the fangs didn't match.

'I don't think much of the dictates of politeness. In the time I come from, that didn't exist. Nonetheless, I have taken on the role of a Lord and am willing to follow your customs. I expect others to do the same.'

'Lord Eldric,' Aleksander resumed, 'may we assume that you wish to end the conflict you had with my late brother? Especially considering you are undertaking the traditional visit in person?'

Eldric pulled himself together and loosened his fingers. He had to concentrate on the conversation. Perhaps Sartiria was willing to cooperate under certain conditions.

'That is indeed my wish,' he said slowly. 'However, the prerequisite for this is a certain willingness on your part ...'

'The law says that no one may kill the Lord of another family.' Aleksander shook his head regretfully. 'With all due respect, we cannot simply ignore that.'

So they wanted to take this track. He raised his eyebrows. 'That offence has been committed on both sides.'

'Has it?' Aleksander asked with an innocent expression.

Tripp growled. 'The whole operation was a trap. You wanted to kill El. That you didn't succeed doesn't change the fact that you tried.'

'As far as I am aware, Farkas only ... detained you, Lord Eldric.' Aleksander wiped invisible dust from his sleeve. 'The man with the intent to kill was Morton.'

'Besides, you are still alive,' Nusa added. 'While our Lord, may his accursed soul find rest, is dead. As is my brother.'

Was that why she had kept quiet? Did she feel betrayed, or partly responsible for Ned and Farkas' deaths through her correspondence with the enemy? The few lines they had exchanged spoke neither in favour nor against her involvement in the whole affair.

'I understand your logic,' Eldric replied coolly. 'But it fails because of the simple truth that I did not kill Farkas ...' He turned directly to Nusa. 'On that note, I didn't kill Ned either.'

Nusa blinked and fell silent.

'Even if it wasn't you personally,' Aleksander objected, 'the blame remains with your family, Lord Eldric, and is thus your responsibility.'

They had anticipated this reasoning. He deliberately addressed his next words to the Lord on her half-throne. 'Sartiria, are you a vampiress of Finsterwald? That would make me your Lord, of course.' This idea would certainly grate on her.

'No,' she replied as expected.

Beside her, Aleksander drew an audible breath. 'Lord Eldric, are you claiming—'

'Correct.' He held Sartiria's gaze. 'You may not remember this, but Albert told us you killed three vampires in one fell swoop ... and paralysed his hand in the process.'

How brave you were. If only you could remember.

'Can we believe your statement if your brother is the only eyewitness?' Aleksander objected.

Everyone flinched as Sartiria jumped up unexpectedly. 'That wasn't me! It must have been the human female who owned this body before. And she did it with a Light bomb!'

Tripp and Lola exchanged surprised glances with him. Yes, Albert had described it that way. But Sartiria's reaction seemed somewhat disproportionate.

'Traitor! The arrowheads, the stars ... Where there are some, there must be more. The humans are planning another war, and you smuggled your lover equipped with Light weapons into this castle!'

He forced himself to sit still, even though his powers also demanded more freedom. 'I didn't smuggle anyone here. I came to rescue my kidnapped daughter.'

'Then how do you explain those Light weapons?'

'Archaeology. Albert digs up old ruins and unearths strange finds in the process. The silvery glass ball – I assume that's what you are talking about – and all the other objects are all artefacts. He brought them with him to test their effects. There are no modern versions.'

Nusa and Aleksander knew nothing to object to for the time being and put their heads together. Sartiria's chest continued to throb furiously. Was she so caught up in her old time that she could see another war breaking out with the use of a few ancient objects?

Then the new Lord of the Crimson Plains sank back into her chair. 'None of you have ever seen Light weapons that didn't come from ruins?'

'No.' Eldric watched her intently.

An unsettled pause followed the general nodding of heads.

Sartiria slowly regained her composure and crossed her arms. 'How can anyone be so stupid as to try out Light weapons on vampires?'

As there was no reply from anyone, Lola recapped. 'As far as the killing of a Lord outside one's family is concerned, we are in the right, and we think we will have sufficient counterarguments before the Council. It would be up to you to prove that this woman you refer to as Lord Sartiria was not the one who killed Lord Farkas.'

Aleksander pressed his lips together. 'The losses we have suffered—'

'Don't talk to me about losses!' He had sworn to protect at least the two lives that meant the most to him, for which he was most responsible. Instead, she had had to protect *him*, to free him, and had paid for it with her life ... with the body that a stranger now controlled and paraded before his nose.

Lola skilfully continued the conversation. 'We see the situation as balanced in the sense that on one side Morton tried to assassinate Lord Eldric and failed.' She made a first gesture in his direction and pointed to Sartiria with a second. 'And on the other side, there was a clash between the old and the new Lord of the Crimson Plains, which you, Lord Sartiria, decided in your favour.'

'If you are willing to forget the perceived affronts of Finsterwald, Lord Eldric is willing to forget your ambush.' Tripp flipped the splinter of wood he had been playing with outside the semicircle of chairs. 'In other words, we propose to clear the air and start anew with Lord Sartiria's takeover.'

Aleksander's nose twitched warily. He turned to Sartiria with a questioning look, and she inclined her head as if to show mercy. 'As you wish.'

So far, so good. Eldric stood up. 'If you have no objections, I would like to discuss the last point alone with you, Sartiria.'

Nusa jumped up with the sleeping infant in her arms. For an anxious moment, Eldric thought Sartiria would flatly refuse. But then, turning to the vampires of the Crimson Plains, she said, 'All right. Go!'

Lola and Tripp also left, and Eldric stepped closer to Sartiria. He waited until the door closed before lowering his voice. 'How did you do it? I have thought about it for a long time, but you must have known incantations in your time that have since been lost.'

The books and ancient writings had told them nothing about how she had managed to store her powers and soul in an object and transfer them to another body when the time was right. If she gave him some clues, he might be able to deduce, with Albert's help, how to repeat the process and free Liliana.

She sized him up for a long time.

What she really wanted, he still didn't understand. She might have joined forces with the vampires of the Crimson Plains, but wasn't that rather a way of achieving something else? Had she simply adopted Morton's plans to subjugate the Continent, or was she pursuing an even grander goal spanning across different periods of time?

'Apart from me and my closest liegeman, Kral, nobody knew about this possibility,' she finally said. 'We first had to find out whether it really worked.'

This implied that she was an isolated case and that they were not dealing with an invasion of vampires from the Four Hundred Years' War.

'Suppose I would like to transfer the soul of a vampire into another body. What would I have to take into con—'

'Are you talking about *my* soul?'

Eldric winced. Hallowed acid! He had been too direct, too obvious. Fine, he would speak more openly to make some progress at least.

Sighing, he ran his fingers through his hair. 'Maybe we can negotiate. Do you like the body you are in now?'

She squinted her beautiful eyes. 'It serves my purpose.'

'I happen to like it, as you have probably guessed.' He smiled yieldingly. There was no point in denying this fact. She had felt it the last time they met and could definitely smell it now, barely an arm's length away.

'It is my wish that you relinquish it to me,' he continued. 'In return, I could get you another one. You can choose a body perfect to your liking, and we will both be content.'

'Unfortunately, that is not possible,' she said lightly. 'Not without a Lightsmith.'

Eldric took a deep breath and immediately regretted it. It was *her* scent ... and somehow not her scent. Almost through no intention of his own, he leaned forward and placed his hands on the armrests of her carved chair. She didn't push him away this time, which gave him hope. Her heart even began to flutter a little.

I miss you, Liliana. His gaze was constantly drawn to her mouth; to those lips that he hadn't kissed for far too long.

'A Lightsmith makes Light weapons?' he asked quickly.

'Yes. But since there don't seem to be any newer Lightsmith weapons, the Lightsmiths must have disappeared, too. Or have they not?'

Newer Light weapons ... The priests' acid was the only thing they knew of. 'If I brought you a Lightsmith, or the modern-night equivalent of one ... would you allow yourself to be transferred into another body?'

She showed her teeth in a hungry smile. 'I would consider it.'

That was in no way a binding answer, at most a vague, temporary agreement to his proposed deal. But she had given him a few hints.

Eldric endeavoured to maintain a meaningless expression. 'I shall look into the matter.'

'What about the Light chains?'

'What Light chains?' So she had been looking for them, too. What did she want with them?

'The chains with the ring. You were held prisoner with them by your blood brother. We cleaned the dungeon thoroughly. Not a trace. Someone has stolen them.'

'Should they fall into my hands, you will find out.'

He might have use for them at some point. Liliana was not in a position to free herself from Sartiria's vampire soul. She needed him. And he needed his Liliana as she had been, as she should be.

He pushed himself off the armrests of her throne chair and took a few steps backwards before tearing his gaze from her and leaving her behind in the room. *Hang in there, Liliana.*

The twins had not been mentioned at all, so he could assume that they had not been exposed. If they were clever, they had saved themselves the diversion via the letterbox and Herder would be waiting for him with a message.

Chapter Eleven

'How about this, Miss?' Sebastian held up a sixth dress, and Annie shook her head. 'No.'

'Or this one?'

She shook her head more vigorously. 'No, Bastian! No. When is Mummy coming?'

'I'm sorry, Miss. I do not know.'

The child's brown eyes filled with tears. Sebastian crouched down a little helplessly in front of the chest that had temporarily replaced Annie's wardrobe and patted her head. He had dark circles under his elongated eyes and blinked suspiciously often. 'She will come back when she is ... not held up any more.'

'Mummy's not here so long!'

Eldric walked over to them with his shirt only half buttoned up and took his daughter into his arms. Annie howled against his sternum. 'Mahaaaaaaaa ...'

'Do you remember what I told you? It was very difficult for all of us when the evil aunt and uncle took you away and locked you up in that other castle. You cried a lot, I screamed and fought a lot, and Mummy fought hard to free us, too. Now she is very tired and a little ... funny in the head. She needs to rest for a long time until she can be with us again.'

He had toyed with the idea of letting Annie talk to Sartiria, because Liliana's spirit might stir at the sight of her. But he couldn't do that to Annie after everything she had been through. He didn't want to risk severing the strained bond between them.

While he waited for her to calm down, he stroked her back out of habit. 'We will do everything we can to make her feel better. Would you like to make another drawing for her tonight?'

'Yeeeeahhh,' Annie sobbed, rubbing her snotty nose on his shirt.

'Would the Miss like anything else to eat?' Sebastian offered her apple slices in a porcelain bowl, and Annie grabbed a handful.

When there was a knock at the door, he carefully placed the bowl on Eldric's narrow desk and opened it a crack.

'Lady Kathleen? And—'

'My brother wanted to see me,' the same announced.

'Our Lord and his daughter are not yet fully clothed. One moment, please.' Sebastian pushed the door shut, but not before half of Aunt Prim's face had appeared there to catch a curious glimpse of Eldric's chambers. A fragrant mixture of iris, musk and carnation wafted in. What was his aunt doing here? And who was the third person whose presence he sensed?

'Do you intend to let the ladies in, Mylord?' Sebastian asked with a doubtful undertone.

Eldric looked down at himself. Annie was still in her underwear and the hem of his half-opened shirt was hanging loosely over his waistband. There was also a nice trail of snot stuck to him. With the hand that had been stroking Annie's back, he fished a note out of his trouser pocket. 'If you could please give this to Kathleen ...'

The valet passed the folded paper through the crack in the door. The twins' message was brief and rather cryptic.

Training for guards
Fighting for the freedom and supremacy of vampires
S plans more recruitment than just increasing guards
Greetings to Mum

It sounded as if Sartiria was actually pursuing the plan for which Morton had enlisted Farkas. In any case, she was making preparations for further confrontations.

'Just greetings?' Kathleen complained outside the door. 'Not kind or warm or friendly greetings to your beloved mother?'

It rustled as she pocketed the note. Neither she nor Prim nor the third person moved away.

Sebastian coughed dutifully. 'Is there anything else I can help you with?'

'There is indeed a matter of which our Lord should be informed, good Sebastian,' Kathleen replied. 'As soon as possible.'

Prim's tone of voice seemed undisguised when she added, 'It's about Medina. I just don't know what to do any more.'

Eldric sighed and rose from the bed with Annie in his arms. The valet interpreted his intention correctly, opened the door, slipped out into the corridor behind him and immediately closed it again.

Prim was dressed discreetly in grey – possibly as a symbol of her grief over the loss of her daughter. To liven up her appearance a little, she had pinned up one side of her chin-length hair with a decorative comb, and a silver powder sparkled on the lids of her close-set eyes.

Kathleen had spoken out in favour of not officially denouncing Berlinda as a traitor, admitting that she had played a part in Morton's escape but understating this for the sake of peace in the family. Prim had lost two of her children within a year; first Tiomon, when the Crimson Plains had invaded their territory to kidnap Liliana, and then Berlinda, when Liliana had used one of Albert's ancient Light weapons to rescue him and Annie. Even though Eldric hadn't ever observed Prim to be an overly caring mother, that must have been a hard blow. He himself had hacked at anything that tried to come between him and his daughter in the Crimson Plains when her life was in danger.

Another vampiress was waiting next to Kathleen. She stood bent over, wearing the strict, black uniform of the servants and her grey hair twisted into a knot over her wrinkled face. Camilla.

The women raised their eyebrows at the sight of him; Kathleen amused, Camilla slightly reprimanding and his aunt somewhere between appreciative and insinuating. Eldric ignored all three.

'What is so urgent that it can't wait until I am in my study? Have you found Medina?'

Prim tilted her head to reveal the back of her neck. Unlike Rosalia, Eldric surmised that she did it subconsciously and not on purpose. She seemed to have forgotten her worries for a moment, however.

'Found and lost again.' Kathleen poked Prim in the side.

'She suddenly returned,' his aunt hurried to say. 'But she locked herself in her room for several nights. And when we finally broke down the door ... Oskar thinks it's just a phase, but ...'

'And what do you expect from me?' He fixed his gaze on Kathleen. 'Solving these kinds of problems with the appropriate sensitivity falls more into your area of expertise.'

His sister smiled benevolently. 'What Medina lacks is a good father figure.'

That might be an apt observation. He could hardly judge the situation himself, as he had never exchanged more than brief words of greeting with her. Oskar, who was always in a bad mood anyway, understandably didn't care much for Medina. Even if it wasn't common knowledge that Boras had fathered the girl with his aunt, the one-armed vampire must have had his doubts about who Medina's biological father was. But with everything that was going on ...

'At the moment, I can hardly do my actual daughter justice!'

Kathleen's smile became a little shrewder. 'I didn't mean you specifically, Eldric.'

'Then why is there a need for me to intervene?' He really had better things to do than deal with the whims of an adolescent.

'She won't listen to me.' Prim folded her arms, and a steep, frustrated crease appeared on her forehead. 'She won't listen to anyone.'

Eldric switched Annie to the other side of his body. 'Why should she listen to me?'

'Because you are her Lord,' Kathleen said. 'A word of power from you could shake the girl up and soften her in favour of other proposals. My theory is that she is struggling with Berlinda's death. We all have our own ways of dealing with grief or shock. Medina's way, however, is not sustainable and the repeated running away makes it difficult to talk.'

He knew very well the need to withdraw in difficult moments. 'In other words, you want me to intimidate her because she is grieving in a way that doesn't suit you?'

Prim did not answer immediately and uneasily shifted her centre of gravity from one foot to the other. 'You'd best see for yourself, Eldric.'

'I thought you didn't know where she was.'

'No, but she left something in her room.' Kathleen took a step to the side, accompanied by an inviting hand gesture.

He let out an indignant growl but relented. 'Fine. You will have to wait until we are ready.'

'I wouldn't want Annie around if I were you.'

Eldric started to make a biting remark. Then he realised that the bronze in Kathleen's eyes was no longer challenging, but caring. So, he sighed again. 'How long will it take to show me whatever it is you want me to see with my own eyes?'

'I want to see, too,' Annie protested.

Camilla stepped forward and bent her crooked spine even further in front of Eldric. 'Lady Kathleen has asked me to give you a hand, Mylord,' she said in a brittle voice.

He eyed the vampiress. Yes, he did need a nanny. So far, despite his and Sebastian's weariness, the position hadn't been filled because he didn't trust anyone enough. Since his sister had brought her along, he had to assume that she would demand a favour in return at some point, be it from him or from Camilla.

Kathleen put a hand on the servant's shoulder to gently straighten her. 'Camilla took excellent care of my sons when I was otherwise occupied.'

As well as of Axton and Tripp, as he had recently learned. Only she hadn't been decrepit then. Perhaps that was a harsh judgement. She seemed mentally alert. Still, he doubted the hunched vampiress would be able to catch Annie if she decided to run away. If she dropped the silverware while cleaning because her hands were shaking, it didn't matter. But if she had a mishap with a child ... How many years did she have left before the Curse would have consumed her flesh? And how would she cope with having to stay awake during the day? Could he still teach an old woman like her the necessary mastery of demonic powers?

'She helped Mother out with us at times, too, by the way.'

He cast an astonished glance at the silent servant. She showed no reaction at all. What relationship could she have had with Amalia of Finsterwald? The idea that this almost frail woman might have carried him around and comforted him fifty years ago seemed a little strange. He must have been too young to remember her later on.

Finally, he nodded to Sebastian, and they withdrew with Camilla. While Eldric put on his shoes, finally straightened his shirt and Sebastian wiped Annie's snot with a moistened handkerchief, the girl eyed the old woman next to whom he had set her down. She was still holding the apple slices in one hand.

'Why are you doing like that?' Annie mimicked Camilla's hump.

Eldric refrained from reprimanding her and instead watched Camilla's reaction. She showed her fangs and giggled. 'Because I am old.'

'How old?'

'Very old.' The servant pointed to Annie's belly. She seemed to have tuned out her Lord and Sebastian and was focusing solely on the little girl. 'Where is your dress?'

'I don't know.' Annie raised her arms. 'Bastian didn't given me it.'

'I'm sorry?'

'*Hasn't given*,' Eldric corrected her reflexively.

'Oh, Sebastian hasn't given you a dress,' Camilla repeated. 'Why don't you show me where your clothes are, and we can have a look together?'

Annie laughed and pointed to the open chest with an outstretched finger. 'There they are!'

'Oh.' Camilla groaned and shuffled off in the opposite direction to sit in Eldric's chair.

Sebastian muttered discontentedly to himself, pocketed the handkerchief and brought Eldric a new shirt with braces and a summer jacket.

'Not there,' Annie shouted and ran after the nanny. 'Over there are my dresses!'

'Will you be so good, dear Annie, and show me which one you like best? I can't bend down very well any more.'

Annie nodded and poked her head into the chest. Only now did Eldric realise that the old vampiress didn't address Annie as Miss. Well, if it helped them to make friends more quickly, he could ignore it for the time being.

'I need to help Aunty Kathleen with something, Annie. I would like you to stay here in the meantime and show Camilla your things. Can you do that for me?'

The girl raised her head in alarm. 'You going, Daddy?'

'Not far. I'll stay here in the castle. Sebastian will stay here, too, and ... tidy up a bit.'

'Yes, Mylord.' The valet inclined his head.

Eldric kissed Annie on the forehead and hurried out to Kathleen and Prim. Behind him, he heard Camilla ask if she could wear Annie's dress, seeing as Annie didn't want to wear it.

Together with Prim, he followed Kathleen through the corridor and two floors up. The moonlight cast long streaks of light through the lancet windows. Something smelled strange … like cabbage, or …

Kathleen stopped and pointed to a door twenty feet away at the end of the corridor, where Medina's chambers were located. She grimaced as she did so. 'Please, see for yourself.'

Prim didn't move one step further and suddenly looked pale under her face powder. Her heart skipped a beat.

Eldric straightened his shoulders and walked on. The closer he got to the door, the more pungent the smell became. He closed his fingers around the door handle, raised the elbow of his other arm in front of his face and slowly pushed it open.

Chapter Twelve

Although he had braced himself against the stench and dampened his sensory perception, it nearly made him gag. A nauseating combination of ammonia, fish, garlic and rotting eggs, sweet and foul at the same time – the unmistakable stink of rotting flesh.

Two undressed bodies lay at the foot of Medina's bed, a man and a woman. The waxen skin had begun to peel and break open. At least it wasn't anyone he knew. He couldn't be completely sure, though, because they were bloated almost beyond recognition and full of movement; maggots and flies crawled everywhere. Well, it could have been worse.

Nevertheless, the bodies must have lain here for five to eight days. How had they remained undiscovered for so long? The awful smell should have seeped through the door, and someone should have noticed.

In his time, Eldric had left many mortal remains for animals to devour. Wolves, bears, wild boars, foxes, vultures, ravens, crows and jackdaws – nature had its use for them. But that was in the wild, not in the bedroom of a noblewoman.

You had an opponent's head preserved as evidence against Farkas, he heard Liliana say. She would have vomited loudly at the sight of this. But Albert knew how to preserve organic matter. This was disgusting, even by Eldric's standards. It was ... not right.

He held his breath and took long strides over the dead to take a look in the dressing room before pulling aside the curtains around the bed. Medina was not there. He opened her balcony door wide and left the room before the decay brought tears to his eyes.

As he stepped over the threshold, he noticed a layer of wax along the entire door frame. Medina had locked herself in and sealed her door from the inside.

He quickly closed the door behind him, but only lowered the arm in front of his nose and mouth when he reached Kathleen and Prim. 'The bodies must be cleared away immediately. I'm afraid we are going to have to replace the entire floor.'

Prim shuddered. 'Medina locked herself in. When we broke down the door, she ran away.'

'Where to?'

'We don't know for sure. But the guards didn't see anyone fly away.'

'Well, if she has spent several nights in there with them, and is still here in the castle, she shouldn't be too hard to find this time.' And he knew a good nose who *should be* interested in helping Medina. 'Has she shown any signs of insanity?'

'N-no.'

He agreed with Kathleen's assessment that Medina's behaviour was a reaction to recent events rather than a belated spurt of powers. Still, strong and erratic emotions always meant susceptibility to demonic madness and the accompanying loss of control over one's powers.

'Tell the servants to tidy everything up,' he charged Kathleen.

As always, when he gave her a direct order, she smiled smugly. 'Of course, Lord Eldric.'

'Tripp can instruct them if necessary.' For a vampire with impressive powers, he had a surprisingly insensitive nose and a stomach of steel. 'I will find Boras.'

At the mention of his name, Prim slapped her hand over her mouth. 'That ... That is ...'

Kathleen also frowned. 'Eldric ...' she began warningly.

'He will find Medina the quickest. You asked me to take care of this, and I will do so as seems right to me.'

He marched off, not allowing any objections. Boras' rooms were not very far from here, and Eldric knew of no duties he had to attend to tonight. Of course, he could have flown out. In which case, he would begin the search by himself.

Sensing a heartbeat behind the door in question, he knocked. The wood trembled under his knuckles. The mere fact that he was standing here in person rather than sending a servant spoke for itself. Nevertheless, he called out. 'Boras, I have an urgent task for you!'

'I'm coming,' his cousin's smoky voice replied.

When he slipped out to Eldric a moment later, he kept his broad shoulders slightly stooped so that his stringy hair fell into his face. The scent that surrounded him was composed of soft candle smoke and colour pigments. Boras detested strong odours in the place where he slept. Accordingly, his rooms were sparsely furnished. In place of curtains, wooden shutters blocked out the sunlight. There were no carpets, books or other dust collectors, and the only decoration consisted of his own whimsical paintings, which leaned against the walls around the easel and everywhere else. The windows and the balcony door were always open at night.

'Help me find Medina,' Eldric said without beating around the bush.

Boras stared at him from his deep-set eyes. Those irises were the closest thing to the colour of madness Eldric had ever come across. Sometimes he wondered if the Primordial Demon himself was looking back at him from those eyes. Fortunately, this appearance was deceptive, for Boras' powers were nowhere near as powerful as his and he had a stable personality.

'Why?' he muttered at last.

'Because she appeared and disappeared again. I strongly suspect she reeks of decay.'

'Like you?'

Eldric wrinkled his nose and sniffed his sleeve. Was it because of his cousin's extraordinary sensitivity to smells, or had the stench burnt itself into his nose so badly that he had become temporarily impervious to it? 'Well, we made an unpleasant discovery in her chambers.'

Boras continued to return his gaze like a hungry hawk, not blinking once. 'Do you have any more clues for me?'

'Sadly not, no. Do you remember Medina's signature smell?'

He grunted indignantly. Eldric might as well have asked him if he had memorised her name. 'Where should I start?'

'The starting point would be the chambers I just mentioned, but I guess that would be too much for—'

Boras raised a hand and shook his head. He was dressed from head to toe in black, as if he feared too much patterning on his clothes might interfere with his artistic work. 'Not necessary.'

He turned his head jerkily in one direction, then the other, and rushed off. Eldric followed him into the west wing, where Morton's former safekeeping chamber lay at the back. He stopped in front of this chamber. Rather than going in and checking on his daughter, he let Eldric enter first.

Medina cowered on the ground with her back to them, her eyes fixed on the bricked-up hole from which Morton had escaped. Her demonic powers were pulsing strongly. Her heart began to beat faster, so she had noticed them.

'Medina.'

She did not react.

He looked over at Boras, but his cousin shook his head almost petulantly. Eldric sighed and turned to the silent, black-haired figure. 'You know the ban on bringing *dead* people into this castle.'

Medina continued to crouch rigidly without acknowledging their presence.

As a warning, he loosened his shoulders and cracked the knuckles of his left hand before unleashing his powers. Medina involuntarily ducked her head as she felt the menacing, invisible force rolling over her. He took on the anger, submitting to it a little without being tempted to transform into his demon form.

'Medina,' he thundered. 'You have broken an important rule of Finsterwald Castle, and I will hold you accountable. Get up!'

Eldric sensed her fear, and yet she did not obey. He reached her in four quick steps. Medina backed away and slid round to him on her buttocks, her arms raised protectively in front of her face. Where was her fighting instinct? One well-directed cut, one bite, and she would be dead.

He was tempted to grab her, but restrained his powers, tugging at the leash until they complied and subsided. Then he crouched down in front of her. She stared at him from under her curtain of hair, her eyes wide. A hint of rot had settled in her hair; traces of urine and cold sweat stuck to her clothes.

'You will work off your punishment as hours of labour in my library,' he said in a calm, friendly voice. 'Now that I have your attention ... Would you like to know how exactly your sister died?'

Disbelief spread across her features. Her heart was still pounding. Eldric could not give Berlinda back to her. Even if he could, he wouldn't. She had betrayed him, murdered Martha, and would have killed him, Liliana and Annie without remorse, or gloatingly watched while it happened. What he could offer Medina was clarification.

She didn't nod, but he thought he could read agreement in her staring eyes.

'Then clean up and meet me in the library. Albert will show you his collection. Or at least, what is left of it.' He rose and nodded to Boras on his way out. 'Thank you. Make sure she takes a long bath. She is to be billeted in one of the guest rooms until her own rooms are habitable again.'

Chapter Thirteen

Tilting her own head, Medina tapped a long fingernail against the glass behind which Geza's head was floating in formaldehyde. Albert had obviously forgotten it was still standing here in the mess, covered by one of his scarves, despite its smell. The girl's face was obscured by stringy black hair. At least now she was surrounded by the odour of rose petals rather than decay.

As he watched Medina, Eldric tried to organise his thoughts. He had meant to spend this night following the trail of the Lightsmiths. The only records that existed from the time of the war were the fragmentary diary entries of an ancestor who had gone into hiding and somehow survived the purge by the humans. They spoke of Sartiria's disappearance and of her having held a Lightsmith captive to pursue some sort of crazy scheme. So far, that was consistent with what the vampiress had revealed.

On the human side, Lightsmiths must have been an important part of the war machine. Albert had unearthed throwing stars, arrowheads and a spear in and around the ruins of Schattenfels. These all seemed to be suitable for attacking enemies at a certain distance; melee weapons were of less use against flying opponents. They had not yet discovered any armour or shields, but that didn't necessarily mean that such had never been in use.

Nowanights, there was no longer anyone forging weapons. One of the first conventions of the Vampire Council prohibited the manufacture and possession of weapons in all territories of the Continent. Of course, certain tools, knives, scythes and the like, could be misused as weapons, and the outdated use of bows and arrows was still occasionally tolerated for hunting game. But objects that had no obvious non-violent use were forbidden – in the name of peace. Vampires did not need tools to kill, and it was in the interests of the noble families that humans prospered and did not decimate one another. Eldric found that the ban on weapons was, in fact, conducive to peaceful coexistence among humans, and the Curse demanded its victims, no matter how peaceably or aggressively they behaved towards each other.

Assuming this particular forging skill had not been passed down in secret over the centuries – which was not impossible, but extremely unlikely – there were no Lightsmiths left. The only people who knew some kind of Light magic were priests. Eldric doubted that any of them had the power or knowledge to transfer a vampiric soul from one body to another; unless Sartiria knew the exact steps and could guide them, either under duress or by baiting them with a nice story.

Whether Sartiria would keep to her part and leave Liliana's body voluntarily remained to be seen. Perhaps if he found a human woman who was tall and had the strong build of a feared general ... Sartiria was definitely pursuing her own plans. What could she want with a priest if he got her one? During Eldric's official visit to the Crimson Plains, she had mentioned a renewed war against humanity, but that was an obscure idea. The vampires already ruled the Continent. The only reason for recruiting additional guards was to prevail against other families and stand alone at their head, as Farkas and Morton had planned. As if the two of them could ever have shared such power ...

Footsteps approached, and Albert entered. The sleeve of his scarred but usable hand was slightly singed, and his suit stank, but Eldric's nose was dulled for the night, and anything that didn't trigger a cough seemed pleasant enough.

Medina raised her eyes without lifting her head and scrutinised the eldest of her uncles from below.

'What have I done to deserve your visit?' he asked in a way that left open whether he was referring to a pleasant surprise or a punishment.

'I want you to show Medina the orb that killed Berlinda,' Eldric said bluntly.

'That's impossible. The remains of that Light bomb lie buried in the dungeons of the Crimson Plains.'

'Not that Light bomb exactly,' Eldric specified. 'I assume what is left of the first one is still lying around here somewhere?'

Albert didn't ask why, but plucked at his tangled, greying beard as he looked at the mess spread across several tables and the floor. His bedchamber always looked as if a gust of wind had just swept through it. How he was able to locate his notes, vials or pieces of equipment for his experiments was a mystery to Eldric. He and Liliana had used some of the excavated relics to free Eldric and Annie, but there were enough curiosities left to examine.

'Ah, here.' Albert bent down under one of the tables and picked out a tied bundle of cloth to hand to Medina.

The girl took a step back, her eyes fixed on the velvet bundle.

'The Light has already escaped, so it doesn't pose any danger,' Albert assured her.

Eldric refrained from remarking that he often claimed such about objects which later turned out to be very dangerous.

Medina hesitantly took the cloth bundle and sat down on the spot to untie the cord.

'The glass is silver-plated. When the bomb is functional, it contains pure Light. This Light eliminates everything demonic that it falls on within a radius of ... maybe fifteen feet, I would estimate.'

Medina uncovered the wrapped shards and held up the largest with pointed fingers. The light from the lamps and candles burning between the fossils and test tubes shimmered on the surface.

'Show her your hand.'

Albert raised his left arm. His hand hung limply from it. For some strange reason, it wasn't dead, just paralysed. 'This is the effect of the same bomb that killed your sister. Much to my chagrin, I can no longer use what was once my writing hand. It's completely numb.' He looked around as if searching for a sharp object with which to prove his point.

'Exactly,' Eldric continued quickly, 'and if the same thing happens to vital organs, the person in question dies.'

Medina turned the shard this way and that, seemingly lost in contemplation. As she asked no questions, Albert turned away to look for something else. Eldric hoped it wasn't a letter opener or the like.

He sighed. His daughter's safety and the fact that the Curse wasn't manifesting in her in a normal way were enough for him to worry about. He wasn't exactly looking forward to what it would be like when she reached Medina's age.

Albert found what he was looking for, which, fortunately, was a pile of scribbled papers. Eldric recognised the barely decipherable list of effects they had observed on Light weapons so far. Nothing with a Light spell on it could be touched by vampires. Shimmering acid, or consecrated water as the humans called it, burned worse than any other substance they knew, and wounds caused by Light weapons did not heal.

How much of the truth could he tell Medina? If she learned that Liliana had used the Light bomb, she might seek revenge. On the other hand, it would be unfortunate if she found out from someone else, and since the Crimson Plains had been told, he no longer controlled access to this piece of information.

He cleared his throat. 'Your sister helped Morton escape. When Albert and Liliana tried to free Annie and me, she tried to kill them and died herself. Liliana ...' He swallowed. '... dropped one of those Light bombs in the fray, hoping it would somehow help them.'

Medina continued to bend over the shards and showed no emotion. What could be going through her head? Why had she kept those dead bodies in her bedroom? Did she condemn Berlinda for her actions, or did she hate those who were responsible for her death? Although Tiomon had been closer to her in age, his death had affected her less. Or was it because both of her siblings were gone now?

'Hmm.' Albert was no longer studying his notes, but instead the girl in front of him on the floor. 'Have you stopped talking?'

To Eldric's astonishment, she nodded.

'Then ...' Albert fished a quill pen out from under one of the cloths, turned over the front page of his paper and placed both next to the shards spread out on the velvet. 'You could try writing.'

Rather than emphasising that this was a ridiculous suggestion because Medina did have the ability to speak and only refused to communicate with them, Eldric silently placed the inkwell he had spied precariously tucked into the corner of the table next to the quill. After all, he had hoped Medina would gain confidence in Albert's presence.

She carefully tied the pieces back together into a parcel and handed it to Albert. She didn't write anything but took his pen and weighed it in her hand.

Albert waited a moment before returning to his remaining pile of papers. Something crackled softly in the background like the bursting of countless dry bubbles.

'We don't set up bans to annoy anyone,' Eldric said. He was not naturally prone to impatience, but right now his skin was tingling. 'They serve to regulate our actions in a way that makes it easier for us to live together. We don't tolerate dead bodies in the castle because it is extremely unappetising. In the wild, they are fed on by animals, but here they contaminate everything.' Turning to Albert, he added, 'We have had to remove two rotting corpses from her chambers.'

'How annoying,' Albert said, unconcerned.

Eldric folded his arms. 'Medina ... If you are interested in the anatomy of death, our library has several colour-illustrated body studies and records of the stages of decomposition. And you will have to spend a few hours there as part of your punishment anyway.'

'The anatomy of death,' Albert repeated, nodding appreciatively. 'You really know how to use words.'

Medina's gaze flitted over to the glass with Geza's head, which Eldric had covered again. Albert noticed it. 'You can have that if you want. I have no more use for it.'

Her previously apathetic eyes filled with a lively lustre. Eldric pressed his lips together and remained silent once more, even though the head belonged to him, to be precise, and he had instructed Albert to take it away months ago. He decided that this was the right moment to make a deal.

'Albert could teach you how to properly preserve organic matter ...'

Medina awkwardly turned her head towards him. Those eyes ... When she looked up at him like that, there was no denying the resemblance to her biological father.

'If you can promise me two things. Firstly, you will obey Albert and follow the rules of our castle at all times. And secondly, you will communicate with your mother. In writing, with hand gestures, or however else is convenient for you. She cares about you.'

Medina's mouth twisted barely noticeably.

'Nod if you agree to these terms.'

She snorted and slowly moved her head up and down.

'Good.' Eldric turned and placed a hand on Albert's shoulder. 'I will leave her in your care for now. Please do not concoct anything that might lift our roof off.'

With that, he left the two. Perhaps Albert could channel Medina's macabre interests into more sensible studies.

Chapter Fourteen

Annie giggled as he sailed with her just over the heads of two ducking guards, circled over the courtyard and landed near the fountain. He had wanted to take her on a trip for a long time, to give her his undivided attention for at least one night and perhaps make up a little for Liliana's absence. He had sent Lola to Thomlin in his place to check their books.

Eldric didn't know exactly what made a man a good father. But he had at least resolved to do what he would have liked Thormund to do better. Firstly, he would spend more time with Annie right from the start. And secondly, he would give her more appreciation for things that weren't directly related to demonic powers or excelling at something.

Sunrise was imminent, so the family were retiring to their chambers. Unfortunately, Camilla still regularly fell asleep when she suppressed her powers without starving, but she managed to stay awake a few hours into the day. Once summer was coming to an end, the nights would slowly get longer again.

Eldric set Annie down on the edge of the fountain and held her by the upper arms so that she didn't fall. The water splashed merrily into the pool from the golden dragon's mouth.

'Annie,' he said seriously, looking into her big brown eyes, 'I want to tell you something important, so listen carefully.'

'Yes, Daddy.' She looked at her feet, visibly tempted to dip one of them in the clear water.

'I want you to know ...' The words felt unnatural and didn't want to roll off his tongue. Why was this so difficult for him? It was ridiculous. She was a small child, and she was his daughter. Of course he loved her. And there were no other listeners.

'That I ...'

'You what, Daddy?' She lifted her head and reached out to tug at one of his coat buttons. The expectant, open way she looked up at him conjured up Liliana's image, accompanied by a dull ache in his chest.

He cleared his throat and made another attempt. 'I love you, Annie. I love you just the way you are. With or without powers.'

'I love you, too!' She threw herself forward and wrapped her arms around his neck.

Surprised, he caught her. She had definitely inherited this willingness to open her heart to others from her mother. Eldric could not remember ever having made such a confession. As a child, he had probably reassured his mother Amalia that he loved her. But he possessed no clear memory of it.

'When is water hald?' Annie asked as he crossed the square with her.

'I'm sorry. I don't understand what you're trying to say.'

'Hald. Hawwd.'

'You mean hard, like when it turns to ice?'

'Yes, Daddy! Ice!'

Eldric grinned. 'When winter comes, Annie. In winter, it gets cold and snows. And the water freezes to ice.'

'How much long?' She put her fingers so close to his face that he instinctively jerked his head back. 'That long?'

'We say *how long*, Annie. And it depends on the weather. At least three months, probably longer.'

'Oh.'

He sprouted his wings and brought them to the height of the second floor, where he entered the corridor via one of the doors with a landing.

As far as he was concerned, love was a complicated and dangerous affair, both a curse and a blessing. There seemed to be no clear dividing line that defined when affection, admiration or concern for a person turned into love. And yet he knew with frightening certainty that he also loved Liliana. There was no other explanation for his behaviour and his feelings. He loved her, he missed her, he ... he smelled her.

Eldric stopped abruptly. His heart stopped for a moment. She was here? Since when? How...? His legs carried him by themselves, following the beckoning trail. Around the next corner, a blonde mop of hair hurried towards him.

'El! There you are at last.' Tripp tossed an empty glass from one hand to the other. 'Your . . . well, Sartiria's here. I tried to intercept, but Kathleen was on the spot, of course.'

His sister usually played hostess and looked after visitors, but she risked Sartiria noticing the resemblance between her and the twins and becoming suspicious of her supposed recruit. Besides, the idea of Kathleen talking to Sartiria in private triggered an oppressive feeling in his centre. So the new Lord of the Crimson Plains had returned the favour of his surprise visit to her. Well, if he hadn't flown out half the night, he could have prepared himself thanks to the border guard's light signals, as Kathleen had undoubtedly done.

'What is she doing here? What does she want?'

'Apparently, she wants to visit our library and find out how the Four Hundred Years' War ended.' Tripp yawned heartily.

At first, Eldric assumed he was trying to demonstrate how boring the subject was. Then he realised the pink glow through the windows and the rising heaviness in his consciousness.

'I'm off then,' Tripp grumbled promptly and set off in the direction he had come from. 'Just wanted to fill you in.'

'Who is Satidia?'

'Who is Sartiria,' Eldric repeated automatically as Tripp's footsteps faded. 'She is ... a woman who looks like your mother but isn't your mother.'

'Mummy's coming back?'

He forced his powers to pull back, ignoring their resistance, squeezing tightly with his mind until they bent to his will. Annie instantly became heavier in his arms.

'Not yet. But soon. I'm working on it.'

Expressed like that, it sounded pitiful. He hadn't achieved anything yet, hadn't made any progress in regard to the requested Lightsmith. The logical next step was to approach a priest directly. The thought did not particularly appeal to him. Would the priest from Heidenried speak to him if he learned that he wanted to help Liliana?

Eldric had killed two villagers: Hans and a young woman called Marie, as far as he remembered correctly. Both had thrown his warnings to the wind, and he had in no way violated his principles. Marie had been the first hunting victim after his memory loss, and Hans had aimed his spear directly at Eldric's heart, which marked a clear intention to kill. However, he doubted that the priest would understand. Well, it didn't matter. He would know how to spin the situation so that he helped him anyway. And if not, there were other priests; their churches were in almost every village.

Sartiria's soul in Liliana's body remained unpredictable. Although they had officially agreed to reconcile, she had gone on the offensive with her recruitments and the spontaneous visit here. Was she trying to spy on Finsterwald? To see how many guards he had and whether there were any other Light weapons in his possession? Did she think he had already found a Lightsmith but was withholding him from her? Or ... was there a part of her that longed to see him, too?

Eldric paced back and forth in his study. He had stayed awake all day, partly to instruct and admonish Camilla to keep her powers under lock and key, and partly to make several rounds of the castle in case Liliana came looking for him. But if she had done so, they had missed each other, which could easily happen in the winding corridors without powers.

Currently, Sartiria was in the library with Albert and Medina. Right next door, only fifty or so steps away ... Eldric cracked the knuckles of one hand, then the other, and finally slid both in his pockets. Should he join them after all?

He had pretended not to be available in order to stall a little longer. Every encounter with Sartiria stirred him up, every confrontation harboured the possibility that Liliana's soul could somehow shine through, and at the same time, there was always the risk that he would give away more than intended with a thoughtless remark ... that Sartiria would take advantage of his weakness and play him.

Eldric was torn from his thoughts by a knock. Three vampires were waiting outside the door. He closed his eyes briefly to concentrate. No, even his powers were unable to recognise anyone by their heartbeat. He quickly sat down at his desk and picked up a document he had started from his pile of papers. He took a few deep breaths to calm his heartbeat.

'Come in.'

One of the servants opened the door, and Aunt Prim entered with Oskar. Judging by his sour expression, the latter was not here entirely voluntarily. He stared at Eldric with narrowed brows. The blood rushing through his veins promised trouble. His goatee seemed to have grown since the last time it had properly caught Eldric's eye, further elongating his rather gaunt face. The striped suit jacket was tailored exactly to his stature, including a closed shoulder on the side of his missing arm. The smell of fresh mint caressed him. Could it be that he was making an effort to win Prim over?

With a resolute hand gesture, he indicated to the servant that he should also enter and close the door behind him.

'Thank you for seeing us.' Prim cast an astonished glance at the servant and stopped in front of his desk. She smiled broadly, although her fingers kept restlessly turning a rolled-up sheet of paper.

'You are welcome,'

He didn't want to draw too much attention to his presence here by having vampires congregating outside his door. Neither Prim nor Oskar explained themselves, so he briefly skimmed the document he had just picked up. It was a permit authorising an aspiring merchant from Klarbad to transport medicinal plants and tinctures across the territory border into the Lakelands. He had negotiated six such licences with Indira. She probably saw a satisfying symbolism in the number. Six licences, six noble families.

Finally, he lowered the letter with a sigh. 'How can I be of service?'

'Medina has written a letter to me.' Prim managed to wave the small roll of paper in a manner that seemed anxious and flirtatious at the same time. 'Consisting of exactly three sentences.'

She minimally honoured this part of the deal then. 'That sounds like a breakthrough.'

'Yes. Yes, it is.' Prim gave Oskar a sideways glance. 'She writes in the first sentence that we shouldn't worry. And in the second ... that there is no difference between dead vampires and dead humans. I don't know what she's trying to say.'

Eldric contemplated this as he added another line to his writing before looking up again. 'I guess we will have to extend the rule about dead humans to dead vampires.'

The wrinkles on Oskar's face deepened. Prim blinked. 'Why?' she whispered.

'I can only make assumptions. But I think the most obvious explanation is that at least one, if not both, of the corpses were vampires – strays.' Of course, common vampire sense should have told her that dead vampires were also taboo in the castle. 'Medina has seen many dead humans before, but apparently no dead vampires. I imagine the loss of her siblings has triggered a strange fascination with death in her. She has tested the question of what happens when our soul leaves the body with a practical experiment and has come to the conclusion that human and vampiric bodies are no different in death. Both decay and decompose to the same extent. The demonic powers are bound to our soul and disappear with it.'

Prim and Oskar stared at him as if these thoughts were completely unfamiliar to them. The servant at the door pretended to look at Eldric's stained-glass window with great interest.

'However, you would be better advised to ask Kathleen for her opinion. She has more experience when it comes to—'

'There is still the third line,' Oskar growled.

Prim reprovingly clicked her tongue. Interrupting a Lord, whether one's own or that of another family, was considered insulting if one did not hold the same title.

Eldric carefully put down his quill pen. The real reason Oskar was standing in his study was about to be revealed.

'Please,' he said with a cool smile, 'enlighten me.'

'Medina ...' Prim brushed a strand of her hair out of her face with her free hand. 'She, er, writes that her sister was killed by a human weapon made of Light.'

Of course. Medina had mentioned the Light bomb, which was what had upset Oskar. Perhaps it had been a miscalculation to let her in on this. He hadn't explicitly kept the discoveries relating to Light magic a secret. Albert's curious pastimes had simply not interested anyone but him. Unfortunately, that would soon change, seeing as Sartiria had searched for the Light chains and enquired about Lightsmiths. In addition, some of the survivors in the Crimson Plains must have realised what a centuries-old ball and a few throwing stars could do.

If he wanted to prevent the other families from storming his gates to gain access to mysterious weapons and information about the human Light magic, he would have to devote considerable resources to diverting general attention.

'You made us all believe that Berlinda died in an honest fight.'

'She did,' Eldric replied.

'With a human weapon?' Oskar's volume swelled. His beard bounced up and down as he spoke. 'Humans aren't allowed to have weapons!'

'That is correct. The Light weapon that Medina mentions is a relic Albert dug up and used to come to my aid. It shattered when it was used. We haven't come across any others.'

'And what about sacred acid? If you'd taken care of those sinister churches and the mob that meets there sooner, I wouldn't have lost my arm.'

'You wouldn't have lost your arm if you were a better hunter.'

Eldric watched with quiet satisfaction as Oskar's face turned red and his heart began to beat a furious rhythm. 'Four of those filthy peasants ambushed me, swung their scythes and doused me with acid. And what does our Lord do? Nothing! You neglected your duty from the start because you'd rather mount human tarts!'

Eldric bared his teeth. His powers crawled around the restrictions imposed on them and filled the room with a creeping chill. In situations like this, he felt as if he were catching his opponent cheating in a card game and turning a blind eye. He didn't feel like arguing with Oskar. He wanted to be angry; he wanted some of his power to escape through his fingers and put Oskar and his ridiculous beard in his place. Alas, he couldn't truly unleash his powers, as that would have revealed his exact location – and state of mind – to everyone in the castle, including Sartiria. But a little taster was usually enough of a demonstration for someone like Oskar, who hid behind a loose mouth.

One moment Oskar looked as if he wanted to spit at his Lord's feet, and the next he smelled as if he was going to stain the floor with his faeces instead. Luckily, he did neither. Prim avoided looking at both men and remained silent, while the servant in the background only dared take shallow breaths.

'At least our territory isn't in ruins, as it undoubtedly would be if someone like you or Morton had been allowed a free hand.' If his threatening tone didn't send a clear message, equating Oskar with a slain enemy would.

Oskar grumbled and growled to himself but no longer uttered any identifiable words.

When there was no reply, Eldric turned demonstratively to his letter, picked up the pen again and signed the document with a flourish. Shuffling, the rustling of clothes and finally the snapping shut of the door revealed that Prim and Oskar had understood his silent request.

He only entered the library after Sartiria had left. Albert and Medina were sitting opposite each other at one of the tables in the centre. They were having a written conversation about taxidermy, as a quick skim of the open pages of her notebook revealed. Their ancestor's diaries from the Four Hundred Years' War huddled forgotten at the head of the table. That had been one of the reasons he had asked Berlinda and not Albert to keep his library in order.

Liliana's slightly altered scent still danced delicately in the air. His demonic powers stirred, thirsting for the being that exuded it. Eldric swallowed and turned to Albert. 'What ... did you show her?'

Thoughtfully, he picked up the thin gloves lying next to him.

'Sartiria?' Albert looked up and pushed the notebook to Medina. 'She wanted to see the diaries from the Four Hundred Years' War. Regrettably, she hardly responded to my questions.'

'I can see that. But what was she looking for in the diaries?'

'She wanted to find out more about battle saints. In particular, why they disappeared.'

Eldric slipped on his gloves and pulled up a chair to leaf carefully through the tattered little books. The term *battle saints* had caught his eye previously. From the context, it had to be a kind of special unit that had been deployed in the fight against the vampire armies. The fact that they were no longer used after the end of the war made intuitive sense. Why did Sartiria suspect a special cause for their disappearance?

'Did she find what she was looking for?'

'No. I would describe her mood before and after consulting the diaries as impatient and annoyed, if not frustrated. She reckons these battle saints could still be lurking somewhere or could come back for some reason. She said this type of human could summon pure Light at will.' Albert tugged at his beard. 'They must have been involved in making these Light bombs.'

'Pure Light?' Eldric paused as he turned the yellowed pages and raised his eyebrows. That was a terrifying concept. Pure Light as they knew it from the Light bombs killed any vampires exposed to it in an instant. A human who could create or summon that out of nothing would be the perfect predator for vampires – a hunter of hunters.

'Exactly. Fascinating, isn't it?'

'Well, humans don't live for centuries. The knowledge of their battle techniques could theoretically have been passed on, but if there were humans able to make pure Light appear, we would know about it. Because we would not be ruling the Continent.'

'Hm, no, probably not.'

Eldric found the smell of the centuries-old leather and paper stimulating and mysterious. He leaned back in his chair and tried to imagine himself in the world of that time. The battles, the war tactics ... One side armed with the Curse, the other with Light magic. The vampires needed human blood. The best outcome for them was the subjugation of humans, the suppression or rather eradication of their Light magic. The humans, on the other hand, fought to end them all.

Lightsmiths, battle saints, ancient weapons ... Sartiria believed another war against humanity was imminent. The resentment and contempt with which she spoke of humans was a testament to how much she thought of herself as the vampiress from her original timeline. By assuming that she was continuing the plan of her predecessor, Farkas, he would be misjudging her. No, that wasn't thinking far enough. Sartiria saw the world differently. For her, the fronts were still divided into humans versus vampires. She had accepted his bargain with her body and the Lightsmith because she saw Light magic and its potential resurgence as a real threat. She didn't want to recruit additional guards to seek revenge on Finsterwald. What did skirmishes among the noble families mean when you had habitually faced an enemy who was bent on utterly destroying all of your kind? Sartiria was a general, and she wanted an army under her command.

Eldric laughed, whereupon Medina, who was writing a question about stuffed mice or the like in her notebook, looked up in confusion.

'What is it this time?' Albert asked. 'Are you trying to relax?'

'No,' Eldric replied with a grin. 'I think I understand to some extent what Sartiria is doing. I'm just not entirely sure *why* she is doing it. She has had her soul encased in glass beads in a self-experiment. This method could be refined into a process that approaches immortality. Then again ...'

'Immortality? Yes, hm ... Yes.' Albert stared absent-mindedly into the air.

Eldric started to turn the pages again and ran his gloved finger over the edge of a particular section.

The humans have left. They see themselves as victors and no longer fear us ... We haven't met any of our kind for two years. I think we are the only survivors ... We don't know where the battle saints are. Perhaps they are holed up in the Lowlands, building their settlements. Perhaps they are chasing refugee ships across the sea to finish off those who escaped. We hide and wait.

The humans had won the war as such and had destroyed everything of vampiric origin apart from these diaries. However, by doing so, they had also allowed their own knowledge of vampires to dwindle over generations and had apparently also largely lost the skill to fight vampires.

In the face of imminent defeat, Sartiria had endeavoured to hide and store her soul. She feared that the lost knowledge of Light magic would return and the humans would once again be victorious in war – and this time end their existence completely. So what did she do? She tried to prevent this from happening. But did she have to do it from inside Liliana's body, of all places?

Someone approached in the corridor, and Boras walked in. Medina shrank a little at the sight of him. Despite the monotony of his voice, his vital functions indicated that something had shaken him up. 'El ... Sartiria and her counsellor have left.'

Eldric nodded curtly. He had hesitated too long and, if he was honest, had knowingly risked missing her.

'In a north-westerly direction,' Boras added. 'She met Oskar in secret before she left.'

By the Primordial Demon, how had Oskar learned so quickly that Sartiria was looking for Lightsmiths and human weapons? The castle of the Crimson Plains was south-west of Finsterwald. No vampire was so badly mistaken in the cardinal direction of their flight path. If they took a diversion, it was with good reason. What had Oskar told her?

Boras' nostrils quivered. 'Rosalia followed them.'

Eldric returned the stare of the golden yellow eyes. A cold calm settled over him. 'Are you sure about that?'

'Her smell was the strongest in the horse's den. It spoke of determination, aggression and ...' Boras broke off. His hair fanned out over his broad shoulders as he turned his head abruptly towards Albert and Medina and then towards the door through which he had entered. How much else might his nose be picking up that he preferred to keep to himself?

'Thank you for coming straight to me with this,' Eldric said, brushing off his gloves and rising to his feet. 'We have no time to lose.'

Chapter Fifteen

Shadowprancer had gained a considerable lead over Boras' mount. Since Lola had not yet returned from Thomlin, he had left Tripp as his deputy at Finsterwald Castle. Narrowing his eyes, Eldric watched as the distant speck he had been following descended out of the cloudy sky. A bad premonition prickled at the back of his neck. Liliana's home village of Heidenried was situated in this area.

He spurred Shadowprancer on even faster. The stallion panted and snorted over the sound of his mighty wings. Suddenly, smoke filled the air that rushed past them.

Eldric leaned forward over the horse's neck. That charred building on the hill, that was the church. Figures moved around it. One of them radiated demonic power into the night like a beacon. Sartiria.

His keen senses took a closer look at the scene. Several people were moving away from the smouldering ruins – humans, villagers. One of them was being carried. Two lay on the ground, dead. Screams rang out. Liliana's voice laughed with pure glee. The demonic sound went right through him.

For a panicked moment, Eldric thought the demonic madness had overwhelmed her. But no, she was still acting purposefully. But what was she doing? By the Primordial Demon, was she intent on spreading the knowledge of their existence throughout all of Finsterwald? Was this the expected act of revenge on the part of the Crimson Plains? To set fire to his villages and incite the humans against them?

He was now close enough to recognise faces and caught a glimpse of Liliana's cousin Valerie running past in the background. That cherry-red hair – that was Rosalia, and she was fighting Sartiria! What was she thinking, pursuing Sartiria on her own and then getting involved in combat? She was an ancient vampiress, an accomplished warrior who had promptly risen to become Lord of a territory.

Sartiria deflected one of her attacks and hurled her against the church wall. Rosalia screamed as the Light spell repelled her soul. The effect must be similar to the protective spell Liliana had made him test on the threshold of her father's house. He had retreated in agonising nausea.

Rather than fleeing in the face of her more powerful opponent, Rosalia picked herself up and charged at Sartiria once more. But her attacks were skilfully parried, and she was driven back to the church, where Sartiria pressed her against the blessed wall again.

Suddenly, Sartiria's claws shot out. Blood spurted. Rosalia shrieked and slapped her hands in front of her right eye.

Eldric acted without hesitation. He unleashed his own powers, released his left boot from the stirrup, pulled his leg up and pushed himself off the side of Shadowprancer's back. Arms over his head, he dived down, hurtling towards the ground like a hunting falcon in a dive.

'Watch out!'

Aleksander's warning rang out, and Sartiria shot to the side. Eldric tore open his wings and landed hard between her and the kneeling Rosalia. What did she venture to do in *his* territory? Plucking out Rosalia's eye had been completely unnecessary. She had been in control of the situation and could have simply defeated her opponent and left her lying there in shame.

The roof of the church was completely burnt down; smoke still rose from the inside. The priest of Heidenried lay sprawled on the ground, impaled. One of the farmers had a pitchfork in his chest. The smell of Liliana's family hung in the air, and blood ... so much blood.

It was more instinct than conscious perception, but his demon did not forget the signature scent in a human's blood, and it whispered Cedi's name. Eldric couldn't spot Liliana's younger brother anywhere. With so much lost blood, his chances of surviving were precariously low. What had she done? Her own family, the priest and the church ...

Rosalia whimpered behind him. She was also losing more and more blood. *Blood* ... He could almost taste it. The demonic powers burst the cage of his constricting control, giving him his demon form. His jaw grew, making room for the sharp teeth, the muscles swelled and tightened under his skin.

Sartiria grinned at him, chin covered in blood. Her eyes gleamed glassily as if she were intoxicated.

'Put another finger on her, and I'll tear your throat out!' Eldric roared, spreading his arms and wings to shield Rosalia.

Sartiria straightened up from her crouching position and bared her teeth. 'Ha, you won't. You'd ruin this body you've been trying to get.'

Her challenge only sharpened the powerful shards of cold in his veins. The demon's desire to attack mingled with his anger. Did she seriously believe he would sit idly by while she trampled the people he was in charge of? And abused Liliana's body to do so?

He made a threatening lunge. 'That's where you're wrong. I will not stand by and watch you torture Rosalia and set fire to *my* land! She is under my protection, and so is this village!'

Your village, Liliana.

'Oh yeah? If you think I'm impressed by empty words ...' She was still giggling to herself.

Anger and power welled up inside him. 'I warned you!'

Sartiria was a powerful vampiress, but he would prove that he would not tolerate this just because she had taken Liliana hostage. Eldric drew in his wings and shot towards her.

She escaped his first blow. The second one slashed her side below the ribcage. Her blood coloured his perception. *Drink her. Kill her.*

Horror gripped him but was displaced by his instinct to fight when her claws rushed towards his neck and caught his shoulder. He growled from the pain.

Sartiria's powers flared up, reaching out to him in a way he had never experienced before. It was as if they were trying to force themselves on him. The powers of another vampire were always palpable, their extent, their malicious will. But only his own powers, the ones that flowed in his blood and had connected with his soul, could affect his body and influence his desires and feelings.

Sartiria whirled around and struck again with the momentum of the spin. He dodged and pushed her elbow away so that her back was to him. She ducked under his next hit and rolled to the side.

Her joy in fighting was clear to see. She was in her element. But so was Eldric. He blocked the strange approach of these powers and stepped towards Sartiria. His boot struck the arms she had raised protectively in front of her face. She was heaved backward, rolled again and, grinning, prepared to leap at him.

Before she could do so, Aleksander, who had been watching in bewilderment, decided to get involved after all and hurled a charred plank at Eldric. He caught it with one clawed hand and turned his attention to Sartiria's counsellor.

'If you attack our Lord, you disregard the declared peace between our families,' Aleksander shouted in a trembling voice. His handsome face was tense. *He* was aware of what his Lord had done here.

Eldric dropped the plank and stomped towards Aleksander as he retreated, step by step. The confrontation may only have lasted a few moments, but while he fought with Sartiria, Rosalia had suffered and lost precious blood. And though it would be foolish, the villagers could return. This was his opportunity to chase the intruders away without further collateral damage.

He roared with all his might and pointed at Aleksander with a threatening gesture. 'Leave now or die! Your choice.'

Sartiria looked alternately at Eldric and her shaking counsellor. If she didn't capitulate before he pounced on Aleksander, she would lose him. Whether she was attached to him at all, Eldric did not know. But it was worth a try.

Putting a hand to her bleeding side and without taking her eyes off him, she straightened up and walked towards Aleksander.

'Come on, let's go,' she finally hissed, taking the vampire by the arm and turning her back on Eldric and Rosalia.

She either relied entirely on the prohibition against killing the Lord of another family, or she was, despite her injury, convinced that Eldric would do her no lasting harm. And she was right. Even that one successful hit had shaken him. The look of pained disbelief on her face; her blood on his hands. He stared at the claws of his right hand and clenched it into a fist. Liliana's blood ... *Drink* ... It smelled so strangely human and yet cursed. *Taste* ...

Suddenly the world seemed to consist only of the red on his fingers and his desire for it. The seeping human blood in the grass mingled with it, and he held his breath as he struggled to contain his powers.

Stop that! Rosalia needs you. He slumped a little as the counter-pressure subsided and his human mind took over. Only then did he dare to breathe again.

He hastily opened his hand, wiped it on his thigh and returned with a mighty leap to Rosalia, who was kneeling on the ground, whimpering. She looked incredibly pale, as if she was going to lose consciousness at any moment.

'Rosalia.' He grabbed her by the shoulder. 'You need to focus your powers on healing your eye socket. Can you do that?'

Her panting was shallow; her heart fluttered, and her pulse was weakening. Eldric gripped her harder. 'We must prevent you from falling into bloodrage,' he said firmly.

Generally speaking, the demonic powers did a good job of healing their hosts, as they wanted to keep the body that allowed them to exist in this world alive. If a vampire threatened to die from blood loss, however, the powers reacted with a hunger so fierce that the person in question fell into bloodrage. But if one were constantly losing blood, this only increased the likelihood of survival if there was a suitable victim in the immediate vicinity. In any other case, the vampire only sentenced himself to death with his raging madness. If a vampire panicked or teetered on the edge of consciousness, the risk of losing control of his powers was high, too.

In addition, demonic powers were unable to make an intelligent decision about where healing could temporarily be neglected in favour of a more critical wound.

'Concentrate on the eye socket, on stopping the bleeding there. Breathe into it if you can.'

He felt her weight tilt to one side.

'Rosalia, concentrate!'

She gasped, and the healthy eye focused on him.

'Good,' he said more calmly, 'good. Stay awake, stay here with me. Forget the thirst for blood. Focus all your attention on the injured blood vessels. Direct your powers there. Make them understand what they need to do.'

He paused for a few breaths. He couldn't see the wound behind her hands, but she seemed to stabilise, her balance, her heartbeat ... And no more fresh blood ran down her cheek.

'Good,' he repeated. 'Keep it up. Think only about healing.'

He gently moved one arm under her knees and wrapped the other around her upper body to lift her up. They were probably hiding in their Light-protected houses, but if the inhabitants of Heidenried turned up with reinforcements, he didn't want to be here. They hadn't been on good terms with him before – to put it mildly – and the fact that they had now seen Liliana as a supposed vampiress didn't exactly defuse the situation. If Sartiria had killed Cedi ...

It was a real pity about the boy. Eldric had liked him. And Liliana would return to a painfully changed world. What had happened tonight could not be made up for with a nice apology. A feeling of heaviness pressed on his lungs.

How many officials would he have to bribe or let go to prevent the metaphorical fire from this church spreading to the neighbouring communities? Aleksander had claimed that he was disregarding the reconciliation between their families by attacking Sartiria. Yet it was they who mocked said reconciliation.

As he rose, Boras landed on the small grassy area in front of the church. He remained seated on the horse and paid no attention to the dead but stared in disbelief at his sister in Eldric's arms.

'Rosalia?'

She didn't answer, just buried her head feebly against Eldric's shoulder, as if trying to hide her condition.

'Find Shadowprancer,' Eldric called to him. 'I'll fly back to the castle with her.'

He could have taken Rosalia through one of the rear entrances or straight to her balcony. But sometimes a little staging helped to justify the steps he was about to take in front of the family.

With a grim expression, he walked across the courtyard, past the fountain and past the natural piece of rock on which a few bushes and pines grew.

'Lord Eldric?'

Startled voices rose as the guards and several servants stopped on their way from one building to another. Windows and doors opened.

'Is that Lady Rosalia?'

'What happened?'

'El?' Tripp landed light-footedly at his side, leaning towards him as he walked to get a better look at Rosalia. The question he was about to ask was interrupted by a sharp cry.

Ismelda ran towards them. Her pinned-up hair came loose in strands and blew behind her like a tattered scarf. 'Rosalia! My daughter! Is she …? Will she …?'

'She'll recover,' Eldric said. He didn't stop as Ismelda frantically palpated Rosalia's head, arms and hips. 'Please bring her something to drink. Quickly!'

Ismelda dashed off like a trained hunting dog. She was immediately replaced by Lola, who had obviously just returned from Thomlin. Her heart was pounding with no less horror than that of the worried mother. Her voice trembled as she cursed and asked what had happened.

Eldric didn't reply but turned around when he reached the end of the courtyard. 'Oskar is banished from Finsterwald, effective immediately,' he thundered loud enough for all the onlookers to hear. 'If he ever sets foot in our territory again, he will be treated as a stray and killed at first sight.'

Ignoring the general confusion, he turned to the vampires at his side. 'Lola, Tripp, escort him off the castle rock.' With that, he turned and growled softly, 'If I do it myself, I might rip out not just his eyes, but all his limbs, too.'

Tripp just grinned and skipped away, while Lola made a face as if she would love to do some ripping out of limbs herself. 'By the blood of my ancestors back to Ragna herself, this son of a stray deserves it!'

Eldric carried Rosalia to her room, which smelled so much like her that he felt as if she were wrapping him in a gigantic embrace. Ismelda overtook him and drew aside the curtains. Their dark green contrasted pleasantly with the raspberry-coloured bed linen. He laid Rosalia down on her bed, but when he tried to straighten up, her fingers closed around his wrist. He paused in the movement.

Her hair still in a loose mess, her mother sat down on the edge of the mattress and coaxed Rosalia to sit up a little and start the bottle of diluted blood she handed her. At first, it looked like she would refuse to drink. Then she released her hand – not the one around his wrist, but the one covering her eye – and greedily gulped it all down.

Eldric took the opportunity to take a look at the eye socket, where an encrusted hole now gaped. Bloody tissue was visible around the edges and on the outer side. He couldn't see the torn optic nerve. 'Maybe it should be scraped out? Should I send for Wade?'

The members of the noble families didn't like doctors, because those who harboured enough power in their veins didn't need cures. Still, there was usually one among the servants who took on this role unofficially for those vampires who needed a little more help with healing or wished for procedures that were aimed at enhancing outer beauty.

At Finsterwald Castle, that someone was Wade, who also cooked on the side. Although his interests partly overlapped with Albert's, the two saw each other more as rivals and rarely exchanged ideas. Eldric had never asked him to look after Liliana. A doctor who lusted after his patient's blood was not particularly suited to the task. Besides, Liliana wouldn't have let a vampire near her anyway. Since she knew her way around medicinal herbs and her injuries hadn't required any major interventions, he had preferred to keep her away from all possible sources of danger, including an unofficial doctor he didn't fully trust.

'No,' Rosalia said in a weak voice. She let herself sink back onto her pillows and turned her head away. The hand with the empty bottle went limp at her side.

Ismelda took it before the last of the drops stained the sheets. Meanwhile, the door opened, and Horatio sat down on an armchair behind them. In addition to the basic furnishings consisting of a bed, a tiled stove and a chest of drawers, an expansive dressing table full of perfumes and tinctures and a sofa with five armchairs stood in Rosalia's bedroom. The furniture was covered in violet-red silk brocade with gold threads weaving patterns of intertwined tendrils, roses and birds.

His uncle's expression remained stony, but the fact that he made no complaints or accusations directed at Eldric spoke for itself.

'Thank you,' Ismelda said and grabbed Eldric's other arm. Tears glistened in her eyes. 'Thank you for bringing my Rosalia back alive.'

'Of course,' Eldric, who would have quite liked to resign but was now being seized by both mother and daughter, replied. At least the earlier disagreements between him and Rosalia's parents seemed to be forgiven and forgotten for now.

'Oskar did this?' Horatio's deep voice rumbled through the room like boulders in a mountain stream.

'He didn't,' Eldric replied over his shoulder. 'But he *caused* it. Sartiria, the new Lord of the Crimson Plains, tried to burn down one of our villages. I assume Rosalia tried to stop her.'

'Oh, why did you have to do that?' Ismelda let go of his arm and bent over Rosalia. 'Our Lord or the guards would have taken care of it. Why did you have to be so brave?'

Eldric had asked himself the very same question. A small, suspicious part of him wondered if Rosalia had thought that killing Sartiria in battle was an acceptable way to get rid of Liliana. But that would be illusory. Even if she hadn't known who Sartiria was, she should have realised from the extent of her powers alone that the Lord of the Crimson Plains was stronger than her. Nor could she have relied on Eldric or anyone else to come to her aid in time, should she not be able to deal with Sartiria on her own. The more obvious explanation was that she had been looking for an opportunity to prove herself.

He looked at her averted face. Had Rosalia risked her life so recklessly just to ... win his favour?

Her long hair framed her neck and shoulders. He only now realised that some of the eyelets of her nonsensically tight hunting blouse were torn and her blood-soaked shift was showing in places.

She had closed her remaining eye and appeared to be asleep. But when he tried to gently release her cool fingers, they twitched and gripped him with greater urgency. So, he settled on simply holding her hand. That seemed more dignified than being clasped.

'I don't see what Oskar should have to do with the Lord of the Crimson Plains,' Horatio grumbled.

Eldric sighed. 'We will have to find out more about that.'

When a knock sounded, Ismelda slipped into the corridor, where she chatted to Selby, the maid who usually attended to Rosalia's needs. She then came back in, not fully closing the door.

'Selby will wash you if you feel well enough,' she said.

Eldric did not quite manage to push aside the image that forced itself on him of Rosalia getting into the bathroom undressed while she continued to clasp his hand so tenaciously.

To his relief, she rejected the proposal. Ismelda contented herself with taking off Rosalia's blouse, which apparently also served as a corset. Eldric did his best to stare at the canopy above them. No one suggested that he should leave, whether because he was their Lord or because Rosalia clearly refused to let go of him. After Selby had placed the bowl, water jug and two more drinking bottles on the bedside table, Ismelda set about removing the worst of the bloodstains from Rosalia's cheeks and forehead with a damp flannel. The maid was attentive enough to push one of the armchairs near her Lord so that he no longer had to crouch at Rosalia's bedside.

Ismelda fussed over her daughter for a while longer, but the night was coming to an end. Horatio was the first to rise and put a hand on Ismelda's shoulder. 'She'll be better tomorrow. Sleep heals many wounds.'

His vowed partner nodded, kissed the top of Rosalia's head and let him lead her out of the room. Selby followed them, and Eldric also pushed back the armchair. But as soon as he let go of Rosalia's hand, she felt for him again.

'Don't go,' she whispered, 'please.'

He flinched as the door slammed shut. The sudden silence was odd. Seeing Rosalia lying there, injured and exhausted, left him with a sinking feeling in his stomach. She could have died. And all because she was hoping to get closer to him.

He should leave. Staying alone in a room with an almost defenceless woman was one thing. But falling asleep next to her without the bond of trust the vow provided was against all etiquette, no matter what one might do or not do between the sheets. Nevertheless, her parents had left him here at Rosalia's side without a second thought. Perhaps it was a gesture of reconciliation because he had saved her life. Or perhaps they were not as averse to the idea of seeing their daughter involved with the Lord of Finsterwald as one might have assumed.

Of course, Liliana had once discovered him asleep in the library. But he had hidden his initial embarrassment well, he thought. Besides, she didn't know the unwritten rules of the nobility, nor had she realised how much he had already fallen in love with her at the time and how trustingly he behaved towards her.

Rosalia, on the other hand ... He should leave. Otherwise, he would send the wrong signals, raising hopes that he was not prepared to meet. Liliana would come back. He would make sure of that.

'I don't want to be alone.' Rosalia continued to grope for him without turning around. Her voice sounded so lost.

Eldric sighed and sat down. He would stay awake for another day. 'Sleep,' he said indulgingly, and took her hand. 'I'm here.'

Chapter Sixteen

This flowery scent felt familiar. His powers stretched out to explore his surroundings. The room only slowly took on sharper contours. Eldric flinched as he realised where he was. He hadn't ...? No, no, he was alone, and at least this was Rosalia's sofa. He hastily got to his feet, smoothed his suit and provisionally untangled his hair.

What a bother. The days spent awake with Annie had caught up with him. As long as his powers gave him a boost, he hardly noticed his fatigue. That changed when the sun came up.

He was tempted to slip away but could already hear soft moans and the rubbing of fabric from the bed. Rosalia was awake and would be able to both smell and feel his presence.

'Will you help me up?'

She had sat up behind the half-open curtains. He slowly stepped towards the bed and offered his arm. She swayed briefly, leaned on him and moved forward. Once in the dressing room, she detached herself from him. He thought she was going to sit down on the padded stool in the centre, but she wobbled towards the tall, gold-framed mirror. She stretched her trembling fingers towards the reflection of her face, bumped rather roughly against the glass and blinked uncertainly before touching the surface with more care.

'It looks ... awful,' she mumbled.

'We all have our scars,' Eldric said. 'Some of them on our faces.'

His own body was covered in scars, on his arms and legs, stomach and chest, and more recently on his back. Thanks to his powers, they had all healed perfectly. Depending on the lighting, the long, fine line that divided the left side of his face was barely visible.

He shrugged his shoulders. 'You can see it as a flaw. Or you can see it as a symbol of having escaped a worse fate.'

Rosalia remained silent. Her remaining eye was fixed relentlessly on her image in the mirror. Admittedly, Eldric was impressed by how composed she remained. She could have sobbed and sunk to the floor. She could have wailed and pitied herself. Instead, she stood there with her head held high.

After a while, she lowered her hand and walked backwards until she collided with Eldric. Instinctively, he held her by the shoulders.

He felt the need to say something soothing, to reassure her that she was still beautiful or that true beauty went deeper. But before he could find the right phrase, she closed her eye and leaned against him.

'I was beautiful,' she whispered, 'and what good did it do me?'

'What ... are you saying?'

'Can't you even deign to comfort a friend?'

Not if she was attractive. And certainly not if he had to assume strong, lingering feelings on her part due to what her words seemed to imply.

Rosalia tilted her head to the side and rested it on his shoulder. She was not Liliana, did not exude her irresistible scent, nor did she possess her empathetic and inquisitive nature. But he was used to watching his own reactions, and it would have been foolish not to admit that the lure was there. If he hadn't known what it was like to feel torn and yet completed in someone's presence ...

He cleared his throat. 'Does it still hurt?'

'Yes.'

Opening her feline eye, she met his glance in the mirror, and Eldric realised that she was not referring to the injury of her missing eye.

As if she could read his thoughts, the movement of her chest accelerated under her breath. He felt the warmth of her body against his. What he smelled from her wasn't exactly lust, but it was dangerously close. Longing, perhaps. His powers began to whisper, to fuel those desires inside him that he didn't want. Her blood couldn't fuel the Curse, but alone the feeling of his teeth sinking into her neck enticed him. And the curves under that gauzy shirt ... Her body felt soft. *Willing. Desirable.*

'I have to go now.' He backed away so suddenly that Rosalia staggered, and he had to catch her again and place her on the stool. 'Selby will be here any minute to help you dress,' he assured her.

Rosalia let out a hissing sob. 'I tried to be the woman you would want by your side. But even that is not enough.'

He swallowed hard. 'I am sorry. I really am. If things were different ... Rosalia, please, don't waste your efforts on me.'

She lowered her head and remained seated as he backed out of the dressing room and then abruptly turned to leave. But her defiant voice followed him into the bedroom. 'I still haven't figured out if you're that cold by choice or if you're just hiding behind it.'

Eldric fled from Rosalia's chambers, cursing inwardly as he took long strides along the corridor. He had promised Liliana that he would turn Rosalia down, even offered to send her away. Just because her feelings and her hurt were real, it didn't mean she wouldn't use that in her favour.

You should have removed yourself from that situation much earlier, Liliana's emotive voice said in his head.

Yes, he shouldn't have stayed. But he was, hallowed be, not heartless.

When he arrived at his chambers, he swung the door open with more force than was necessary and stood rooted to the spot. Empty, completely empty! Annie's missing odour gaped like a big hole in the air.

His heart started hammering even harder as his nervous system flipped from one overwrought extreme to another. Of course, she would disappear as soon as he relied on a nanny to look after her! He spun on his heels.

Thinking rationally, it seemed unlikely that Annie was in any danger. Still, he felt like he was once again rushing through the tunnel to the dungeon in the Crimson Plains. His powers pulled and tugged at him, urging him to unleash them. If something had happened to her ...

Where to? The library? He ran, jumped out of one of the stairless doors into the courtyard, blew open another and skidded past some servants who hurriedly made way for him, heading for the library.

No sign of Annie or Camilla here either. Where else? Where else? He raced back through the corridor and out into the courtyard, where suddenly the smell of cooking wafted over from the kitchen.

Eldric stopped and breathed a slow sigh of relief. Before he could take the first, more leisurely step towards the kitchen, his instincts called out a warning. From above! He jumped to the side, activating his powers. Something heavy and gleaming silver in the moonlight crashed onto the paving stones beside him. Eldric stared at the object.

Was that an ... anvil? He raised his eyes and saw outstretched claws and blond hair peeking out of a window in the tower above him. Olin. What was going on in his head remained a mystery to Eldric. But it looked as if he had run out of patience. He had given up trying to pressure Eldric into the duel and instead tried to exact his revenge in other ways.

Eldric adjusted his jacket – just another inconvenience on his long list of unresolved problems.

He hurried through the back entrance into the kitchen. Annie was standing on a chair at one of the kitchenettes, stirring the contents of a boiling pot, while old Camilla held her by the skirt, so she didn't get too close to the fire. No blood, no crying ... She was fine.

Kathleen stood on the other side of the fire in front of a wall on which various cooking utensils such as pans and sieves were hanging, snacking on nut-and-honey cubes from a porcelain bowl. Sebastian chopped carrots and parsley at one of the long tables in the centre. He looked up and lowered his knife in apprehension as soon as he saw his master's scowl.

'What are you doing here?' Eldric asked. 'What is the meaning of this meeting?'

'Mylord,' the valet hastily replied, 'when I went to your chambers this evening, you were not there. The young Miss complained of hunger, and on the way here we ran into Lady Kathleen, who was also looking for you. I can assure you we are taking care of Miss Annie to the best of our ability and have not let her out of our sight for a second.'

Of course, his sister managed to turn up as soon as he wasn't spending the day in his own bedroom. He really shouldn't care if rumours started about him and Rosalia and yet, anger welled up inside him.

'Calm down.' Kathleen licked her fingertips with relish and held out the bowl, which Sebastian immediately took from her. 'Nobody here wants to hurt your Annie.'

'You should have let me ...' Eldric broke off. No, it was his fault. He should have been back in time to make sure his daughter was looked after and guarded around the clock.

'You're cute when you worry about Annie, but too much paranoia won't do you any good.' Kathleen smiled and sauntered over to Camilla and the girl.

Before he had a chance to retort, Annie turned to him with a beaming face and called out, 'Daddy, I'm cooking!'

She lifted the ladle with such enthusiasm that he had to duck under splashes of brown liquid. He hadn't seen her this cheerful since they had left her mother behind in the Crimson Plains. If he isolated her because of his fears, he would be doing her an injustice.

'You know ...' Kathleen stroked Annie's head and combed her fingers through her thick, slightly curly hair. 'I always thought I should have had a daughter after Zac and Zic. But a pretty niece is acceptable, too.'

Eldric crossed his arms. He didn't know what to make of this remark. 'I can't help but wonder how Oskar could have known that Sartiria would want to talk to him about Light magic.'

Kathleen had been the one to receive Sartiria as a visitor, and apart from Tripp and Lola, had been the only one to be informed of the former general's special interest. She hummed a few notes before letting go of Annie's hair and glancing into the soup pot.

'You know, when a pot is simmering for a long time, it is sometimes wiser to lift the lid before it boils over.'

Eldric growled. 'An open attack on a village is not boiling over, in your opinion?'

'I just wanted to make sure what kind of dish was in there. It smelled a little burnt and I knew you would finally get rid of a meal if it proved to be bad.'

'You wanted to get rid of Oskar?'

Kathleen's smile turned sour. 'Only if he really represented a burnt dish. So, I provided him with an opportunity.'

The frustration he had just felt turned to full-blown anger. His powers demanded to be used again. Why was everyone playing these games? Sartiria had killed Liliana's brother while wearing her face. Rosalia had lost her eye. And Kathleen was standing here in the kitchen, amusing herself with sweets.

'Rosalia could have died in the process. Some of the villagers have died, and the rest will have a hair-raising story to tell about one of their own who turned into a monster!'

'Monster?' Annie shouted and the ladle clattered to the floor.

'Not here,' Eldric hastened to say. If he trusted Sebastian and Camilla with his daughter, he could probably trust them to keep some secrets. Nevertheless, it was not a good idea to discuss the details of the incident in front of everyone present.

Camilla patted Annie's arm and pointed to the ladle. 'Annie, can you pick that up again, please? I can't bend over with my back.'

While Annie climbed off the chair, Eldric grabbed his sister by the elbow and pulled her with him to the back of the kitchen.

'I'm sorry it has come to this.' A frown replaced Kathleen's smile.

Apart from Rosalia's precarious condition, she hadn't known what had happened. That meant she hadn't tried to squeeze Boras – or Rosalia for that matter – but had rushed to him at the earliest hour of the evening and stayed close to his daughter, where he was bound to appear sooner or later. Eldric could almost see the cogs turning in her mind as she tried to put the pieces together.

'You could have informed me of your intentions,' he hissed, 'rather than secretly pulling random strings to see what would happen!'

'Pulling strings is my role, Eldric. If I discussed anything and everything with you first, I wouldn't be of any real help to you.' Kathleen shook off his hand and tossed her dark waves of hair over her shoulder in a gruff gesture. 'If you don't want my help, all you have to do is say so. Then I'll have a nice little house built for me and Richard near Dimas and never bother anyone again.'

Was that a subliminal threat or had he truly offended her this time? Eldric looked at her enquiringly and smoothed out his quick-tempered feelings. If she had asked his permission to entrap Oskar, he might have agreed. Sartiria had completely overreacted. A sensible Lord from their time would never have interfered so brazenly in the affairs of a foreign territory without prior consultation, and in full view of everyone. The proliferation of churches on his land was his problem ... at least as long as they didn't pose a threat to the entire Continent and the preservation of the vampiric way of life.

'I need your help,' he said in a sincere tone. 'You know that.'

'That's right. Don't forget it.' Her smile returned, this time conciliatory. 'Intent alone wasn't enough. Oskar had to prove himself guilty of an offence before he could be removed. Besides, she might not have been so nasty if you had deigned to talk to your visitor yourself.'

Eldric ignored her last remark. 'I want you to get in touch with Herald. He is the only one who hasn't officially recognised her as a Lord yet. See if you can influence him to delay doing so. That will give us room to put her in her place.'

'Certainly.'

Oskar had whispered to Sartiria about where Light magic was still practised on a small scale. Why he had mentioned the church in Heidenried of all places remained unclear; presumably out of pure malice, to spite him and the humans he was oh-such-good friends with. He could not believe that Liliana's memory had led her there, for if she had been present in Sartiria's mind, she would certainly not have allowed her home to be attacked and her brother to be killed. Unless she had access to her memories without Liliana's consent, which was a terrifying idea.

Unfortunately, Sartiria had killed the priest of Heidenried with whom he had wanted to speak. What might he have told her? Eldric saw her before his eyes, her grin smeared with blood and pulsing with demonic power. He had relied too much on the fact that a powerful vampiress like Sartiria would easily survive his attacks. She had, of course, and yet ... And yet he had veered too close to disaster. Sartiria might be a battle-hardened vampiress, but that didn't make her invulnerable. Any injury he inflicted on her would also affect Liliana. The question of what else she might be doing in her body was beginning to wear him down, especially with a handsome counsellor like Aleksander in close proximity.

Chapter Seventeen

'Give your dad a good pinch on the leg, Annie.'

Eldric gave Tripp a scathing look.

'He is right,' Kathleen said. 'Will you stop moping?'

He sighed and turned away from the early autumn drizzle outside. The weather matched his mood. He had never imagined freeing Liliana from Sartiria would be easy. But neither had he expected to have to actively limit the damage she would do in the course of her mad schemes or ruthless vendettas. The uneasy feeling that the more influence Sartiria exerted over this time, the more difficult it would be to get Liliana back refused to leave him. He still didn't understand whether the open attack on Heidenried was due to her hatred of humans or was a warning to him; probably both. In any case, she had clearly taken pleasure in it.

Sartiria would not give up Liliana's body. Why would she? She now knew where she had to start in order to track down Light magic. And she liked having leverage against him. No, she would only leave Liliana voluntarily when her body was no longer functional, and he couldn't let it get that far. He urgently needed a plan.

'Are we almost there?' Tripp looked up at the ceiling, bored, while he flicked a gold standard into the air and caught it again.

'I want to play, too!'

Annie, who had made herself comfortable on Kathleen's lap and was fingering her necklace, crawled over to him on the bench and tried to grab the coin. Tripp made the gold coin disappear into his pocket with a lightning-fast movement.

'That's mine, you little magpie.'

Meanwhile, Kathleen opened the carriage window. She held out a letter, tore off a tiny piece and threw it out. 'Do you want to help me with this?'

'Oh yes!' Annie slid back to her and took the paper.

Kathleen smiled smugly and said to Eldric, 'I will be her favourite aunt before this journey is over.'

Neither he nor Liliana had another sister, and the other aunts in the castle were either his aunts, such as Prim and Demelza, or were in fact even more distant relatives, such as Aunt Prisca and Aunt Penelope. Consequently, Kathleen was Annie's only real aunt and therefore both the favourite and the least favourite.

Although it was nice that she made an effort with Annie, the memory of how Liliana had played with her still hurt; the sparkle in her eyes when she told Annie one of her fairy tales.

'Goodbye, paper. Goodbye!' Annie waved at the scraps from the window and giggled. The letter was a brief note that had reached them through the letterbox from Zac and Zic.

Nobody knows us in this sleepy little town. The nightingale is silent, but a limping pigeon has found asylum. More and more new ones are arriving. We take good care of your puppy.

Translated, this probably meant that Viktor had kept quiet and their cover had not been blown yet. Sartiria was recruiting more and more vampires as future soldiers. The puppy had to be Liliana, and the only person who would have reason to seek asylum in the Crimson Plains was Oskar ... Oskar, the limping pigeon. Eldric grinned at the comparison, although Sartiria had once again taken someone under her wing who knew more about Finsterwald than he would have liked. This turn of events did not come as a complete surprise. *Let her deal with this killjoy.*

The rocking and shaking signalled that they had left the road, and the carriage wheels were now rumbling along a forest path. He remembered this turn-off.

'We should be there in an hour,' he replied to Tripp's question, somewhat belatedly.

'At last ...' Propped up on his knees, Tripp leaned towards him. His whisper kept only Annie from hearing him, because with her vampire ears, Kathleen could easily eavesdrop if she wanted to. 'Is what I heard true?'

'That depends entirely on what you've heard.' Reluctantly, Eldric lowered his voice as well.

'Rosalia has hooked you after all?'

Eldric raised his brows. 'Excuse me?'

'Because you were obviously with her. You know ... during the day.'

So there was talk behind his back. Although Rosalia could have fuelled such rumours herself. Eldric glanced over at Kathleen, who was so engrossed in her game with Annie that it seemed suspicious.

'That shouldn't really matter to you.'

'It just seemed like you were all about your Liliana. Rosalia tried to kill her, after all, and she was quite nice ... for a human girl.' Tripp clicked his tongue.

'Let me make it clear that Rosalia is just a friend, nothing more.'

'If you say so.' Tripp usually believed everything Eldric said, but this time there was doubt in his eyes.

Eldric snorted. 'Humans don't have inhibitions about falling asleep around someone else, by the way. Liliana watched over me sleeping for many hours while I was among them.'

Tripp let out a whistle.

'She wanted to nurse me back to health. In my condition, I was completely at her mercy anyway. And my rhythm was all over the place. I stayed awake most days and tried to sleep at night.'

'Is that even possible?'

'If you permanently suppress your powers and are exhausted enough, yes. Then your body behaves just the way a human body without demonic powers behaves.'

'Tripp!' Annie pointed to his mouth. 'Do it again, with your lips!'

Tripp straightened up and whistled a short tune. 'You mean like this?'

'Oooooh, how you do that?'

'How *do you* do that,' Eldric corrected her and noticed that Kathleen had set out to do the same.

Annie spent the rest of the journey copying Tripp's whistling noises in every possible way, while Eldric kept his eyes fixed out of the window. Tara had provided them with a carriage from a small town not far from Alfort, as a token of their friendship. They had accepted the offer mainly due to the weather. Rabenmoor Castle was hidden in a perpetual fog, making it difficult to find even from above. The area beyond the mountains looked like the dissolved shapes of a watercolour and offered no clear landmarks.

The coachman knew exactly which meadow to cross and where to look for the gap in the hedge of thorny bushes to finally reach the plank road. This was the only way that led to Rabenmoor Castle by land.

Every vampire castle had a more or less effective defence to prevent the common folk from simply wandering in. In Rabenmoor, true to its name, it was the moor itself. Without night vision, it was a treacherous landscape where one could get miserably lost. The ground was too soft, too uneven and too often interrupted by waterholes for vehicles on wheels but would also never allow a boat to pass. The stories that surrounded the moor were a further deterrent. Some of the sightings of beasts and dead, bloodless bodies were based on truth, of course.

For Eldric, the moor harboured a grotesque kind of beauty. He could not decide whether it was a sleeping, overgrown giant slowly rising from the water or whether, on the contrary, the landscape was drowning inexorably over the centuries.

The eternal humidity had bleached the colours here, and they peeled off like an old canvas. Tufts of tall grass stood out as rust-red and pus-yellow splashes between greyish pools and carpets of pale green moss. Half-submerged tree stumps and branches lay scattered about, resembling the remains of creatures that had crawled here purposely to die. They were pursued by an army of scrawny birch trunks marching stoically through the white swathes.

And then there were the birds, the guardians of the moor. Tara used ravens as messengers and was warned by her crows when someone or something approached her home. Their cawing followed them, sometimes closer, sometimes further in the distance.

Only when the castle itself came into view – which in these conditions of poor visibility meant it was less than a hundred feet away – did the plank road turn into a cobbled driveway. This was flanked on both sides by wrought-iron fence tops rising from a knee-high wall and stone pillars with onion domes.

Eldric got out as soon as they stopped and gave Annie a hand to help her climb down. Kathleen gave him a rare genuine smile when he offered her the other arm. After Tripp had jumped out of the carriage behind them, they walked together towards the steps.

Rabenmoor Castle was less formidable or ostentatious than the other family residences and instead nestled, lurking, in a light wood dominated by ancient pines. Overall, it appeared as if someone had lined up many small houses, connected them with black beams and added a few towers on top. The first and second floors were each enclosed by a single long balcony that connected all the doors and was covered by the balcony above, or the protruding roof, respectively. Wooden pillars and carved struts completed the picture. The shape of the building was narrow at the front and widened towards the back, making the entrance section look like a head, in which the gate waited as a dark maw.

Before they reached the stairs, that maw spat out Tara and her grandfather. The old man leaned on a stick and blinked at them from wise eyes. Rumour had it that Angus was already over two hundred years old.

Eldric was relieved not to see her half-sister Hina anywhere. He would rather have taken on ten vampires in bloodlust or the annual report of all Finsterwald Castle's household expenses than talk to Hina.

Tara wore the traditional face paint, which today consisted more of black and red pigment than blood. Her flaming orange-red hair was tied up with a leather cord. The black feathers on her coat shimmered, although the moon only shone as if through milky glass. The unmistakable smell of peat permeated the air, coupled with that of moss and pine needles. Fine rain lay as a delicate layer over their skin, hair and clothes.

Tara spread her arms and grinned. Her powers swirled around her, and her croaky voice matched the scenery perfectly. 'Welcome! Please, come in. Warm yourselves by the fire.'

She turned around and waved her guests behind her with an imperious gesture. As damp and uncomfortable as the weather could be in Rabenmoor, the interior of the castle was all the more cosy. The entrance hall, with its collection of clothes racks, mirrors, umbrellas and shoe racks, had been designed with practicality in mind. It led into a room that was more living room than hall.

In lieu of an expansive chandelier, small lamps were placed in every conceivable nook and cranny. A friendly fire crackled in the fireplace, and a herd of leather armchairs occupied the room. Stuffed deer heads and antlers adorned the wood-panelled walls. The floor was almost completely covered with carpets, as was the back wall, where a woven depiction of the local Sibling Rock hung. According to legend, the siblings Tauron and Darlena had separated there to colonise the Continent. However, this legend was based more on the imposing appearance of the colossal rock split in half than on fact. Thanks to the Four Hundred Years' War, there were no sources to prove or disprove it.

Liliana would have appreciated the warm ambience. While Kathleen thanked Tara for the carriage, Annie marvelled at everything with wide eyes and climbed onto the first armchair. Tripp's fingers flashed the gold standard again. If he was trying to provoke Tara because of her financial predicament, that was pretty boorish.

Rather than sitting down, Eldric nodded to Tara. 'Since we can't stay long, we had better get down to business quickly.'

'Sure,' Tara crowed, motioning to a servant who was weaving his way between the armchairs to place his tray full of glasses on a low cupboard next to Kathleen and open the nearest door for them.

As soon as Eldric had followed her into the room, the servant blocked the way. Kathleen had naturally expected to follow them and grimaced. But as Tara's grandfather also stayed behind in the room with the armchairs, she didn't argue. Apparently, the Lord of Rabenmoor insisted on speaking to him alone.

Annie was in good hands with Tripp and Kathleen. Still, he winced as the servant closed behind him. Eldric hadn't visited Rabenmoor Castle in person since ... well, since the night Tara had filled him in on Hina's secret.

This was Tara's study, and it seemed like a natural extension of the lounge. She had a bookshelf that wasn't as large as his, but it still held around fifty books. Her desk was massive and not nearly as untidy as he would have expected from a Lord who didn't have a proper grip on her income and expenditure. A houseplant squatted in a clay pot in the corner, looking like a tall cousin of the tufts of grass out on the moor.

He sat opposite Tara. After Liliana had whirled into his life, only the rare interactions with the Lord of Rabenmoor had reminded him of Hina. As far as he knew, she had returned to Rabenmoor Castle, which meant she was most likely within these walls.

Tara glared at him from across the table. 'What business did you want to get to so hastily?'

Eldric pulled himself together and focused his attention on the task ahead of him. All thoughts of Hina could wait.

'My daughter was kidnapped, and I was almost killed trying to save her. I would like to hear a good explanation as to why my supposed ally lured my capable fighters away with her false call for help, thus playing directly into the hands of our enemies.'

Tara showed her vampire fangs. 'As I have already explained to Kathleen, this message flew out without my knowledge or permission. Gunnaryn has paid for his betrayal. I think it is you who owes me an explanation, a reason why our alliance was discovered so soon.'

'The reason was Berlinda.'

'She is dead, too, I presume?'

'Correct.'

They stared at each other as if they were in a practice duel. Tara had dared to make a similar manoeuvre with Gunnaryn as Kathleen had with Oskar. And just like Kathleen, she had been prepared to take the risk that his betrayal would have serious consequences. She could have exposed the suspected cousin in other, less dramatic ways. So there had to be a good reason why she had put the alliance with Finsterwald on the scale as well.

Tara had wanted to speak to him in private, paving the way for an open confrontation. She appreciated directness. Eldric straightened his spine and leaned his upper body towards her without breaking eye contact.

'You wanted to put us to the test,' he said, realising.

Placing her hands flat on the tabletop, Tara leaned forward for her part. 'Allies you can rely on are worth their weight in gold. Those you can't rely on are worth less than a lump of peat.'

'Why sign if you didn't know whether you were getting involved with gold or peat?'

She grinned like someone who had secretly hoped to be caught out. 'Because I have always liked you. I just had to make sure you had said goodbye to being a wimp on all counts.'

Eldric's eyebrows shot up. Had everyone set out to snub him today? 'What have I done to deserve this praise?' he remarked dryly.

'What do you think?' Tara looked around the room in a playful search before fixing him with her gaze again, a challenge sparkling in her eyes.

Hina. Eldric groaned inwardly and sank against the back of his chair. 'A lot has happened since then.'

'Obviously.'

Perhaps he deserved a verbal jab or two. Although everything could have gone differently if Hina had been as open as her half-sister that night. He crossed his arms. 'May I assume I have passed the test?'

'Yes. Because you answered the call for help immediately. Because you killed your stupid brother. And because you're sitting here now, in person.' She grinned, satisfied.

'Fine.' He crossed one leg over the other and smiled matter-of-factly. 'Then I'll take the liberty of testing you, too.'

Tara laughed her rasping laugh, her feathered shoulders shaking. 'It's not a particularly difficult test, if you give me a heads up.'

'I will even whisper one of the answers to you.' His tone became more serious. 'As you know, Herald has called an extraordinary council to discuss the legitimacy with which Sartiria has taken her title.'

'Ah yes.' The lines of her face paint rippled as she grimaced irritably. 'That promises to be fun.'

'As it happens, Sartiria visited us and set fire to one of my villages on her way back.'

This news elicited a surprised sound from the Lord of Rabenmoor. 'Why?'

'I'm not sure. Sartiria has a hidden agenda. But telling you all the details would make the test too easy. Besides, your surprise would no longer be genuine.'

Despite snorting indignantly, Tara accepted the compensation he asked for. She nodded, tapped the tabletop twice and stood up. 'It's a deal. I will take your test.'

With that, she strutted towards the door as if suddenly in a hurry. Eldric followed her into the common room, only half listening to her remark, ‘By the way, you’re not the only wimp who’s been rehabilitated.’

It was a movement out of the corner of his eye, coupled with the scent of heather, similar to lavender, with a hint of honey and smoky undertones, that made Eldric stop in his tracks. The vampiress, who had been talking quietly with Kathleen, rose and smiled hesitantly.

‘This isn’t a test, by the way,’ Tara hissed in his ear, ‘just an opportunity for a long overdue heart-to-heart.’

Chapter Eighteen

Eldric turned up his collar to shield his neck from the steady rain and put his hands in his pockets. To avoid the many prying eyes and ears of the castle, he had suggested going for a walk. Facing Hina after all these years was strange enough without Annie climbing on his lap, Kathleen throwing meaningful looks around and Tara giving her unsolicited opinions.

She had pulled her slate grey hood over her head and trudged ahead of him under the branches of the pine trees. Even if the reason for this walk had not been to talk, he would have kept close to her. This endless moor was the only place on the Continent where he didn't trust his sense of direction. If he took his eyes off Hina for even a moment, her shape would melt into the landscape and her scent would disperse in the acidity of the moor.

He was comforted by the fact that Hina's heart thumped just as awkwardly as his own. Presumably, Tara had somehow forced her to have this conversation, too. They had nothing to say to each other.

'How, um, are you doing?' she finally asked.

'Good,' he said. 'My title and the obligations that come with it keep me on my toes. But I'm sure you hear that often enough from Tara.'

'Yes.' She smiled; it was still the same smile, albeit a tad sharper.

They walked on in silence. Eldric sank in with every other step. Although his boots had solid heels and were fairly waterproof, his toes already felt clammy.

'You have changed,' she said. 'You've matured.'

She said it with such astonishment that he raised an amused eyebrow. 'I should hope so.'

The attribute *matured* also applied to her. Her scent still charmed him, but Hina had changed. She held herself differently, looked older. She resembled her half-sister in that she had the same agile physique, the same porcelain-coloured skin tone and the same golden-brown eyes. Hina behaved more calmly, spoke more softly. However, her courteous manners should not be mistaken for patience or composure. Her temper could boil over just as quickly, and when she argued, she did so with passion.

As he looked at her from the side, he suddenly noticed other similarities, features that she had in common not with Tara, but with Liliana. The silky, rich brown hair, that delicate neck, the pointed chin, the teasing mouth. The mere comparison stung him.

Knowing every speck of iris, every birthmark on a person and then meeting them again after a leap of two decades was a strange experience. He had once known everything there was to know about her: who she admired, where she felt most comfortable, her childhood memories, her likes and dislikes ... Now they were separated by countless unshared experiences and events. Or at least he'd thought he knew her so well back then. But she had kept one crucial fact to herself until the end.

He cleared his throat. 'And how are you? You have returned to Rabenmoor.'

'Five years ago, yes. Orson cheated on me several times with a blood-young vampiress from Mirror Lake. I ... struggled with myself for a while.' Hina's offended expression changed to a self-satisfied grin. 'At last, I reclaimed the heart promised to me and silenced it.'

Her powers danced around her as she stepped over a clumped tuft of grass. Before she set it down, a frog hopped out from under her boot. Of course, Eldric knew the gist of the story. But he was out here on the moor with her, and he preferred to listen rather than have to talk himself.

'Tara supported me in this decision. Unlike my father, she never cared much about Orson. She even secretly practised with me for the confrontation. You'd be impressed by my fighting skills.'

Lord Ualan had fathered three other half-siblings in addition to Hina and Tara. He had been the driving force behind her vow with Orson of Evernight Valley, which Hina had never condescended to mention. If it hadn't been for Tara, he would have waited in vain at their meeting place one night, never received a reply to his last raven letter and only later learned in a roundabout way that Hina had moved to Evernight Valley and sworn herself to another man. Did she regret having chosen Orson?

The details had faded now. Still, he remembered Morton's announcement that the wild brat from Rabenmoor was standing outside the gate calling his name. Tara hadn't calmed down until Eldric had let her into his rooms.

Hina wants to swear herself to that slimy sack from Evernight Valley in two nights. You have to stop her!

And Tara had always resented the fact that he hadn't tried. He was still alive, however, while Lord Ualan had wandered off into the moor exactly one year later for no apparent reason and had never been seen again, and Orson had literally paid with his unfaithful heart.

Should he have fought for Hina? At the time, it had seemed out of the question. Thanks to Tara's overzealousness, Morton would soon have discovered their hidden love affair. But what was more important, Hina had decided against him and in favour of someone else. You didn't take a vow with someone you had no feelings for. Not only that, but she had also kept the fact from him that he wasn't the only one she was seeing, thus deliberately denying him the opportunity to change her mind and win her over.

Tara had seen it differently, had tried to explain to him that her father had put Hina under pressure, that she needed him and would let him talk her out of this vow. But Eldric's crushed soul had wanted nothing to do with it. That was what happened when one opened one's heart to someone.

The first two or three years after that had been hard. He had withdrawn even more than usual, seeking out the solitude of the mountain peaks and making the odd trip to Trinago, where he had rummaged around in Tesoritown and started meaningless fights with drunken humans during the day.

Little by little, he had managed to suppress the whole affair. What did he care about Hina's betrayal? Their relationship had been doomed from the start. At some point, Morton would have found a way to ruin it. Hina had done it for him. Eldric's life went on as before.

And then Morton had made himself Lord by killing their parents, and he would almost have succeeded in killing Eldric, too, had Liliana not found him.

Eldric had been enchanted by her without knowing why. He had seen her in her home, had seen the strong family bonds, the warmth, the mutual support. It had all seemed so strange and unfamiliar even before he had regained his memory; too good to be true. He had destroyed her perfect little bubble simply by accidentally coming into contact with it.

Where there was power, there was danger, and as much as he had tried to avoid conflict, he had possessed too much of it for Morton to ignore. Once he had decided to intervene, to wrest the title from Morton and take his place, there was no turning back. He could no longer hide and hope that the world would overlook him if he stayed out of other people's affairs. Because power attracted everyone; those who saw in him an opportunity to expand their own power as well as those who felt threatened by it.

Nevertheless, someone had *had* to dethrone Morton and, unfortunately for him, he was the only one capable of doing so. He had thought he would be able to protect Liliana and her family, but he'd been wrong.

During his recovery, his protective inner walls had crumbled. His consciousness had forgotten what it meant to be betrayed and under constant attack. Neither his demonic powers nor his well-practised apathy had been able to prevent this wonderful young human from finding a gap, squeezing through and strolling right into his heart to make herself at home there.

Even after his memory had returned, his feelings for Liliana had not dwindled. If anything, these feelings had grown, despite his desperate attempts to keep his distance.

'El?'

Eldric realised that his thoughts had wandered and he had either missed Hina's last words or had let too long a pause pass. Such inattention was not only impolite but also problematic depending on the person you were talking to.

She misinterpreted his furrowed brow and blushed as she caught his gaze. 'Sorry, I mean ... Lord Eldric.'

'No, that ...' He smoothed his expression and made a dismissive gesture. 'Forget the formalities.'

Hina headed for one of the waterholes, which reflected the bleached grass and the general grey. 'Tara let it slip that you're cultivating a ... complicated relationship with the new Lord of the Crimson Plains?'

'One could say that.' He didn't really want to talk to her about Liliana or Sartiria.

'I guess we are both a touch unlucky in love.' Her melancholic smile stirred the pain of remembrance in him.

He could only guess why Lord Ualan had insisted on a connection between Hina and Orson. Some kind of barter, better relations with the neighbouring territory – he didn't care all that much. The question that was still burning in his mind was not about Hina's father, but about her.

He stopped abruptly, and Hina turned around to face him a little further ahead. The moor enveloped her in its tendrils of mist.

Eldric brushed through his damp hair with his fingers. In the ethereal silence, his voice seemed far too loud. 'Why did you choose Orson?'

Hina paused and stood still like one of the many birch trunks he had seen in passing from the carriage. He felt tension in his stomach. Finally, she took a hesitant step towards him. A soft gurgling came from under her feet.

'I thought you'd never ask me that.' She raised a hand as if contemplating touching him and then placed it against her chest. 'Seven years ... and you still wanted to keep our relationship a secret.'

Eldric remained silent to encourage her to continue.

'In the beginning, our covert meetings were exciting. I was fascinated by your mysterious, unapproachable personality. But you can't build a relationship on that. At some point, I began to wonder whether you really cared about me. You knew how to use beautiful words and yet you never openly admitted your feelings. Orson was ready to lay his heart at my feet. He was open, he was honest. He called a spade a spade.'

'Honest, huh?'

'Oh, he lacked enough other qualities. But yes, at the time, he was.'

'Or at least that was the impression he wanted to convey. Isn't it more reprehensible to feign openness than to hold back when you cannot be open?'

She sighed and looked at him sincerely. 'Yes, of course. But we are talking about you, not Orson. El, you ... loved to argue, to discuss all kinds of topics, only when it came to your person, you simply blocked, dropped and avoided everything that was difficult for you. I unintentionally waited for the night when you would drop me, too, because I became too difficult for you.'

He suppressed the sudden, bitter laugh that rose in him. 'How can you accuse me of lacking candour when you were the one who never mentioned Orson or his proposal to take the vow?'

Hina lifted her chin. Her tone became more heated. The fingers on her chest clutched at the fabric. She had been waiting to say all this to his face. 'You didn't do anything anyway, even after Tara told you about the planned vow. It may seem ironic or hypocritical to you now. But that was how it was for me! I treated you the way I felt you were treating me.'

How much more criticism did he have to take? He was a wimp, dishonest, secretive, cold, avoidant and, yes, why not, a victim who allowed the will of others to be imposed on him. Morton would never have tolerated such insolence. *Morton is no role model. Stop comparing yourself to him. You asked her and she gave you her answer. That is simply how it was for her. It doesn't have to make sense to you.*

Rather than snapping at her, he clenched his hands into fists in his pockets and then spread his fingers to dispel the tension and tingling of his powers that encouraged him to use his claws.

'If you want openness, you shall have it. You hurt me deeply, Hina. And you offended my pride. So I withdrew to lick my wounds. You could have decided to go against your father's wishes. You could have refused the vow. You could have come to Finsterwald to tell me yourself. Or ...'

Eldric looked at her, and for a moment the Hina of the present merged with the Hina of the past. 'Was that a test, too? You didn't think I would appear as the dreamy hero on the night of your vow and snatch you from Orson's arms, did you?'

Hina blinked back tears. 'Yes,' she breathed, as if only now admitting it to herself. 'A little. Not believed, but ... hoped against all odds.'

In his blinded grief, he hadn't seen through her behaviour. But now the proverbial fog was clearing. Tara hadn't come of her own accord; they had just made it appear that way. Hina had sent her sister to him.

Eldric's breath caught for a moment. Once again, he forced himself not to laugh. What irony. 'We were pretty stupid, weren't we?'

She returned his sad smile. 'Yes. We were.'

Somewhere above them sounded the thin hunting cry of a falcon.

'I found in Orson everything I would have wished for from you,' Hina said quietly. 'And I overlooked his faults.'

'Do you regret ...' He broke off and shoved his hands deeper into his coat pockets.

'Do I regret my decision?' Lowering her head, Hina took another step towards him. 'In hindsight, you could judge that it was the worst mistake of my life. Orson betrayed me, and you are now Lord of Finsterwald, but ... I couldn't wait forever for something to change. That would have been just as stupid.'

'I see.'

She raised her eyes and studied him before continuing. 'Perhaps this is no longer relevant. If I had one thing to say to the Eldric of all those years ago, it would be this. You don't have to be afraid of difficult feelings, nor be their slave.'

Eldric nudged the moss beneath him with the tip of his boot. 'I know my feelings. I monitor them. The extent of my powers compels me to do so.'

'I would have liked for you to be willing to give more of yourself.'

'More?' He looked into her eyes and a familiar, reluctant fear gripped him.

'You could be so warm and attentive,' Hina said. 'And then again cold and dismissive, like a completely different person.'

Eldric suddenly shivered as if a bitterly cold gust of wind had blown through him. 'Why do all of you struggle to understand this? You can't have powers like mine without suppressing your feelings and desires. Do you know why Morton didn't have much trouble with his powers? Because he was born that way, without remorse, without the need for a real connection, without the conflict between human and demon. He truly did not care, and never believed that he should moderate his urges. He just put them off until he found the best way to get what he wanted. The perfect vampire. I, however ...'

His hands had freed themselves from his coat pockets. Hina didn't flinch when he grabbed her. 'You can't grow up around Morton and show insecurity! He knew me. He knew all my reactions, every little telltale. Keeping a neutral face is not good enough. There is no pretending with Morton. He can feel your sacred heartbeat! He smells your misery! He draws the right conclusions. I had to convince my own body that I didn't feel any of it. And you can only do that if you truly don't. If you can stop feeling. I had to learn it – or break under it!'

He let go of Hina, alarmed at the vehemence of his own words. His heart was racing as if he were in the middle of a battle. He swallowed and forced himself to breathe calmly. He needed his ice. 'With powers like mine, you have to be able to keep your emotions below the surface, even when others are provoking you to the point of drawing blood. Or else the madness will take you.'

She brushed a strand of hair behind her ear but didn't look away. 'I didn't realise it was like this for you.'

Eldric snorted. Their roles from the past seemed to have reversed. 'Well, Morton prepared me well for what it means to be a Lord at the pinnacle of power.'

'Morton is dead, El,' Hina said quietly. 'You finally decided to take action against him. He is gone, and that changes things. Even if you still have to be careful with your powers.'

'I wouldn't have killed him if he hadn't ...' If he hadn't threatened Liliana and Annie's lives. And if he hadn't made the mistake of attacking first.

'It's all right,' she said quietly. 'I just felt the need to say it. I think you have a better understanding today of who you are and ... of who you want to be. Tara would never admit it, but she's impressed with how you are handling being Lord.'

Eldric cleared his throat. He had voluntarily revealed all this to her, and yet he now felt oddly naked and exposed. 'That is ... good to know.'

Hina looked around searchingly. She hopped a little to the side, where she bent down and picked a stalk. Heather with bright, pink-coloured flowers. He hadn't even noticed it.

She lifted it to her nose before rubbing the flowers between her fingers. The scent that had already surrounded her intensified. 'Your daughter is adorable.'

'Thank you.'

He wished to return to the company of the others, where Hina could not elicit any more confessions from him. Besides, they would have to leave soon if they wanted to be back at the border before sunrise.

'Come.' He pulled himself together and carefully put an arm around her shoulders. 'We should get back.'

She let him take her with him and even seemed pleased with their physical closeness. They walked back across the marshy ground. Hearing what Hina would have liked made him ponder. The circumstances had changed. *He* had changed. Would he be able to do it now? Could he lay his heart at the feet of the woman he loved?

Something small with a rapid heartbeat scurried across the ground behind them, perhaps a black grouse. After a few steps, Hina lifted her head. She grinned and nudged him in the ribs. Her finger pointed to the left into the mist.

'You're going in the wrong direction. It's that way.'

Chapter Nineteen

The farewell was cordial by Tara's standards. She assured her visitors from Finsterwald that they were always welcome at Rabenmoor Castle, which Eldric did believe. She also didn't fail to whisper to him that Hina could leave her occupations at any time, as they were by no means *binding*. In other words, this probably meant that her sister was not too attached to the vampires with whom she amused herself on lonely nights.

As Eldric and Tripp approached the carriage where Kathleen and Annie were already waiting, Tripp flicked his coin in the air again. He glanced over his shoulder at Hina, who stood behind Tara and beside Angus at the front gate. She had thrown back her hood, and her hair shone in the light of a solitary moonbeam that had fought its way through the blanket of mist.

Tripp turned back around and whistled softly. Then he grinned at Eldric from the side. 'Are two not enough?'

At first, Eldric just shrugged his shoulders. Although he had been uneasy about a possible encounter with Hina, a weight had been lifted from his chest. As Tripp gave way to his Lord to board the carriage, Eldric plucked the gold standard out of the air in passing.

'I don't need chests filled with gold,' he said. 'I just want my one coin back.'

They spent the day in an inn just across the border that Kathleen deemed acceptable. After she and Tripp fell asleep, Eldric set off with Annie. There was one more matter he wanted to investigate before the extraordinary council meeting convened by Herald.

They had left the horses in the forest, so he had to go on foot to the next village. It was an opportunity to spend time with Annie, plus, he would appear more friendly with a child at his side. He didn't know the name of the village, only that it was at the northern end of Thomlin's administrative area and that there was a quaint little church on the outskirts.

He asked Annie to knock on the door of the neighbouring cottage. When no one answered, she ran to the church door, banged on it and demanded to be lifted up to peer through the windows and – just to be on the safe side – bang on them at least twenty times with the flat of her hand. Well, nobody could accuse his daughter of not doing her job thoroughly.

'Everyone gone, Daddy!'

'It looks like it. Should we ask in the village?'

'Yes!'

Eldric put her down and suddenly heard a voice behind him.

'Are you looking for me?'

He turned around and put on an approachable face, although he didn't like how easily others could sneak up on him when he had to forgo the use of his powers. The man nearing them was recognisable as a priest by his crisp white robes. To halve an estimated vampire age in humans was a gross oversimplification; after all, vampires still aged normally in childhood. Nonetheless, it served as a helpful rule of thumb. This man looked to be about sixty, so he had to be somewhere around thirty. He carried a small pouch in which metal clinked, and there was a small cut on the edge of his left hand that had stopped bleeding only recently.

'If you are the priest here, then yes.'

'That's me,' the man replied, patting the sleeves of his robe, secretly amused. He didn't seem as if he often threw acid around. 'Priest Arnfried.'

'How do you do, Priest Arnfried?'

'Hello!' Annie beamed and pointed to the church behind them. 'We knock and knock, but no one was there.'

Priest Arnfried couldn't help but smile back. 'I was looking after another child, one who's currently ill. I was just on my way back.'

'Is it better now?' Annie asked anxiously.

'The child? I'm sure he'll be better soon, yes.'

Eldric made a vague gesture towards the road. 'I've left my horse further ahead. We are just passing through and needed a break. I thought I'd take the opportunity to pander to my curiosity. We don't see churches in the city, but here, out in the countryside, they are quite popular. Why is that?'

The priest made a quick appraisal of Eldric's expensive clothes and proceeded to speak more slowly, suddenly deciding that Eldric must be struggling with his dialect. 'For one thing, because the building regulations in the cities don't allow churches.'

'Really?'

Priest Arnfried nodded gravely. 'People here enjoy more freedom and are more open to the words of Light.'

His brows furrowed as if he were contemplating this, Eldric tapped his chin. 'I've heard that battle saints are even more powerful than priests. Is that true? Can we see one?'

'Battle saints?' Priest Arnfried asked, puzzled. 'That must be an urban myth. The last war was many centuries ago, and the only saint I know of is a lonely wanderer who has nothing to do with violence.'

Eldric added wonder to his voice. 'Can he fight demonic monsters and heal people?'

'Heal the monster!' Annie shouted.

'But no, Annie. Healing people and driving away monsters.' Eldric laughed and patted her on the head, hoping she wouldn't start to babble on about his wings or bloody battles.

'Our saint is the most peaceful man I've ever met. But ...' The priest hesitated and scratched his chin. 'Have you heard of any demonic sightings?'

'I think these sightings are limited to Roinnenstadt, where people are a bit, well, crazy,' Eldric said offhandedly. 'But a powerful healer would cause a stir.'

'Oh, he doesn't like any stirrings about his person. Most people who are healed by him don't even know where their healing comes from. He travels around teaching us priests so we can teach our congregations. He never announces where he will appear next.'

'But you have met him?'

'Yes. Shortly after I completed my training, he came to consecrate me. And later he visited the village once. A kinder and humbler man does not exist in the Highlands. His words are inspiring, and his healing powers are beyond what we priests can offer. In any case, he doesn't need a ceremonial knife or life force from his blood. My stomach ache went away on its own, and none of the Eggers had club feet any more.'

'What does he look like? Does he have a long beard like you?' Eldric looked back and forth between Annie and the priest to give the impression that he was asking for her.

'A medium-length beard. He must be from the south, with his black hair and brown skin. He looks a bit like a tramp.'

'Does every territory have a saint responsible for it?'

'Not that I know of.' The priest smiled, but his gaze drifted to his hut and then to the church. 'I'm happy to continue this conversation, but I have other things to do. Our church hasn't seen a broom for a while and there's a terrible draught ... Yes, so, helping hands are welcome, but if you have to get on with your journey, I understand ...'

He had obviously had enough of being questioned. If Eldric wanted to know more, he would have to turn to another priest with a story moving enough to warrant further details.

'We really should get going to arrive before nightfall. Thank you for the chat, Priest Arnfried.'

'You're welcome.'

With Annie on his arm, Eldric returned to the inn. If Sartiria had taken on the priest of Heidenried, he had to assume that she had gathered similar information. This saint did not sound nearly as dangerous as the elite soldiers who had spread fear and terror among vampires in times of war. Their magic had probably withered over the centuries. Lightsmiths had become priests, and battle saints ... healing vagrants. Unless he was hiding on purpose to avoid persecution by the nobility. But why would they persecute someone who did no harm?

He locked himself in the rented room and, as he prepared himself and Annie to go to sleep, he felt disappointment rather than relief. He should be glad that they were in no danger from a superhuman being of Light. But ... if this saint had been the terror from the diaries, he would certainly have wielded the power to expel a vampire soul from a human body. Priest Arnfried's answers seemed to point more to a senior priest with extensive skill and experience. Well, as long as his healing skills surpassed those of an ordinary priest, there was hope. Eldric would have to examine those skills for himself.

On their return, Finsterwald Castle had three surprises in store for him. One came in the form of a formal report. He hadn't thought it a good idea to personally turn up in Heidenried and had instead asked Roinnenstadt to send an official to write a detailed report. Most of what he read didn't surprise him, except for the number of casualties. Two. Only two bodies ... He lowered the letter, liberated.

Cedi was still alive! Eldric had not seen his corpse. The fact that he had survived such blood loss was nothing short of a miracle. But Liliana's family seemed to attract miracles. Or perhaps he had been mistaken about the amount of blood spilt.

The second surprise burst into his study, bringing with it the third surprise.

'This was on your doorstep,' Zac announced, placing a bulbous bottle of amber glass on his desk. His dark curls stuck to his head and, like his brother, he smelled of excitement and exertion. Both still wore the uniform of the guards from Crimson Plains Castle.

'And this was next to it,' Zic added, handing over a torn piece of paper.

GIFT was written on it in black ink and further down, linked by an arrow, *from an anonymous admirer.* Pretending that he had already heard of the twins' return, Eldric inspected his gift. It had only recently been bottled and corked, and the contents smelled bitter, a touch like the herbal ointments Liliana and her grandmother had rubbed on him back then, except badly fermented.

'Who do you think it could be from, Uncle El?' Zac grinned broadly and wiggled his eyebrows.

He could compare the writing on the card with samples from letters and the entries in the library register, but Eldric was pretty sure he already knew who had left him this toxic concoction. 'Olin.'

'Olin?' Zic repeated.

Zac widened his eyes. 'Who would have thought it! His, er, tastes must have changed since Luella.'

Eldric sighed and put the bottle in the cupboard before interlacing his fingers and looking at his nephews expectantly. 'Well?'

Zic immediately stood at attention and nudged his brother in the side so that he straightened up, too. Had they actually learned discipline under Sartiria?

'Lord Eldric,' Zac shouted eagerly, 'we have returned from our mission because ... well, the object of our observation has found out that we were watching her.'

'And she just let you go?'

'It was daytime, and all the other guards, the ones who would have been on shift, had been cleared out of the way by Marika. She tried to—'

'She wanted to stab Liliana,' Zic interrupted. 'Or Lord Sartiria. But we stopped her and her henchmen. We had to give up our cover to do that, though.'

'Wait a minute.' Eldric raised his hand. He could feel himself turning pale. 'Marika, mother of Farkas and Aleksander, tried to stab her Lord in her sleep?'

Zic nodded excitedly.

Eldric swallowed. He had feared Sartiria might make enemies with her heedless, domineering actions. And anyone who threatened Sartiria's life also threatened Liliana's. 'Why?'

Zac put his hands on his hips, as his mother often did. 'Jeno said—'

'Who is Jeno?'

'Nusa's son, of course. He helps train the soldiers and was always there during the exercises.'

Right, Nusa also had a son, who had to be about the same age as the twins.

'Yeah, so, Jeno said that Marika had been railing against Sartiria the whole time because she had appointed herself Lord despite being an outsider,' Zac continued. 'Not just an outsider, but also one who previously had ties to Finsterwald. If you know what I mean.'

It was possible that she blamed Sartiria as well as him for Farkas' death. That still didn't explain how she had managed to break into her Lord's chambers during the day. Sartiria couldn't have been so careless not to lock herself in. 'How did Marika get to Sartiria?'

'Oh, she must have got herself a key. Sartiria has moved into Farkas' old rooms.'

'Maybe she could have copied it beforehand,' Zic suggested innocently.

'Maybe,' Eldric confirmed. 'Please describe what happened in more detail.'

'Sure. Imagine this! Me and Zic always did some catching up just after dawn, so we'd be on the same page and all. Then we suddenly hear cries for help. Sartiria would never call for help if the situation weren't serious. We grab the servants' keys for the main entrance and run over to the castle. Oddly enough, no one else reacts. But we don't think much of it, because we're trying to get to Sartiria as quickly as possible.'

'Two servants and a guard were in cahoots with Marika,' Zic continued. 'Because they assume everyone was asleep or lying poisoned on the wall, they have left the door wide open. One of the servants is already bleeding from the neck. The other two have cornered Sartiria on the balcony and are pinning her arms against the parapet while Marika holds the dagger to her throat.'

The twins paused for dramatic effect. Zac's cheeks lit up with excitement.

'Go on,' Eldric demanded impatiently.

'We distract them, of course,' Zic said. 'Sartiria bites one of Marika's henchmen and stabs Marika in the chest with her own dagger. Zac takes the baton from the bleeding servant and finishes him off. I push the renegade guard over the parapet and send the servant who lunged at Sartiria to the ground with a well-aimed kick.'

Zac shuddered. 'Fighting without powers is ... scary.'

'Yes,' Zic said. 'That man was terribly heavy!'

'And afterward? How did she react? Was she angry? Grateful?' Would anything change if she knew that Eldric had sent someone to watch her and protect her? She would probably see this as confirmation that he was still attached to her – or rather, her body.

'Er, a bit of everything. But she was mostly taken aback when she saw both of us at once.' Zac shrugged apologetically. 'We took the opportunity to get away unpunished.'

Eldric nodded slowly. Everything about him had tensed, ready for battle, and he hadn't even been there. In a way, he was almost glad. *She could have died*. That realisation alone made his heart race. What this also meant was that Liliana's consciousness did not return even in daylight. She had become Sartiria.

He cleared his throat. 'That was a brave and stalwart intervention. What else do you have to report?'

'We silenced Victor by regularly threatening him. He knew that one of us was lying in wait at all times.'

Zac giggled. 'Oskar lives with the servants.'

'Sartiria was training us all to become soldiers. She wants to raise an army.'

'She thinks you instigated the extraordinary council being held.'

'And she wants to make you look incompetent. We just don't know exactly how ...'

'Hm, what else?' Zac gave his brother a questioning look.

'She kidnapped, interrogated and recruited a lot of priests.'

'Yes, exactly! And whoever is collecting these priests, also sets fire to their churches.'

Eldric's brows drew together. 'In the Crimson Plains?'

'Yeah.' Zac scratched his head. 'Sartiria seems to really hate humans.'

Such a radical approach could quickly lead to riots and unrest. Unless a satisfactory explanation could be found for the general population. Surely Nusa and Aleksander would not allow Sartiria to openly kidnap humans and set fires.

'Are there any other events or circumstances that I should be informed of?'

The twins shook their heads.

Sartiria's claims about Light magic were not completely made up, and he would do well to properly assess the extent of the danger. She could indeed make him look bad in front of the other Lords if she harped too much on the fact that he had known about Light magic for some time and tolerated it in its current form. On the other hand, as the church fires inside the borders of her territory proved, there were not only offshoots of the Light religion in Finsterwald. So he wasn't the only one who could have discovered it. If he wanted to track down the saint and ask for help on Liliana's behalf, he had to prevent a search for him on a grand scale, as that might cause him to go even further into hiding. He would also risk not being the first to get his hands on him. Last but not least, he was well aware that Liliana would not be very pleased if he actively contributed to harming a group of humans she deeply respected.

He gave his nephews a broad smile. 'You have done excellent work. This information is valuable. And I can't thank you enough for saving Sartiria's life, and therefore Liliana's.'

Zac glowed with pride, while Zic averted his eyes and shrugged his shoulders as if to suggest it wasn't a big deal at all.

'And now, off to your mother, if you don't want to mortally offend her!'

Chapter Twenty

The castle of the Silver Coast, like everything Herald surrounded himself with, radiated an unapproachable elegance. It had been built on a spur of the cliffs and was only accessible from the land through a single high, iron gate. With its slender towers, graceful bridges and arches, it looked like something that had grown in a stalactite cave and had been placed here on a pedestal for all to admire. At the same time, it fitted amazingly well into the picture of the light-coloured cliffs and the deep blue of the ocean in the background. Or at least it usually would have, but the fog had followed them from Rabenmoor all the way here to the other side of the Continent.

Kathleen disappeared as soon as they had been received, and Eldric spent the time before the Council began reading Waldemar's *Reflections on a Pine Forest* on his bed. One couldn't call the page-long descriptions of tree bark exciting. However, he didn't read it for its entertainment value, but for its calming influence. Besides, Waldemar wasn't a much-praised poet for nothing. Be it pompous ballads, insinuating poems or strings of incoherent thoughts – everything he penned showed his typical playful use of language.

They had discussed their approach to the Council at length, and Eldric had gone over every argument, every question and every accusation in his mind. Now all that remained was to wait for Sebastian to bring him his freshly ironed clothes.

That moment came sooner than he had hoped. Eldric continued reading in the bathtub and even squinted at Waldemar's lines while Sebastian shaved his chin.

'Everything fits perfectly, Mylord,' the valet said with a final bow. It was his way of letting his master know that he had considerably contributed to his dashing appearance.

'Thank you very much, Sebastian.'

Eldric checked his reflection in the mirror, loosely ran a hand through his hair and left the guest room. He was dressed in an ensemble of dark brown tones, which – as Master Bertrand had assured him – emphasised the colour of his eyes. Over it, he wore his favourite coat.

While Sebastian guided him to Kathleen's rooms, he went through his physical signals. Breathing, pulse, facial expressions, muscle tension. He let the cold rise inside him to calm and relax everything.

Kathleen turned up unusually punctually. She widened her black-framed eyes in an exaggerated manner. 'What a handsome brother you make!'

He raised a single eyebrow. 'Don't act so surprised.'

'And where is my compliment? You'll have to work your charm if you want to impress Sartiria.'

'*Sartiria?*'

'Yes, yes, you heard me right.' Kathleen started moving, and Eldric walked alongside her.

'I'm not suggesting that what she did in our territory was in any way acceptable,' she continued. 'I'm just looking for opportunities. And the fact that the Crimson Plains have a Lord you formerly entertained a close connection with should suit you.'

'She is a different person,' he replied sharply. 'With different feelings, memories and intentions.'

'Certainly. But in terms of smell and appearance, she hasn't changed much.' Kathleen lowered her voice enticingly. 'Frankly, you should welcome this development, my dear. She can still grant you the same pleasures, except that she is a vampiress now ... a powerful vampiress with the title of Lord.'

He felt tempted to slam his sister against the wall. Instead, he said coolly, 'I don't welcome this development one bit.'

'But Eldric, think of all the benefits. You wouldn't have to curb your appetite any more. She will age at a normal rate. She will understand you and be an actual, helpful ally to you.'

The fact that he had kept Liliana, a human, by his side and obviously felt more for her than was appropriate had always been a thorn in Kathleen's side.

'If we join forces with her, we could finally put an end to the interminable rivalries. Then we would already have two territories on our side. Wouldn't that be desirable for future Council meetings?'

'You are a faithless soul, Kathleen. So quick to move from Mirror Lake to the Crimson Plains.'

'I am only trying to incorporate your personal preferences in our strategy.'

It wasn't like he couldn't understand the logic behind it. Of course, it would be better for the preservation of his position if he had a powerful vampiress at his side. Apart from her overzealousness and high-handed manner, Sartiria did possess useful qualities. She was battle-hardened, passionate, decisive and knew how to take the lead. But accepting her would mean giving up Liliana. And he was not prepared to do that.

'She's still your Liliana,' Kathleen said. 'She's two women in one. And if you manage to swear her to you, no one will come between you again.'

Eldric growled. 'I would rather douse myself with sacred acid than let you interfere in my love life.'

They remained silent the remainder of the way to Herald's council room. As Eldric had never entered it before, he looked around with interest. The special architecture continued here, with grooved pillars protruding from the wall and meeting high at the ceiling. They drew the eye upward and lent the room a sense of spacious weightlessness. The room was minimally decorated with an ornamental window, inset with the painting of a starry sky in place of a real opening. A mixture of citrus fruits and sea salt refined the air.

They had done without a table and only set up white chairs, arranged in a circle and adorned with cushions in midnight blue. Herald and his underlings Darwin and Elvina were already present. Kathleen greeted them endearingly, and Herald even deigned to raise his hat briefly to her and Eldric.

They didn't have to wait long before the next Lord joined them. Tara rushed in, wearing her feathered cloak, accompanied by her grandfather, Angus. Tonight's facial paintings covered almost her entire face.

The door had barely closed behind them when it opened again and Sartiria stepped in on Aleksander's arm. Her demonic powers blazed around her. The black dress, embellished with indigo lace, cinched tightly around her waist and showed off her hips. Liliana would mourn the loss of her long hair. At least her ends were now trimmed to an even length. On her chest, the obsidian of the Crimson Plains gleamed.

Eldric breathed calmly as he studied her under half-closed eyelids. His thoughts were spinning like cartwheels. Had the confrontation with Marika shaken her? Had she sustained any injuries? Powers like hers had already made any bruises and scratches disappear, but, yes, there were signs of healed cuts on the fingers and palm of her right hand.

He caught her gaze, and his heart made a leap. Hastily, he interlaced his fingers and turned to Tara, who had just sat down at his side. 'Long time no see, Tara. How are you?'

The Lord of Rabenmoor laughed. 'Very well, Eldric. Don't you worry about my well-being.'

Although it had changed somewhat, he could detect Liliana's scent immediately, even in a room full of scent-clouded nobles. She was still beautiful; beautiful and domineering … and yet a little nervous. She showed a confusing mixture of that strange, scowling look and small familiar gestures, like chewing on her lower lip or smoothing her clothes.

'And Hina, how is she?' he added, turning to Tara and watching out of the corner of his eye as Sartiria and Aleksander chatted with their host.

'You should ask her yourself. After all, you write inspiring letters.'

This remark drew his attention away from Sartiria for a moment. Hina hadn't shown her his letters, had she? Tara's grin did nothing to allay his suspicions.

'I assume you are not talking about our latest correspondence regarding a steam drive.'

Tara laughed again. 'I knew that Hina was seeing someone back then,' she whispered, which wasn't particularly quiet in her case. At least the others were already talking, except for Kathleen. 'We are sisters. She just wouldn't tell me who it was. So I intercepted her raven. Unfortunately, this letter skilfully omitted everything that would have indicated its sender.'

Sartiria and Aleksander sat down on the middle two of the vacant chairs, and Eldric tried to ignore how close she seemed with her counsellor.

When Indira entered, everyone in the room seemed to shrink before her. Her powers commanded respect and, as always, she made an impressive appearance. Her snow-white hair wrapped around her neck and shoulders in a stately braid like a necklace growing from her scalp. Isabella wore hers loose except for two simple braids as a crown around her head. Both had squeezed into tight, wine-red robes that looked flattering but couldn't possibly be comfortable.

Baldrich then marched into the room and made himself comfortable on the last chair next to Sartiria, poncey and with legs wide apart. His shirt stretched across his shoulders and the open buttons revealed his hairy chest. A gigantic buckle in the shape of a bear's head glinted on his belt.

He whispered something to Sartiria. Aleksander's all-too-familiar touches had been harmless compared to the eager looks the Lord of Evernight Valley bestowed on Sartiria. Eldric pressed his lips together so as not to make any biting remarks. He had smelled Baldrich's lingering interest at the last Council, and now it had shifted from one kind of hunger to another. Both were well-nigh offensive.

'Since everyone has assembled, let us begin.' Herald's mouthpiece, Darwin, stood up and unfurled a piece of paper, which he held up with both hands. 'Honoured Lords, as you all know, this is not a regular meeting of the Council, so we will not be following the usual protocol. Rather, as *seemingly* the only family that takes the agreements surrounding the succession of titles seriously and accordingly has doubts about the legitimacy of the recent change of leadership within the Crimson Plains, we feel it necessary to clarify certain points in this regard. We suggested doing this in an official forum, so that everyone may participate.'

Herald had more or less already stated this in his letter. Sartiria looked at Darwin with an expression of indignation.

'We have heard certain rumours that must be refuted if the Silver Coast is to recognise Sartiria as a new Lord.' Darwin aimed the tip of his nose at her.

'As far as we are concerned, this is not customary,' Sartiria said, sitting bolt upright in her chair. Hearing her voice in that authoritative tone was still odd. 'Other Lords have no say in who becomes the new head of a family.'

Darwin lowered his roll of paper. 'Your case is highly unusual. And there is certainly a need for discussion, as proven by the fact that every family is represented here tonight.'

'It will be our pleasure,' Aleksander said, 'to refute any of the petty offences you take at our Lord's assumption of power.'

Baldrich grinned approvingly, and Kathleen smiled almost encouragingly at Sartiria's counsellor.

Darwin cleared his throat. 'I shall start with the first two points. The Council's agreements stipulate that a Lord must firstly be of noble blood and secondly come from the family of which he or she wishes to become head.' With an inviting gesture, he gave the floor to everyone in the room and sat down.

Aleksander parried without hesitation. 'Lord Sartiria is a vampiress by birth, which fulfils the first criterion.'

Sartiria fired up her powers so that everyone present could feel the full extent of her aptitude. The other Lords more or less reluctantly took note of her demonstration. A human-born vampiress could never have survived such a powerful Curse. Eldric had to give her credit for living with such powers without being overcome by madness. At the same time, after the incident with the burning church, he wasn't entirely convinced how stable her sanity really was – nor what that meant for Liliana's mental welfare.

Darwin shook his head in amazement. 'How is that possible? We met *Sartiria* as a human at the last Vampire Council.'

Herald shot Eldric a sharp look from under the brim of his hat. But his thoughts were preoccupied with the question of what state he might find Liliana in once Sartiria was gone. Being exposed to the Curse, even indirectly, could have devastating consequences for her mental health. The idea that he might succeed in bringing Liliana back, only to have her be drooling and thrashing about ... no, he didn't want to entertain that idea.

'Had you bothered to seek us out in person to ask this question, you would know that Sartiria is a general from the time of the Four Hundred Years' War who transferred her soul to this vessel.' Aleksander made a gesture from Sartiria's shoulders towards her feet.

Vessel? Eldric's powers protested. But he held them back relentlessly. He had to keep a cool head to achieve what he wanted to achieve here. He had to concentrate on the conversation.

Darwin looked at Herald before sighing and continuing at his behest. 'All right. But how are you going to establish family affiliation?'

'As a native vampiress, she should belong to a family and the only reason she does not is because of her special circumstances. Since she lived long before our time, she could theoretically be an ancestor of any of our families.'

'I guess that fact is and remains a matter of interpretation,' Indira's voice spoke up. 'I believe a vote is in order.'

Aleksander nodded. 'We agree with that. I would like to point out though, that we, as the family of the Crimson Plains, have unanimously claimed the privilege of accepting Sartiria as our ancestor.'

'And I am honoured to be adopted into said family,' Sartiria said with a grin that looked too wolfish to seem truly grateful.

'I don't see nothing wrong with this mutual understanding,' Baldrich grumbled.

Eldric, on the other hand, did see something wrong with that. After all, Liliana came from his territory, as did the necklace in which Sartiria had stored her soul. Consequently, it could and should have been assumed that she – the body and the soul – belonged to Finsterwald. To emphasise these circumstances, however, would have been unwise right now.

'Darwin,' Indira said, 'if you would be so good ...'

'Certainly. Dear Lords, you will now vote on whether Sartiria ought to be considered a family member of the Crimson Plains ... Lord Tara?'

Tara took her time to answer. She likely would have preferred not to be the first to cast her vote. Finally, she sighed. 'Yes.'

'Lord Eldric?'

'Yes.' He sat up straighter and stifled a smirk when Sartiria took a breath to start a verbal rebuttal and then slumped against the back of her chair, perplexed, as his answer sank into her consciousness. In a multi-layered dispute, Sartiria was just as easy to take by surprise as Liliana.

'Lord Baldrich?'

'Yes.'

'Lord ... well, Sartiria, you do not have a voice in the Council yet. Lord Indira?'

'Yes.'

'Lord Herald?'

'In view of the arguments presented, yes.'

Despite her satisfaction with the result of this vote, Sartiria watched Eldric with narrowed eyes. She waited for resistance from his side. Well, he would meet her expectations soon enough.

'The third point is a rumour we received from a certain source. It was claimed that Sartiria is secretly acting as Lord Eldric's puppet.'

'*Puppet*? Of *that man*?' Sartiria made a rude gesture, aimed at him.

Eldric let her aggression roll off him. The right time had not yet come. Besides, Darwin was not staring at Sartiria, but at him.

'If a secret takeover has taken place, the Council must intervene,' the same emphasised. 'Otherwise, the resulting imbalance could become a threat to all other parties.'

'There is no connection beyond the nature of the usual Lord-to-Lord negotiations,' Aleksander hastened to say, seeing as this accusation was as unacceptable to the Crimson Plains as it was to Finsterwald.

Sartiria bared her teeth. 'If you think I would let that creep order me around, you must be an absolute imbecile.'

Eldric put on the same cool, bored expression he had used to deflect Morton's provocations. 'Any connection that existed before has been severed with Sartiria's takeover of this human body.'

'We hope, of course, for active co-operation in the future, should Sartiria take over her position as Lord irrevocably.' Kathleen beamed first at Sartiria and then at the others in the room. 'However, we can assure you that Finsterwald is not exerting any undue influence over the Crimson Plains. On the contrary, some conflicts have already arisen and have yet to be successfully resolved.'

'Can anyone else vouch for that statement?' Darwin wanted to know.

Tara leaned forward. 'Vouching is an exaggeration. But I've seen with my own eyes the damage Sartiria has done in Eldric's territory. Lord or not, she owes him compensation.'

That was more than he had expected. Since she didn't specify the damage, she provided him with the opportunity to fill this gap as he pleased – with truths, half-truths or even brazen lies.

'Indeed.' He leaned back, allowing his powers more room to manoeuvre. 'What reason would I have to order her to cause trouble wherever she goes? Especially *in my own territory.*'

'If you want to be considered as a Lord, you have to abide by the rules we have agreed upon.' Tara raised her chin defiantly and crossed her arms, the feathers on her cloak rising outwards.

Indira jumped at this. 'And what rules are these?'

'That we keep the commoners in the dark about our existence,' Eldric said.

Herald spoke without using Darwin to deliver his message. He sounded sober but interested. 'In what way was this agreement broken?'

'Sartiria set fire to one of my villages and bit the local priest in front of its inhabitants,' Eldric growled.

'This priest already knew about vampires,' Sartiria replied. 'I didn't reveal anything that these humans didn't already know.'

'That they *were apprehensive of,*' Kathleen corrected her. 'Thanks to you, that fear became a certainty.'

Herald frowned. 'If this certainty were to spread ...'

Despite Aleksander's warning glance, Sartiria flew into a temper. 'Why should we need to hide from the humans?'

'To rule over them in peace and quiet.' Kathleen smiled with calculated condescension.

Immediately, Sartiria's demonic powers flared up. She glared around indignantly. 'Peace? Vampires and humans cannot live in peace! One race wants the death of the other. The war will continue until one has subjugated or wiped out the other.'

Sartiria had clearly not come to terms with the past. She wanted to drag the war from her original time into this one. There was a brief silence, then several persons present raised their voices.

'The common folk are not in a position—'

'What can they possibly do?'

'Eradicate? That's ridicul—'

'We *need* human blood!'

Demonic powers boiled up with everyone's emotions and merged into an angry, chaotic mush. Sartiria's eyes shone again, like on the night Eldric had driven her out of his territory. A warning pulsed through his body.

'I mean, we have to reduce their numbers!' She reared her head. 'Subjugate them. Breed them. Rule them with an iron fist. None of this playing hide-and-seek and granting dangerous liberties ...'

Throw-ins and counter-throw-ins flew across the room. Sartiria jumped to her feet and pointed a furiously trembling finger at Eldric.

'Do you think the humans don't know how to utilise their freedom? You are content with a fictitious truce! You have no idea what humans are capable of. Eldric is keeping you in the dark about their Light weapons!'

Chapter Twenty-One

Eldric remained seated. Now he had her where he wanted her, upset and unthinking. The points Darwin had mentioned were mere paragraphs. Although no tongue had posed it yet, the question that had drawn everyone here was why the Crimson Plains needed a new Lord in the first place. One of *them* had died, and no one outside the two territories involved in the incident knew what had really happened.

'The world has changed while you slept in your necklace,' he said. 'Apart from acid, Light weapons are no longer in use these nights. You are stuck in the past.'

'And what about the spread of the churches? The cult of Light, which almost destroyed us in the war. It still exists!'

'Is that how you legitimise your actions? Razing those churches one by one and turning commoners against us?'

Sartiria faltered. Either she hadn't realised how much of her machinations Zac and Zic had observed, or she had neglected that part in her preparations for tonight's arguments. At last, she gave in to Aleksander's tug on her sleeve and reluctantly sat down.

'You will find,' her counsellor said, 'that all attacks have been human led. Furthermore, Lord Eldric, your interference in this matter is not welcome.'

'Neither was yours,' Eldric replied.

'Churches? What's that supposed to be?' Baldrich scratched his chest.

'Recruitment bases for the followers of Light magic,' Sartiria hissed, and Eldric replied, correcting her, 'A building where the countryfolk meet once a week to gossip and be exhorted by a priest to help each other out.'

Baldrich looked back and forth between them and shrugged his shoulders. 'And what's the problem if they do or don't exist?'

'They are secretly plan—'

'That is an utter—'

'*Friends!*' Indira's demonic voice shook the walls. 'Let our hosts speak.'

Darwin coughed audibly. 'To avoid the discussion getting out of hand here, let us return to the starting point ... We feel it particularly necessary to resolve the issues surrounding Lord Farkas' death, specifically with regards to the unclear connection Sartiria has or has had to Finsterwald. We would like those involved to inform the Council of the exact events.'

Such impatience ... Farkas' death really was weighing on their minds. All the better for him.

Baldrich must have thought along the same lines, because he started to laugh out loud. 'Why don't ye just ask him directly what ye really want to know?' He turned to Eldric. 'Did ye kill Farkas? Yea or nay?'

'I did not.' As much as Baldrich's lapidary directness amused Eldric, his domineering behaviour annoyed him more with every passing minute, especially whenever his knee bumped against Sartiria's leg.

'Are there any eyewitnesses?' Darwin asked.

'One, yes,' Kathleen replied unconcernedly. 'Albert.'

'Albert, your brother?'

'Correct, my dear Darwin.'

Indira raised a hand. 'And who was responsible for Farkas' death?'

'Well ...' Kathleen paused, pretending to deliberate the question. 'If Sartiria is considered a member of the Crimson Plains, as just approved by vote—'

'It was the human!' Sartiria glared at the other vampires – Eldric most of all. Her anger was so palpable, she might as well have been reaching across the centre of the circle for him. He had to admit that he still preferred that to her whispering with Baldrich.

Darwin's eyes widened. 'The human?'

'Impossible!' Tara stared first at him and then at Sartiria. Well, he had promised her a surprise, hadn't he?

Sartiria saw her opportunity. 'Absolutely possible with the help of Light weapons. Do you finally realise how dangerous they are? A noble Lord was killed with them!'

'A relic, a remnant from the ruins ...' Kathleen sighed. 'Unfortunately, rummaging through them for ancient artefacts is one of Albert's favourite pastimes.'

'Are you trying to tell us that Lord Farkas died in an accident with some ancient weapon?' Indira put two slender fingers to her temples. 'Crimson Plains, what do you have to say to that?'

'The incident can't be called an accident,' Aleksander continued. 'It seems more like my brother—'

'The human detonated a Light bomb, which took the lives of three vampires.' Sartiria interrupted him. 'If we don't stomp this new movement to the ground, we'll soon find ourselves confronted with an arsenal of—'

'Is that your excuse for the army you are secretly building?' To immediately divert the topic, Eldric needed to trump her objection with an accusation of even greater interest. Unlike the humans, other Lords and their perceived dominance were a source of danger that they were used to and would be quicker to take seriously.

As hoped, Tara's feathers ruffled. Herald and Darwin exchanged a worried glance.

Indira also gasped indignantly. 'The Crimson Plains are amassing an army?'

Sartiria clenched her fists. 'Someone has to do something! You are all resting on your pretence of peace. What will you do when the humans suddenly march up with their priests and battle saints?'

'What my Lord would like to say,' Aleksander added, 'is that we had to increase our guards again after the unfortunate incident with Eldric of Finsterwald. We see their expansion as a necessity in the longer term.'

'That may be how you are trying to sell it to us,' Eldric growled. 'As a neighbour, I see it differently. Who is to say you won't continue the megalomaniac plan your brother and Sartiria's predecessor pursued?'

'What plan?' Darwin asked suspiciously.

'The reason we – Albert, Liliana and I – were in the Crimson Plains in the first place was that I was intended to be the first victim of a scheme that Farkas had engineered with Morton. They planned to undermine the stability of the families and, in due course, establish themselves as rulers over the entire continent.'

Herald rose to his feet, eyes flashing, and Baldrich leaped up as well. The powers of those present roared and burned and rumbled in such a discharge of energy that dust trickled from the ceiling. Eldric suppressed a smile. It had almost been too easy.

'What plan?' Darwin cried, while Indira hissed, 'Excuse me?'

Eldric shrugged his shoulders. 'As far as I am aware, the plan was simply to bring us down one by one ...'

'... and to seize power over the Continent in the resulting chaos,' Kathleen added.

'And you knew about this?' Tara's remark was addressed at Aleksander and Sartiria, not at him.

Even Baldrich clenched his fists. The attraction that Sartiria exerted on him had temporarily been overruled by anger.

'I had nothing to do with that!' Sartiria also rose and glared at everyone, as if she expected to join some epic battle.

'How deep did this plot go?' Indira ignored her and addressed her question to Eldric. 'And why are we only being told about this now?'

Sartiria grabbed Aleksander by the arm and forcibly pulled him up beside her. 'Speak!'

Aleksander adjusted his sleeves before he began. 'My brother was not someone who freely shared his secret plans with the family. All those who were privy to the matter with Lord Eldric are dead. I would like to point out that the parties involved have agreed to make a fresh start with Lord Sartiria's takeover. In my eyes, death is a just punishment for the offence on hand, and we have *cleaned up* on both sides. Since no one else has been harmed, we hope that the other families will also grant us this fresh start.'

His rational answer had a pacifying effect. The others probably remembered that Farkas and Aleksander had never had a close relationship. The demonic powers calmed down. Slowly, the vampires sat back on their chairs, except for Darwin, who clutched his document like a rare treasure.

'So you expect us to believe that you have sorted everything out internally?'

''Tis how I'd do it,' Baldrich grumbled, already grinning at Sartiria again. 'Act first, limit the damage and talk 'bout it later.'

Indira looked thoughtfully at Aleksander. 'Fortunately,' she murmured, 'none of the other families came to any harm. I wonder if the two Lords could have overpowered the rest of us ...?'

'With a secretly assembled army, perhaps.'

Silence spread in response to Kathleen's pointed remark. The eyes of the other Lords turned gradually to Sartiria again. Baldrich's entire upper body jerked around to face her. The tips of his moustache trembled angrily.

'This has *nothing* to do with this Farkas and his blessed plan,' Sartiria roared. 'It's about the humans and their Light magic. I cannot and will not allow them to overwhelm us unprepared!'

She may have been right in her warnings, but as long as she held Liliana hostage, Eldric could do without her help. As far as he was concerned, they were pursuing different goals.

'Then you should have brought this matter to the Council before you acted on your own authority,' Tara crowed.

'I couldn't agree more,' Indira said.

With her menacingly bared teeth and formidable powers, Sartiria was not nearly as delightful as Liliana when she was angry. 'Well, I'm doing it now!'

'We can understand you just fine, *Sartiria*.' Darwin pressed his free hand to his ear.

She jumped up again. 'No, you don't understand at all!'

'I think,' Herald's mouthpiece continued stubbornly, 'we have heard enough to make a decision. Please share your final votes before we conclude with a binding decision regarding the proposed new Lord of the Crimson Plains.'

Sartiria trembled. Eldric could almost taste her ire. Her powers licked at her like flames, stretching to the ceiling, hungering and searching for a way to feed. But she mastered the demon's rage and sat down, breathing heavily. She couldn't afford to antagonise the entire Council by shouting like a madwoman, making threats or getting violent in the middle of a meeting – not that it would have been the first time a member had physically lashed out at another.

'I don't care who the new Lord of the Crimson Plains is,' Tara said with an appraising glance sideways at Eldric. 'However, I would like to know that this person can abide by the rules of the Council.'

Indira lifted her chin. 'I second that. Since we have all agreed to her affiliation with the Crimson Plains, there is only one thing that speaks against Sartiria's suitability as Lord of the Crimson Plains, and that is the implementation of rash decisions that require backing from the Council.'

'So the question is,' Eldric said, as if the thought had only just occurred to him, 'whether Sartiria can promise us to behave as a real Lord should in future.'

Darwin cleared his throat so that Herald could speak. 'What do you think of the following proposal? We recognise Sartiria as the new Lord of the Crimson Plains if, in return, she reduces her army to the number of guards they had before Farkas' death and refrains from attacking human churches ... or at least pauses the latter until the next official Council, to enable us to get to the bottom of it all.'

Murmurs of approval followed, which Darwin took as an opportunity to initiate another vote. Eldric leaned back. The die was cast, and the council's decision would curb Sartiria's ambitious plans. He had not been able to prevent her from bringing up the churches and the Light magic, but he had weakened her position enough, and not just out of self-interest. True, he had to find the saint before she did and prevent the deaths of innocent people for Liliana's sake. But on top of that, none of the families would want to subordinate themselves to a single leader, as was no doubt ultimately Sartiria's intention. She may have different reasons for it, but her goal was sufficiently similar to what Morton had wanted to achieve to warrant a formal reprimand. The other Lords could sense this, too.

'Lord Tara?'

'Yes.'

'Lord Eldric?'

'Yes.'

'Lord Baldrich?'

'Yes.'

'Lord Indira?'

'Yes.'

'Lord Herald?'

'Yes.'

'*Lord* ... Sartiria?'

'Yes,' she snarled, glaring at him as if everything that wasn't right in her world was his fault alone.

Chapter Twenty-Two

As soon as the Council had officially ended, Elvina took up position next to the door. 'Honoured Lords, dear guests …' She clapped her hands, and two servants opened from the outside. 'Due to the improvised nature of our gathering, we are unable to provide entertainment on the scale you are accustomed to at the annual meetings. But we hope you will stay for a musical performance by our opera company before you leave. Please follow me to the theatre.'

The Lords rose and strode towards the prospect of drinks and entertainment. Eldric strolled out of the circle with Tara and Kathleen but found himself stopped by Isabella. Just like her mother, she exuded an intense scent of vanilla. She put a hand on his elbow and leaned closer to whisper something.

'I hadn't expected to see you again so soon after our last parting.' She batted her eyelashes at him. 'What a pleasant surprise!'

Eldric smiled at her through force of habit but glanced back at Sartiria, who had remained seated between Aleksander and Baldrich. Despite just having been accepted as a full member of the Council, she furrowed her brow and looked as unhappy as Liliana had when he had told her that it was too dangerous to visit her family. Yes, he had clipped her wings, but he could have been much harsher on her.

Isabella hooked her arm up with his and said something about the opera and the ballads the people of Mirror Lake sang about the mysterious Princess of the Lake. He let her chatter wash over him.

Indira's daughter had not once spoken during the Council. She could hardly have abandoned her plans to forge a deeper bond with Finsterwald, with the possibility of swearing herself to him in order to produce exceptionally powerful offspring. Although, the fact that his human lover had turned into a Lord was an added complication. Indira and Isabella would see it the same way Kathleen did. Unlike a human with no influence, a vampiress in the circle of nobility was a serious competitor. What Eldric actually wanted mattered little in their game plan. The question was only how they could get him to do what they wanted.

Herald's servants were waiting in the anteroom to the opera hall and distributed a rare blood wine. Eldric wasn't particularly interested in where the grapes came from or in which hole in the ground they had ripened, nor what the humans had been doing until shortly before the blood harvest. His demon enjoyed the flavour, and the human in him paid attention to the influence the drink had on his mental faculties.

'Excellent,' he proclaimed after the first sip, and toasted Isabella while keeping an eye on the door through which they had entered.

Baldrich and Sartiria were the last to join them on the red carpet. Her cheeks were still slightly flushed with anger and excitement. Individual strands had come loose from her pinned-back hair and the tips were tickling her chin.

Eldric felt his muscles involuntarily tense as they walked past him and Isabella. The Lord of Evernight Valley reeked like a bull in heat. Eldric would have liked to drag him away from Sartiria by force. He had not expected that she would enjoy his company this much. Liliana had never shown any interest in him. But, by the Primordial Demon, she was no longer Liliana.

The only thing that finally drew the bull away from the object of his desire was the blood wine. As soon as he had left Sartiria's side, Indira took his place.

'What about you, Lord Eldric?' Isabella took a small sidestep, obscuring his view of Sartiria and her mother. 'Are you an admirer of the opera, or what kind of music do you prefer?'

'My mother used to play the organ,' Eldric replied. As he could only catch snatches of Sartiria's conversation with Indira, he focused his senses on her heartbeat instead to keep in touch with her. 'I don't seem to have inherited her flair for music though.'

'You must have inherited other natural abilities. My mother says that Amalia of Finsterwald had a wide range of interests and talents.'

'Well, I shall leave that to others to judge.'

'You are too modest, Lord Eldric,' Isabella warbled, and Eldric had to smile.

He did possess many useful qualities, but modesty was not one of them. The fact that he generally held back his powers was due to the principle of thrift. Those who were wasteful with their powers passed this wastefulness on to the human lives they consumed. If he appeared modest, it was only because everyone around him had their arrogance oozing out of their ears.

'The fact that you interpret my words in this way speaks more for your excellent manners than for my character.'

'Children inherit many of their parents' good qualities.' Isabella casually brushed her fingers over the trim of her neckline, no doubt to draw his gaze there. 'I hope you will reconsider my mother's request?'

His diplomatic response had rejected Indira's proposal to form an alliance between their families through a vow. But the point of a diplomatic response was that it could be reinterpreted according to the circumstances. And, admittedly, the circumstances had changed.

Eldric sighed inwardly. Before he had risen to become Lord, he had never received such concentrated attention from the opposite sex. Or did he suddenly appear available and accessible from the outside because he had taken a human lover?

Isabella was pretty. She was powerful, had an impeccable demeanour and smelled pleasant. Yet everything she did was so calculated; every laugh, every gentle touch purposeful. He found it hard to see more in her than an agreeable distraction at these gatherings. Where was the real Isabella behind the perfectly polished diamond? He wasn't convinced she existed.

At her back, Indira whirled around. Whatever she had discussed with Sartiria seemed to have irritated and puzzled her in equal measure.

'I don't think that will be necessary,' he finally answered, while Sartiria waved Aleksander over and walked by his arm into the opera hall.

Eldric followed them at a distance, and Isabella joined him. 'Patience, too, is a virtue,' she replied with friendly equanimity. 'One that my mother passed on to me. Where do you prefer to sit, Lord Eldric?'

The chairs had been reduced to the exact number of Lords and their companions, making the hall seem even more spacious. The balconies were unoccupied. The smells of the respective vampires were joined by old fabric, make-up powder and rose petals. A violinist in a brightly coloured outfit slipped through the curtains that concealed the stage.

Eldric headed for the second row. In front of him, Kathleen was conversing with Herald and Elvina. As soon as the first notes sounded, however, she left the vampires of the Silver Coast and sat down next to him.

The plaintive melody alone didn't mean anything to him, but when the curtains opened, he recognised the scene: the silver-haired beauty Paresina on her throne, surrounded by servants and bathed in reddish light, symbolic of her passion and the blood that would soon be spilled. It was the first act of *The Fall of the Silver Lord,* the story of a former head of the Silver Coast who was ultimately torn to pieces by her countless jealous lovers.

How fitting ... Eldric sank deeper into the cushion and crossed his arms. Was it his fault that everyone suddenly wanted to force themselves on him? Kathleen giggled beside him, as if she were able to read his mind.

His mother had made him read this play in his adolescence to teach him some hidden lesson. This had been one of Amalia's favourite methods of education. She had passed on her advice and wisdom through the lines of others, be it in the form of poems, novels or scientific treatises. His father had read to understand how the world functioned. His mother had read to understand how they functioned in the world as individuals. Sometimes she and Eldric would have whole arguments, taking turns recommending books to each other. Every now and then they would present each other with something that contained no message at all, as a kind of practical joke simply to let the other person puzzle at nothing.

As the star of the night began her song, Sartiria hissed in the back row. 'By the Primordial Demon, why is she screaming like that? Are we watching torture? Of *vampires*?'

Darwin gave a piqued cough, and Baldrich let out an amused grunt, while Aleksander spoke to his Lord in a whisper. She obviously didn't appreciate this modern art form.

On the stage, Paresina swayed back and forth, singing her own praises. Before she had finished her introductory performance, Eldric felt Sartiria's powers slip away. Aleksander had failed to persuade her to stay.

Although everyone present would notice, Eldric was tempted to follow her simply to keep an eye on her and ... to have a word with her. Though he didn't have much to say, really. It was Liliana he wanted to talk to; Liliana whom he wanted to feel close to.

'Go after her,' Kathleen whispered, nudging his elbow.

He ignored her and pretended to follow the performance with great devotion.

'Eldric, don't be stubborn. We don't want to miss this opportunity. Remember what I told you. Find out what she plans to do next. If you don't go, I will.'

Isabella shifted in the armchair on his other side and casually brushed against his arm. Of course she hadn't missed the whispering. Couldn't they both just leave him alone?

Silently and refraining from any further comments, he rose and left the hall, where he felt increasingly watched and cramped. After the servants had opened the double doors to the anteroom for him, Eldric wandered aimlessly through the high, bright corridors of the castle. Some fresh air would do him good.

He crossed the empty courtyard, nodding to one of Herald's servants who was watering a row of dahlias in terracotta pots. Only once he was on the steps to the castle wall did he realise he had inadvertently sought out Liliana's scent and followed it here. He hesitated, stopped for a moment, then climbed the steps anyway. Sanctified! Like a moth to the flame ...

The sentries watched with mild interest as he strode along the wall walk, his head bowed and his hands buried deep in his coat pockets.

The moon lit up billows of mist, and the rising wind swirled them around like paint dripped into water. Eldric breathed in the salty freshness and stopped again when he spotted her at the south-western tip of the wall. She was standing on a battlement, leaning forward, her eyes fixed on the waves thundering against the cliff below. With this peaceful expression, she looked more like the real Liliana than ever before. She closed her eyes, while Eldric could hardly take his away from her. His instincts called him to hurry. She was too close to the edge!

When she noticed him, she spun around. He didn't stop but returned her gaze with feigned indifference and hopped onto the narrow battlement next to her. She wouldn't fall, and even if she did, she could summon her wings. It made no sense and yet knowing that all he had to do was stretch out his arm to keep her from falling reassured him immensely.

'Marvellous view,' he remarked.

Sartiria scowled at him. She was likely annoyed at having to look up at him when standing this close. 'And what's *your* excuse for being out here?'

Eldric straightened up and smiled mockingly down at her. 'I prefer to read the story in book form.'

She remained silent but didn't retreat to another battlement. Her heartbeat rang in his ears. Was she agitated or angry? Her scent implied both.

'You are a waste of demonic powers!'

'I use them as I please.'

She creased her forehead. 'Why do you enjoy putting obstacles in my way?'

She wasn't Liliana, and still ... He missed the stimulating discussions he'd had with her, and it was good to be able to have a relatively normal conversation with her. Sartiria saw him as a rival, not an enemy.

Eldric raised his brows. 'You place them there yourself. I simply point them out.'

Sartiria growled in response. Her powers ignited. She grabbed him by the front of his coat and pulled him even closer until their faces were almost touching. He could just kiss her. He could ...

'If you think ...' Sartiria began. A few tips of hair, moistened by the sea air, stuck to the corner of her mouth.

The wind changed direction, and her nostrils trembled. The sudden surge of confusion and lust that rose from her was overwhelming. Her cheeks flushed, while her lips remained half open. Her heartbeat pulsed in time with his. Even her powers seemed to reach for him, as they had during their brief battle outside the burnt church in Heidenried. The Curse gleamed in her eyes, golden green instead of blue.

Struggling for composure, he remained still. It was her body, not her soul, that reacted to his proximity. Or was Liliana coming through? What if she had truly merged with Sartiria, and the two souls could not be separated any more? Was Kathleen right and he was the one who was terribly mistaken? What if *he* was stuck in the past, mourning something that was already lost?

Eldric staggered, stupefied for a moment. No, he ... That couldn't be. He couldn't give up on her.

Abruptly, he straightened up; his coat slipped from her fingers. He cleared his throat to make sure his voice sounded normal. 'Let's settle our differences in a less ... physical way for the time being.'

Staring steadily at a point above the crown of her head, Eldric tried to collect himself. What was he supposed to find out again?

'What are you going to do ... now that you have officially acquired one of the highest positions on the Continent?'

Sartiria clenched her fists. 'I will prove to you – I will prove to *all of you* that I'm right! Once I've found the battle saints and uncovered their secret preparations for war, you'll be begging me on your knees for help and forgiveness!'

Such doggedness ... After she had almost thrown herself at him. His heartbeat was calming down. She sounded almost as vainglorious as Morton. He very much doubted her judgement when it came to the alleged preparations for war. But if this saint the priest had told him about really existed, he would find him. And if he was as powerful as she claimed, it would be she who regretted her decision not to cooperate with him.

He pursed his lips and leaned forward to whisper in her ear. 'We shall see who is going to beg who.'

Heavy stomping boots caught his attention. With a hasty step back, he withdrew onto the nearest battlement and glanced at the approaching figure. Baldrich. Of all people ...

The Lord of Evernight Valley waved at them. His hairy chest was, as so often, exposed under his open shirt. Why did he bother wearing a coat at all?

'The opera has just ended,' he exclaimed.

'Excellent,' Eldric replied tonelessly.

Baldrich stopped and crossed his muscular arms. 'Seeing ye squabblers together like that, I assume ye've already made up since the Council.'

Eldric remained on his battlement, but Sartiria raised her chin and jumped down in front of Baldrich on the guard's walk. She plucked at her dress for a while before she spoke. 'We do our best.'

Baldrich's eager gaze lingered on her buttocks. He stroked one of the ends of his moustache. 'I wanted to invite ye for a bloody drink ... in my room.'

That blessed bastard! With difficulty, Eldric suppressed a growl. His powers swelled along with his rage, and he had to hold them back with such force that his stomach tightened and the fingers in his coat pockets twitched.

'It would be my pleasure,' Sartiria purred. She leaned into the arm Baldrich put around her and sauntered off without looking back even once.

Chapter Twenty-Three

Eldric watched them leave. It took all of his mental capacity not to let his demonic powers overflow. He breathed heavily, temporarily unable to move without running the risk of losing control of his motor functions.

He had to intervene. He had to stop them. He had to ... *kill him, tear him to pieces ... drag his headless body across Herald's courtyard.*

Where was his composure? His thoughts kept running wild. Was she just doing it to provoke him? Would she really accompany Baldrich to his room? Was she going to enjoy herself with another Lord to punish him for the outcome of the Council meeting?

Her tongue in his mouth. He ... in her. Eldric forbade himself the idea. Anger gripped him; icy, mindless anger. The demonic powers raged within him. He dug his nails into the heels of his hands, hoping the pain would bring him to his senses.

Jealousy etched its way up through his oesophagus. But it was more than that. Liliana would never want that. Would she? No, she would find the thought repulsive. What Sartiria did to her body, she did to her. And Baldrich – he knew exactly who Sartiria had been before, whose body she was in.

A goal ... he needed a goal to hold on to. He would separate them, with words, or if necessary, with violence. In doing so, he would reveal that she had him in the palm of her hand with such a simple act, or even just the threat of it. But he couldn't bear the alternative. And what if Baldrich bit her in a fit of hungry passion?

He pulled his hands out of his pockets, spread and moved his fingers. No claws – his powers obeyed him. He whirled around, jumped off the wall and caught the impact on the patio with springy knees and a surge of demonic power. The servant tending to the potted plants dropped her secateurs in shock.

He crossed the sandstone-coloured courtyard with long strides. Two more of Herald's servants hurried out of his way with expressions of dismay.

'Lord Eldric? Where are you going in such a hurry?'

He barely noticed the white-haired woman who grabbed his wrist as he walked past. Isabella.

'Will you finally leave me alone?' he hissed and snatched his arm away.

He heard her gasp indignantly behind him, ignored it, marched straight to the guest wing and tore open the door before anyone could open it for him. On the other side, he almost collided with Kathleen.

'Eldric, I just saw—' She broke off. Rather than flinching from the storm of power inside him, she opened her arms and blocked the way. Her bronze-coloured eyes shone warningly.

'Whatever you're about to do, I can sense it is a terrible idea,' she said calmly, as if she were talking to a spooked horse.

He bared his teeth. 'Sartiria is ... with *him* ...'

His sister knew immediately who he meant. Her expression remained serious. 'You will not cause a diplomatic incident after we have manoeuvred ourselves into such an advantageous position in the Council.'

Eldric growled and forcibly pushed her aside. When Kathleen grabbed his arm, he reacted instinctively, seized her hand with his and swung her around so that she was hurled against the wall. The impact knocked the air out of her lungs. Kathleen gasped. He turned around to continue on his way. But she didn't give up that quickly. Eldric saw out of the corner of his eye how she ran her fingers over a scratch on her cheek, pushed herself resolutely from the wall, gathered the layers of fabric on her skirt and caught up with him in three lightning-fast steps.

'*Eldric*,' she hissed and immediately switched back to a beseeching tone. 'Please, calm down. I'll take care of this.' She made a curt hand gesture to someone further back in the corridor.

Hasty footsteps echoed off the walls and the high, pointed ceiling. He identified Ava and Sebastian.

'Mylord ...' Sebastian's broad face appeared beside him. He looked worried, almost pale under his light beige complexion.

Eldric caught himself at the sight of his loyal valet. The familiarity of his smell and the austere uniform, the tied-back hair and the dark golden, narrow eyes helped him to come to his senses. Perhaps he associated Sebastian's presence with retreating to his own chambers at home in Castle Finsterwald.

Eldric took a deep breath and pulled hard on his powers. There was no need to let the whole Silver Coast feel the extent of his Curse. He had to keep his composure.

Kathleen sighed and held still so that Ava could pin her partially loosened waves of hair back into place. The graze on her cheek was already healing. 'Please accompany Lord Eldric to his guest room,' she instructed the two servants. Addressing him, she continued, 'Stay there until I return. I'll lure her away from him.'

He gritted his teeth and nodded, whereupon Kathleen hurried away, relieved.

'Mylord, if you would follow me.' Sebastian took the lead, while Ava trudged behind Eldric.

Now that his tunnel vision had cleared, Eldric discovered seven other individuals scurrying through the corridors with their pounding hearts. Once in the guest chamber, Sebastian and Ava stopped at the door. He refrained from glowering at them because they were behaving as if he couldn't be trusted. He deserved it.

'Leave me,' he said coolly.

'Yes, Mylord,' came back the replies, in two voices and hesitant.

After they had closed the door behind them, he dropped onto the bed. He closed his eyes and concentrated once again on his vitals, staying with his heartbeat and his breathing until he had clamped down on his powers fully. Gradually, he released all muscle tension and welcomed the heaviness in his limbs. From the outside, he could have been mistaken for a human who had fallen asleep fully dressed on his bed.

There was a knock, and Kathleen slipped in. 'Eldric?'

He opened one eye and watched as she cautiously approached. Her heels clacked on the tiles. 'Sartiria has decided to leave. You should know she's not averse to an alliance with Finsterwald.'

'I see.'

'However, you should also know that she will make such an alliance with Evernight Valley in one week's time should you not act accordingly.'

'Hm.'

Eldric closed his eye again. Although Kathleen had prevented him from doing anything unreasonable, Sartiria had realised she could torture him by abusing Liliana's body. She could have threatened self-harm or even suicide. But that would have harmed her, too, as long as she did not have the option of transferring her soul into a new body. In comparison, she probably felt that whatever Baldrich wanted to do to her was a more pleasurable option, because while Eldric still harboured the same feelings for her, or for the person inside her, she had no attachment to him.

He felt the unwanted tension returning to his muscles. Perhaps it had only been a matter of time before she turned to blackmail. Now she could play him and Baldrich off against each other just wonderfully.

Groaning like an old man, he sat up and ran his fingers through his hair. 'I ... apologise for the rough treatment earlier.'

His sister smiled. She had never seemed intimidated. Honestly, he was amazed at how much trust was generally placed in him to keep his powers under wraps. Well, as Herald's servants had proved, most vampires had no idea what he was really capable of. After all, he always made an effort to remain unobtrusive. Kathleen, on the other hand, knew. She had seen him grow up. And she had seen what such extraordinary powers had made of Morton.

'I drowned Harlan in a lake,' she replied. 'I can handle a passionate argument. However ...' She crossed her arms and drummed the fingers of her right hand against her upper arm. 'You obviously owe someone else an apology.'

'And who would that be?'

'Isabella. She just now turned away from me in a huff when I tried to greet her in passing.'

Right ... He had also lashed out against her in his anger, but in his opinion, she deserved it more. Still, he would conjure up the decency to apologise.

'You don't want to upset the ladies of Mirror Lake by treating them rudely in addition to your hasty rejection. I hope you didn't throw her against walls, did you?'

Ignoring her last question, Eldric stood up and walked past her. He paused briefly at the door. 'Tell Sebastian to pack my things. We'll leave as soon as I am done.'

Eldric unleashed his powers just enough to catch Isabella's scent and saw her step out of her guest room around the first bend. She was wearing her travelling attire, breeches, blouse and jacket, and the young vampiress at her side was balancing her luggage – a small chest and a carpet bag – in her arms.

Both women curtseyed to him. 'Lord Eldric.'

He nodded in the direction of the room they had just come from. 'A word, Isabella.'

She made a huffy sound. 'You said I should leave you alone.'

'Isabella, please.' Eldric sighed and stretched out a hand towards the door handle, whereupon the maid quickly made room for him. 'I would like to apologise.'

Isabella glanced down the corridor as if expecting to see her mother appear at any moment. Then she bowed her head. 'As you wish, Lord Eldric.'

He held the door open for her, and she complied with feigned submission. As soon as they were both inside, he pushed the heavy wood behind him into the lock with his boot and turned to face her.

The room looked completely unused. The bed was made and there wasn't a single hair or a speck of dust to be seen. If it hadn't been for the scents of the two vampiresses mingling with the omnipresent salt and citrus notes, he would have assumed it hadn't even been entered.

Isabella's snow-white hair shimmered in the moonlight that fell on her through the high window on the far wall. As she stood before him, proud and upright and the epitome of loveliness, she was quite the legendary Princess of the Lake.

He cleared his throat. 'Forgive my harsh words earlier in the courtyard. My anger was not directed at you.' ... Or at least not primarily directed at her.

'You sound like you have more on your mind.' She smiled expectantly.

'I do.'

Eldric hesitated. The message he wanted to convey remained essentially the same. He wanted to be left alone. But in order for it to be properly received, he had to present it in a way that was acceptable to his counterpart. He could have approached Indira directly; however, he believed he could achieve more with Isabella.

If he simply repeated what he had already said, she would smile and say yes but continue to faithfully follow her mother's plans. He had to draw her out of her shell, and the best way to do that was with a shocking dose of candour.

The ladies and gentlemen of the noble class in general could stand a little more candour, in his opinion.

The conversation with Hina haunted him still. Strangely enough, it was only then that he had truly realised. If Morton had been able to shape people and circumstances around him, so could he. After all, that had been his original intention. He had wanted to make his home a more pleasant place for Liliana's sake, a place where she could actually live. As far as her safety was concerned, he had failed more often than not. Nevertheless, most of the vampires at Finsterwald Castle had accepted Annie and Liliana after some initial resistance.

He was Lord of the central territory. Whether intentionally or not, people were watching him, taking note of what he did, what he said. He could no longer hide. This also meant that he could bring about change with his personal behaviour alone.

'I am tired of acting as if we were on stage,' he finally said.

Isabella blinked, this time out of surprise, not coquetry. 'I do not understand what you are hinting at.'

'And I imagine you are tired of dancing to your dear mother's tune, too.'

Her mouth twisted. 'Insulting my mother is not a very good apology, Lord Eldric.'

'My comment was neither intended as an insult nor an apology. It is my honest, heartfelt opinion. Isabella ... I don't want to have a child with you, and I strongly suspect that you don't really want that either. Why don't we stop this theatre? Then maybe there could be room for real rapport between us, for the benefit of both of our territories.'

'Maybe that is exactly what I want!' She threw her head back defiantly, only to immediately cast her eyes down and blush. 'Have you not considered that I might be trying to win your favour of my own accord, because I am attracted to you?'

At first, Eldric was taken aback. Was it possible? No. Her scent remained too neutral. He knew how intricate and subtle love could be; how deep true passion burned. This was neither of those things.

His tone became harsher. 'Our union is at best an idea that you are not too averse to. That is not what I want for my future.'

'How cold you are!' When Isabella raised her eyes, the copper irises sparked. The sudden change was almost uncanny. But Eldric sensed that he was slowly getting to the heart of the matter.

'You can't walk in your mother's shadow forever,' he replied. 'I refuse to give up my personal happiness for someone else's intrigues. And you? Who are you but Indira's daughter?'

Her indignation, too, melted away like another excess layer. What remained was a contemptuous line around her lips. 'If you assume that I am Lord Indira's straw doll like everyone else, you are not half as insightful as my mother thinks you are.'

'Is that so?' Eldric masked his surprise by adopting her mocking tone.

'Yes.' She casually put one arm to her side. There was no sign of the supposedly enamoured Isabella left. 'It was my idea! I whispered to my mother how beneficial it would be to unite the Curse running in our families.'

She snorted. 'You have no idea with how many men, in how many positions and moon phases I have tried. My sacred cousin is about to give birth to her third child. And I, *I* am not getting pregnant.'

'That must be difficult.'

Isabella wiped his expression of empathy out of the air with a brisk wave of her hand. 'My mother has no idea, and if she finds out after this conversation, I will know exactly who told her!'

'I can keep secrets to myself.'

'Good.' Her powers expanded into the room as she continued to speak. Her heartbeat did pick up speed now. 'Our bloodline will not end with me! I will have a daughter. She will be the most powerful Lord the Continent has ever seen. And if I have to spend my life loveless to achieve that, so be it! I will raise the next Princess of the Lake.'

Eldric let a short pause pass. Was the servant outside in on the secret? That was probably why she continued to stand on the other side of the door, making sure no one was eavesdropping.

'I am sorry that you are struggling with these difficulties. But what does that have to do with me? One would assume that your chances of getting pregnant would diminish if you vowed yourself to any one person.'

'You are not just any one person, though, Lord Eldric. After my many attempts, you suddenly appeared out of nowhere with your outrageous manifestation of demonic powers. And you have fathered a child already. With a human, even, and after only a few months of acquaintance.'

Of course, Isabella was aware of such details ... 'I'm afraid you have turned to the wrong party.'

This was not the first time he had been amazed at how much information vampires largely ignored or simply overlooked about their prey. He himself had only grasped the connection afterward, when he had found out Annie was *his* daughter. Perhaps it was because vampires believed themselves to be superior to humans in all respects that Isabella attributed the high fertility to him.

Her eyes narrowed. 'How so?'

'As much as I would like to boast about my masculinity, it is not me who is exceptionally fertile.'

Isabella stared at him in horror. 'You mean I would have to mate with a human to ...' This time, her embarrassment was more clandestine, which made it all the more genuine. The tip of her nose twitched.

'I am not completely sure.' He hadn't expected the conversation to go in this direction, after all. 'But I suspect that vampires produce less semen than humans. And what I can say with certainty is that human women bleed about once per lunar cycle.'

'That often?' The hand on Isabella's waist slipped.

Eldric grinned. Thanks to Liliana's stay at Finsterwald Castle, this fact should be more or less known to anyone living there with a functioning olfactory organ. 'Roughly speaking, that should increase their chances of conception sixfold.'

Isabella opened and closed her mouth as if she no longer understood how the world as a whole worked.

'I can't say why it is that way. Maybe the fact is owed to our slowed ageing. Fertility could possibly be increased with the targeted use or relinquishment of demonic powers. To be honest, I haven't done much research on this particular subject so far.'

'Their lifespan is shorter, thus ... humans live and procreate faster. Like rabbits.' Isabella tugged at her crown of hair as she looked at him, first in amazement and then with increasing frivolity. 'Is that to your taste, Lord Eldric? Is this the reason you sought a human lover?'

'Whatever you are implying, I assure you it had no bearing on my decision.' Eldric cleared his throat and took a step back. 'In any case, I apologise for my rude behaviour. And I would also like to reiterate in no uncertain terms that I do not intend to enter into the kind of relationship with you that you propose. I like your company, and I think we can build a better connection between Finsterwald and Mirror Lake if we stay on platonic terms.'

Before she could say anything in reply, he indicated a bow. 'I bid you farewell. Your mother, as you can tell, is on her way. I wish you a good night and a pleasant journey home.'

Chapter Twenty-Four

On the way to his study, Eldric swung the keys around his finger to make them jingle. Where was this saint? He had pulled all the levers. The guards at the border towers had been alerted, and the street watchmen in all his cities and towns were on the lookout. But there was no sign of a vagrant who performed miraculous healings.

Was he chasing a phantom? Was there nothing but stories left of these battle saints that Sartiria was so afraid of? Something the priests told the poor farmers to comfort them? Something he also wanted to believe because it comforted *him*? The thought tightened around his chest like a metal band.

Although he had been hunting not so long ago, an inner restlessness drove him from one place to the next. He had already been at his desk, then in the library, on the wall, back in his chambers, and also in the forest room, where Annie was playing with Zac and Zic under Camilla's supervision. He had brought them Silver Biscuits in a pretty tin; paper-thin, caramelised wafers decorated with the imprint of Herald's coins. On the Silver Coast, even food was stamped like money. But they were, he had to admit, delicious, and just like real money, they were good for bribing others.

In a week's time, Sartiria would meet with Baldrich to negotiate an alliance. Much to his chagrin, he could imagine all too well what else might happen during these negotiations. That bastard had snatched Liliana as soon as she had acquired enough power to be interesting to him. Sartiria did whatever she liked with the body she had taken possession of. Of course, that had been the case from the start, but now she was rubbing it in his face, and he couldn't just sit idly by. He had to stop her somehow.

But if he couldn't find the saint, what else could he do, short of downright attacking another family? Kathleen had mentioned that Sartiria was also willing to negotiate with him, but ... on what basis? Everything stood or fell with an untraceable vagrant.

Taking three steps at once, he climbed the stairs. Aunts Prisca and Penelope were whispering in their favourite alcove, and he could feel their eyes following him to the door where Lola was waiting for him. She wore a grey checked waistcoat over her shirt, a tie and fashionably pointed shoes – more like something he would have expected Richard or the twins to strut around in. Was he mistaken, or had she become more experimental with her fashion choices recently?

'News?'

She looked him thoughtfully up and down. 'I'm afraid not.'

Eldric snorted. 'Then why are you standing outside my door?'

'Would you like to play a game of Lordboard?'

He raised his brows. 'Now?'

'Yes, now.'

'No thanks, I'm busy.'

'With pointless wandering around the castle?'

By Tauron and Darlena, wasn't his irritable dejection a good enough reason to avoid him?

Eldric started to retort sharply, but his guilty conscience pricked him. He had offloaded many of his regular tasks onto Lola and sent her away on assignments, which meant that they had only seen each other in passing and for reports. Lola was reliable, discreet and the most sensible person he knew ... at least as long as her mother, Demelza, wasn't nearby. Eldric couldn't remember playing with his cousin as a child, but as adults they had naturally found each other, probably because their personalities were alike.

He couldn't rule out that Kathleen or someone else might try to usurp the title. However, there was an unspoken agreement between him and Lola that she would take over the leadership of the family if he were incapacitated or killed. Accordingly, he made sure that Lola was up to date with the most important developments in Finsterwald and had an idea of where to look for which type of document. While Kathleen took care of the network of relationships within the family and the dialogue with other territories, Lola was the one who was most adept at dealing with numbers and resources.

'Fine. A game of Lordboard it is.'

He pulled out the keys that were already in his hand, but Lola stopped him with a wave of her hand.

'Not here,' she said, 'downstairs.'

By *downstairs*, she probably meant the cellar that had once been known as Morton's gambling den. Eldric had never felt comfortable there, but the others kept the room as a favourite meeting place even after Morton's arrest and his later death.

He had no desire to sit down there and push little pieces back and forth on a board. What was he doing here in the castle anyway? If there was no progress to report on this saint, he might as well have flown out. He felt restless and found everything unsatisfying – the fruitless search, the events surrounding the Council, Liliana's continued absence, the expectations that weighed on him, and all the other entanglements.

'A little distraction will do you good,' Lola promised, and quickly took him by the arm.

He allowed her to pull him along, past Prisca and Penelope and down the stairs.

'How is Rosalia?' he asked, in truth to enquire how Lola was doing with Rosalia. The fact that this topic was taboo and could only be touched on was another unspoken agreement between them.

'Unchanged. I mean ...' She stubbornly looked straight ahead and continued to pull him through the entrance hall. 'She has recovered remarkably well.'

He translated that as *I don't want to bother anyone with my feelings and I don't want to talk about them, especially not to you, after all, she adores you, whereas she'll never see me as anything more than a good friend. But if you really cared about her wellbeing, you could have sought her out yourself to see how she is.*

'I'm glad to hear it,' Eldric replied as a neutral signal that he had understood the verbal fence and accepted her silence.

It was hilarious – or exasperating. Lola had long had a secret crush on Rosalia, Rosalia didn't want to give up her feelings for him, and he pined for Liliana. If Liliana or Sartiria had fallen in love with Lola, they would have made a tragic quadrangle of unfulfilled romantic longing.

Rarely in his life had he been so tempted to bang his head against the wall to banish a particular image from it. Sartiria and Baldrich walking away together ... that scene was permanently carved in his mind. Yearning for someone was one thing. But to have your yearning served up as a means of blackmail because that someone was possessed by another soul while you were seemingly condemned to idleness ...

Glum and brooding, he followed Lola. They had reached the centre of the hall when a wing of the entrance gate burst open, and Tripp rushed up. 'There you are. I challenge you to a practice duel! Since the Silver Coast, you look like you need to blow off some steam.'

'We were just about to play Lordboard,' Lola interjected.

'That can wait!' Tripp put an arm around Eldric from the side and patted him on the shoulder. 'We haven't banged heads for fun in ages. Well, what do you say?'

Eldric slipped out of this half-embrace. It was well-intentioned, no question, but that did nothing to dampen his irritation. 'No, listen, I just want to ...'

Before he could raise his objections and emphasise that he wasn't really in the right mood for either, the cellar door opened this time, and Boras glided in.

'El, I was looking for you,' he announced in his muffled voice. 'I thought tonight might be a good night to start on a collaborative project. You know, art is enlightening to the mind and soothing to the spirit.'

'Or you could join me,' Rosalia said, appearing behind her brother in the doorway and leaning against it, a wine glass in one hand and an already opened, tantalisingly fragrant bottle in the other. 'And wash away your worries.'

Eldric looked from one to the other. Where had they all come from at once? 'I don't need ... whatever this is supposed to be.'

Rosalia smiled. In lieu of a glass eye, a golden marble sat in her now healed eye socket. It made her look more daring. Her black dress consisted of a fluffy, silky top and a tight, calf-length skirt. 'Just one glass?'

He cleared his throat. 'I'd much rather be on a mountain top somewhere ... *alone.*'

'Come on, El.' Tripp's elbow took aim at his ribs, and Eldric dodged mechanically. 'I'm getting out of practice.'

'I could explain to you where I get the inspiration for my paintings.'

'If you beat me at Lordboard, I will let you choose my wardrobe for the next banquet.'

'It would really do you good to forget Liliana for a few hours at least.'

'If you stopped moping for a minute, you could—'

'*That's enough,*' Eldric hissed, and the group fell silent. A chill spread through the emptiness of the hall.

'Stop trying to cheer me up. I ...' He registered the half-disappointed, half-worried faces and took a deep breath. Then he exhaled and resigned himself to his fate. 'Fine. Why not? And why not everything at once?'

Lola and Tripp exchanged a meaningful glance.

Eldric gave Tripp a push and waved Rosalia and Boras over. 'Come on, to the courtyard. Bring drinks, paints, easel, the game board ...'

Boras dashed off with as much enthusiasm as he could muster without ceasing to be Boras. Meanwhile, Rosalia and Lola hurried into the gambling den to fetch their respective equipment. They met a little later in the courtyard, where Eldric waited and Tripp had already started prancing from one foot to the other. Rosalia sat down at the edge of the fountain with glasses and what looked like half the storeroom, Boras installed himself by the trees, and Lola put down one of the little tables and chairs from the forest room.

Everything began in a reasonably orderly fashion. Eldric made his first three moves with Lola and then sauntered over to Boras to be shown how to hold the brush properly while Rosalia poured him some blood wine. In addition to the easel, the canvas stretched over a wooden frame and there was an excessive selection of brushes. Boras had brought a box with compartments that could be folded out. The vials, tubes and pouches stored in it looked more like things one might find in Albert's room. They smelled of oil, salt and crushed metals such as iron and copper.

Tripp was almost bursting with impatience and stomped towards them. 'What kind of practice fight is this?'

Eldric took a sip from his glass and grinned at him. 'One where you won't land a single scratch.'

Of course, Tripp immediately dashed towards him at that. Eldric let him rush past with a sidestep, downed the rest of the wine and threw the empty glass to Rosalia, who had sat back down on the edge of the fountain. She caught it skilfully and uncorked another bottle. The loose sleeves revealed a teasing portion of her shoulders.

Tripp's fist hurtled towards his head, and Eldric ducked. 'Move one of my guards forward,' he shouted to Lola.

'Left or right?'

He dodged two more of Tripp's blows. 'Either.'

'All right! I've positioned my stealth hunter behind your first front line.'

'Here is your glass,' Rosalia announced from the fountain and held it up.

He whirled around and ran towards her, but Tripp was two steps ahead of him, grabbed his glass and jumped onto the edge of the fountain, grinning.

Eldric did not slow down but used a small amount of his powers to support himself with one hand on the stone edge and swing his right leg upwards. He hit Tripp's kneecap.

His friend buckled and fell backwards into the water. Rosalia giggled as he jumped up with a snort, wine glass held above his head. 'Do not worry, nothing spilt!'

While Tripp savoured the rescued contents, Eldric hurried back to Boras and handed him the brush. 'Assuming I want cornflower blue, what would I have to mix together?'

Boras tilted his head so that his long, stringy hair fell even more in his face. 'You mean the kind of blue that Liliana's eyes were?'

Eldric gritted his teeth. Of course ... the first colour he had thought of was Liliana's former eye colour.

'Yes,' he grumbled. 'That is exactly the kind of blue I want. And that—' He swerved instinctively as one of Tripp's boots flew right past him.

He jumped out of the well and shook drops out of his straw-blond hair. 'Come back and fight properly!'

'You say that, but you haven't even assumed your demon form yet.'

'Ha!' Tripp wrestled with his wet shirt, tugged it off his body with some difficulty and slapped it over the golden gargoyle.

'Don't get any ideas about imitating Axton,' Lola shouted from her gaming table. 'We don't need you both parading around stark naked in the cold to prove how tough you are.'

'No complaints from me,' Rosalia said with a chuckle. The hostile tension between her and Tripp had apparently eased.

'My frontal fighters will attack your guards,' Eldric instructed Lola.

'You can only move one figure at a time, so ...'

'On the side you placed your stealth hunter.' Perhaps he needed to take a quick peek at the board after all.

However, Tripp had now shed all his clothes except for his trousers and transformed. Strands of muscle bulged under his skin. The jaw grew and his facial features distorted. Rosalia ducked her head to avoid being hit by his wings. The pressure of his powers spread across the courtyard. This time, he rushed towards Eldric with such speed that he was forced to release his own powers.

They strengthened him and yet made him as lithe as a cat. He dodged Tripp's claws, allowed himself to be pushed towards the main entrance, leaped over Lola's table, moved his Lord figure and rolled backwards as Tripp chased after him.

Lola leaned back in the chair to be safe and crossed her arms. 'I can't say that this is a very interesting game from my side.'

'Feel free to paint or drink, too.' Eldric laughed, jumped to his feet and had Tripp chase him across the courtyard. Tripp's blows pounded at him, and he squirmed here and there to avoid them.

Tripp stopped and bared his teeth, whereupon Eldric smirked at him. For he knew full well that his opponent hated it when he didn't attempt any attacks of his own.

'I mixed your cornflower blue,' Boras informed El in his flat tone of voice. 'With radiant lapis lazuli from Velusia.'

Eldric turned his head and immediately stumbled back as Tripp's foot dug into his stomach. The second foot followed, aimed directly at his temple. He groaned, jerked his arm up, staggered to the side and pushed himself off the ground as he used his powers to heal. Wings shot out of his back and carried him into the air. When Tripp landed a hit, his strength could do real damage.

'Not a scratch. As if ...' Tripp mocked from the ground. 'And you claim to have ripped Morton's heart out of his chest?'

Eldric flew over to Boras, retracted his wings and landed next him. He could have sworn he heard Rosalia's murmur as he did so. 'Oh, El is skilled at ripping out hearts.'

In a flash, he pulled the palette out of Boras' hands, dipped his claws into the colour trough with the blue and sprayed it across the canvas. Boras mumbled something indistinct.

Eldric could already feel Tripp approaching, so he threw the palette in the air, dropped into a crouch at just the right moment and rammed his shoulder into Tripp's hip. His own momentum caused Tripp to topple forward, and with a little strength from his legs, Eldric catapulted him over his back. Boras caught the palette and clasped it protectively to his chest but couldn't stop Tripp from taking the easel with him as he rolled to the ground.

Boras objected at the rough handling of his paraphernalia, but Tripp scrambled to his feet, grabbed the canvas and smashed it over its owner's head so that he ended up wearing it around his neck like some sort of strange collar.

Tripp wiped sweat from his forehead with the back of his hand and grinned mischievously. 'Shall we call this art, too?'

'I think it looks pretty lifelike.' Lola grunted with laughter.

Although Boras growled and angrily extricated himself from the painting, he then held it up, seemingly contemplating the validity of Tripp's question.

Meanwhile, Eldric strolled over to Rosalia at the fountain, grabbed one of her uncorked bottles and put it to his lips, paying no attention to the glass she held out to him. He drank casually at first, then more and more quickly. The blood rushing down his throat was a relief, as was the wine. He swapped the empty bottle for a new one and noticed that some of the spectators, whom he had previously only sensed at a distance, had joined him.

Annie ran across the square, and Camilla limped after her. Zac picked up some brushes and the colour palette that Boras had just carefully put down and threatened his twin brother that he would beautify his ugly face. On the second floor of the main building, a window opened, and Aunts Prisca and Penelope stuck their heads out, no doubt to get a better view of Tripp, who had changed back into his vampire form and shook himself like a wet dog. Even Horatio had made himself comfortable in the courtyard, apparently attracted by the unfinished game of Lordboard. He sat down opposite Lola, lifted one of Eldric's pieces and circled it over the board before setting it down.

Eldric smiled as Annie briefly hugged his leg, then immediately dipped both hands into the fountain. Zac and Zic smeared each other with the paint, which Boras tried to wrest from them with much gnashing of teeth. Eldric waited until everyone was sufficiently distracted and he didn't feel any eyes on him. Then he patted Annie's head and retreated silently towards the castle wall.

Chapter Twenty-Five

He stretched out on a link between the main roof and one of the smaller towers and watched the night sky above him. Only once winter came would snow fall on the castle rock. The mountains, on the other hand, were already powdered and emerged like fins from the sea of forest. The spectacle of colours of deciduous trees among the evergreen firs may have been more intense during the day, but it also warmed the scenery at night.

Up here, the noises from the courtyard on the other side, the jostling and the laughter, barely reached his ears. He did feel more cheerful, thanks to the well-meaning company of the others and the wine.

It didn't take much knowledge of the Curse to realise that anything that interfered with his ability to keep his powers under control was inherently risky. Therefore, Eldric had never really set out to test this. Being slightly tipsy did not tend to disturb his inner balance much. But the more his senses and his capacity to hold back the demonic powers diminished, the sooner they would remove the toxic substance responsible for it from his body. Admittedly, this did not happen as quickly as if he had initiated a deliberate detoxification. But it meant that even if he tried, he would probably never be truly drunk. Not like humans or vampires with minor powers who occasionally lost consciousness completely or vomited ... which was the body's attempt at limiting damage. No, there were other states of inebriation for vampires like him, as Morton had proven that night in the grotto.

Eldric shuddered and sat up. An hour of mild tipsiness was all the wine could provide for him, and it was also all he would allow himself. There were plenty of examples of noblemen who had done things while liquored up that they later regretted, or never had the opportunity to regret.

He flinched, realising too late that someone was approaching to disappear unseen. Rosalia scrambled up to him on the roof ridge, clambered around the chimney and brandished a hip flask. She must have gotten onto the roof from a window.

'Look what I've found! This must be one of Grandad Edgar's.'

She held on with her free hand, lowered herself down and skidded across the tiles towards him. He bent over hastily, blinking as the roof beneath him swayed briefly, and grabbed her by the elbow as her foot slipped. At the same time, he used his powers to diminish the influence of the wine sooner than he had hoped.

'Thank you.' Rosalia knelt and swung her legs over the side. The fact that the tight skirt slid up to her thighs didn't bother her in the slightest. She supported herself with her free hand and angled her upper body so that her lush red hair fell down her back and showed off her silhouette perfectly.

'Can I offer you a drink?'

'I'll pass.' He was still focussed on eradicating the remaining percentages in his blood.

Meanwhile, Rosalia treated herself to a sip. 'Gin,' she established, giggling and holding the flask out to him again.

'You know that trying to get me drunk is a pointless endeavour, don't you?'

She smiled and shrugged unconcernedly, whereupon the delicate, loose fabric slid further over her right shoulder, exposing it completely. 'Maybe I'm not trying to get *you* drunk.'

Eldric swallowed, tore his gaze from her and fixed it on the chimney further up. 'In which case ... I suggest you don't try that up here on the roof. A fall from this height is fatal for any creature, cursed or not.'

'Fortunately, you are here to catch me,' she purred and moved closer.

'Or to give you a push.'

She laughed, then immediately turned serious and reached out for him. 'You know,' she whispered as her fingers gently touched his cheek, 'I would do anything for you, El. Anything.'

Near her, his head couldn't clear fast enough. He wanted to back away and instead found himself leaning towards her. Her fingers caressed his jaw, his neck, reached the collar of his coat and began to undo the buttons, while her healthy eye held his gaze. The deeply golden speckles in it sparkled as if they reflected the starlight.

The gin and the floral perfume partially masked her natural scent. Nevertheless, he felt his body respond eagerly to the invitation – to her heartbeat, to the softness in her voice and in her movements.

By the Primordial Demon, Rosalia possessed a sixth sense for picking just the right moment. She had smelled his frustration, his unmet needs. And she wasn't half as drunk as she pretended to be. *Watch out. This is her style of hunting.*

'You would do anything,' he repeated, struggling to focus his spinning thoughts. 'Except respect my wishes.'

'El ...' She slipped her hand through the gap in his open coat and stroked over his shirt from the pectoral muscle to the ribs. Her voice sounded indulgent. 'Be honest with yourself. Liliana is not coming back. If there was a way, you would have found it by now.'

'I'm still working on it,' he mumbled.

'I just want you to be happy. But you clearly aren't. You are lonely.'

'No, I'm merely ...' He broke off. There was no point in denying it. 'I have told you what I want, or rather what I *don't* want, and you ... are ignoring it.'

Rosalia tilted her head and looked at him under dark eyelashes. Her skin almost glowed in contrast to the black dress.

'I'm not doing anything.' She pulled a pout.

The sudden memory of Liliana hit him like a whiplash. The tears in her eyes, the betrayed expression on her face ... He had wanted to spare Rosalia's feelings.

He had wanted to preserve their friendship, to not burn this bridge. But he couldn't do it at Liliana's expense. She was the one coin; the book written just for him. As long as his heart had the strength to beat, it would long for her. Just because she was not present, didn't mean he could act as if his behaviour didn't affect her.

'Yes!' Eldric pulled his legs up and abruptly got up. Fortunately, his sense of balance had been restored. 'Yes, you are. And you know it.'

He looked down at Rosalia resolutely.

'To put an end to your puzzling, I will tell you one thing. What you perceive as emotional frostiness is neither arbitrary nor me hiding. It is simply me being rational and acting consistently. If I already know what the consequences of a certain action will be and I don't want those consequences, then it would be extremely unwise to take said action anyway.'

'You can never really foresee the consequences.'

'No, but I am fairly good at judging. This also serves as a protection. From pain, from madness, from anything that would be worse. If you cannot respect my boundaries, I will lock you out to prevent worse things from happening.'

'Lock me out? That wouldn't be rational at all. That would be overly dramatic.'

Eldric growled. 'It wouldn't. Because who knows ... if you try long enough, you might eventually get what you want. I am not immune to your charms. But do you have any idea what will happen if I give in?'

She smiled promisingly. 'We should find out.'

'Fine.'

He summoned the cold, reaching out to the part of him that could remain indifferent to Morton's mockery; the part that turned away from his dead parents, for whom life simply went on after Tristan's disappearance, too.

Then he crouched down in front of her, looked intensely into her eyes and placed his index finger under her chin. 'Stand up,' he ordered and slowly straightened up.

She obeyed and followed his lead until they were standing close together. He directed his senses entirely on her physical signals and neared her lips. Her heart pounded feverishly.

'I will lift you to the highest heights and plunge you into the deepest depths.'

He unleashed his powers and continued to focus his full attention on Rosalia. The gin bottle slipped from her grasp and clattered down the sloping roof as the demon's power wrapped around her, seeking a way to consume her. The cold crept over her skin, embracing her.

'You may be able to recognise clues from my smell,' he hissed. 'But I will know exactly how you feel, as if we were one body and one soul. I will ruin you.'

More than his own sensations, he enjoyed the reactions he could trigger in her: the soft knees, the trembling and pulsing, the desire and hope humming in her chest. And he enjoyed knowing that he could snatch it all away from her just as easily.

'I will take what I can get, and you will give me everything. I will feast on you. I will suck you dry. I will bring you rapture and ecstasy. But I will never fall asleep next to you.'

Eldric released his hand from her chin and grabbed the hair at the back of her head. His powers engulfed her, freezing her in place.

'You will love me,' he breathed into her mouth. 'You will hate me ... And you will despair. Because you will know that you are not the true object of my desire.'

He allowed his powers even more freedom. The voice boomed through the Darkness behind his thoughts. *Yes ... Take her ... Drink ... Crush her heart ...* Anger and desire competed within him. But he didn't care. Rosalia's scent shifted from arousal to fear.

'And when Liliana comes back,' he stated soberly, 'we will both be unhappy. You, because you are chasing after something you can't have, and I, because I will have betrayed the trust I've worked so hard to earn. The trust of the only person who ever truly made me feel like myself.'

Pushing back his powers bit by bit, he let go of her hair and took a step away from her. Rosalia gasped and stared at him with one eye wide open.

He put his hands in the pockets of his open coat and continued to wrestle down the demonic powers. They hissed and struggled for a while, but he kept a firm grip on them until they calmed down and he no longer heard their whispers.

'So, go ahead. Take advantage of my weakness. Trick me into doing something I'll bitterly regret ... and see how that works out for you.'

Rosalia stood rooted to the spot in the silence above the castle. Then she began to back away from him, foot by foot, until she bumped against the slope of the main section. The silk of her top ripped as she summoned her demon form and spread her wings. Without another word, she leaped up and flew away.

Eldric waited. Only when her last wing beats had faded did he sit down on the connecting section and lean back against the main roof. That bridge was well and truly burnt. Without his cold, he felt empty and exhausted. The moon glared down at him reproachfully. Had he gone too far?

Telling her hadn't been enough. He had to make her feel it. Morton's voice rasped in his mind. *She has herself to thank for that.* That was exactly how his sainted brother would have handled the situation. No ... no, that wasn't true. He wouldn't have shown her, he wouldn't have warned her, he would have simply acted on his momentary urges and then blamed everything on Rosalia.

Why did the people around him so easily forget who he could be if he didn't consciously and continuously choose not to become like Morton? From a logical viewpoint, he seemed to have done the right thing. So why did he feel like he had regressed?

'What do you think, old friend?' he asked the moon.

It remained silent as always, round and patiently waiting.

'I know we haven't spoken in a while. I've been busy taking care of some minor issues down here.'

So now he had started talking to himself out loud again and not just in his head. He laughed and repeated the advice his father had drilled into him. 'Always watch out for the first signs of madness.'

Yes, he knew that other vampires didn't hear their demon speak. Not even Morton had done that, although he had once mentioned intrusive images. The demonic powers only conveyed impressions, impulses and desires. They knew no language. This voice was just the way it manifested for him. Different vampires gave their powers different characteristics. They all struggled with their own kind of madness. His mind translated it into a voice. And the clearer, the more articulate this voice became, the more his self disappeared and threatened to be swallowed up by it.

His powers were not separate from him; they had merged with his soul. They did not create anything new in him, only reinforced what was already there, the feelings and desires that corresponded to the nature of the demon.

'I can let my feelings consume me,' he explained to the moon. 'At best, I become irascible like my drunken grandfather. At worst, I fall to the demon's madness. Or ... I can *not* feel. Then I follow in Morton's footsteps.' He sighed deeply. 'My life is a constant balancing act between these two opposites.'

Liliana had disturbed this balance precisely because she had managed to stir strong feelings in him. And in return, he had taken refuge in avoidance and in his cold. Had it been the same with Hina?

'I wouldn't know how else to deal with it,' he confessed. 'Do you think there is a third way?'

This third way was likely the slow and arduous process of finding this balance anew in every precarious situation, acquiring it bit by bit at a higher level like a weightlifter who alternately added weights on each side of a barbell.

In relation to his lake, it was madness to simply jump from the boat into the deep. He had to start on the safe shore. He had to dip his toes in the lake and slowly get used to it; then step in with both feet, stand still, stabilise himself. Once he felt safe, he could take the next step, wade in up to his knees, hold out until he found his balance again. Then up to his hips, up to his chest, and finally dive in completely. At some point, he would probably have to try out those strange, frog-like movements humans used to stay afloat.

'You are right as always, my shining friend.' He lifted an imaginary hat. 'If I want to keep Liliana, if I want to start a family with her and Annie, I will have to learn how to swim. I have no other choice.'

When he had become involved with her – body, heart and soul – Liliana had shown him a different version of himself; a version that could tread this third path. In a way, she was like the Curse, perhaps his personal counter-curse. For she reinforced his good qualities, his desire to protect and preserve, his compassion and his determination to act and truly participate in life, in the world around him.

Only, she was no longer here to create the safe space in which he could feel without losing himself. In other words, she had led him into the water and then left him standing with wet feet.

'Do you understand?' he murmured, this time including the stars, too. 'She *has to* return. Her work here is not done.'

Chapter Twenty-Six

Although he didn't think it a good idea to interact directly with Liliana's family, he remained at least somewhat informed on what was happening in Heidenried – as he had done when the villagers had driven him away and he had worried about Liliana's safety from afar.

The church had slowly been rebuilt, with one of the timber companies having been inspired by an anonymous benefactor to distribute a load of roof shingles very cheaply. The stories told about the fire changed with increasing distance. In Grünau, people knew that a fire demon was hiding in Heidenried. In Roinnenstadt, the fire demon had become an arsonist who was also responsible for the burning of two barns, a granary and last summer's forest fire. And south of the mountains, all they heard was that the people in the countryside were crazy anyway.

In addition, Zac and Zic had tasked themselves with eavesdropping on the people outside the inns in case word got out about a healing vagrant. Eldric didn't have high hopes for an unsystematic approach of earwigging, but it couldn't do any harm either.

When he learned that the old herb woman from Heidenried had died, he sent the two of them to covertly investigate whether this death was somehow related to Liliana's disappearance or his influence on the village. That didn't seem to be the case, and yet this new stroke of fate further weighed on his already disgruntled mood. He owed his survival of Morton's first attempt to kill him not only to Liliana's helpfulness but also to her grandmother's homemade remedies.

He was occupied with these thoughts when the guards alerted him of a light signal from the western border – a level 2 from Tower 25, signalling an incident or unauthorised intrusion that did not require the deployment and alert of their entire armed forces, but nevertheless did necessitate rapid intervention.

Had they found the saint? Flustered, Eldric instructed the guards to inform Lola of the signal and that he would leave immediately.

He reached the area of Tower 25 in record time. The guards took formation in the air as soon as they spotted him. As he approached, he recognised the uniforms of the Crimson Plains roaming the area seemingly aimlessly. What were they doing circling over Finsterwald?

As luck would have it, Boras, the vampire with the best nose, was on watchtower duty. Eldric instructed him to land while the others stayed on the lookout. Then he steered Shadowprancer towards a lonely shed that stood in a harvested field not far from the edge of the forest. The air smelled fresh, but also damp, infused with straw, wood and the remains of the grain planted here.

He swung from Shadowprancer's back as Boras drew in his wings. 'Sartiria is here. Along with her guards. I did not engage in battle but thought it best to wait for your orders.'

Sartiria? Not the saint? She had to have deliberately kept her powers hidden for him to not have felt her presence. Eldric snorted and handed him the reins. 'What does she want?'

'That I help her find a human, a battle saint.'

So he had been found! *She* had found the saint – found and lost him again? Or was she only chasing after memories from the war?

Boras cast an uncharacteristically hurried glance at a figure that landed twenty feet away and immediately marched towards them. She had apparently left her guards behind. 'When I refused to help her, she threatened to kill us if you didn't show up in person.'

'Well,' Eldric sighed. 'Here I am.'

He nodded in the direction of the forest, motioning Boras to retreat and leave Sartiria to him. Only then did he turn to the Lord of the Crimson Plains, suddenly brimming with demonic power, and snapped at her bar any formal greeting, 'You have encroached on my lands again. Explain yourself!'

She stopped in front of him and planted her legs firmly on the ground, showcased by the dark hunting trousers. 'With good reason. I warned you – all of you – about the battle saints. Now I've found one and tracked him here from the Crimson Plains.'

'Where is he? I want proof, not excuses.' If this saint really existed, he had to witness his abilities himself.

Sartiria gasped indignantly. 'You would have had your proof by now if you hadn't turned a blind eye!'

'Whatever you thought you saw, the ground you are standing on is under my territorial jurisdiction, and you are obligated to ask permission if you want to enter it, let alone organise some mad hunt! All the more so if your guards are involved.'

Although the Council's agreement allowed Lords to enter a foreign territory in principle, they could be expelled at any time on account of *undue circumstances*. And he could not allow Sartiria to find this saint without him being present.

She grimaced. 'I'm asking now.'

'Then my answer is, withdraw your guards! I will deal with this.'

'Ha!' Her demonic fire flared up. 'The way you've dealt with it so far? One could almost think the battle saint fled here on purpose to find shelter.'

'If that is the case, it won't do him much good.' Eldric endeavoured to keep his face calm and his breathing steady. It was better if she didn't realise how much he also wanted to find this saint. 'Describe to me what I need to look for, and we will take it from there.'

'*I* will find him,' she huffed. 'And you will admit to the assembled Council that you were wrong!'

'I may do so ... *if* I was wrong.' He turned his back on her and started walking towards the edge of the forest.

'Oh, you'd like that, wouldn't you? For me to just leave so you can continue pretending there are no battle saints and no preparations for war! I demand to be part of the search!'

'No.'

'That monster took my arm and made me unfit to fly!'

He stopped and turned around, '*This* battle saint?' That was bizarre. Not even vampires lived that long. Sartiria's hatred of humans had made her delusionally paranoid.

'That's what I said! I recognised him! It was him, exactly the same man from the war back then.'

She was completely serious about her claim. But humans couldn't possibly live that long. Unless ... Could prolonged exposure to the Light cure someone so completely that they became practically immortal? The thought both disturbed and intrigued him.

'You are just imagining thi—'

'I am *not* imagining things! I'll never forget his face. I have to be there when he is caught!'

'Give me one good reason why I should allow this after the fiasco you left behind on your last visit.'

'Don't forget, Eldric, I have something you want ...' Without any transition, she began to open her jacket and threw it to the ground.

He froze. What in the ...?

Although her powers continued to flare up around her, a smile crept onto her lips. She placed her hands on either side of her waist and slid them down to her hips while she slowly approached him. Her fingers played with the hem of her blouse for a moment before she pulled it over her head and threw it off.

Liliana ... His thoughts faltered. That was her scent, and at the same time, he could feel her strange demonic powers circling him, searching for a way to connect with him again. He did not believe that Sartiria was deliberately sending them out to penetrate his soul. It was probably because she wasn't fully anchored in Liliana's body after all. That was a good sign, wasn't it?

She blew the short hair out of her face and unfastened the piece of cloth crossing in the back that she wore instead of a lace-up bodice. As her fingers encircled the hem of her shortened chemise to part with the last layer of clothing, Eldric stepped forward and grabbed her by the wrist.

Now her, too? By Ragna, mother of all vampires, did he have a sign hanging around his neck that said he was in rut and looking for a partner?

'What are you doing?' he growled. 'Stop that!'

'I told you what I want. And you told me what *you* want.' Sartiria looked up at him and placed her free hand on his chest. 'Please excuse me, my love. I completely forgot to play the part.'

She sank against him with feigned weakness. Her body pressed against his, and he sighed with every fibre of his being. *At last.* He felt his heart pump and spread heat through his body. His blood flowed to all the wrong places.

It was only natural that he was attracted to her. She had taken over Liliana. Nevertheless, he was unsettled by how easily he responded to her.

'It's me, your Liliana. A helpless human female who can't possibly resist your demonic charm. Take me in your strong arms!'

Anger boiled up inside him, and his demonic powers began to writhe under his grip. Each overwhelming emotion made it harder for him to control them. Lust and rage, however, were the most difficult; the combination of the two was even worse, for it matched the demon's raging hunger so excellently.

'Don't you dare! Someone like you could never—' He broke off as Sartiria giggled. 'I don't have time for your games.'

Eldric pushed her away from him and kept tight rein on his powers.

'You want this body!' Sartiria pushed against his chest.

With his powers suppressed, he had nothing to offer in opposition and staggered past the rickety shed to the back.

'You have no idea what I want,' he pressed out between clenched teeth. *And you'll regret trying to shamelessly take advantage of what doesn't belong to you!*

'Ha! You said it yourself. You like my shell.'

She pushed him again and again and he stumbled into the deserted field, still struggling to hold his powers back. The muddy ground soon stuck to his soles.

'You're fooling yourself if you think you can suppress your demon this stubbornly forever. Do you think I can't sense your hunger?' She licked her lips. 'Do you think I don't know how much you hunger to unleash the power within you? To give in just this once? To take what you crave?'

Now she even had the audacity to tempt him with Liliana's blood! Would it satisfy the Curse under these circumstances? He wasn't sure. His powers, on the other hand, were keen to find out and stirred even more fiercely. Their cool prickled under his skin. He gritted his teeth again.

His blood level was low, but not *that* low. He wouldn't—

Sartiria shoved him so hard he instinctively stabilised himself with a surge of power and caught her arms. In turn, she grabbed his arm with one hand and his coat collar with the other and let herself fall backwards, clutching him tightly. He fell with her, rolled over and landed in the dirt on his back. Sartiria rolled with him and landed kneeling on his chest.

He thrust her knees away with both hands, so she had to support herself with hers to keep balance. Then he clasped her waist and rolled her around. Grabbing her hands, he pressed her against the ground with his body weight. She doggedly tried to free herself, and he had to use more and more of his demonic powers to keep her there. His hunger grew.

The way she squirmed beneath him ... The sight made his mouth water in more ways than one. That healthy, beating heart, that beautiful skin, the blood in her veins ...

She stopped resisting. There was no longer scorn or animosity in her eyes, but undisguised desire. Eldric knew that expression. That was Liliana during their most beautiful moments. He bent down to her. Her chest brushed his with each quivering breath. The touch sent shivers through his body. Entranced by her presence, her sensuality, he approached her lips.

No, not Liliana! Sartiria. It was Sartiria who was controlling her; Sartiria who had taken up residence in this body. He had to pull himself together. He couldn't allow them to mix in his perception.

Then again, would it be so bad? If he kissed her, he would kiss Liliana, too. If he touched her, if he loved her, feasted on her ... Would it really hurt Liliana if he allowed himself a sip? Sartiria was already cursed. If their souls had truly joined ... If this was all he would ever get of Liliana again ... His powers pulsed in his head, in his limbs, increasingly clouding his thoughts. *Enticing. Appetising.*

She turned her head to the side to offer him her neck, and this simple gesture drove him over the edge.

He was no longer in control of the situation. His powers began to slip away from him, shaking off his restraints and rearing up. The demon's power exploded in his veins and expanded in all directions. The Darkness encircled him. Icy veils permeated his consciousness. *Mine ... My prey ...*

He felt his claws grow and couldn't halt the transformation. No! No. He had to contain it. Her odour was overwhelming. Her blood sang to him. He wanted nothing more than this very body, this very life beneath him.

Slowly, he approached her neck, breathing her in. The demon's voice boomed in his head; the demonic desires flooded his own desires.

Take her. Kiss her. Drink her. Now.

'Do it,' she hissed.

She wanted it! She wanted him to bite.

He stifled a groan and clutched her hands tighter, pressing them into the damp earth. He couldn't allow his powers to ... But he wanted her so badly it hurt. His whole body trembled with desire and his effort to suppress it. He wanted to devour her, skin and hair and blood and heart ...

Take her! Bite her. Tear her clothes off. Penetrate her. Sink your teeth into that delicious throat. Drink. Drink. Drink.

His mind was boiling over. All he wanted to do was scream, shout, take, drink, chop, destroy.

Then he heard another voice; a soft but firm voice.

Giving up is not an option.

Although his father had taught him to fight and wrestled him down when his powers threatened to overwhelm him, it was his mother's words that guided him through the worst of it.

Eldric, you can't give in. You simply cannot. Your life depends on it. And one night, others will depend on you, too. Be it an entire territory or just one person, one night someone will depend on you and your ability to keep back the madness. You must not give up. You must not give in.

He gasped. With almost unbearable effort, he pulled back, pulled everything back. His powers fought, hissing and slavering. But he wrestled them down, gave everything to this fight. He forced the Darkness down, into his core, until they finally gave way, and he slumped down.

Eldric struggled to push himself up and stumbled away from her. He could only see shadows.

'Boras!' His own voice sounded unfamiliarly throaty in his ears.

Boras was waiting somewhere nearby. He would never interfere on his own accord. But he would answer Eldric's call.

Eldric felt weak and short of breath. His head, heart and muscles throbbed as if he had just finished a duel.

Sartiria jumped up and clenched her fists. Her expression was one of fury and disappointment. He hated that she had managed to merge the two instincts in him, bloodlust and libido. She would have given herself to him in both ways, and not just out of cunning. For her smell, her physical reactions couldn't lie either. She lived in Liliana's body and had thus taken over her weakness for *him*, too.

He had to admit that he had never been so relieved to see Boras as he was now, when he took position between him and Sartiria.

'You take over here,' Eldric instructed him, rubbing his face with one hand. 'See to it that we find this saint, wherever he may be.'

'I will be the first to get my hands on the battle saint,' Sartiria hissed.

'As you wish.' Eldric looked past her as Boras continued to hold his ground. 'We will let you know once we've found him. Now get out of my territory ... Along with your guards.'

He turned away from her, and Boras followed him towards the forest.

'Then make sure you find him quickly!' Sartiria called after him. 'Because in three nights' time, I will withdraw my offer and negotiate with Baldrich!'

Chapter Twenty-Seven

In three nights... Eldric leaned against the trunk of a beech tree while Boras relayed his orders and the saint's rough description to the border guards. In three nights, he would show up at Castle Evernight Valley, no matter what else happened.

What would it have been like if Liliana had been one of them, a vampiress? Would they still have fallen in love with each other? Would everything really have been easier? At least, no other vampire soul would have been able to possess her.

Sartiria had taken him by surprise with her genuine attraction and willingness to act on it. He found it increasingly difficult to conjure up Liliana's voice. Instead, he could see Morton's grinning face in front of him. *What's your problem? It wouldn't have been* infidelity. *They are* one and the same person. *And it wouldn't have hurt her, either; she already has the curse inside her. You're* a fool *anyway if you think she'll* ever be the same *after all this.*

Detaching himself from the tree, Eldric shooed his brother from his thoughts and walked over to Shadowprancer.

Why don't you show yourself, Liliana? At least a little bit. So that I know you're still there ... that there's still hope.

This hope was now pinned on a human; on someone who would be either completely overwhelmed by this task or – if he really was a powerful being that was a thousand years old – wanted him and Sartiria and all other vampires dead.

He untied Shadowprancer and absentmindedly rubbed his neck before mounting.

Assuming the saint was able to save Liliana ... he had to firstly bring Sartiria to him and secondly contain her somehow, so that she wouldn't kill him immediately and the ritual could be performed. Since Sartiria insisted on being present when they confronted the saint, the first aspect was easy to manage. The second, however, presented a hurdle. Holding her by force could end in someone dying or being seriously injured. But there was another possibility, for which he only needed two ingredients: a normal human blacksmith and a Sartiria who was distracted for a few moments and in his immediate vicinity.

The best lies were close to the truth; sometimes uncomfortably close. Just like Rosalia, Sartiria knew his vulnerability and wanted to exploit it. But he could turn the tables. And if she thought she had him completely in the palm of her hand, he would hand her over to the saint for purification.

To realise this, he first had to return to Finsterwald Castle. Eldric steered Shadowprancer out into the open field.

He brought Tripp and some additional guards from the castle. It was one of these guards who, rather out of breath, had reported a suspicious glimmer in a stable in the early hours of the second night.

Eldric could have kissed the young vampire with relief. If that was him ... If he could free Liliana ...

He immediately had himself led there. His pulse quickened as they landed at the back of the building. The young guard pointed to a gap in the wooden wall, and Eldric approached quietly to peer through. There, in the hay, among mice and cows, the outline of a man shimmered out. He stretched as if he had just woken up. This had to be him!

Although Eldric held back his powers to avoid detection, he felt a creeping unease rising within him alongside his wild hope. This man was filled with pure Light, continuously. That alone was remarkable. If he could summon his Light anywhere outside his body, too, that made him a dangerous opponent indeed. Sartiria had been right: they still existed, the battle saints from her time. The only question was why they were in hiding and, as far as he could tell, doing nothing to oppose the nobility. Was there something to her crazy idea that the humans could secretly prepare for war?

Well, he could worry about that later. For now, what mattered was that this unwashed man with his frizzy beard could be Liliana's salvation; and that he didn't lose sight of him until the next sunset.

As the third night fell, he sent the castle guards back. He made sure Boras picked up the saint's signature scent and stuck to his heels until he returned with Sartiria.

He himself flew hurriedly with Tripp to the castle of the Crimson Plains, only to be told by Nusa that Lord Sartiria had already departed. He would have loved to grab and shake her but turned on his heel and spurred Shadowprancer to top speed, in a straight line of flight towards Evernight Valley.

Tripp refrained from making any mocking remarks; partly out of solidarity and partly because his horse, Tarantula, could barely keep up with Shadowprancer. Either Baldrich's border guards took their job as seriously as those in Finsterwald under Morton, or they had found a good spot and enough height to fly over. Either way, nobody bothered them as they entered the territory and kept heading east.

Eldric found it fitting that the humans called this *the Harshlands*, not only in reference to Baldrich's predations on his own citizens, but also in reference to the rugged landscape. The Evernight Valley was the longest of the rifts that divided the area here, leading like a funnel towards the castle at the end. It began as a wide, wooded swathe with a stream running through the centre and ended as a narrow gorge with steep, sharp-edged walls.

The castle itself was built into the rock. It consisted of only a front and a system of hollowed-out rooms and tunnels behind it. From the outside, it resembled a many-eyed stone giant with towers and bays as teeth and horns.

With no one to stop them, Eldric and Tripp landed on a small platform on the left that led into a horse den. They tied their animals next to the others on iron hooks, and Tripp nearly stumbled over someone snoring away in the straw.

Eldric resolutely entered the passageway that led to the castle interior. He had avoided Castle Evernight Valley since the incident with Hina and before that he had only visited it once. Of course it was one of them who wanted to steal his lover again.

Hearing laughter at the end of the tunnel, he prepared to use his powers. But the two men who should have been standing guard wore dirty clothes over each of their heads and were staggering around in circles.

Tripp caught up to him with a grin. 'I'll ask Boras what he thinks of this art form. I didn't realise they were so cultured in Evernight Valley.'

Eldric twitched the corners of his mouth and headed for the gate, behind which the noise of wild festivities was emanating. The smells from inside stung his nose: roasted meat, spices, smoke, sweating bodies, saliva, beer and wine and ... blood. Liliana's blood.

He growled, pushed open one of the huge gate leaves and hurried through. It took him a moment to take in what was happening. The noble family celebrated with toasts and belted out barely harmonising songs, while the servants helped themselves with their bare hands to the remains of the game sizzling over a huge fireplace on the side wall. Bowls and gnawed bones skidded across the floor, kicked away by rowdy dancers. Two busty women swung their skirts on top of the banquet table, while a couple rolled passionately under the table. A cook, swinging a poker, chased a boy who stuck out his tongue at him and, in turn, received a poorly aimed fist to the back of the head from a brawl behind him.

Out of the corner of his eye, Eldric noticed Aleksander holding one side of his tailcoat protectively over a roll of paper. But his attention was primarily drawn to the throne at the other end of the hall. It was carved from the same wood as the pedestal and canopy. Sartiria reclined on it while Baldrich himself knelt in front of her and licked something from her bare legs. Her eyes were closed, and she was wearing nothing but a red vest, more like a corset with overlong frills. Eldric gritted his teeth. *That bastard!*

Behind him, Tripp let out a whistle that broke off under Eldric's murderous stare. He scratched his head and shrugged at the same time. 'Don't do anything I wouldn't do.'

Eldric shot off in a flash, moving between the staggering and caterwauling members of the family. His powers reached into his consciousness as waves of Darkness. Shards of ice clawed at him from the inside out. *My blood. My woman. Kill him. Get her.*

He stopped right by the side of the wooden structure and paused for a couple of heartbeats to steady his breathing. 'I found him,' he said in a hard voice, his clenched hands buried deep in his coat pockets.

Sartiria opened her eyes and sat up. She blinked dumbfounded for a moment and gasped as she realised what he had just said. 'You have ...?'

'What are ye doing here?' With a growl, Baldrich jumped to his feet and stopped between Sartiria's legs. 'I didn't invite ye! How did ye get in here?'

Eldric suppressed the impulse to run his claws across Baldrich's face. Instead, he raised his brows and surveyed the headless confusion in the hall. 'Is that an earnest question? I walked past two guards wearing their underpants on their heads.'

'As ye can see, we're busy. So get lo—'

'You found him?' Sartiria asked again.

Eldric averted his eyes from Liliana's body in this nothingness of a garment. 'Boras has taken to his heels. If we hurry, we shou—'

'Did ye think I'm just going to let ye march into my castle and steal this appetising creature off me?'

Even as Baldrich spoke, Sartiria wriggled out of his grasp and leaped from the throne. 'You haven't done anything yet, have you? He doesn't know we have him?'

'No,' Eldric replied curtly.

'Lovely!'

She took a step towards him when Baldrich grabbed her from behind. Eldric knew only too well the smell of anger and greed that rose from him. But Sartiria escaped his grip with a smooth twist.

'Our pleasures will have to wait.'

Baldrich's expression darkened. 'What for, eh?' he barked at Sartiria and then fixed his gaze on Eldric. 'Ain't it funny how ye're always the one messing with the other Lords.'

'The same could be said of you.' Eldric crossed his arms.

Baldrich's neighing drowned out the festive noise but stopped as suddenly as it had begun. The Lord of Evernight Valley reared up in front of Eldric and raised his stubbly chin defiantly. 'Ye won't leave my castle without my permission!'

Sartiria took a step towards Baldrich and leaned against him with a sigh. Smiling suggestively, she curled her fingers into the hairy chest under his waistcoat and ran them down to the waistband of his trousers. 'I'm not made of stone, Baldrich. I'll be back as soon as we're done with the battle saint. After that, we can feast on each other until we're sick.'

Eldric felt sick just hearing those words. Was everything that had a pulse from here to the Southern Expanse out to irritate him to death? He wouldn't let her and Baldrich do whatever they wanted to Liliana's body!

He imagined twisting Baldrich's throat, how he would ram his claws right into his torso ... Darkness pulsed through his veins. His powers roared with rage and eagerness to put this fantasy into action. *Blood. Kill him. Kill him!*

Baldrich's features also took on a determined look; he kept his powers ready for battle. His moustache trembled with disgruntlement.

Eldric's twitching fingers had freed themselves from his pockets. With the exception of hunting, he had never killed anyone who had not attacked him first, thereby revealing his own intent to kill. This self-imposed rule served as a clear line between self-preservation and the abuse of power. As much as he itched to, he would avoid a violent confrontation with Baldrich to the best of his ability ... But, by the Primordial Demon, he hoped Baldrich would not hold back.

'Give me a reason,' he muttered. *Please, do it. Attack me. Give me a reason to impale you on your own blessed ribs.*

Sartiria broke away from Baldrich, who did, in fact, charge at him. Eldric turned quickly, grew his claws and struck. Baldrich fended off the first hand, but the second cut him across the jaw.

If Baldrich had thought he would be able to beat him with his bare fists, he now realised his mistake. He backed away, grinned with his chin dripping blood and transformed into his demon form.

'Yer tricks won't do ye much good. I'll take ye apart!'

Eldric laughed, half as a taunt and half in relief at finally being able to act on his urges.

They shot towards each other. Baldrich knew how to crush skulls and tear out arms; he was not Lord of a family of nobly dressed bandits for no reason. Eldric's powers craved more bloodshed. With pent-up rage, he struck at his opponent's massive body, taking grim satisfaction in every hit.

They could not kill each other in front of so many witnesses. That would result in a trial before the Council for the survivor, in which he would be stripped of his title and, depending on the circumstances, even punished with death. But the rule said nothing about mutilation.

Eldric caught Baldrich by the arm and felt his claws sever flesh. More blood spurted and filled his senses.

Baldrich's subsequent attempt to clumsily bite him in the neck he rewarded with an elbow to the face. His claws ran over Baldrich's waistcoat and ribs, but Baldrich managed to grab him by the shoulder and throw him around. He then used his own body as a battering ram. Eldric hit the wall carved out of the rock with his back, and something cracked suspiciously. Immediately, he sent his powers to the spot in his spine where pain shot up as he dodged Baldrich's next strike.

Growling, he pushed himself off the wall and jumped at Baldrich, throwing him backwards against his overly ornate throne. The wood cracked, and within seconds the structure collapsed on top of them. Eldric rolled away just in time. Baldrich, on the other hand, was buried by his own canopy at the waist and legs. One of the decorative spikes pierced his wing.

It took much more to incapacitate a vampire like Baldrich, though. He kicked away the wooden debris, bent over and tore the spike from his wing. With an angry roar, he got back to his feet and spread both wings threateningly despite the wound.

Their Lord's roar brought the other members of Evernight Valley to the scene and their powers slowly swelled in the hall. Growling and hissing replaced the previous singing, belching and laughing. Eldric was vibrating with power and felt on top form. Whatever Baldrich had done to his back, it was no hindrance.

But the sensible voice inside him urged caution. He had not come here to wreak havoc, but to get Sartiria out of Baldrich's clutches and to lead her to the saint. Crouching, he waited for Baldrich's next move.

It was another attack. Eldric snorted and leaped towards him.

'Stop!'

Sartiria stood between them and kicked Baldrich so hard that he was hurled backward. Startled, Eldric realised that he had too much momentum. He just about managed to slow down and deflect his claws but still collided with her. As

Sartiria had not yet found her footing, she staggered. Eldric grabbed her wrist and pulled her to him to prevent them both from falling over.

His face directly in front of hers, he hissed, 'That was a sacredly close call!' What was she thinking? He could have seriously injured her!

She looked at him with that familiar, astonished expression, whereupon he swallowed hastily and wiped the sweat and blood splashes from his cheek with the back of his free hand. Only now that she had interrupted the battle, did he realise how hot he had become from all the exertion.

She quickly yanked her wrist away. 'As if you could seriously hurt me!'

Meanwhile, Baldrich got to his feet behind them. It had become quiet in the hall. The Evernight Valley waited for an order from its Lord. Then a single pair of hands began to applaud. Eldric didn't need to turn around to know that it was Tripp, who was treating their skirmish like a rousing performance.

Baldrich bared his teeth in a snarl, and Eldric growled back a threat. But Sartiria stretched her arms out impatiently in both directions. 'Save your quarrel for later. We have a battle saint to capture!'

'Noble Lords, I implore you ...' Aleksander also raised his hands and addressed them in appeasement. 'We cannot let this unique opportunity pass us by! Lord Eldric has, it seems, tracked down a battle saint. This human could be the key to understanding and stopping the spread of the churches among them.'

Raising his upper lip, Baldrich turned to Sartiria. 'And the opportunity just happens to coincide with the signing ...'

'The timing doesn't matter!' She snorted and threw her chest out, marching between the confused vampires towards the exit. Her powers radiated into the room for all to see. 'I want nothing more in this world than to have this battle saint in my hands. He will suffer for all the crimes he has committed! Starting with my mutilation! We know where he is. So we will capture him *now*.'

Aleksander rushed to her and let out a loud, 'Yes, Mylord!'

As they passed Tripp, he joined them, clearly in good spirits. Eldric took a deep breath, exhaled and dampened his powers a little. Then he followed the three of them through the hall, keeping his senses alert to react to any surprise attacks.

Nobody else moved. No chairs were pushed back, no drinks sipped. Even the flames at the fireplace had turned to nothing but glowing coals. Would the Lord of Evernight Valley let them go, for Sartiria's sake?

Finally, Baldrich shook off his resentment and laughed out loud. His moustache twitched. 'Capture him, huh ... So 'tis about a *hunt*?'

The last word spread around the room, pricking up ears and loosening tongues, flitting from one end of the table to the other. Hearts pounded, and minds brightened. Standing next to his collapsed throne, Baldrich began to smite his fist against his broad chest. In time to his tapping, a chorus of chants arose from among the vampires of Evernight Valley.

'Hunt! Hunt! Hunt! Hunt!'

Suddenly everyone, tired or awake, drunk or sober, pushed past them towards the gate until, apart from the non-family vampires, there were only two servants and Baldrich himself left in the hall. The jeering shouts moved away through the tunnels to the outside. Eldric did not envy those whose duty it was to clean this pigsty of a banqueting hall.

Baldrich sauntered past Eldric as if he had completely forgotten his existence and cockily put his arm around Sartiria. 'They always behave as if we'd already cornered our prey.'

Chapter Twenty-Eight

Sartiria seemed less than impressed by Baldrich's behaviour. 'Call them back!' she hissed and brushed off his arm.

'Nah, there's no going back.' The Lord of Evernight Valley took one last lecherous look at her thighs and trudged into the tunnel behind the boisterous crowd.

She caught up with him, and Eldric followed them swiftly. Tripp and Aleksander brought up the rear in silence.

'You don't understand,' Sartiria hissed. 'This battle saint will detect you immediately and wipe us all out before we get anywhere near him!'

Baldrich only gave his whinnying laugh in response. 'With his holy acid, or what? Ain't nobody afraid of that here.'

'A battle saint doesn't need a medium for his Light. He simply lets it appear wherever he wants. *Wherever*, get it? Right inside your sacred thick skull, for example. Then you're –' Sartiria snapped her fingers sharply – 'dead as a doornail!'

'If humans could do that, we would've noticed.'

The flow of the crowd came to a halt in front of the horse cave, as there was only enough room inside for a certain volume of bodies.

'I'm the only one who's ever fought a battle saint. You have no idea what you're getting into!' Sartiria tugged at Baldrich's damaged waistcoat and threw the bloody fabric to the ground when it ripped completely. 'And I won't let your rampaging horde of wild boars spoil my triumph!'

'We will not back down from a good hunt!'

The first riders and their horses threw themselves off the platform in front of the cave. Their joyful shouts echoed through the night. Baldrich communicated with one of his men by shouting and hand signalling before he joined the others. Presumably, he was ordering them into a specific formation.

'You are leading your soldiers to their death,' Sartiria claimed angrily, to which Baldrich replied with a guttural growl.

'Listen, ye're underestimating my people. We can be careful.'

'Not only can he kill us instantly with his Light, he can also heal himself. A battle saint is as good as invulnerable!'

'And how were *ye two* going to hunt him down if he's supposedly invincible?'

Eldric took this question as his chance to get involved. He needed to know what she had in mind so that he could adapt his approach accordingly. 'I would like to know that, too. You do have a plan, don't you?'

She crossed her arms. 'There's only one way to kill a battle saint, and that is instantly, in one fell swoop. However, there is an alternative that I like even better, and it doesn't put any of us in danger.'

Sartiria's lips curled into a smug grin. 'It's not as if he doesn't feel pain. We can make him suffer until he runs out of Light – or gives up.'

Baldrich plucked his moustache thoughtfully. The stable behind him gradually emptied and the horses that had stayed behind snorted. 'How are ye going to do that?'

'Light can't harm humans. And I have a number on call who are willing to do anything as long as the pay is right. I'll tell them to keep him prisoner and work on him in every way possible. We could bury him deep underground or sink him in the depths of the sea. Without air, he can give up and die or *remain dying* for the rest of his miserable existence.'

Baldrich hesitated. Then he turned away from them and towards his horse. 'Humble me likes the first option better.'

Without getting any further involved in the discussion, he jumped on his unsaddled mount and joined his pack outside. Sartiria looked as if she was about to burst with anger. 'That brainless carrion has no idea! The way they swept our troops away before them ...'

She clenched her fists tensely until drops of blood welled up under the nails digging into her palm. *Blood. Tasty. Drink.*

Eldric froze. The smell alone made his demon rise up, mad with greed. But his demon was mad anyway, so it was no big deal. He *could* handle it ... Provided no other aggravating circumstances came into play.

She noticed his gaze, snarled and wiped the blood off on her bare knee. 'This battle saint deserves to suffer. After all he's done ... the thousands and thousands of vampire lives he's destroyed!'

Aleksander approached them and drew an audible breath, but Eldric cut him off before he could get a chance to speak. 'For once, I agree with you.'

'You weren't there when the pathetic, ragged remnants of General Zaron's army sought refuge with us! Whole regions littered with the carcasses of our people! The fear, the paralysing fear in the eyes of even my most capable soldiers!'

'You are right. The plan you proposed, the second option, sounds promising.'

'The humiliation, the escape, the ...'

Sartiria's powers crackled like wildfire. Was she about to surrender her sanity to the curse? No one possessed such a degree of power without occasionally flirting with madness. The thought filled Eldric with sobering dread. If he lost Liliana because Sartiria lost control of her powers right before the confrontation with the saint ...

Fortunately, after a few moments of dull staring, she was distracted by Tripp, who flicked his finger against his cheek in the background to produce popping noises.

'Stop that!' she snapped.

He lowered his hand. 'Stop what?'

Eldric quickly cleared his throat. 'I have a suggestion.'

'Yes?'

'I like your plan ... Very much so.' If her goal was not to kill the saint immediately, but to torture him a little first and then bury him, that gave him a chance to hold on to her. Besides, the disagreement between her and Baldrich gave him a good reason to get rid of him. 'We will hardly change Baldrich's mind. But since we have to spend the day somewhere before we reach the border, we are presented with an excellent opportunity. If we sneak away while he and his family are asleep, we can gain a small head start and make them lose our trail with an unexpected change of direction. Then we can deal with the battle saint unimpeded.'

'Don't you have any better ideas?' Tripp started to protest but was stopped by El's punishing look.

Aleksander pulled on a leather strap that was sticking out of the pile of loose saddles next to the tunnel opening. 'I wouldn't—'

'That could work.' Sartiria grinned, ignoring her counsellor, who set about saddling one of the animals. 'Tell me where the battle saint is, and I will instruct my humans accordingly.'

'One thing at a time.' Eldric pulled on the thick riding gloves he would need later. 'First, we shake off Baldrich and find your humans. *Then* I shall reveal where the target is.'

'I won't be able to follow you if you ride on by day,' Aleksander interjected.

'Then stay here.' With an indifferent expression, Sartiria walked to the animal that her advisor had just prepared for travel and pulled herself up on it. 'Or fly back to the Crimson Plains directly.'

Weighing up his options, Aleksander didn't answer. The shouts outside the cave became more impatient.

'You can take Victor and your valet with you.'

The bridle already in his hands, Eldric found himself staring at Sartiria's exposed legs wrapped around the horse's rump. He pressed his lips together, not really wanting to comment, and reminded himself that he shouldn't be hiding the weakness Sartiria was trying to exploit right now. So he pointed to her outfit with a glove.

'Don't you at least want to put on a jacket?'

She looked down at herself and put on an innocent expression. 'Is this not appropriate?' Turning to her counsellor, she added, 'What do you think?'

Aleksander smiled smugly. 'You look delightful, Mylord. But I'm afraid you are a little stained with blood wine. Facing the humans like this might raise unnecessary questions. I will have something more suitable brought for you ... including a jacket and a pair of boots.'

Shortly before sunrise, Baldrich's riders dived down and gathered under a broad rocky outcrop, where they sought shelter for the day. They were probably familiar with this spot, as it was well shielded by undergrowth and trees. As agreed, Eldric, Tripp and Sartiria left their resting places as soon as they could be sure the others were asleep.

Tripp visibly struggled, but after a few moments was able to assume his usual upright posture. Although in theory, he had known for some time how to dampen his powers to avoid being drawn into deep sleep, in practice he found it difficult and usually relied on fasting from blood.

Baldrich would be anything but understanding when he realised at sunset that they had disappeared. But that, too, could be dealt with later.

They led the horses on foot down the wooded slope. In her eagerness, Sartiria wanted to press on immediately. But Eldric had demanded a lot of Shadowprancer by travelling to the Crimson Plains Castle and then into

Evernight Valley, and he was keenly aware that he hadn't allowed for enough longer breaks. Tarantula also trotted along behind Tripp with her head hanging low.

Pushing the tired horses further would increase their risk of injury, especially if they had to cross uneven terrain rather than swinging through the air with the power of the Curse. Therefore, he insisted that they rest.

Left to their own devices in their familiar surroundings, vampire horses fell asleep in time with the rising sun, just like their owners. Not wanting to create rivals for their prey, the vampires had experimented for several centuries until they found the smallest possible manifestation of the Curse that still gave the horses powers and wings. Today's breeding horses were content with smaller rodents and small amounts of human blood dripped into their drinking water.

While Sartiria sulked and waited for the journey to continue, Tripp discovered a small trickle where the animals could drink. Eldric patted Shadowprancer, and he lowered his head to press it against Eldric's chest. Later they settled down next to each other in the stony grass. Shadowprancer wasn't the most affectionate of stallions, so it meant all the more when he deigned to show affection. Tripp passed the time by aiming stones at various objects and occasionally nudging Tarantula so that neither he nor his horse would fall asleep unawares.

Sartiria's impatience also made Eldric nervous. Would his plan succeed? Was it selfish of him to bring Liliana back, possibly at the expense of all vampires?

You are a miserable moron, Morton grumbled in his head. *Sartiria risked her* soul *to warn you of these battle saints. Don't you realise the danger? You've seen him with your own eyes, you've felt* his power. *And you want to sacrifice her just to get your* human lover *back, who – as we both know – will decide a month or a year after you save her that she* can't love *a vampire* like you *anyway.*

When would his brother finally stop talking? Eldric closed his eyes and listened to Shadowprancer's strong, reassuring heartbeat. Thinking of all the things that could go wrong wouldn't help. They had found someone who possessed the power to save Liliana. He had to focus on that.

Chapter Twenty-Nine

With the head start they gained by staying awake all day, they left Baldrich and his riders far enough behind to fly on undisturbed at night. At the border to Finsterwald, they parted company with Tripp, whom Eldric tasked with alerting the watchtowers for a possible confrontation with Baldrich. He promised, grumbling, that he would avoid any bloodshed and only delay Baldrich's advance for as long as possible. Lola would have been better suited to this undertaking, but Eldric had to trust that Tripp would hold back as ordered.

'Don't do anything I wouldn't do,' he called to him in parting, and Tripp grinned wryly at the repetition of his own humorous advice.

'Not me!'

For the success of her plan to capture the saint, torture and interrogate him in every way possible, Sartiria wanted to enlist the help of the gang that had demolished the churches in her territory. The light could not harm humans; on the contrary, it could only heal them. So it was worth spending some time trying to find them.

Before Sartiria's band joined them from the Crimson Plains, they had to leave their winged horses in the forest so as not to cause panic. Eldric said farewell to Shadowprancer and told him to look after Sartiria's beast ... just in case.

Sartiria instructed her gang to fetch shovels and a large crate, and Eldric set off in search of Boras. The peaceful, sleeping landscape below him, the villages and pastures at night, stood in stark contrast to the tension he felt.

He limited his search to the immediate vicinity of the churches that lay in the direction the saint had previously travelled. After almost two hours, he found Boras waiting for him. He reported that the saint was staying in a priest's hut in a nearby village and was sleeping peacefully.

Eldric flew back to Sartiria and led the gang on the back of a horse they had borrowed to the edge of the village in question. From there, he let Sartiria take the lead.

'Listen to me carefully,' she commanded as she pulled her horse around. 'Tonight, I'm giving you a special assignment. In this village, in the priest's hut, there is a dangerous man. He may not look it, but he is a ruthless murderer who has many of my family and friends on his conscience. So be careful and, above all, don't believe a word that comes out of his mouth. He calls himself a saint but is a criminal of the worst kind!'

The group grumbled uneasily and Sartiria continued, 'He will probably tell you that he is innocent, that he means you no harm or that he is just helping. But those are all lies! He tries to instigate riots, sets people against each other and kills without hesitation if it serves his cause. Tonight, we will put an end to his misdeeds. We will tie him up, gag him and blindfold him. Then we will take him to the designated location and beat a confession out of him. Yes, we will!'

She thrust her fist into the air and roared. 'For your courage and loyalty, I will reward you twice as generously as usual!'

Aleksander had apparently taught her how to motivate people of a certain calibre. She pointed at herself, him and Boras. 'We will oversee the entire operation. Now get to work!'

The church stood between a quietly rattling mill on the other side of the road and the priest's cottage with its carefully tended garden. Sartiria's men – and the one woman – stopped right in front of the hut and jumped off their horses. The onslaught was anything but orderly. Half the gang tore at the door at the same time and squeezed through the narrow entrance. The woman stood ready with ropes and two of the crooks waited with cloth to gag the saint. The others held the horses or trampled aimlessly over herbs and flowers.

Sartiria ducked behind her horse, and Eldric joined her. Boras retreated to a distance where he could still hear and smell them but otherwise stay away from the action. The saint's Light flashed from inside the hut in the melee. A horrified voice rang out and was immediately drowned out by several other harsh shouts.

Eldric peered over the back of the mount he had borrowed. It neighed and kept its ears stiff as if it sensed something being off.

'Leave him alone!' the priest implored, whose white robes Eldric could spot through the open door. 'What are you doing? Don't you know who that is? He's a good man, a saint!'

But his plea went unheeded. Wood splintered and Sartiria's men dragged a half-clothed man with tangled hair out into the open.

Sartiria hissed and grabbed Eldric by the arm. 'That's him.'

'Are you sure?'

'Most sure I've ever been in my life! Can't you see the glow on his skin?'

Of course, Eldric could see it; he could *feel* it. And he could even believe that this man with the unfathomably dark eyes was several lifetimes old.

Those eyes were bound shut as instructed. The saint did not resist as they tied his wrists with ropes, slapped his face and kicked him in the back of the knees so that he fell into the mud. Hopefully, he would listen to Eldric's concerns despite this rough treatment. He couldn't intervene now without arousing suspicion. The continuous Light healed every scratch and bruise on him instantly.

The priest kept trying to intervene but was pushed away. Even the heated vapours of unwashed bodies could not mask the smell of his fear. More Lights flashed as the saint tried to heal and strengthen his friend. Sartiria undoubtedly knew what she was doing and hadn't merely blindfolded him to hide her identity. Without being able to see, he struggled much more with accurate placement of his Lights. Meanwhile, the gang of mangy humans seemed completely blind to the glaring Light.

The inhabitants of the village had not missed the commotion. They started to gather and were slowly advancing, armed with torches, scythes, pitchforks and other implements. Eldric suddenly felt reminded of the night they had driven him out of Heidenried. It was time to leave and not involve any more civilians in this affair. He mounted the borrowed horse and spurred it towards the end of the village, telling the gang that they needed to move quickly. They heaved the saint onto the back of one of the horses and followed him.

Sartiria stopped and watched the villagers with that malicious grin. Eldric was afraid she was going to attack them, but at the last second, she turned away and followed him.

The place designated for the interrogation was an abandoned bear's den in the forest. Five of Sartiria's men dragged the battle saint inside. The alleged criminal was to confess to them what he had already done to prepare for war and who else was involved in it.

'Find out how many other so-called *saints* are hanging around and where we can find them,' Sartiria ordered.

They sent the rest of the gang to the edge of the forest to dig a hole long and deep enough to forever bury the saint, nailed in his box.

Unwittingly, Eldric groped for the weight in his right pocket. Then he released his powers and focused on Sartiria, intending to make her feel them.

'I must confess, I was wrong about you,' he said. 'This human is indeed capable of making Light appear, and his capture is strategically extremely valuable.'

'Ha! I told you you'd be grateful. And you had better offer your gratitude officially before the next Council if you don't want to become a laughingstock.'

Eldric sighed playfully. 'What would we do without you?'

It would be a delicate balancing act. He could not give in to his impulses to such an extent that he jeopardised Liliana's dignity or well-being. Their last encounter had made that more than clear. But he had to give in to them far enough for Sartiria to feel safe and block out the rest of the truth. Her hatred of humans and her rigid thinking would blind her to what didn't fit her narrative, namely that a powerful vampire like him would give anything to save a mere human soul.

With his arms folded, he leaned against the lichen-covered rock at the entrance to the cave. He raised a gloved index finger to his lips. 'Listen!'

Sartiria closed her eyes and grinned gleefully. The saint's groans echoed off the cave walls. By the Primordial Demon, if only these thugs didn't smash his skull out of sheer coarse incompetence ...

Eldric granted his powers more freedom. *Kill. Kill him. Drink them.*

The sounds of pain from the cave became more piercing, followed by a dull thud. The saint's voice sounded distraught. 'Why are you doing this?'

'Shut up! Tell us where the other saints are hiding!'

Gagging and more moaning followed. Sartiria basked in the prisoner's misery. Her powers blazed with such force that Eldric feared he would soon hear *her* voice in his head as well.

He joined in her demonic joy at hearing her archenemy suffer. *Kill the saint. Dismember him. Snuff out his Light.*

'Too bad we can't sound him out ourselves,' he remarked. 'What satisfaction ...'

One of the crooks approached the cave exit with bumpy steps, sticking his hollow-cheeked head out of the opening. 'We won't get anything out of him no more, mistress.'

'Go on,' Sartiria barked with a mad glint in her eyes.

'He's passed out.'

'How?'

'Tobi hit him o'er the head. A bit too hard.'

She snorted. 'Then go and help the others shovel! I'll come get you when he wakes up.'

The hollow-cheeked head called the other gang members out of the cave. They took with them their instruments of torture – an assortment of clubs, hammers, nails, torches and a shovel – as if they were objects of considerable value.

Sartiria rubbed her chin feverishly, and Eldric's heart began to race. She moved towards the entrance, which could only mean one thing: She was going to kill the saint while he was unconscious. He hastily pushed himself off the rock and intercepted her.

'Not yet!'

Sartiria growled but stood still. This was it. This was the moment.

While she hesitated, Eldric leaned over her. He allowed his powers to spread, to invade his mind and escalate his desires.

'That body of yours belongs to me!'

The hunger of the Curse seized him, wanting to devour everything that had life in it – the bushes, the trees, the insects in the air, the animals crawling under the earth, the moss and the mushrooms ... and above all this appetising half-human, right here in his grasp.

'You wish!' Sartiria bared her teeth.

'What are you going to do? Stand here bored until he wakes up from his nap?'

The demon's power coursed through his limbs. He pushed her against the outside of the cave and pressed her hands against the stone. 'Whatever you gave Baldrich, I want a thousandfold!'

Her heart was beating wildly now, but she still resisted.

'Later.'

No. He had to distract her to the point where she was no longer paying attention, no longer noticing what he was up to. Eldric surrendered to the hunger, allowing the Darkness to fill him almost completely. He wanted her blood; he wanted her passion. And he wanted it—

'Now!'

He was playing with fire. But he had to misdirect a vampiress who could smell his emotions. His powers wrapped her in an eager embrace. Sartiria felt his desire and savoured it. He inhaled her neck, and she pushed him away. But his strength grew with his powers, spiralling higher, craving her all the more. *Kiss her. Take her. Drink her.*

Eldric sank against her and kissed her lips. His ice melted into her fire, and Sartiria surrendered to the surge of power and the sensation of the kiss. Good. She smelled it, she felt it, she ... she believed him.

When she broke away to catch her breath, he whispered, 'With you in her body, I can do whatever I want. Live out all my desires. *You* are cursed with the same power. You share my hunger!'

He slid his hands over her arms, down her waist, to her hips. Those curves, the movement of her pelvis ... No, too much. *Pull yourself together!* He had to hold back; he couldn't allow his powers to take over any further.

Hastily, he wrestled the Darkness down and continued to talk, his lips still against hers, repeating all the things that had been whispered to him; the things Liliana would never be able to offer him as a human. 'You will not age prematurely ...'

Ring ... the ring. He had to ... Heart pounding, he groped for the object in his pocket, wrapped in a woollen scarf so that it wouldn't give off a suspicious glow. Had she noticed something?

'My family will accept you. I can restore my reputation.' He pressed her closer to him, away from the rocky wall, to open a gap behind her back where he could pull the ring up with both hands. His tongue wanted to run over her skin. *No, keep talking!*

'You are not weak and helpless. You have the power and ambition to be at the top. *You* are my equal.'

She clawed one hand into his hair and the other into the front of his shirt. Had she become suspicious or ...? The moment he slipped the scarf off to put the ring around her neck, she instinctively ducked under his arms and stumbled to the side. Primordial Demon! No!

Her gaze fell on the shimmering ring, which had been separated from the matching chains. The metal shone in the moonlight. Eldric froze. He had failed. She had sensed the Light in it and caught him at the very last second.

'You wanted to trap me with *Light chains*?' Her eyes widened in disbelief. Her heart beat hard with anger.

He didn't give her a chance to think about it any longer and leaped forward to close the metal around her neck. Sartiria hissed, kicked at him and knocked the ring from his fingers. She then put distance between herself and him and assumed a fighting stance. Her expression was one of genuine shock. She hadn't seen it coming.

Eldric tried in vain to control his breathing. Holy Lights, he had tried to prevent exactly that! But a confrontation was unavoidable now. He took off his gloves with his teeth and threw them to the ground so as not to shred them when using his claws. He never took his eyes off Sartiria or the shimmering metal ring of Light on the ground.

Sartiria assumed her demon form. 'How dare you play such a dirty trick on me?' she hissed, fangs bared.

'What did you expect?' He watched her carefully. 'Playing with other people's feelings seems fun ... until you start losing.' She was the one who had meant to exploit his weakness, his affection for Liliana.

'Losing?' Her voice almost cracked with indignation. 'I'm going to kill you!'

She raced towards him with a fierce scream. He swerved to the side, and she crashed into the rock behind him, but nimbly pushed herself off again and came after him.

She fought with the ease of a seasoned warrior and the vengeance of a rejected lover, while he had to time each of his attacks precisely. If he inflicted a fatal injury on her in the heat of battle ...

Sartiria intuitively deflected his blows, no matter how fast he struck, and for her part, did her best to slash him. Her claws sliced through the air just next to his ear. She fought resolutely and seemed to anticipate most of his advances. Even his father or Morton had not adapted so flexibly to changing angles of attack and sequences of blows.

The longer they fought, the more Sartiria's anger waned in favour of her pugnacity. His had also dwindled, giving way to the concentration and thrill of the battle. His heightened senses perceived everything more clearly: Sartiria's scent, the quickened pulse, her every movement, every sound.

His reserves of power helped him to evade her attacks or at least block them. But he would have to knock her unconscious if he wanted to take her to the saint. How on earth was he supposed to do that without seriously jeopardising Liliana's life?

Soon they were both panting with exertion, and Eldric felt beads of sweat on his forehead despite the autumn temperatures. The power of the Curse clashed against itself in the form of two different bodies. It filled the air with oppressive tension.

Any animals nearby had fled. As a precaution, he had agreed with Boras that he would send Sartiria's gang away with a bogus order – and an alleged advance payment. So he wasn't worried about any interference from them. In any case, it seemed more likely that they would run away screaming at the sight of two monsters fighting.

Eldric channelled his concentrated powers into his right arm and caught Sartiria on the shoulder. Her blood stood out, sharp and enticing, against all other odours. His demon was torn between the desire to tear and kill and the desire for her quasi-human blood. *Drink. Drink it.*

Hissing in pain and anger, she jumped out of his reach. Fortunately, he hadn't severed anything vital. If only he could somehow drag her into this blessed cave.

He lunged forward and grabbed her, but as soon as he got hold of her arm, she whirled around and sank a foot into the pit of his stomach. His claws slipped as he was thrown back by the force of her kick. Eldric staggered and straightened up, breathing heavily. He spat thickened saliva onto the ground and ran his tongue over his teeth.

They once again threw themselves into the ferocious interplay of ducking, striking and defending. Sartiria seemed to be watching his reactions more closely now. Suddenly, she jumped back and began to laugh.

'You can never defeat me if you aren't going for the kill!'

She knew it. Blessed again, she knew he had to regulate the severity of his attacks.

Sartiria's powers burned even brighter. Her eyes flashed in the demon's feverish frenzy. She giggled as she dashed up and hacked at him. Eldric's stomach tightened. Was she deliberately not healing herself? Would she risk her life just to—

She wasn't dodging! Horrified, he rotated his arm, and his claws scraped along the side of her ribs rather than digging deeply into her ribcage ... leaving his side unprotected.

He swung his arm upward, but Sartiria threw herself forward, blocked him with both hands and opened her mouth.

Her teeth dug deep into his neck. Pain overwhelmed his senses. She drank his blood! He pushed her off; she bit down with even more force. Skin, artery and muscle fibres tore as he violently freed himself from her.

Sartiria stumbled back in his clouded vision, spitting out shreds of flesh and grinning with a bloodied face.

He pressed both hands to the wound gaping at the side of his neck. Warm blood oozed from between his fingers and soaked his shirt and coat collar, seeping down his front. He struggled for breath, pushing aside the rising panic and the demon's fury with all his might. *Concentrate ...*

Eldric staggered and sank to his knees. Darkness engulfed him, cold and bitter. The sounds around him became distorted. All his attention was concentrated on the wound on his neck. He had to direct the full extent of his powers on staunching the bleeding and couldn't do anything else.

He barely perceived Sartiria's giggling. While he underwent the vital healing, he was defenceless, completely at her mercy. In other words ... he was as good as dead.

Chapter Thirty

Eldric drew in a shuddering breath. When he opened his eyes and his sight returned, Sartiria had been swept off her feet. Life left his body in trickles and no longer in gushes. He could only have been gone for a few moments, not unconscious in the true sense, but entirely absorbed in the healing process. Still, those moments would have been the perfect opportunity for Sartiria to finish him off for good. Why hadn't she done it? What had happened?

No time to think – he tore a strip from his shirt and wrapped it around his neck as an improvised bandage to stop the blood mechanically and free a part of his powers for other purposes.

Boras had come to his aid and was wrestling with Sartiria on the ground. She hurled him off with a kick. Eldric slipped on a glove and dashed forward, his powers now fully engaged in speed. He picked at the metal ring in the moss, threw himself at Sartiria and rammed the clasp closed around her neck. She clawed at him, but by the time her hand reached his face, it was already human, leaving only scratches on his cheek.

She gave a choked cry and tried to push him away. But even with his powers mostly focused on healing again, he easily caught her wrists. Her demonic powers were neutralised.

Eldric stared down at her. Against all odds, he had succeeded ... Thanks to her hesitation and Boras' help, he had managed to capture her in the Light chains. He felt dizzy with relief. Or maybe it was the loss of blood. Why had she hesitated? Did Liliana have something to do with it? Or had Sartiria not been able to bring herself to actually kill him?

He rose and dragged her to her feet. Boras was already recovering; his heartbeat sounded healthy and strong in the background. Heartbeat ... *blood, blood, drink* ... The sudden bloodthirst of the Curse hit him with such force that he gasped.

Soon ... He just had to end this now ... hold out until the saint took care of her.

Eldric dragged Sartiria towards the cave in the rock. She struggled, throwing herself back and forth like a human who had just been bitten, but without her powers, she had no chance of opposing him.

'You're working with *him*?' she hissed. 'You're even worse than the battle saints themselves! A traitor, you are! A traitor to your own people, your own race! Filthy rat! Scum! Human whore! Vulture!'

She paused to take air. Before she could utter the first syllable of a cry for help, Eldric pulled her close, wrapped one arm around her and pressed his gloved hand over her mouth with the other. Sartiria bit at him, but his grip was hard and the thick leather that had shielded his skin from contact with the Light chains also protected it from her teeth.

He peered inside the cave and hesitated. Although he had observed the saint's abilities, he did not know what awaited him in there. What were this superhuman's intentions? Would he kill them both if they got within his reach? Well, so be it ... he had come this far. He would not turn tail now.

Determined, he dragged Sartiria into the cave. Their footsteps echoed dully off the damp walls. She still struggled, ramming her head against his chest and clawing at the wound on his neck. But her feet slipped on the loamy floor and her slender, human arms were too weak.

The saint stirred on the ground and groaned.

Eldric swallowed. 'Please help us! Please help my friend.'

Sartiria gasped and choked with the effort of trying to free herself. He carefully climbed over a large bump with her and, keeping a safe distance, stepped up to the saint.

'If you are who we think you are,' he said loud and clear, 'you can help her with your Light.'

The saint sat up, trembling. The Light returned along with his consciousness, presumably to heal his battered body thoroughly. He seemed instantly more lively.

Eldric backed away. The demonic forces within him hissed and shied away from the light.

'If you help us, I will see to it that you are released.' Eldric went to his knees before the saint and pushed Sartiria down with a hard grip. His powers wanted to revolt in anger, but he ignored them. 'I beg of you, heal my friend! She is possessed.'

Sartiria shouted something into the hand he held pressed over her mouth; nothing intelligible came out. It was likely she hated him for humbly asking their supposed common enemy for his help almost more than for his betrayal.

The saint merely looked at them for half an eternity. The gag and blindfold had been removed, but his hands were still bound together with thick ropes. It was only when he groped for the cave wall and slowly stood up Eldric realised that, like all other humans, he could barely see in the dark.

'I know what you are,' he said in the most neutral accent Eldric had ever encountered. 'My Light will kill her.'

'No,' he quickly contradicted. 'This woman harbours two souls. One belongs to a vampiress, the other to a human. If you drive out the vampiress with your Light, the human will be free. I will spare your life if you save hers.'

Their souls had not connected. They couldn't have connected. So it had to work ...

The saint stared with narrowed eyes and an unclear expression at a point above the crown of his head. He did not indicate whether he thought these conclusions were correct or not. 'What's stopping me from sending you into the ether as well? The way I see it, you are asking for two lives for one. A poor trade-off.'

As much as he was reluctant to grovel to a human as this was going against both his innate and learned tendencies ... he had to prove that he meant no harm; that he was dependent on his help and would submit to his terms.

Eldric cleared his throat but did not stand up or loosen his grip on Sartiria, instead, looking up at the saint from the ground, he said, 'That is why I kneel before you as a supplicant, saint.'

The curly-bearded man's face almost broke into a smile. 'Untie me, and I shall help you.' He held out his bound arms to Eldric.

Why did he demand that? He could free himself if he rubbed the rope long enough over a sharp-edged stone. Was he setting a trap for him? Surely, he could, just as he had suggested, simply summon Light directly into his head if he wanted to kill him? Or did he not trust his marksmanship in the dark and wanted to catch him at the right moment to make sure he would strike true? Was he secretly waiting for Eldric to attack him first so he could obliterate him without a guilty conscience?

Sartiria noticed his uncertainty and escaped his grasp to claw at his eyes. He jerked back and forced her arms down with his elbows without releasing her mouth.

'If you know who I am,' said the saint calmly, 'then you must also know that I cannot lie.'

Why shouldn't a saint be able to lie? His behaviour increasingly confused Eldric. But he did not seem averse to his request to help a human soul.

Eldric took his hand from Sartiria's mouth, and she immediately screamed. 'Of course he's lying! He's going to kill us both!'

But if it meant he could save Liliana, he would do anything. He would kneel, he would beg and, if necessary, lay down his life for her. The clarity of this realisation surprised him. Of course, she had saved his life several times, which meant he had a debt to repay. But his willingness went beyond that debt ... He loved her. It was as simple as that.

Eldric leaned forward, one arm still pressing Sartiria tightly to him, and cut the saint's ropes with his claws, careful not touch him.

Instantly, the saint pulled his hands apart and the ropes fell away from him. He shook out his arms and his features hardened. 'She's right, supplicant. Unless you get out of here. And as quickly as possible.'

He would help her! 'Thank you.'

Eldric let go of Sartiria and moved away step by step. He had to leave her to the saint. It was the only way.

He retreated, keeping his ears pricked. When he reached the cave exit, he paused, his gloved hand on the stone. The saint's voice only reached him softly and indicated interest.

'A possession? I'm not familiar with this phenomenon.'

Although he was tempted to stay and listen, he stepped out of the cave and breathed in the fresh forest air. This superhuman had the ability to kill him, and his tone had made it clear that he would. And why wouldn't he? They were natural enemies ... And Eldric was in no shape to face an opponent like him. His powers were still busy healing his wound, and his blood levels were so low that the curse would run away with him as soon as he stopped actively fighting it.

He dragged himself over to where Boras was waiting, sank into the moss beside him and leaned against a boulder.

'For a moment there, I thought ...' Boras began and then fell silent under his curtain of stringy hair.

'I was going to die?' Eldric muttered.

'Hm ... yes.'

He tried to wave it off nonchalantly, but the result felt feeble. 'That was nothing.'

'If you say so ...'

'Could you please get our horses now? You can bring all three.'

Boras nodded stiffly and disappeared between the trees.

Eldric had to find some unfortunate human before the bloodrage caught up with him. But first, he wanted to give in to his exhaustion for at least a few minutes and simply sit here.

Have you been watching, Morton, from wherever your cursed soul is wandering around now? Three to zero. This is the third time I've narrowly escaped death. What do you say to that?

And Morton was silent. Eldric laughed quietly. At last, he was silent ...

How long did it take a saint to exorcise a vampiric soul? Not much seemed to have happened so far. In any case, he heard no screams or scuffles or incantations. However, he had out of necessity reduced his powers, and therefore his senses, to the absolute minimum.

He leaned his head back against the damp stone and closed his eyes.

Who would come out of this cave? Sartiria, who had somehow killed the saint? Liliana, just as she had been before she had absorbed Sartiria's soul? A Liliana who hated him again for everything that had happened? Or a Liliana broken by demonic madness, who would no longer recognise him and no longer be able to speak a coherent sentence?

Worse still, what would happen if he was terribly mistaken? If the two souls had united, the saint's attempt to help her would kill them both.

Eldric had never felt the desire to pray. Apart from the fact that he found the Light repulsive, it would never listen to him anyway. And if, for some unfathomable reason, it did listen to him and came to haunt him, it would be detrimental to his health. But ... it was *her* beacon of hope. And as such, he needed it to work its miracles for her. That was his supplication.

Chapter Thirty-One

Liliana fell and hit something soft. She felt as if she'd been swallowed, digested and spat out again. Was she still alive? She felt cold. She felt dark. Someone was holding her.

'It worked,' a friendly male voice said close to her ear. The battle saint – no, the saint. 'Are you all right?'

Her legs trembled and refused to stand upright, as if they were still waiting for Sartiria's orders. The smell of mould filled the air. The metal ring hung heavy and cold around her neck. An abyss opened up in the darkness. Images and other sensory impressions crept out of it, clawing their way into her mind. Laughter echoed in her head. Her fingers severed tendons and muscles. Her mouth filled with warm blood.

Choking, she tore herself free from the arms that held her. She staggered back, hit the ground and stones and threw up. She sucked the life force out of innocent people. She set the church on fire. She wrapped her legs around Baldrich. She condemned the priests to become vampires. She ... had killed Cedi!

She gasped, scrambled blindly, scraped her palms and crawled on until her head hit against a rock face. What had she done? She cupped her bloody, dirty hands to her face and sobbed. The distorted fragments came together to form a picture of horror. What had she done?

Another choke interrupted her sobs. Her stomach wanted to rid itself of the horrible lump that was squatting inside it. But apart from bile, she had nothing to spit out. The bitter flavour stuck to the roof of her mouth.

Sartiria had left her wicked mark on the world – and Liliana had made it possible. She had witnessed it all, experienced it all as a prisoner in her own body. She had thought, felt, acted like the vampiress who inhabited her. She had shared her lusts and her desires, let the demonic fire eat through her insides until she was burnt out. Charred, black, empty.

Cedi ... Liliana clutched her knees and rocked back and forth in the dark. She banged the back of her head against the wall again, this time on purpose. But the sharp pain that flashed through her skull was meaningless. Cedi ... Priest Mathias ... Urs, the loyal neighbour ... the kidnapped people in the Crimson Plains dungeon ... four pregnant women and a whole host of other people who had died at Sartiria's hands.

She tasted salt on her tongue. And pain, bitter pain. All the suffering, all the death brought about by the attempt to save her daughter. And El ... The cold and the darkness drew tighter and tighter around her, wanting to crush her combined with the weight of what she had experienced. It hurt so much. It hurt so much!

She curled up even more. A vague voice surrounded her. A hand touched her arm, and Liliana instinctively pushed it away. The next time she took a breath, she felt as if a warm breeze stroked over her skin. Something soft warmed her from the inside and at the same time wrapped itself around her like an immaterial woollen blanket. The pain eased a little. Her cramped hands loosened. She clung to this vague warmth. Please help me! Don't leave me alone!

'What is your name?'

The question was repeated several times, and Liliana struggled to answer. Where was she? The cave ... The saint ...

'You don't need to be afraid. I won't hurt you.'

When she focused on the voice, on the benevolence in it, the images faded a little – Cedi, the blood and the dead on the battlefields ... She had even shared Sartiria's memories whenever they had come up.

'The demoness is not coming back. I can promise you that much.'

'I let her in.'

'What do you mean?'

She was glad she didn't have to see his face. 'There was no other way out.'

The saint remained silent, and Liliana continued to speak, shoving back the terrible images and grimaces that crept around her under the cover of darkness. 'To save my daughter. How could I have known what she would do, who she would kill or torture ... my own brother ...' She whimpered, squinting her eyes as if she could unsee and by doing so rewind the events. 'How many lives a single decision can destroy ...'

'Do you regret this decision?'

She held her breath. The back of her head throbbed oppressively.

'Now that you realise the extent of the impact, would you make a different decision?'

She put her head on her knees. How could he ask her that? Her daughter's life against the lives of other people ... She defiantly swallowed the nausea that was rising up again. That spiteful laugh ... shouldn't it have disappeared along with Sartiria? 'I love Annie more than ... I am responsible for her ...' She broke off and mumbled barely audibly, 'But how could I ...'

'You don't have to answer me. If, in hindsight, with the knowledge you have now, you would decide differently, then you have learned from the experience. If you would still make the same decision ... well, then – be it justified or not – you have no reason for regret.'

'I couldn't have foreseen the consequences! How can a single decision affect so many other people?'

'All our decisions affect others. Our lives and actions are always interwoven with others. No one lives in complete isolation. And even if we did, our absence, too, has an impact on the world.' He sighed. 'Believe me, I would know.'

'I didn't want all this!' She buried her wet face against her knees again. If only she could undo all those terrible things. As long as Annie remained safe, as long as she had saved her beloved Annie.

'It should have been me, no one else!' She hadn't given it much thought, she had simply acted; out of her desperate hope of saving those she loved, she had grabbed the only lifeline available to her. It hadn't occurred to her that there could be an afterwards.

Nothing stirred in the darkness for a while, and Liliana began to suspect that she had imagined the saint in her confusion. In truth, she was alone, trapped in some in-between world into which the Light had hurled her when Sartiria was driven from her body. After all she had brought upon the world, she should not be surprised that the Light rejected her as well.

'I feel your grief, Liliana. Would it help if you told me what happened?'

She winced. 'No.'

'What would help you?'

'I don't know.' Annie's little hands, outstretched towards her. Mummy! And her distraught little face. She didn't understand why her mother had suddenly pushed her away and handed her over to Albert like an unwelcome bundle of straw. 'Annie ...'

'Your daughter?'

Where was she now? Sartiria had never met her again after El had escaped with her. Hopefully, she remembered her mother. Hopefully, she was all right. And hopefully, El hadn't turned her into a vampire!

'Is she still little?'

'Yes,' Liliana said. 'Almost four.'

If only she could hold Annie in her arms, hug her and reassure herself that her little girl was all in one piece.

'Can you get up?'

Wondering again at the soft warmth around her shoulders, Liliana rubbed her clammy cheeks dry with her sleeve. She groped for the cave wall and pulled herself up.

'Shall we go outside?' The saint took a few steps and waited. 'It's pretty dark in here, although it must be getting towards midday.'

'What?' She followed him, staggering. 'Midday?' Impossible ...

But when they stepped out into the forest, the sun was already at its highest point. Liliana blinked and looked around as if in a dream. Had she been sitting in the dark for so long?

She stared at her feet, her feet that felt just as numb and twisted as everything else. Was she really standing here on the mossy forest floor? Were the bare, tangled branches real? And the ashen grey sky behind them?

The saint also had a look around. 'My tormentors have not returned. I wonder why.'

Liliana stared at him. She understood what he was saying but couldn't formulate an answer. Why was it so quiet? Where were the birds, where was the wind? Did the world know what she had done? Or was she stuck in a fantasy? A fantasy that protected her from having to witness the other atrocities that Sartiria had used her body to commit? Perhaps she was still lying paralysed on a bed, hallucinating.

'I would like to ask you to accompany me for a while on my journey.' The saint smiled, and the smile seemed outrageous to Liliana. The dark branches above her knotted together. The moss beneath her feet squelched hungrily. How could he be so nice to her?

'Why?' Her voice trembled.

'I'm hoping I might be safer if you stay close to me. But, more importantly, I would like to talk to you a little longer. Is that all right?'

She wrapped her arms around herself. Why was he hoping for safety near her? He was the one who could summon Light. Nevertheless, she nodded tentatively.

'I'm Inay, by the way.'

Inay? The saint blurred before her eyes and took shape again. Shaggy beard hair sprouted on his chin. His skin had a darker tone and showed hardly any wrinkles. Only in the depths of his eyes did the centuries show.

She nodded again, and he started walking.

Chapter Thirty-Two

She followed Inay down the slope like a doll with no will of her own. Without him, she would have sunk to the nearest patch of ground and simply stopped moving. The forest slid past her as a dirty grey mass. She felt as if trapped in a glass box. None of the sounds or smells reached her. Vines tugged at her clothes and stinging nettles pricked her skin. She felt none of it, only the strange competition between the cold penetrating from the outside and the inexplicable, comforting warmth from inside her.

Above their heads, the clouds thickened until the sky sagged with heaviness. She expected to feel drops on her forehead at any moment. But everything remained dry.

At some point, she stumbled out onto a country road. The saint looked in both directions and picked one. Liliana followed him. Although the ground here was level, her feet seemed to be wading through a treacherous swamp.

'I would like to take this ring off you.' The saint turned to her and pointed to her neck. 'Unfortunately, we need the key to open it. And that key, I suspect, is in the hands of the vampire who put it on you.'

Confused, she felt for the metal. Sure enough, it was still there.

'Walking provides a good opportunity to talk.' The saint slowed his steps to stay by her side. 'I cannot make sense of what happened. I've seen a lot in my time, but ... A powerful vampiress has risen from the past, and another vampire is supposedly risking his own life to save you – or at least to get rid of that vampiress. If he knew what I was capable of, why did he let me go? Where are her companions? I hope you can shed some light on the matter.'

Liliana continued to look down at her shuffling feet. Her thoughts were in desperate chaos, from which she had retreated as far as possible.

'Too soon?'

She nodded, put one foot in front of the other and stared at the ground in front of her. Could life simply go on after all this?

They didn't pass any larger villages. Instead, they came across two ox carts, crossed a group of hikers and were overtaken by a stagecoach. Liliana barely noticed any of it. Whoever talked to the saint seemed to move on a little more upright. Once, he came back to Liliana with bread and encouraged her to eat. Her bile surged up again immediately, but she forced herself to chew slowly. It took a while for her jaw to get used to the movement. Later, they drank water from a small stream.

As the dreary afternoon darkened into eve, a rider sped past them at high speed, and Inay pulled her to the side of the road as a precaution. In passing, she realised that the road had taken them out of the forest and was now running through harvested fields. His hand remained on her shoulder. The warmth inside her increased for a moment, and Liliana took a deep breath. He made another attempt to start up a conversation with her.

'I understand that it must be difficult for you. Nevertheless, it is important that I find out what is going on.'

She nodded timidly and avoided his gaze.

'It seems Sartiria was seen as a threat by the other vampires. They are always competing among themselves. Still, I can't shake the feeling that there is more to it than that. How did you get involved in all this?'

El's voice wafted through her head. *I beg of you, heal my friend. She is possessed!*

The thought of him made Liliana's stomach ache. He had freed her, but would he still ...? And would she ever see him the same way? The strange relationship between him and Sartiria left her with an unpleasant feeling that she couldn't quite name.

'Please tell me what you know.'

If there was anyone she could confide in, it was a saint. And yet the truth would not cross her lips. Although she no longer really knew what the truth was. So she wrapped her arms around herself and spoke the first thought that formed in her head. 'Is what you said true? That a saint can't lie?'

'It is.'

'Why not?'

'Because if I lied, I would no longer be a saint.'

'So you can stop being a saint?' Liliana had to admit that she had never given much thought to the life and nature of a saint. In fact, these saints that Priest Mathias had spoken of had seemed more like legends to her. Neither she herself nor any of the people she knew had ever met one. But that was how it had been with the vampires at first, too. She dug her fingers tighter into her arms. If Inay knew that she had the deaths of several priests on her conscience ... No, she couldn't see it that way! Sartiria had done that. And yet she could feel her teeth in Priest Mathias' flesh. The acid in her stomach shot up to her throat again. And Cedi ...

She swallowed and stumbled over her words as she continued. 'S-so you will ... you will stop being a saint if you tell a lie?'

'Yes and no.' He took his hand off her shoulder. She could see him looking at her thoughtfully out of the corner of her eye. 'It's not like there's someone constantly watching me, ready to punish me if I do something wrong. You have to think of it like the change of the seasons ... When you see the first flower poking its head through the blanket of snow, is that spring?'

'No. But I know that spring is nearing.'

Inay smiled. 'The flower is one of the many aspects that make up spring. Longer days, awakening insects, the first butterfly ... Spring comes slowly, and yet, there is a day when we say now it's spring. Similarly, lying is a sign of what is happening inside me. I wouldn't stop being a saint because I told a lie. I would tell a lie because I stopped being a saint.'

Sursprisingly, that made sense. Liliana breathed a little more easily. She wanted to ask the next question before he continued to enquire about El and her role in the nightmare that had ensued. And she had more than enough questions.

'What makes you a saint then?'

'So you believe that I am a saint?'

'Yes.' She didn't believe it, she knew it.

'And why do you believe that?' Inay set off again, inviting her to walk beside him with an inviting gesture. Liliana hoped he had a destination. She herself was completely disorientated.

'You exorcised a demonic soul out of my body with your Light,' she said.

'Did you see the Light? Did you perceive it while she was inside of you?'

'Yes.'

'Do you see it now?'

Liliana squinted sideways at him. He looked like a normal, slightly scruffy man, probably raised in the south of the Continent. Apart from his friendliness and his neutral accent, there was nothing to suggest that he was anything special. In her imagination, a saint wore bright priestly robes, gave poetic speeches and sported a long, white beard on his chin. Although his comparison about spring wasn't too far off being poetic.

'No, I don't see anything.'

Inay held out a hand in front of him as if he were holding an invisible ball. 'That's the funny thing. I can't see it either. I can only feel it.'

For the first time since they had set off together, she raised her head. 'Are you holding Light in your hand now? How do you do that?'

He lowered his hand and looked at her. 'I'm asking for it. It's little more than a prayer.'

'A prayer?'

'In prayer, we make contact with a higher power, and we ask this power for help.'

Liliana nodded. That was what Priest Mathias had taught them.

'When I pray,' he continued, 'I communicate with the Light. That is the purpose of every prayer. The more in tune I am with the Light, the easier it hears me and responds.' He read Liliana's expression and grinned. 'Who says a prayer has to be long or even put into words?'

How was she supposed to imagine a prayer without words? Even if she didn't speak out loud, she would use words in her thoughts. 'But how can you be in harmony with the Light? How can you pray without words? Priests always say their blessings out loud.'

'They do that largely for the benefit of their audience.' He smiled amicably. 'Besides, what priests do and what I do are two different ways of working with Light. I ask the Light to appear in a certain place. Once it has appeared, it disappears again immediately, because just like the original demonic power, pure Light is not of this world. Although the Light that is in our world gives life to plants, animals and people, it is always bound to matter. If this connection does not exist or no longer exists, it goes back to where it came from. Can you follow?'

'I think so.'

'Priests work with bound Light. They bring about a certain effect of the Light by instructing it with specific words and transferring it from one state to another. Bound Light never develops the same strength as pure Light, but the effect lasts as long as the object to which it is bound exists.'

Liliana was able to assimilate what he said with what she already knew. Her thoughts flowed more easily when they weren't focused on her momentous decision and Sartiria's misdeeds. Because priests could not summon pure Light, they needed the Light bound in their blood for blessings. This method robbed them of their own life force, but had the advantage that – as the Light weapons Albert had discovered proved – it retained its effect for centuries. That was probably why there were both priests and saints.

'If the Light only appears at one point and disappears again immediately, how could you fill my whole body with it? Or hold Light in your hand?'

'Holy Light is in some ways like the light we can see. It radiates in all directions. The intensity simply decreases the further away you get from it.' He pointed into the distance. 'At night, you could see the glow of a single lamp on the hill there. But you would have to be a lot closer to be able to feel its warmth. It can shine through certain things that stand between you and the light, and it can be obscured by other things. If I want to hold Light, I have to summon it continuously.'

She was a little surprised that he was so willing to tell her all this. Did he simply trust her because she was human? He knew next to nothing about her.

'In the beginning, I prayed like we teach it in the churches. I assume you have attended a church? Otherwise you wouldn't know about priests and blessings. By now, I am deeply connected to the Light and my intention alone is enough. I can make Light appear in such rapid succession that it seems continuous or spread out.'

'Where does this deep connection come from?'

'Practice. And by drawing closer to the Light in my daily thoughts, feelings and actions. That's what I mean when I say you have to be in tune with the Light so that you can communicate with it.'

He turned onto a side street that looked remotely familiar to Liliana. 'That is the purpose of every sermon.'

She stopped abruptly. 'That means ... you're covertly teaching us how to become saints?'

'There's nothing particularly covert about it.' He winked. 'After all, everyone and anyone is free to sit in a church and listen.'

Apart from vampires, of course. Had Sartiria been right after all with her suspicion that the other side was recruiting in secret?

'Then there are more saints like you?'

'I'm afraid not.' Inay waved to encourage her to move on, and Liliana set off obediently.

'Why not?'

'If only I knew ...' Inay's voice remained soft but lost its chatty melody. Should she not have asked that?

'But you can't be the only one.' With so many people, that seemed just too unlikely. Also, Sartiria had spoken of saints in the plural.

'There were four of us.'

She stared at him in dismay. Only four? How had only four humans managed to defeat entire armies of vampires? These saints must be incredibly powerful. No wonder Sartiria had feared them.

'What happened?'

'That is a long story ...'

Although he continued to walk with the same vigour as before, the exertions of the previous night were suddenly visible on his face. Liliana realised that they had arrived in a village and were heading for the church in the centre. This was the village from which Sartiria's band had abducted him! It didn't seem wise to return to the same village the very next day.

'Won't you be easily found here?'

'I want to reassure and comfort the people who had the misfortune of witnessing it all.'

Just as the last of the sunlight disappeared, Inay knocked on the door that Sartiria's band had forced open. The garden looked sad with the trampled flowers and herbs, chopped-up fat-hen plants and four badly battered pumpkins. The agitated voices from inside broke off.

'Yes?' someone asked through a narrow gap. 'Who ...?'

The door was pulled open and the priest – a thin man with a nearly bald head – beamed at Inay. 'You're back? We didn't know if ... And nothing happened to you? We searched everywhere, but had no luck.'

Behind him, curious faces peered out of the hut. Half the village – children, women and men – seemed to be crammed into the small space. Yet the church was right next door. Perhaps they had moved here to light a warming fire.

'I'm fine.' Inay hugged the priest warmly and patted him on the shoulder. 'How are you?'

'Us? Good.' The priest turned to his swarm of visitors as if they hadn't observed the entire greeting. 'The saint is back! He's back!'

'Come in,' shouted a woman with two children on her lap.

The fact that she was accompanying Inay was obviously reason enough to invite her in without reservation. He gave way to Liliana. She took two steps and stopped because she couldn't find anywhere to sit down. The bench and the only two chairs in the room, the priest's bed, the cot on the side wall and the entire otherwise free-standing floor were occupied. If she had wanted to sit down, she would have had to make do with the table. The room smelled of smoke and sweat. Her unconventional outfit, the trousers and high-necked blouse, earned her a few puzzled looks. The metal ring around her neck probably couldn't pass for jewellery either. However, the general attention was focused on the saint, who was inundated with questions as soon as the priest had locked up behind him.

'What happened?'

'Who were those bandits? What do they want?'

'Will they come back?'

Inay smiled. 'Do not worry. Maybe Liliana can answer some of these questions. She was kidnapped, too. Albeit in a slightly different way.'

All eyes darted to her, and Liliana would have loved to sink into the ground. Fortunately, Sartiria had hidden behind a horse and hadn't attacked anyone herself. She didn't know what she should divulge to these people, though. How much could she say without endangering anyone or making things worse? Did the village know about vampires, or would she cause a panic by mentioning them?

'I ... It ... These bandits are riding around, burning down churches on someone else's behalf. Especially in the Lowlands.'

Inay nodded, as if to confirm her words. 'I wanted to make sure they hadn't crossed the border, but they seem to have done so now.'

'Why?'

'Our church is still standing!'

An older man bent forward on the bench. 'I don't mean to be rude, but ... your protective blessing isn't working, Priest Adom. Otherwise they wouldn't have been able to break in here.'

'The blessing doesn't stop humans,' Inay said. 'Only demonic creatures.'

Fear and astonishment rolled over those present. 'So they really do exist?' a girl whispered from the floor. 'The dark, winged creatures of the night?'

Inay looked at Liliana from the side, as if considering asking her about her experiences in front of everyone. Her stomach tightened. She shook her head in panic. So the saint patiently turned back to the tense faces.

'Yes, they do exist. That is why it is so important not to go outside at night and to pray to the Light every day. The blessings of the priests will protect you to some extent. But what can truly protect you is your own connection to the Light.' He nodded to the room in general. 'I ask you to pray with me and then go back to your own homes as soon as possible. If the bandits do return, you will be safer there.'

Murmurs spread among the villagers. Priest Adom raised his hands in the air and shouted to drown them all out. 'Let's pray together!'

Eager hands found each other, and heads were bowed. Liliana joined in and closed her eyes.

'Holy Light, we ask for your protection. Heal our infirmities, purify our hearts and accompany us on our paths ...'

As Inay spoke, warmth filled Liliana; not the heat of the fire or of the many bodies in the confined space, but a greater portion of the comforting warmth that seemed to surround her since Inay's arm had touched her in the cave.

'... So that we may all be united with the Light, now, in life, and one day, in death.'

She felt the warming comfort all the way to her toes and fingertips. Inay and the priest wished everyone a good night, and the villagers pushed past her. She remained huddled against the wall until the voices outside had faded away.

Priest Adom closed the door and sat down on a chair at the table where two men had previously squeezed together.

'May I ask what delicacy is hidden in there?' Inay pointed to the cauldron over the fire.

'Of course, Master Inay. Please help yourself to the remains of my simple bean stew, as much as you like.' He jumped up to fetch plates, but Inay signalled him to stay seated and reached for the hob himself.

The saint filled a plate, placed it on the table and reached for another. Meanwhile, Priest Adom rested his underemployed hands on the tabletop and asked, 'So you think they might return?'

Inay did not answer directly but crossed the room with the second plate and held it out to Liliana. He studied her with his endless dark eyes.

'What do you think, Liliana?'

Chapter Thirty-Three

She almost dropped the stew he had just handed her. Clutching the edge of the plate with both hands, she stuttered, 'I-I don't think the bandits will turn up here again ...'

Or would they? El could have recruited them for his own purposes after Sartiria disappeared and sent them out to fetch her. That way he could avoid a dangerous confrontation with Inay.

'And the other vampire? The one who brought you to me?'

Liliana swallowed. Did he know? Did he sense that there was more between them? Perhaps the Light somehow helped the saint to divine her thoughts or her heart's desires. If so, he knew more about Liliana than she did.

She lowered the plate in her hands. 'I think he will come.' And hopefully, he wouldn't bring Boras with him.

Only the fire crackled in the silence that followed. The village had gone to sleep. Priest Adom shifted uneasily in his chair. Inay's expression became thoughtful.

'If you know their plans, you should share your knowledge with us.'

'Sartiria's plan was to bury you so deep that you would never have been able to free yourself.'

Inay nodded. Turning towards the priest, he explained, 'Sartiria was a vampiress. She sent the bandits to get me. I severed her soul from Liliana's body, and we escaped.' He turned back to Liliana. 'The vampires haven't paid attention to me in a long time, so she managed to take me by surprise. I had no idea there were survivors from that time.'

'I don't think any other vampires besides her have been bound to anything.'

'Can you describe how it works?'

'She somehow modified the skills of a Lightsmith and transferred her powers – and therefore her soul – into a necklace. I wore this necklace as jewellery, and it took possession of my body.'

The plate was getting heavy, and she had thoroughly lost her appetite. Inay politely stepped aside as she shuffled past him and placed her food on the table. Priest Adom looked at her with concern.

'I was trapped in her head, if you like, while she controlled me,' Liliana continued with more composure than she would have believed she was capable of. 'Her goal was to continue the war and win it. She was convinced that the battle saints were still alive and secretly recruiting an army to wipe out the vampires. Is that true?'

Priest Adom looked from Inay to Liliana and back again. His expression resembled that of a child trying to follow a conversation between adults despite having long lost track of all the unfamiliar words.

'No, she was wrong.' Inay approached the table, hesitated for a moment and then sat down next to Priest Adom. He gestured for Liliana to sit down as well. 'I have no intention of starting another war after all these years.'

On the one hand, Liliana was relieved to hear that. Sartiria's memories had taught her to fear war. Then again ...

'Why not?'

'Because there are no winners in war.' Inay sighed and tilted his head as if he was suddenly weighing heavier. 'A wheel that keeps turning describes the same circle over and over again.'

'What do you mean?'

He looked at her across the table, contemplating. 'What happens if the vampires win?'

'They rely on human blood, so they can't kill us all.' Liliana deliberated. She could imagine all the things that unscrupulous vampires like Sartiria could have done to humans if they had won the war. 'Keep us in cages, breed us, buy and sell us ...'

'Until it all boils over and the people take up arms again. What happens if we win?'

'Then there are no more demons!' Priest Adom slapped the table with the flat of his hand.

'For a while, yes ...' Inay shrugged sadly and turned to his portion of stew. 'Fifty years, a hundred or even two hundred. Then it starts again ...'

'Why should it start again?' the priest asked.

'That is simply what history, the last eight hundred years, have proven.'

'H-how?' Priest Adom stared at Inay, as if it was only now dawning on him how long the saint had been wandering the world.

Liliana couldn't leave it at that either. 'Why shouldn't a victory over the vampires last? What about the other saints? Where have you been all these centuries?'

Inay brought a spoon to his mouth, chewed and swallowed, while Liliana and the priest waited impatiently for him to enlighten them. 'It is, as I mentioned, a long story ... with only one saint remaining in the end.'

'So, you are the only one.' And Sartiria would have managed to get him out of the way if El hadn't thwarted her plans! 'Is that why you aren't fighting the vampires? Because you are alone? But saints are so powerful!'

'Powerful, yes ... But we can't be everywhere.' Inay's gaze turned inward as he rolled out the past before them. 'A war is waged by hundreds of thousands of people, including Lightsmiths and soldiers, and battle tactics. Not cleaning up properly after our victory and celebrating us as heroes, as invincible, even infallible ... that was the beginning of the descent for humanity, who was at the top of the wheel back then.'

'Why?'

'Because only one vampire has to survive for everything to start all over again. And because arrogance is never wise.'

Liliana would have liked to shake him like a plum tree so that the answers would finally fall into the grass. He had been there! He had witnessed the end of the Four Hundred Years' War and all the history since then.

'What happened?'

Inay gave up eating and put down his spoon. 'As soon as our victory became apparent after the Four Hundred Years' War, disputes crept in between the people who cared about prestige. A new world order had to be created, and not everyone envisioned it to look the same way. Various factions formed, and each of them wanted our support. In the beginning, we kept our distance from all of this and only gave advice here and there that nobody wanted to hear. You must understand, many people had never known a time that wasn't soaked in war and bloodshed.'

Next to Inay, Priest Adom nodded eagerly.

'When we saw the chaos that ensued and the disputes slowly turned bloody, Raiden got involved. Ah.' He interrupted himself and added, 'We were four saints then. Raiden, Noor, Solana and I ... Raiden meant well, I'm sure. Over time, unfortunately, the success and attention must have gone to his head. He was sad proof that saints don't just stay saints forever when they no longer live in harmony with the Light. His connection waned and with it, little by little, his reputation. He died a bitter man, bent by age.'

Liliana imagined Raiden as a male version of Indira; a man whose radiance took over every room he entered ... until pride caused his connection to the Light to fade.

'Are you not ageing at all or is the process just slowed?' Priest Adom wanted to know.

'As we get older, the body gradually loses its ability to regenerate itself. The Light takes over this task for me. I suspect my body is still ageing, but so infinitely slowly that it is hardly noticeable. I could age faster if I consciously stopped inviting the Light to be with me.'

The saint sighed, as if reluctant to return to his story. 'That is impressive, of course. Then there are all the other gifts of the Light. Fertile fields, protection from demonic attacks and, of course, healing other people. We can't undo death, but as long as there's a spark of life left in a person, we can heal them – completely and in an instant ... I can understand Raiden's transformation painfully well. When you are praised by everyone and told every day how powerful and smart and perfect you are, you start believing it. At the same time, fear creeps in. Because deep down you know that you are just you. The tension between the powerful but fallible being that you are and the ideal that everyone wants to see begins to tear you apart. You become afraid of making mistakes, of disappointing others. So you don't make mistakes, and everything that goes wrong is someone else's fault.'

He fell silent; his thoughts wandered off into the vastness of his memories.

'And the vampires?' Liliana asked. 'How did they get back? What happened to the other saints?'

Inay winced. He smiled apologetically. 'Noor was murdered almost two hundred years to the day after the declared victory. Someone cut off her head in her sleep. That was a shock. I still don't know whether vampires or one of the more fanatical factions were responsible for her murder. After that, a hunt began for anyone who could have been connected to that tragedy in any way. People began to identify more and more with what made them different rather than what they had in common. Humanity was too busy blaming each other to realise that the vampires were slowly creeping back. As I said, all it takes is one surviving vampire for their kind to spread again. That left Solana and me ...'

Priest Adom continued to nod as if his head were stuck in that movement. The flames in the hearth had gone out, but no one bothered fanning the embers.

'We did our best to make peace, mediate and appease. Over time, we succeeded, but the resulting prosperity harboured its own dangers. Many

Lightsmiths had passed on their craft to the next generation. But it was gradually modified because no one had any use for weapons that fought an enemy who was thought to be eliminated. Instead, they made a living by selling talismans for good health, fertility, and later, luck, true love, success with financial transactions – whatever their customers wanted. The craft degenerated into a farce ... A normal human life is short, and we forget quickly. The vampires, on the other hand, had learned. By the time we realised they were back, they had already established themselves in strategic positions disguised as humans. We found that some people were willing to work with them in order to gain money, power or supposed security. I cannot list all the attempts we made to remove the vampires completely from our midst. Every time we thought we had done it, rumours would start again.'

'What happened to Solana?'

The regret in his voice intensified into unabashed sorrow. 'Solana despaired of the wickedness of the world. She withdrew. She didn't want to fight any more. You get tired after several centuries. And lonely. It's a painful experience to lose the people you love again and again. We can prolong the lives of others, by healing them often. But to actually stop ageing, we would have to constantly pray Light on the person in question and would be unable to do most other things. And there are so many people who need healing and help.'

'She gave up,' Priest Adom realised.

'She decided to lead a fairly normal life. She shut the Light out of her body, got married, had children, grew old with her loved ones ...'

Liliana could understand the saint's desire for a family, especially in the face of a never-ending battle against the demonic. Nevertheless, Solana had condemned the only other saint to even greater loneliness.

'She abandoned you.'

Priest Adom gave her a startled look, as if he would never dare to poke at the saint's wounds. But Inay smiled sadly.

'Yes,' he said quietly. 'Yes, she did.'

The embers threatened to go out completely, and darkness pushed in through the windows. Priest Adom pulled himself together and got up to add wood and get the fire going again. Liliana heard him working in the background, but couldn't take her eyes off the saint, who sat upright and yet infinitely tired in front of her at the table. He was so old, so lonely and so ... burdened with responsibility as the sole remaining bearer of hope for humanity.

'I can't blame her. I felt the same. It's just that now that she has already chosen it, that way out is no longer open to me.'

'What did you do?' Her voice was a devout, compassionate whisper.

'I withdrew for a century and lived on a small island in complete isolation.'

'Oh.' That was a strange way to deal with loneliness; perhaps an attempt to shed the responsibilities and worries of the world. 'But then you came back.'

'I can't deny my calling. Solana may have abandoned me. But I couldn't bring myself to abandon all of humanity. Someone had to carry on. And as long as I am the only one, nobody else can do the work for me. We had been fighting alone for a long time, but when I came back, vampires were seen as nothing but legend.'

'Why don't you tell everyone, everywhere? Surely many more people would join your cause!'

'I tell those who want to hear it. Usually, they are simpler people whose lives are not so comfortable that they cling to their world view in order to preserve it. The aristocracy and all those who have something to say politically suppress that knowledge at considerable expense.'

'Have you given up the fight, too?'

Liliana herself had done remarkably little to publicise the existence of the vampires. However, she had never really had the opportunity to do so. Frederik and some of the other men in Heidenried had spread news of the incident with El as much as possible among their friends and acquaintances but had been ridiculed from all sides. And she had been locked up in the castle for so long that she would not have been able to tell anyone other than her family what was going on with those nobles, who hardly ever showed their faces. On top of that, she was afraid of causing panic or provoking retaliation from the vampires.

Holding her own knees under the table, Liliana rocked gently back and forth. Here, among other humans and in the presence of the saint, she was enveloped in a feeling of community that she had not felt for far too long. Here, she was one of them; accepted, without questioning, without arrogance and without a constant threat breathing down her neck. But if she joined Inay's cause ... after El had risked so much to bring her back ...

She flinched as Inay continued. 'I was never a warrior at heart. Fate just wanted it differently. Have I given up the fight?' He pondered for a moment. His gaze became a little livelier. 'I would say I diverted it. I stopped trying to save the world and started trying to save individuals.'

The fire crackled briskly. Priest Adom patted off his robe and sat down next to the saint. His frown reflected Liliana's incomprehension.

Inay read it and started again. 'Do you know how vampires came to be?'

'The legend of Ragna and her enemy lover.' The painting behind the curtain at Mirror Lake Castle flashed before Liliana's mind as if she had seen the golden-yellow eyes full of demonic madness only yesterday.

'Yes. A ritual born of covetous hatred opened the door for the demonic to enter this world. Or in other words, a human brought vampires into existence with his hunger for power and his lust for revenge. Even if we eradicated all vampires at once – which we haven't been able to do in over a thousand years – someone could come up with the idea of tapping into demonic power again a few centuries later and create a new kind of demonic creature. That is the sobering truth.' He looked at her with a serious expression. 'As long as there are humans, there will be vampires.'

What he said sounded wrong. Humanity was not responsible for the atrocities committed by vampires. But what could she retort? If they believed the legend, vampires had only come into being after humans, and not of their own accord, but because of the decision and malicious actions of a human. At least, without that particular human, vampires would never have existed.

'We have brought the Light into the world, and we have also brought the Darkness. We are capable of both.' Inay raised his hands across the table, palms up. 'After all this time, I have finally understood.'

He turned his penetrating gaze to Liliana, as if he had only come to this realisation because of her. 'The only thing you can truly win is your soul. If each and every one of us realises that the real battle, the only battle we can win, is fought within ourselves ... If you and I and every human in this world did everything we could to win this one battle, then we would win the war.'

The comforting warmth inside her flared. She could have sworn he was reaching out to her, but his physical hands stayed right where they were. 'If everyone let the Light prevail within them, the demonic would have no place. That is why I bring the Light to individuals. That is the message I want to share.'

Priest Adom had resumed his nodding. He kept his eyes closed as if to pay more respect to what his ears were hearing.

'Vampires can kill a saint. It is unfortunate, but possible. However, a saint can neither be bitten nor turned into a vampire. If every soul were bound to the Light, vampires would no longer be able to feed on us or spread the Curse.'

Was this gentle, fluttering hope? She thought she understood the message. The saint was focussing on strengthening the good rather than eradicating the bad. She smiled. Then she remembered the sweetest of children, and the priest's hut began to blur. Annie ... Was she spreading the Darkness? With her Annie? Her daughter, for whom she would give up anything?

Inay sighed as if he'd heard her thoughts. 'Unfortunately, I sometimes fear that humanity doesn't want to let go of the demonic.'

Suddenly the room seemed too small, the fire too hot and the air stifling. The stew smelled as bad as if she were in the early stages of pregnancy again. If he knew ... If he knew what her child was that she so desperately wanted to save! And El ... wasn't just some vampire, he was Lord of Finsterwald.

'Are you feeling unwell?' Inay asked, finally taking the opportunity to empty his plate. 'You should eat something.'

Even Priest Adom eyed her with concern. 'You look pale, good woman.'

Liliana clutched her knees tighter. She looked to the side and mumbled, 'The last few months have been awful.'

'That's understandable,' Inay said. 'If you don't have an appetite, you should at least rest.' He turned to the priest. 'Would you prefer for us to spend the night in the church? So that your vegetable garden is spared this time, in case the aforementioned vampire or someone else turns up.'

'Shouldn't we take precautions?' Priest Adom interjected.

'Ah, of course ...' Inay passed the question directly to Liliana with a wave of his hand. 'What is your assessment? What does this vampire intend to do? Will he come alone?'

'I don't know exactly. But he will want to talk to me or bring me to him. He won't harm anyone ... unless he feels compelled to.'

'And when does he feel compelled to hurt people?'

Inay asked exactly the right questions. Liliana shrugged her shoulders uncertainly. 'He's definitely not going to destroy buildings and ruthlessly kill people like Sartiria would have done.'

'How do you know that?'

'Because he said so.'

'And you believe a demonic creature?' Priest Adom furrowed his brow. 'If I understand correctly, you were possessed by a demoness and freed by Master Inay. What else does this vampire want from you?'

She shrugged again and stood up so hastily that she banged her toes against a table leg. 'I'm happy to sleep in the church.' It wouldn't be the first time.

'Sleep will do you good,' Inay said.

Priest Adom gave the saint a puzzled look, but Inay smiled reassuringly and asked for a blanket, which he handed to Liliana.

'Here. I'll join you as soon as I've given Adom some instructions.' As much as Liliana searched for suspicion in Inay's voice, she found none.

Chapter Thirty-Four

The saint watched her from the doorway, just in case someone was already lurking outside. She walked slowly towards the church, looking around intently. The cool night enveloped her, buildings and trees looming only as silhouettes. Apart from the stream murmuring and the mill wheel softly groaning, the village lay quiet. She hoped El was prudent enough not to show himself openly. Was he here hiding somewhere, or was he still looking for her? What was she supposed to do when he did come? And what if he didn't?

Liliana gripped the woollen blanket tighter. She reached the church door and pushed it open. Her shuffling steps and the slamming of the door echoed off the stone walls. Dark, massive beams supported the roof. It smelled of dry wood, wax and earthy dust. Compared to the church in Heidenried, this one seemed heavy and armoured. She chose the second-backmost bench and curled up in the blanket. Despite itchy eyes and tired muscles, she sat upright and fixed her gaze on the moonlit windows. As soon as she closed her eyes, the terrible images would return.

If only she knew how Annie was doing. Holding her daughter in her arms would alleviate all the pain that plagued her. Forgive me, Cedi ... A dull stupor overcame her. If Inay hadn't joined her a little later, she would have sat there all night like a misplaced boulder.

His footsteps approached slowly. 'I find it easier to fall asleep when I lie down,' he said with mild reprimand.

She kept silent and pulled the blanket tighter. Inay stood still for a moment, then she heard footsteps again and the bench she was sitting on creaked at the other end. She squinted over from the corner of her eye. He was lying stretched out on the hard seat, wrapped up in a winter coat. If she concentrated, she could hear his gentle breathing. She found his presence reassuring; without the comforting warmth she attributed to his connection with the Light, she would have been even more restless.

'Why didn't you kill him?' She asked the question timidly, but the size of the room threw her voice back at ten times the volume.

She turned her head to see Inay's reaction. He continued to lie there with his face motionless and his eyes closed. Perhaps saints were blessed with a particularly rapid onset of restful sleep. He had made some kind of agreement with El to be released. And he honoured this agreement because saints did not lie. Yet she thought she remembered that El's life had not actually been part of that agreement. Inay had only promised to help him, not to spare him. So he could have killed El without contradicting his own words.

'Because he asked me for help.'

Liliana winced; she hadn't expected him to still answer. 'W-what do you mean?'

'He didn't make demands, didn't threaten, didn't try to force or manipulate me. He simply and respectfully asked me to set you free.'

Yes, Sartiria had hated that.

'The motive behind it was probably to get rid of Sartiria. Nevertheless …' Inay continued to speak with his eyes closed. 'I have never seen such behaviour from a vampire before. He didn't ask for his own life, just yours. He made no attempt to kill me or recapture me after I had granted his request … at least not yet.'

'So you don't kill vampires as soon as you see them?'

'I usually act faster. I was still a bit dazed from the treatment I'd been given … Should I have killed him?'

'No!' The word slipped out before she could stop herself. 'I mean, caution was definitely the right course of action.'

'Hmm.'

Something rustled under the bench. Probably a mouse. Her gaze slid back to the window. Where was El? What was he up to? And what would Inay do if he met him again? She was still too anxious to come up with a good plan. But she had to keep the two men away from each other, that much was clear.

'What will you do if—'

A clatter interrupted them. A pebble had bounced off one of the windows. A second one followed. The glass remained intact, but the sound pervaded as if the stone had flown through the window into the church.

She jumped to her feet, her palms moist. It had to be him!

'Looks like we aren't to be granted any sleep after all.' Inay stood up, too.

Liliana had to force herself not to run headlong but put one foot in front of the other at a normal pace. She reached the door before Inay and turned to face him.

'I'd better go and see for myself.'

'Alone?' The saint stopped in front of her. 'That doesn't seem like a wise idea.'

'He won't hurt me,' she assured him.

'How can you know that?'

Liliana swallowed. She could no longer keep the truth from him. She would have liked to hold fast to him, but that seemed absurd given the confession she had to make.

'Because ... because I am the mother of his child.'

In the dim light, she barely noticed a change in his expression. 'You mean Sartiria's child?'

'No. I ...' Her heart was pounding so hard in her throat that she could hardly speak. 'We are ... We were already ...'

She sensed the astonishment spill over from Inay as he began to understand. Something lit up in the dark eyes that she would have called joy for lack of a better term; perhaps the experience that there were still things in this world that could surprise him.

'Is it possible?' he murmured, more to himself. 'This story you are involved in is getting more startling by the minute. What about the child? And how come you are still alive?'

At least to his first question there was an obvious answer. 'Yes.' After a short pause, she added, 'I saved his life. I didn't know what he was then.'

'Amazing!' He thought for a moment and shook his head. 'Still, you can never assume you're safe from a demonic creature. He might change his mind, or even unintentionally attack you in a fit of rage or bloodlust.'

Her stomach tightened as if it absolutely agreed with this assessment. She took a deep breath. 'You asked me when he would feel provoked. I think the risk is lowest if I go alone.' Pleading inwardly for the saint to be persuaded, she added urgently, 'I can talk to him.'

'If you say so.' He put a hand on her arm. 'I'll wait outside the church. But if I hear anything, a scream or even just a whimper, the neighbourhood will go up in Light.'

Inay had claimed not to be a warrior at heart. But the determination in his voice gave her goosebumps. Those were the words of a man who could be very dangerous for the opposite side.

'All right,' she whispered.

They stepped outside together. The moon hung bright and full in the sky. No one was to be seen. She listened carefully. The stream rushed as before, otherwise everything seemed eerily still.

'There!' Inay pointed past her.

She searched for a figure in the dark until she realised that he meant something else. Candlelight flickered on a tree stump beyond the mill. A lantern! Since neither Liliana nor Inay had noticed it on the way to the church, it couldn't have been there for long.

Was that a marker? A signpost?

Inay reached for her hands and gave them a quick squeeze. 'I'll wait here as agreed. May the Light watch over you.'

'Thank you,' Liliana replied, although she hoped she wouldn't have to rely on its protection at all.

With her heart still pounding and the blanket around her shoulders, she stepped away from Inay, crossed the road and approached the mill. Similar to Father's construction, the course of the stream had been forced into a narrow, straight path by a wall so that the water hit the wheel with greater force. The ditch was deeper here, probably to protect the village from flooding. Liliana decided to jump anyway rather than taking the diversions around the mill. She made sure the ground was reasonably level and took a running start. Her foot slipped as she pushed off – the momentum was just enough to reach the embankment on the other side. The metal ring gave her a knock and another object hit her chest under her blouse. She felt for it and realised that she was still wearing Farkas' obsidian.

Liliana reached the lantern and peered in all directions. Was someone hiding here? From her vantage point, she could just make out the saint on the threshold of the church. To her left was a chicken coop. Straight ahead and disappearing to the right behind the mill was a field. No one landed, crept out from behind the mill or rode up on horseback. It was only when she ventured a few steps away from the tree stump that she noticed another light at the end of the field, where cultivated earth turned into woodland.

She grabbed the lantern on the tree stump and marched off across the field. Oil radish grew here after the potato harvest. So she would likely be forgiven for trampling the catch crop a little. As she trudged towards the edge of the forest, she tried not to think about the fact that she was making herself a target with the lantern in her hand. It was El who wanted to lead her to him, wasn't it? Not some elaborate trap, because ... who else could have found her here?

After she had reached the second lantern, she quickly found the next one. She now knew what to look out for. As expected, the trail beckoned her between the trees, where a vampire – or even several – could find cover.

The familiar smell of the autumn forest, damp leaves, mushrooms and rotting wood, greeted her. Nevertheless, she flinched at every crack. The light from her lantern wavered over the trees and bushes, causing the shadows to reach for her and retreat again with the rhythm of her steps. This rhythm kept speeding up. The twitching and swaying of the shadows called up the images. Blood spurted from Cedi's wound, dripped from Rosalia's empty eye socket ... blood on her hands, blood on her clothes, blood on her chin, blood on her tongue ...

She stumbled, caught herself and ran on. Whether she was running towards or away from something didn't matter at that moment. Her feet hurried over the forest floor of their own accord, dragging leaves and branches along.

The pane of glass crashed against her elbow and sent pinpricks across the bone into her arm. The candle went out. Liliana dropped the lantern like a hairy spider and fixed her eyes on the light in front of her among the trees. Rustling and cracking enclosed her and the demon's mad laughter in her head – but she was so close now, almost there, by the next lantern on that mossy stone. Was this the last one? Oh please, let it be the last one. Please let him be here.

Gasping, she fell to her knees next to the stone. Everything blurred for a few breaths. Faces and figures mingled with ferns and tree trunks. And everything danced around her in a wild, menacing frenzy.

When she raised her head, he stood there motionless, as though he had been waiting for her since the dawn of time. He was still wearing the same, slightly crumpled, bloody clothing he'd worn in the bear's den. The collar of his coat was pinned up, his dark hair tidied with skilful fingers rather than a proper comb. The familiar bronze glowed in his eyes.

'Liliana.'

Chapter Thirty-Five

'Are you hurt?'

Concern for her spoke clearly from his gaze, but Liliana also recognised doubt in it. The shadows rippled around him as if his outline refused to take on clear contours. He held his powers at the ready. Her heart was pounding so hard by now that she feared she might collapse at any moment. Hurriedly, she shook her head.

'It is you, isn't it? He has exorcised Sartiria?'

'Y-yes.' Her voice groaned like a rusty door hinge. She lifted herself trembling, blanket slipping off her shoulder.

He eyed her suspicously. 'I don't feel any powers.'

'Sartiria is gone.'

'And where is he?'

'At the church. He's waiting for me.'

El came closer but stopped a good distance away. 'Is it the candlelight or …'

'Where is Annie?' Liliana urged. 'Is she all right? You haven't …?'

'Made her a vampiress?' He raised his eyebrows. 'No. How many times do I have to iterate that? She already is. But her powers didn't awaken while you were gone, if that is what you are asking.'

She could have sunk to her knees again in relief.

'Was Sartiria right?' he asked abruptly. 'Is the battle saint recruiting under the pretence of his religion of Light?'

How cool he seemed! Cool, uninvolved and controlled. After everything she had been through! After they hadn't seen each other for so long … or at least it hadn't been her he had seen. Or was what he'd whispered to Sartiria true after all? That she was weak and useless and not his equal? The shadows around his figure flickered almost hostile now.

Shivering, and very slowly, she reached for the blanket on the floor. Only when she had straightened up again and wrapped the blanket around her did she say, 'Is that all you want to know?'

'Is that all I want to know?' His eyes narrowed. 'Do you have any idea what far-reaching consequences your answer will have?'

She stared at him. Her mind was too bewildered to guess what was going on inside him.

'Liliana!'

The corners of his mouth twitched indignantly. His expressive brows drew together.

'I don't want to kill him if I can help it. You should know that. I didn't even kill Morton until there was no other solution.' He snorted. 'If you won't tell me whether a war is imminent or not, I have to assume the former and act accordingly. If he doesn't want to start a war, you have to let me know!'

Liliana flinched as if he had hit her in the face. She hadn't run here until her lungs were burning for this. Her lower lip trembled. She had thought he would banish the horrible images, be elated to see her again. But no, he had made the lantern trail for strategic reasons. The dimly lit surroundings began to spin around her.

'He doesn't want a war! Is that why you brought me back? So I can spy on the saint for you?'

'How did you come up with such a nonsensical idea? That is utterly …' He broke off.

With a long sigh, he closed his eyes and took a breath so deep that the coat tightened around his chest. His shoulders suddenly slumped. When he opened his eyes again, the cold melted from his features. His demonic powers retreated.

'Forgive me.' His gaze darted to the lantern and back to her. He laughed ruefully and adopted a much softer tone. 'I ... I can't quite believe it worked. Sometimes I find it hard to let go of my mistrust. I have become used to keeping my guard up around you. I mean, around Sartiria.'

'I am not Sartiria!'

'No, I ... I know that. I can feel it. But ...' He ran his fingers through his hair and took a step backwards to look at her from head to toe. The moss smacked under his boots. His eyes shimmered uncertainly in the candlelight. 'There's something strange about you. Something different.'

'Different?'

He nodded tentatively. 'I'm not sure how to express it.' He lowered his eyes and buried his hands in his pockets. 'How ... am I supposed to know whether you are still the same person?'

It was precisely this uncertainty that gnawed at her, too. They couldn't carry on as they had before Sartiria. So much had happened, and Liliana had not yet come to terms with it all. She had met Inay, the last of the saints, and had got to know the Light better. She had also seen a different side to El. His powers were much vaster, much more destructive than she had realised. The same applied to the hunger and greed that he kept locked inside. Sartiria's thoughts and experiences gave her a deeper insight into what it meant to be a vampire; deeper than she would have liked. The madness was always lurking beneath the surface, waiting for an opportunity to break out. Added to that was the utter disregard the vampiress had had for human lives. She knew that El didn't share that. And yet ...

'I don't know either.'

El looked at her silently for a few heartbeats. His pale features looked sharper, as if drawn by an artist's hand. However, the timid affection his gaze started to reveal did her the world of good. She finally felt she had arrived with him.

He cleared his throat. 'You must have been confused to suddenly wake up in a strange place.'

'Not confused, no.' Without warning, her eyes filled with tears. Her shoulders shook. Would the images ever go away? The taste of blood and hatred? The madness waiting to pounce? The guilt she bore for everything?

'What's wrong?'

El stretched out his hands towards her. Feeling him close would make everything better. She let herself fall into his embrace, seeking refuge in the familiar tenderness, his scent and the strength of his body. But as soon as his chin brushed her temple, he jerked back as if he had burnt himself on a hot iron.

Audibly stifling a groan, he pushed himself away from her. 'What—?'

Liliana stared at him through the veil of tears like a sleepwalker. The abrupt separation left her feeling even more miserable than before.

'I ...' He came closer, reached out with his fingertips for her cheek and pulled them back with a stunned hiss. 'I can't touch you!'

She stared at his fingers, at his distraught expression and back again at his fingers. Although the lantern was still burning behind her, the night drew closer around them. The treetops bent menacingly overhead.

'What is that?' El growled from deep within his chest. His eyes glittered dangerously; his well-formed jaw tightened. 'He has recruited you! He made you one of them!'

'W-what?' Liliana rubbed her eyes. 'No. I ... am not a saint.'

'Then it must be a protection spell! What has he done to you?'

'N-nothing ... I don't know. He just sent Sartiria away...' She shook her head and whimpered. 'I didn't want any of this. It's too much, El ... It's too much! I don't know how I ... how ...' Her words were drowned out by more sobs.

El tried to take her hand in his. Just before skin met skin, he cursed and flinched. 'I can't. I ... You have become a walking church.'

He lowered his arms helplessly. 'Liliana ...' This time his whisper sounded just as unhappy as she felt. He pressed his lips together as if not being able to hold her at this crucial moment caused him physical pain.

Something hammered against her temples from the inside. Her head hung heavy. She was suddenly tired, and all she wanted to do was sleep; sleep and never wake up again. Let the forest and its darkness bury her.

El gave himself a jolt and reached into his pockets. Before she realised what he was doing, he had already slipped on his gloves. He lifted his hand to her cheek and pressed the cool leather against her skin. He stayed like that for a moment, then drew in a sharp breath and shook out his hand. 'At least this way I can touch you if only for a little while. Come.'

He hugged and squeezed her, a gloved hand on the top of her head to shield the skin on his neck and chin. Liliana cried into his shoulder until the expensive fabric was soaked. El remained silent. She wouldn't have understood him anyway.

Clutching her fingers in his coat, she gasped for air. 'I was trapped in my own body! I couldn't do anything, just watch ... how Sartiria destroyed everything ... I lived through all of it! The kidnappings, the murders, the laughter ... Why won't it stop? Even her memories of the war! And Cedi ...' Her voice faltered.

El pressed her even harder against him. 'You saved us. Without you, Annie and I would be dead. Do not forget that.'

'Please tell me that I didn't kill my own brother! Please ... tell me that none of this truly happened ... Not because of me ...'

'You are not responsible for what Sartiria did. She alone decided what to do with her chance for a second life. And she paid for it.'

She felt as if all the pain, the pent-up terror, was trying to leave her all at once. Her whole body trembled. But El held her, and the fact that he was here, real and tangible, made it more bearable. His arms, his panting breath, the warmth of his body that she could feel through their clothes – that was her reality. The bloody images, the stench of death and panic: that was in the past, belonged to someone else.

Her pulse slowly calmed down. She concentrated on what she could perceive now. The supple leather on her head, damp salt on her lips, the soft forest floor beneath her feet, his voice, his soothing voice ...

'It's over, Liliana. It's over.'

She closed her eyes and, for the first time since she had been able to control her own body, saw neither severed limbs nor the waxen faces of victims. Instead, a wonderful blackness enveloped her.

El gently detached himself from her. 'Nnnnghh ...'

Liliana looked up, startled, as he staggered back. The colour of his face was even paler than usual under his dark hair. He looked as if he was about to vomit.

'Is it the protective spell? You shouldn't have ... waited so long.'

'Don't worry ...' He hunched over and panted for a while. 'I will be ... just fine.'

Liliana waited, feeling a little lost, and reached for Priest Adom's woollen blanket, which was attempting to slide to the ground again. Having shared in Sartiria's sensations, she knew that the Light – if it wasn't strong enough to kill – caused a kind of mental torture in vampires. No wonder, if it was capable of separating the demonic from the human part and banishing it from this world ...

'You didn't have to do that to yourself, El.'

He smiled painfully. 'A powerful vampire like me can take a lot, right?'

Was he alluding to her own words? Back when she had persuaded him to check the protective spell on Father's house? She laughed with wet eyes. 'Well then, everything ought to be all right.'

'Exactly.' El shook himself like a wet dog. His spirits returned. 'Here.' He pulled something small and shiny out of his pocket and held it out to her: a key. 'To take that ring off your neck.'

She groped for the keyhole. It was tricky to insert the key at the right angle. El took hold of her hand and guided her, just as he had done with Annie in the dungeon. Although Liliana had forgotten about the metal band, the click of the lock opening was liberating. El hastily took the ring from her and pocketed it.

'As for your family, I have good news and bad news. The good news is that Cedi is still alive.'

'He's alive?' How was that possible? She could have thrown her arms around El's neck for joy. But given the circumstances, that wouldn't have been very accommodating.

El nodded indulgently, as if he had read the train of thought on her face.

'He's alive ... That's wonderful!' She had neither directly nor indirectly killed her brother. What a relief! 'And what ... what's the bad news?'

He put both hands in his coat pockets and sighed. 'Maybe now is not the right time to deliver it.'

'You can't mention something like that and then not tell me what it is.' She wrapped the blanket tighter around her shoulders and braced herself for what he had to say.

The candle sizzled and hissed and threatened to go out for a moment. But the flame did not give up and continued to spread its flickering orange light over the tree trunks.

'Tell me, El! Or else knowing that something bad is waiting for me will hover over my head like a sharpened axe, and I'll imagine the worst possible ...'

He hesitated but complied. 'Your grandmother passed away a week ago.'

'No ... no ...' Liliana staggered backwards and almost fell over the stone and the lantern behind her. 'That can't be ...'

'She died of natural causes, as far as I can tell. Your grandmother wasn't that young any more. For a human, she had reached an acceptable age.'

Once again, she had lost someone without being able to say goodbye! Grandmother had died, and she hadn't even been there to comfort her, to hold her hand or rub on her favourite herbal ointments. Now that she knew how easily Inay could heal even the terminally ill when he was present, the loss seemed even more cruel.

'I am sorry.' He watched her reaction closely. 'I know she was important to you. Unfortunately, I won't be able to repay her for all the kindness she showed me.'

There had already been too many tears tonight. Although the message had reached her mind, it hadn't truly reached her heart yet. She had always been able to rely on Grandmother's wisdom and kindness. This wonderful woman had been as much a part of her life as the eternal fire in the kitchen and the grass that grew in the pastures. In many ways, she had been a mother to her. Liliana couldn't imagine a world without her.

El hesitated. Finally, he brought a hand to his chest and then raised it in the air as if toasting the moon in the sky. 'To the dead,' he said quietly. 'And to the living.'

There was something strange about this act, all alone in the forest, surrounded by tall fir trees and scurrying rodents in the copse. Although Liliana did not repeat the abbreviated toast, she recognised the intention behind it and was grateful for his gesture.

Then they both fell silent, half out of respect, half out of helplessness. The candle was nearing the end of its life and burned all the more vigorously. The smaller the amount of wax, the higher the flame rose – or so it seemed to Liliana. A swarm of insects circled the glass box in which it flickered.

'To come back to our current situation ...' El began. 'Can he lift this spell on you?'

It took Liliana a moment to follow his mental leap. 'You mean Inay?'

'Inay,' El repeated ponderously, and her heart skipped a beat. Should she not have revealed his name?

'I, uhm ... I can ask him.'

A rustling behind them made El spin around. His posture changed immediately. Liliana also turned and saw the saint himself step into the circle lit by the lantern. The borrowed winter coat reached down to his ankles and covered his hands to the tips of his fingers.

'The simple answer is no.'

She froze. How long had he been listening to the conversation? Had he overheard them from the beginning, or had he only come closer when she had started sobbing?

'I saw you running across the field and realised that I wouldn't be able to help you from the village,' he explained. 'So I followed you to stay within earshot. And yes,' he added, addressing El directly, 'I, too, can lock my powers away to avoid being noticed.'

El's eyes narrowed to slits; his fingers twitched. Apart from the mild flicker of candlelight on the tense faces, Liliana noticed no change but knew that Inay had begun to glow to demonic eyes.

'Why not?' Although El's expression remained impassive, Liliana could feel his demonic powers creeping in as icy shadows.

The saint planted himself next to a young fir tree and crossed his hands in front of his body in a priestly manner. He wouldn't need to be able to move them in the event of a fight. 'Because I only summoned the Light. I can't say exactly why it stayed. Some things are unpredictable, even for me.'

The rising panic drove away all the tiredness she had just felt. She hastily placed herself in front of El – between the two men – and faced Inay. In terms of sheer fighting power, they represented the peak of what each side had to offer. Under no circumstances could Liliana allow one of them to kill the other! She feared for Inay, the only saint who still defended humanity. El was incredibly fast and brutal when he attacked. If he used his powers to the full, he could rip the head off an ordinary human in the blink of an eye. On the other hand, Inay didn't even have to move to strike and could draw on centuries of experience. El had never faced a saint before. If he got a little too close to the Light, it could easily cost him an arm, a leg or his life. She had experienced first-hand what Inay was capable of.

The tense silence made the hairs on the back of Liliana's neck stand up. And this chain of thoughts was giving her a headache. Sartiria's inclination to analyse opponents had left traces in her way of thinking. She bit her lower lip. A peaceful outcome had to be possible ... one where all three of them left this forest alive.

'So this is the Lord to whom the Highlands pay their taxes in blood and gold,' Inay said calmly.

Liliana's breath caught. Had he gone mad? Was he trying to provoke El? She glanced over her shoulder to see said Lord smiling brittlely.

'The renewed pleasure is all mine, battle saint.'

Inay stayed motionless where he was. 'What happens now?'

'I reckon now we settle on either war or peace,' El growled.

'Nobody here wants a war!' Liliana raised her hands and looked pleadingly back and forth between the two of them. 'Inay, you said you didn't want another war, and you, too, El!'

El's eyebrows shot up. 'Not if it can be avoided.'

'I believe it can,' Inay said.

'Am I to assume that you are not secretly starting a revolution? Arming for conflict, forging weapons, recruiting soldiers?' El obviously remembered that saints didn't lie. Was he testing Inay's reaction?

'No, at least not in the way Sartiria imagined it. Her way of looking at the world is too far removed from mine for her to understand what I do.' Inay eyed El curiously. 'But I can assure you, Lord of Finsterwald, that I will not start a violent conflict.'

A pause followed, during which El probably turned over each of Inay's sentences three times in his head, checking for hidden meanings. Liliana wrapped her arms around herself.

'As long as everything remains as before, you will not have to fear persecution from my side,' El finally emphasised. 'But the other noble families have been made aware of you and the existence of your organisation by Sartiria. If the Council decides that the danger you pose is too great and action is needed,

I will have to comply. If, like me, you want to minimise the risk of an open conflict, you should go into hiding. Cease your mission. Keep any gatherings to a minimum.'

'I don't have a mission,' Inay replied. 'What I do is my life ... It is who I am. I can't just stop that. And I have done well with it so far. Nobody bothered us until Sartiria was summoned from the past.'

'Then do what you think you need to do without stepping on anyone's toes.' El crossed his arms. 'Otherwise, we will meet again in battle sooner or later, a battle which will claim countless unnecessary victims.'

Inay nodded slowly.

'I will stop my pursuit. And I have warned you hereby.' El glanced at Liliana and then quickly fixed his gaze on the saint again. 'That is all I can do as a token of my gratitude.'

The flame in the lantern sizzled, coughed and died out. As small as the light source had been, it had pushed the darkness back surprisingly far. Illuminated only by the soft glow of the moon, the night seemed denser, and Liliana's eyes had to get used to recognising more than just shapeless surfaces.

'You didn't come back to kill me?' There was an indistinct glint in Inay's eyes. 'Just to pick up your friend?'

El raised a single eyebrow. 'I adhere to the principle of reciprocity.'

'Then you are more humane than many actual humans.' Glancing back over his shoulder, Inay released his hands under his sleeves. He didn't look alarmed, but rather as if he remembered a task that needed doing. 'I would like to talk to you in private for a moment, Liliana.'

'Yes, of course,' Liliana said before El could raise any objections.

With a furrowed brow, he watched as Inay retreated between two trees and beckoned Liliana to join him. She silently formed *I'll be right back* with her lips and followed the saint, guided more by her hearing than her sight.

A twig tickled her face, and she bent it to the side. After a few steps, her foot sank into a hidden watercourse. She jumped on hastily. 'Inay?'

'Here.'

He was waiting under a particularly gnarly tree, an old oak. As soon as she reached him, she felt his hand on her arm.

'Is this where we part ways?' he asked.

'No, I ... It ...' She would have loved to continue travelling with him. He had so much experience to share, so much wisdom to pass on, so much warmth to give. 'You have to understand ... I ... have to see my daughter.'

She couldn't decipher the expression on his face. 'You are more like Solana than you could ever know, Liliana.'

Solana, the saint who had let him down? She involuntarily clutched her chest. 'H-how? Why?'

'I don't claim to understand your situation. But I feel obliged to tell you one hard truth.' He sighed. 'I asked you in the cave if you would make the same decision again, knowing what you know now. The answer is clearly yes. You put the lives of those close to you above the lives of others.'

Speechless, Liliana opened her mouth.

'It's not up to me to decide whether this is wrong or right. I just want you to understand. What is true of Sartiria is true of every vampire.' Inay pointed in the direction where El was waiting by the extinguished lantern. 'As long as he lives, others must die for it.'

How could he say that? El was not like Sartiria!

'Without him, someone else would take the position of Lord, and whoever that was, they would definitely make things worse for us humans. He is not like the others.' And Annie most certainly wasn't! 'We should be judged by our choices, not by who we were born as.'

'You may be right,' Inay replied. 'But you can't ignore what he is. All I want for you is to not close your eyes to reality. I want you to open them, truly open them ... so that you can see the influence you have on the events of this world.'

The tears that she'd thought dried up gathered in her eyes yet again.

Inay sensed it and continued gently, 'Think about it. What do your choices say about you?'

'What do you mean?'

'As I mentioned, some things are unpredictable. You may be the start of something new. The fact that you have Light in you now is no coincidence.'

'I ... haven't turned into a saint, have I?'

'If I believed that, I wouldn't let you go with him.' He shook his head wistfully. 'I dare say you wouldn't want to go. But I could be wrong. What I'm describing is only a state as it is now, not as it one day could be.'

The air around them seemed to crackle. Behind Inay, something stalked through the undergrowth. He didn't seem worried, so it wasn't a vampire or a bandit, but a larger animal; a deer or a badger perhaps.

He removed his hand from her arm and let it hover over her chest for a moment. 'Seeing as you are a living being subject to illness and injury, I suppose the Light in you will eventually die down on its own. But remember that Light cannot remain in this world unless it is attached to something. And it doesn't do that on its own.'

What did he mean by that? Liliana still had so many questions she would have liked to ask him. But they all rushed forward at once and because they could only leave her tongue one at a time, they got stuck in her head as a tangle of half-formed thoughts. Even uttering a few simple parting words seemed overwhelming.

He stepped away from the tree, sighed and bowed his head. 'I hope to see you again, Liliana. Now, if you don't mind, I'll return the blanket to Adom. He only has two of them.'

A little stiff and embarrassed that she hadn't thought of it herself, she rolled up the blanket and handed it to him. He walked slowly through the dark forest back to the village.

The saint's silhouette began to blur with the surroundings as he turned to her one last time and called out to her. 'I hope you find your place.'

IF YOU LIKED THIS BOOK ...

... please take three minutes to leave a review on Amazon and wherever else you usually post.

I really appreciate your reviews because as a new author and indie publisher, every little bit of attention makes a huge difference. And I love to hear what my readers think.

Thank you so much for joining the journey!

THANK YOU

To all the delicious humans who have one way or another made this book possible: I thank you from the bottom of my heart!

Dear Alex, thank you for your patience and unwavering support. You are the best. I hope you know that by now.

Dear Riona, you have inspired me to include parenthood as a theme throughout all the books of this series. I love being your mother more than the Curse loves human blood – and that is an awful lot!!

Dear Rhiannon, thank you for reading and for your comments that have made me chuckle countless times.

Dear Mami & Papi, dear Kate, thank you for reading my many writings. I know you are all busy, and I cherish your support.

Dear Melinda, thank you for sharing your thoughts, for reminding me how a normal person would react and for re-kindling the feminist spark whenever mine starts to dwindle.

Dear Samantha, Manuela, and Marei, if it weren't for your honest feedback, I wouldn't have written this book to offer an alternative path. I'm sorry there was not time for a feedback round on this one – I hope you enjoy it :)

Dear Klaudia, thank you for being the kind and supportive friend everyone wishes they had in their lives. And thank you for sharing my love of books and for drawing fantastic fantasy maps.

Dear Lukas, thank you for being flexible to accommodate my requests and creating those beautiful twin covers.

Dear Lauren and Leona, thank you for taking my writing to the next level.

Dear Phillipa, thank you for lending me your keen eye for style and consistency.

WHAT'S NEXT?

In case you are interested in reading this part of the story from Sartiria's perspective, check out A Tale of Something Borrowed: The Path of Resistance.

And if you'd like to hear when the fourth and last book in the series gets published, check out my website www.ataleofbooks.com and sign up for my newsletter!

You can also find me on Instagram as @dsmccolgan (personal profile, in German) and @ataleof_books (English).

Printed in Great Britain
by Amazon

60318070R00184